SINCERELY, WILLIS WAYDE

SINCERELY, WILLIS WAYDE

BY JOHN P. MARQUAND

LITTLE, BROWN AND COMPANY

Boston   Toronto

Published simultaneously in Canada
by Little, Brown & Company (Canada) Limited

PRINTED IN THE UNITED STATES OF AMERICA

Experts in the belting industry may feel that I have not given a full or fair description of this line of endeavor. I have refrained from too complete a study for several reasons, the chief of which is that good fiction is seldom achieved if it follows life too carefully. Thus this interpretation of the belting industry is a figment of my own imagination and the same is true of the characters in this book. They are none of them modeled after or intended to represent any persons living or dead. If a name given one belongs to any individual who reads this book, it is pure coincidence.

I

WILLIS WAYDE, before he went to sleep, could shut his eyes and see every detail of the Harcourt place. He had never owned it and had never coveted it, but as his father might have said in engineering language, it did serve as a base of reference. In engineering when you set out to make a map, you started running your line and reading off from some fixed mark, and in life too everyone possessed some solid starting point. The Harcourt place and everything around it was like this for Willis, and whether he liked the idea or not, it meant more to him than any place he had ever owned or rented.

Though it was customary for people in Clyde, Massachusetts, to think of the Harcourt Mill and the Harcourt place as a part of Clyde, this was inaccurate. The Harcourt place and the mill were three miles up-river in a community by themselves known as Mill Village. The mill buildings were on the riverbank. The house itself stood on higher ground overlooking the small community, a typical picture of early industrial New England. It was not an old place, as places went in Clyde, yet Willis could never get over his illusion that the Harcourt place was old. There are some early illusions that you can never evade, however incorrect.

Willis first saw the Harcourt place late one afternoon in August, 1922, when he was fifteen and when all of New England was an unknown country. He and his mother had arrived in Boston from Chicago in the morning. As long as they were in Boston, his mother said, they might as well spend a few hours seeing the sights, because it was a very historic city. There was a train for Clyde at three o'clock in the afternoon, leaving the North Station. They would send their trunks across the city by baggage transfer, and they would check their two suitcases in the parcel room of the South Station. Meanwhile his mother would buy a map of Boston at the newsstand and she would go to the restaurant and order breakfast while Willis arranged about the transfer company and carried the bags to the parcel checkroom. Willis was big enough to carry the bags, instead of tipping a porter—as long as they weren't traveling with "your father"—and looking after the suitcases and the trunks would be an experience for him. And one thing more, now that Willis was growing up. After getting the parcel room checks he could go to the telegraph office and send a telegram himself to "your father," saying in ten words that they were arriving in Clyde at four-sixteen and please meet them at the station.

"A map of Boston won't cost as much as giving something to a porter," his mother said. "We'll really be getting the map for nothing."

Even at half past nine in the morning it was very hot in the old South Station, and the heat covered his face with a sheet of moisture that dripped from his nose; and his hair, under the old Stetson hat his father had passed on to him, became wringing wet. The restaurant was not cool either, even with the big fans on the ceiling stirring up a smell of over-ripe muskmelon and boiling coffee.

"Heaven sakes, Willis," she said, "you are dripping with perspiration. Get out your handkerchief and mop your face."

"I wouldn't sweat so," Willis said, "if I was to have a haircut."

"If you *were*," his mother said, "and you don't need one yet. You ought to be a girl, the way your hair grows."

Actually it had taken Willis years to realize that a well-groomed man should have his hair trimmed once a week.

His mother's map of Boston with a list of historic spots was spread on the table in front of her. She had opened her bag, pulled out a blue pencil, and was now circling points of interest.

"This is a real opportunity, Willis," she said. "We're going to see Faneuil Hall with the grasshopper weathervane, and the Old North Church, where they put the lantern aloft in the belfry. Then we shall see the site of the Boston Massacre and then the old State House and then the Common. We shall also see the new State House, built by the famous architect Bulfinch. We shall then pass through the Public Gardens, and we shall visit the Boston Public Library. That ought to be enough to hold us for the morning, if we walk. It will do us good to stretch our legs after the train."

His mother was tireless in those days and very light on her feet. She looked cool in her cotton print dress and undisturbed at being a public spectacle, as she held her map in front of her. All that Willis could do was to try to walk two paces behind her, pretending that he did not know her—not a successful device, because she called to him imperiously at intervals, telling him that they did not have all day. Consequently the sights he saw were lost in a blur of twisted, crowded streets that shimmered beneath the August sun. All that morning and afternoon must have been a series of stolen minutes forming a hiatus that took his mother's mind from the immediate future, preventing her from giving a thought to "your father," or how long "your father" would keep this new position.

"Your father, Willis," his mother had said on the train, "is so much more brilliant than most people that it's hard for him to stay satisfied, which explains why he moves from place to place."

As they moved along the torrid streets she might have been teaching American history again, as she had once in Topeka, Kansas. Willis never forgot her expression when she saw the Book of Common Prayer in the Old North Church with the name of the King erased from it. It appealed to her imagination in a way that it never would to his. He could never share that sort of intellectual enthusiasm which could endow the pages of an ordinary old book with life and voice, or a bare room of a stuffy house, like the house of Paul Revere, with vanished people. Willis could only be pleased that he had not lived in an epoch that was completely devoid of automobiles and electricity.

"Now pay attention, Willis," his mother said. "There's the grasshopper on Faneuil Hall, and it really is a grasshopper."

She knew better than Willis did that few things were what you really thought they were going to be, and perhaps the grasshopper had looked just the way that she imagined it when she had read about it as a pretty girl on her family's farm near Topeka.

When they finally reached the North Station, and after Willis had seen about the trunk checks and had put the suitcases in the rack above them in the day coach, his mother told him that it had been a delightful day in Boston, a real holiday and something for him always to remember, but now it was time to put first things first, and she pulled "your father's" letter out of her handbag.

"I wonder what it will be like this time," she said. "Your father always starts by being enthusiastic, and he's enthusiastic now about this Mr. Harcourt. I must say, it's very generous of Mr. Harcourt to let us have a house to live in right on his place. Now, Willis, I want you to be polite. I don't want people to think you're a crude Western boy. Have you lost your pocket comb?"

"No, Mom," Willis answered.

"Then get it out and comb your hair. You look as hot as a boiled beet. Aren't you feeling well?"

"I'm feeling all right," Willis answered, "but I wish I could go for a swim."

"You can't," his mother said. "Are your shoes tight?"

"Yes," Willis said, "awful tight."

"Well, you can take them off and rest your feet if you want to. No one will see you. Why do you always look ashamed when I make a suggestion, Willis?"

"Couldn't I take my coat off instead, Mom?" Willis asked.

"No," she said, "not in the train, Willis."

The train was five minutes late. At least it was four-twenty-one by Willis's Ingersoll watch when they got to Clyde.

Eventually everybody knew about everyone else in Clyde, because most Clyde citizens were endowed with deep human interest, not kindly perhaps, but indefatigable. It was only natural that an authority should eventually appear who could describe the first minutes of the arrival of Willis Wayde in Clyde. This was Bert Barker, who for thirty years ran the baggage room at the Boston & Maine Railroad station, and the older Mr. Barker grew the more clearly he could remember the incident.

Not many people ever got off the four-sixteen, and the four-sixteen was late because they were repairing the track down near Culver Crossing where the roadbed had softened up after a northeast storm. At four-ten exactly the Harcourts' old Locomobile, with Patrick Flynn driving it, pulled up at the station and parked in the place reserved for taxis, just as though the Harcourts owned the whole Boston & Maine. Mr. Barker was just getting ready to wheel out two crates of chickens on the truck, when he saw there was someone else in the Locomobile with Mr. Henry Harcourt's chauffeur. It was that new man working at the Harcourt Mill whose name he hadn't caught yet, a kind of a big-barreled fellow with bushy eyebrows and baggy pants. He remembered the incident perfectly, because this fellow had called him partner and asked if the four-sixteen train was on time, and Mr. Barker had said it was bound to be late because of the soft place on the roadbed. The fellow had said it was a hell of a roadbed all the way from Boston, and Mr. Barker had asked who the Locomobile was going to meet, seeing Mr. Harcourt had not gone to Boston that morning. It could not be waiting for Mr. Bryson Harcourt or Mrs. Bryson Harcourt either, or their two kids, because they would have used their own automobile. The fellow had said that his wife and son were expected on the four-sixteen and that they had been traveling quite a piece. They had been coming all the way from Colorado.

"You come from Colorado?" Mr. Barker said.

"Colorado and other places," the fellow said, "and I could certainly do with a good cold beer."

Those were his exact words, and Mr. Barker remembered them because he could have done with a beer himself, what with Prohibition and everything.

"Say," Mr. Barker said, "you're working at the Harcourt Mill, ain't you?"

"Yes," the fellow said, "as an engineer."

"They tell me Mr. Harcourt's a nice man to work for," Mr. Barker said.

"It seems that way, partner," the fellow said. Those were his exact words.

"He must think a lot of you," Barker said, "to send down his old Loco to meet your folks. He thinks a lot of that old Loco."

The fellow did not answer. He took a bag of Bull Durham out of his coat pocket and rolled a cigarette and lighted a match on his thumb nail.

"How do you like it now you're here?" Mr. Barker asked.

"It's a friendly place," the fellow said. "People here are interested in strangers."

"You look as though you'd been around a lot," Mr. Barker said.

"Yes," the fellow said, "around a lot. If it helps you, my name's Alf Wayde, so you won't have to ask anyone."

He didn't belong around there and he wasn't friendly, but at the same time he was common just like you or me. He raised his voice just when the train was coming in.

"She's got a bad bearing," he said, "and her pistons need packing."

It did not take a minute to get the chicken crates aboard the baggage car and there was nothing to come off except one light case for Fenwick's Dry Goods Store, so Mr. Barker could check on the passengers alighting. The first to get down was Miss Mamie Bowles, who was studying shorthand at the Lynn Commercial School, and after her came Charlie Wilson, who ran the drugstore, and after him, his sister, Minnie Wilson, the high-school teacher. Then a gawky boy of about fifteen, wearing a Western ten-gallon hat, got out of the rear coach lugging two straw suitcases so heavy for him that he came near to tripping, but he turned right around to help down a spry little lady who was on the steps behind him. Then this fellow Wayde shouted out, "Hello, honey," and, "Hello, Willis." Wayde kissed the little lady and shook hands with the boy; and Patrick Flynn didn't seem to know whether to treat the party like guests or like people just working for Harcourt.

"Willis," the little lady said, just when Mr. Barker was rolling the truck down to the baggage room, "give the baggage man the trunk checks."

The trunks weren't on the four-sixteen and that was a fact. "Willis," the little lady said, "didn't they tell you the trunks would come with us?"

"Yes, Mom," the boy said.

It didn't matter what anyone had said. The trunks weren't there and that was a fact.

"It will be all right, Madam," Patrick said. "They'll be coming on the six-two, and Beane is coming down with the truck at six o'clock."

"Let's get going," Wayde said. "You sit in back with me, Cynthia, and Willis can sit up front. This is Mrs. Wayde, Pat, and this is Willis."

Patrick looked startled when the little lady shook hands.

"It's nice to know you," she said. "You shouldn't have hired this big automobile for us, Alf."

"I didn't hire it," Mr. Wayde said. "It's Mr. Harcourt's automobile. Why don't you take your coat off, Willis?"

"Oh, no," the little lady said, "not in the automobile."

Well, that was all there was to it. But anyway, Mr. Barker was the first one to lay eyes on Willis Wayde. You would never have thought that the young fellow would amount to much. You never would have thought that some day he would have his own Cadillac and his own chauffeur. He was just a hot, gawky, red-faced kid with big hands and a big nose and mouth, and he needed a haircut. The fact was that he was in what you might call the growing stage. His body hadn't caught up with his hands nor the rest of his face with his nose. There was no way of guessing then that Willis Wayde was going to come out well set up, almost handsome, and a snappy dresser too. But even then the boy did carry a pocket comb, which was a sign he was particular.

Later Willis came to realize that you could never tell whether Mr. Harcourt's chauffeur, Patrick Flynn, was sad or happy. You always felt that he was not at home in an automobile, which was understandable, since he had been the Harcourts' coachman until they had given up the carriage horses and the old stables had been turned into a garage. Behind the wheel of the Loco, which was a period piece in itself, Patrick sat up thin and straight, an immaculate, elderly man, with his long dish face as stern and watchful as though he were handling a skittish pair that at any moment might need a whip's corrective touch. Whenever Patrick reached for the gearshift of the Loco, you thought of him stretching out his hand to the whip socket.

Just as they were leaving the station Willis's father turned down the heavy plate-glass window that divided the chauffeur's seat from the occupants in back.

"Stop at Wilson's Drugstore, will you?" Mr. Wayde said. "I want a prescription filled. It won't take more than two minutes."

"What sort of prescription, Alfred?" Willis heard his mother ask.

"For a pint of rye, Cynthia," his father said.

"Oh, Alf," he heard his mother say, and then the window turned up again, and Willis and Patrick were alone.

"It's an awful hot day, isn't it?" Willis said. "But it's hotter still in Kansas."

"Don't talk when I'm driving," Mr. Flynn said.

It was all like a foreign country. The street was lined with old-fashioned homes, all neatly painted and pretty close together. The trees were what impressed Willis most. He had seen elms before but never so many big ones looking like green feather dusters, and not a leaf of them was stirring. Outside of town they passed a few small farms in a mean-looking rocky country with fields bordered by stone walls. Then the road ran along the river for a piece, and all at once he saw a group of brick buildings and a tall factory chimney. There was a high wire fence all around them and a row of workers' houses on the other side of the road. They turned left near the factory and began climbing a steepish hill, and a minute later Willis saw the dressed-granite wall that marked the front of the Harcourt place.

When the Harcourt family, like other New England millowners, had become suddenly rich during the Civil War, William Harcourt, Mr. Henry Harcourt's grandfather, had built the Harcourt place. Though the war had added to the family fortune, the Harcourts were already well-to-do. In 1819 William Harcourt had married a Miss Rebecca Atwood, the only daughter of a Boston shipping family, and he had also inherited a substantial legacy from an English cousin. Furthermore he was gifted with sound business instincts that prompted him to build a cotton manufactory in 1850 upon the river frontage of what was then the old Harcourt farm.

William Harcourt had been an old man when he built the Harcourt place—not so much for his own enjoyment as from some vague desire for dynastic security. While on a business trip to England, he retained the services of a British architect, an Oswell Beardsley, whose specialty was country houses, and consequently the Harcourt place always had a slightly foreign flavor. This Mr. Beardsley selected for his site a knoll in almost the center of the old farm acreage that overlooked the mill buildings and the river; and, arbitrarily, he cut off a tract of about fifteen acres of forest and orchard and pasture, surrounding it by a low wall. It was Beardsley who decided which old trees would remain and who supervised all the planting of the new trees and shrubbery that shielded the house and outbuildings. Though the place was walled off from the farm proper, very consciously excluding the old farmhouse and cattle barns, the imported architect had considered all the three hundred acres of the old farm and the mill itself as a single unit, and the granite house he built—with its Gothic windows and Gothic verandas, with its stables and greenhouse, and walled gardens for flowers and vegetables—became the central adornment of the whole.

This vision had been somewhat altered when the land around the mill grew eventually into a small village and more foremen's and superintendents' houses were constructed. Yet anyone who faced the main entrance in the low granite wall and saw the stone gate cottage and the mansard roof and gables of the big house through the trees still understood that the Harcourt place owed its existence to the functional structures by the river. The wisteria vines on the porches and the growth of the trees had softened harder outlines. When Willis first saw the Harcourt place some sixty years had passed over it, and it had begun to have its own atmosphere.

When the Locomobile turned into the drive, the limbs of the beech trees that bordered it made a network of shadow over the freshly raked yellow gravel. Between their pale-gray trunks Willis saw the mowed green fields on either side, with a sheepfold in one space and then a duck pond and a summerhouse. It was quite a while before they came to the lawns and the terraced gardens. From there they turned down the back drive past the greenhouse and past the stable yard, and for the first time Patrick spoke.

"This is the big house," he said, "and down there is the road to Mr. Bryson's house."

"Say," Willis said, "does Mr. Harcourt live there all alone?"

"He does," Patrick said.

"Gee," Willis said, "I don't see what he does in it."

"That's his business," Patrick said.

"I only mean it's so big," Willis said, "with all those other buildings and everything."

Patrick did not answer. The back drive had brought them past the kitchen garden, and Willis saw the garden house just at the edge of a grove of oaks.

"You get off here," Patrick said.

"Gee," Willis said, "is this where we're going to live?"

Patrick did not answer, but he jumped out of the Locomobile more smartly than he had at the station and opened the door formally for Mr. and Mrs. Wayde.

"That's all right, Pat," Alfred Wayde said. "Willis and I can handle the bags."

"Mr. Harcourt told me to tell you, Madam," Patrick said, "that if there is anything you need, to call Mr. Beane on the house telephone. Selwyn has left some groceries to get you started, Madam, and MacDonald has brought a few vegetables."

"That's very kind of Mr. Harcourt," Mrs. Wayde said. "Everything looks lovely, and if we want anything Mr. Wayde can get it in his Ford."

It was the first time that Willis had heard that his father had a car, but now he saw a Ford runabout standing in a small shed beneath the trees.

"Well, if that's all then," Patrick said.

"Yes, that's all," Mr. Wayde said. "Thanks, Pat."

"Oh, just a minute," Mrs. Wayde said, and she lowered her voice. "Alfred."

"Oh, yes," Mr. Wayde said, and he pulled a bill out of his trousers pocket.

"That isn't necessary, sir," Patrick said, and Willis saw his glance fall, unintentionally perhaps, upon the straw suitcases.

"All the more reason to take it," Mr. Wayde said.

"Well, thanks," Patrick said. "Remember, if you want anything, Madam, call up Mr. Beane on the house telephone."

All three of them stood for a moment on the path looking at the garden house. It was a small two-story replica of the big house, built of stone in the same Gothic style with leaded casement windows, and there was a flower bed filled with deep-purple petunias on either side of the front door.

"Why, Alfred," Mrs. Wayde said, "it's like a picture. Is it furnished?"

His father stood with his hands in his trousers pockets.

"You come inside, Cynthia," he said. "We've got a real place for once. There's sheets, blankets, china, and everything."

Willis felt there must be some catch to it when they came into the small front entry with its flight of carpeted stairs and figured wallpaper. On the right was a sitting room with a big fireplace, all furnished with easy chairs, pictures, lamps, and everything. There was a big dining room on the left with a dark-oak gate-leg table and Windsor chairs, and there was a kitchen ell with a fire in the stove and a table covered with groceries and vegetables.

"Do you like it, Cynthia?" his father asked.

"Of course I like it, Alfred," she answered, "only I can't believe it."

There were two bedrooms upstairs, with curtains of shiny chintz, and there was even a chaise longue in one of them—a word that Willis learned later. His mother looked at it all doubtfully, as though she still could not believe it.

"What's the rent on it, Alfred?" she asked.

The corners of his father's wide mouth tightened.

"Twenty-five dollars," he said.

"Well, maybe it's worth it," his mother said. "But can we afford twenty-five dollars a week?"

"No," his father said, "twenty-five a month."

Willis heard his mother catch her breath.

"Why is he only asking that? I don't see . . ." Mrs. Wayde began, and her voice ended on a higher note.

"It's all right, Cynthia," his father said.

"Gosh," Willis said. "Mr. Harcourt must have an awful lot of money, Pa."

"That's no way to talk," Mrs. Wayde told him. "You mean he must be a very kind man, Willis, who thinks a lot of your father—unless there's something we don't know about."

"There isn't anything," Alfred Wayde said.

"Well, I certainly hope not," Mrs. Wayde said, and she sighed. "I'll start things in the kitchen, and, Willis, you take a bath and put on a clean shirt, and be sure to wash the tub. Why, everything's all dusted."

"That's right," Alfred Wayde said. "Two women were here all last week."

"I just can't believe it," Mrs. Wayde said, "I really can't."

Past experience was no guide to what confronted Willis then. He was learning at the age of fifteen that wealth beyond a certain point always created its own small world of unreality. He was caught in such a world that afternoon, one from which he never wholly escaped.

Just as Willis was looking over the bedroom that would be his for a long while but that would always seem to belong to someone else, he heard a knock on the front door.

"I'll go," he heard his father say.

"What was it, Al?" he heard his mother call after the front door had closed.

"It's a note from Harcourt," he heard his father answer. "He wants us all to come to dinner," and then he heard his father laugh, "and we don't have to bother to dress. He knows I don't own an open-front suit. I told him so."

"Oh, Alf," his mother called, "you shouldn't have told him that. Can't we excuse ourselves? All my good clothes are in the trunk."

"We've got to go, Cynthia," his father said, "and anyway it means we don't cook supper."

You never do forget first times, particularly first times when you were young. The sun was setting when they walked across the lawn to the big house. The birds were singing their last songs in the oak and beech trees, and there was a steady late-summer noise of crickets in the grass. His father was telling them not to act as though they were going to church. They had all eaten at big hotels in Chicago and San Francisco, and they knew what headwaiters were like, and Selwyn, who was Mr. Harcourt's butler, was like a headwaiter. Besides they had been to lunch at the Cashes' in Denver, and he would bet that Harrod Cash had more cash than Mr. Harcourt.

"Now, Willis," his mother said. "It's important for your father that you make a nice impression."

"Willis will be all right," his father said. "Just take it easy, Cynthia."

"Now, Willis," his mother said. "Remember what I told you about the knives and forks. Begin with the outside ones, even if they don't look right, and don't be nervous, Willis."

"Don't worry him, Cynthia," his father said. "You'll feel at home in a minute."

"Oh, Alf," his mother said, "you feel at home anywhere because you never notice anything, and there's an awful lot to notice."

There really was too much for anyone to notice all at once. The front veranda with its gray Gothic pillars was cool and shadowy. They only waited a second or two after ringing before the heavy front door opened. The hall with its walnut woodwork was already dusky, but a lighted chandelier gave Willis a glimpse of the staircase, some paintings of land-scapes in heavy gold frames, and a tall clock that ticked loudly in the heavy silence. An elderly man in a black tie and stiff white shirt had opened the door.

"Good evening, Mrs. Wayde," Willis heard him say. "Good evening, Mr. Wayde."

"Good evening, Mr. Harcourt," his mother said. "Isn't it a lovely evening?"

"It isn't Mr. Harcourt," his father said, and he laughed. "This is Selwyn, Cynthia. He's the butler here. Selwyn, I want you to meet my wife and my boy. You've heard me talk about them."

"Oh, how do you do, Mr. Selwyn," his mother said, and she shook hands with him. The scene was not embarrassing, because Selwyn showed no surprise.

"The pleasure is all mine, Madam," he said. "If you will be so kind as to follow me. Mr. Harcourt and Mrs. Blood are watching the sunset on the west veranda."

"Mrs. Blood is Mr. Harcourt's sister, Cynthia," Alfred Wayde said. "This is my boy, Willis, Selwyn. Willis, you shake hands with Mr. Selwyn, too. He's a good man to know around here."

II

THE LUNCHEON in Denver at the residence of Mr. Harrod Cash was an experience which Willis had treasured as something never to be equaled again, but after Mr. Harcourt's house it had the ring of a counterfeit coin. That Denver mineowner's home was vulgarly blatant, compared with the polished solidity of the Harcourt place. Willis was actually facing his first experience with the peace and order of a settled tradition, and also an example of convention, undiluted by unnecessary extravagance. He could feel dignity and permanence compared to which the house in Denver was as ephemeral as the settings of a stage. The broad front hall led directly to another wide passage, which extended the full length of the house. This hall was carpeted with Oriental rugs. Its walls were lined with low bookshelves and gold-framed pictures, and its light came from the open doors of the rooms on either side and from the glass doors leading to the east and west verandas. Thus it was always a shadowy passage, even in the daylight. Willis could still hear the ticking of the clock, because their footsteps were quieted by the carpet. He had a glimpse through open doors of the drawing room and the library, and there was a clean smell to everything, of wax and flowers, that combined with a satiny sheen of woodwork to give a sense of complete security.

As Selwyn led the way to the west veranda, Willis could see his parents ahead of him, his mother stepping lightly and swiftly, moving her head to peer into the library and the dining room. His father walked deliberately, with the careful gait of a man used to traveling over rough country, his hands in his pockets, his shoulders bent slightly forward. When they came to the open door of the west veranda, Selwyn halted, and spoke in a gentle voice that seemed unnaturally loud after the silent progress down the hall.

"Mr. and Mrs. Wayde," he said, "and Master Wayde."

Another silence followed, through which came the humming of the crickets. In the afterglow of the sunset, it was still possible to see the view, mellow and soft through the haze of a hot evening. The lawn and the rose garden in the foreground were clear but the vistas through the oak and beech trees of the fields and pastures to the bend of the river were already indistinct and it was dark enough to see the sparks of the fireflies against the trees.

The disciplined beauty of the view from the west veranda held Willis's attention for only a brief moment. Then there was a creaking of porch chairs as an elderly lady and a gentleman in a dinner jacket rose to greet them. Somehow he was not at all what Willis expected. Instead of being large he was small and almost frail. His gray hair was brushed back from a high, thin forehead. His nose was straight and long, and his pendulous lower lip always twitched before he spoke, giving an impression that he was about to stammer, even though his words were always measured and precise. His voice, which he seldom raised, had a flat nasal ring which still was modulated and agreeable.

"It's very kind of you to come to us at such short notice, Mrs. Wayde," he said. "I hope my note didn't seem like a summons. My sister was afraid it might, but it seemed to me that a dinner away from home might be a rest for you after such a hot day. I hope everything is comfortable at the cottage."

Mr. Harcourt smiled graciously, and looked at Willis.

"And this is your son, is it? What's your first name, Master Wayde?"

Willis cleared his throat. "Willis, sir," he said.

"I'm glad to meet you, Willis. You must meet my grandson and granddaughter tomorrow, but first you must all meet my sister, Mrs. Blood. She's paying me her annual parochial summer visit. She wants to be sure we're not mismanaging the mill."

Mrs. Blood was an inch taller than Mr. Harcourt, and her white hair, done in a pompadour, made her look taller still. Her eyes were dark and sharp and she had her brother's smile. She stood up very straight in her black silk dress with her pearls tied around her throat, and her diamond and sapphire rings glittered in the waning light.

"How do you do, Mrs. Wayde," she said. "My brother tells me you come from the West."

"Oh, yes," Mrs. Wayde said. "Kansas."

"Oh," Mrs. Blood said. "Kansas."

"What shall we have before dinner?" Mr. Harcourt asked. "Shall it be sherry or a dry Martini?"

"Oh, thank you," Mrs. Wayde said, "but I never touch anything strong."

Alfred Wayde laughed loudly.

"Cynthia was born in a dry state," he said.

[19]

"My brother ignores the eighteenth amendment," Mrs. Blood said. "I should like some sherry, Henry."

"If it's all the same with you," Mr. Wayde said, "I could do with one of those Martinis."

When Willis sat apart from the rest of them after the sherry and the cocktails came, he did not feel gauche or shy, because in some odd way the house had offered its protection to him, giving him a feeling of being absolutely safe.

"Will you have another cocktail, Alfred?" Mr. Harcourt said.

"I don't mind if I do," Willis heard his father answer.

"I won't join you, if you don't mind," Mr. Harcourt said. "We're having some wine for dinner—Château Lafite."

"I don't know much about wines," Alfred Wayde said. "It's always hard liquor or nothing on most jobs, except in California."

"It's a very lovely view," Willis heard his mother saying to Mrs. Blood.

Willis did not hear Mrs. Blood's reply, because a large police dog walked slowly up the steps to the veranda, wagging his tail, and Willis patted his long head.

"That's Benny," Mr. Harcourt said. "His real name is Benvenuto Cellini. He doesn't make friends with everybody."

"I get on pretty well with dogs, sir," Willis said.

"You and Benny and I will have to walk around and see the place tomorrow," Mr. Harcourt said. "Well, here's Selwyn with your Martini. Would you mind bringing it with you? We'd better go in to dinner."

When the Harcourt dining table was extended for family birthdays or for luncheon after the annual stockholders' meeting, more than twenty people could sit at it comfortably. The dining room never seemed too small on these occasions, but conversely, when the table was contracted to a small circle, as it was that night, there was never any sense of sitting in too large a room. The marble-top Chippendale serving table, the magenta brocade curtains drawn over the French windows, the family portraits, and the silver service on the mid-Victorian sideboard only seemed to draw closer. Somehow the dining room was never formidable or forbidding, even with Selwyn and a maid waiting on the table.

That night at the big house Willis must have seen the portrait of the clean-shaven old Mr. William Harcourt, standing against a pastoral background, with his hand resting on the head of an Irish wolfhound. He must have seen the less skillful portraits of Mr. Henry's own father, George Harcourt, with his gray sideburns, and of Mrs. George Harcourt, Mr. Henry's mother, in white satin. The Sargent portraits of Mr. Henry and of his wife, who had died in 1910, were in the upstairs hall in those days. He must have seen the screen before the pantry door with its panels done by Lawrence, and the silver tea service and the cans by Paul Revere inherited by Mr. William Harcourt from his Boston wife; and he must have seen the silver coffee urn presented to Mr. William on his seventieth birthday by the stockholders and the employees of the Harcourt Mill. Willis surely must have seen all these objects, but not one of them moved out from the others to obtrude on his consciousness. Instead everything gave the impression of being expected, down to the lace tablecloth and the green Chinese place plates and the Georgian candlesticks and the cut flowers in the center of the table.

The meal was simple enough—cold consommé, guinea hen with bread sauce, and salad, and blueberry pie for dessert, and he was given a glass of ginger ale instead of wine.

"My brother says you can turn your hand to anything, Mr. Wayde," Mrs. Blood was saying to his father.

"Well, ma'am," Mr. Wayde said, "I've been thrown against a lot of stuff in railroading, building, and mining. They all come down to pretty much the same thing in the end."

"What do you mean, the same thing?" Mrs. Blood asked.

"Making what you've got on hand do what it isn't meant to do," Mr. Wayde said.

"Wine, sir?" Selwyn asked him. "Or Scotch and soda?"

"Whisky," Mr. Wayde said, "and water. Did you ever know Mr. Harrod Cash, ma'am, out in Denver?"

"No," Mrs. Blood answered, "I don't know Mr. Cash."

"No reason why you should, I suppose," Mr. Wayde said, "except Harrod—you get to first names fast in Denver, ma'am—he gave me a letter to your brother when I got through at Whetstone. Harrod was always strong for Harcourt belting."

"I'm glad to hear it," Mrs. Blood said, "but what's Whetstone?"

"The Whetstone Mine, the best silver and lead property in the Rockies, ma'am. I was working in the mill when water came in and flooded number seven and six levels. You never can tell where water is inside a mountain, and that's a fact."

"Alf is absent-minded about a lot of things," Willis heard his mother saying, "but never about machinery."

"I've noticed that myself," Mr. Harcourt said. "He's a great comfort to me at the mill. You see, I haven't a mechanical, only a business, mind."

"Some people think Alf is lazy," Mrs. Wayde said. "When I first met Alf, I thought he was. It was at a dancing party at the Y.W.C.A. in Topeka."

Mr. Harcourt's lower lip twitched and then he smiled.

"I'd like to know," he said, "how he ever got to the Y.W.C.A. in Topeka."

"Oh, a contracting firm was building some water works," Mrs. Wayde said, "and some of the young fellows on the job came to the dance. I guess Alf went because he'd lost all his money at poker the night before. I was teaching in the high school and living at the 'Y,' and my sister Nell and I invited him out to the farm on Sunday with another fellow. He just sat on the piazza with his feet on the rail until the windmill broke down and we were out of water."

Mr. Harcourt's lower lip twitched, but he did not speak.

"Well, Alf got right up off the porch and climbed up the windmill. I get dizzy when I look down from a height, don't you, Mr. Harcourt?"

"Always," Mr. Harcourt said, "always."

"You see, Alf doesn't notice where he is, if his mind is on something. I don't believe he knows where he is right now."

They both glanced across the table at Alfred Wayde.

"No, ma'am," Willis heard his father say to Mrs. Blood, "I'm not a mining engineer, but anyone learns something about rocks when he handles dynamite."

"Well, Alf came down with a broken cog or something," Mrs. Wayde said, "and asked where a blacksmith shop was. I said I'd take him down to Sawyer's and we hitched up the buckboard. Ned Sawyer's a Baptist and doesn't work Sundays, but Alf started up the forge himself, and he made a whole new cogwheel right by hand. It took him six hours and he was a sight when he got through, but he got the windmill going."

"Did you say you play bridge, Mr. Wayde?" Mrs. Blood was saying.

"Yes, ma'am, sometimes," Alfred Wayde answered, "but Cynthia would rather talk."

And Mrs. Wayde still was talking.

"If Alf's interested, he can do anything, but when he loses interest he drifts away to somewhere else. I hope you can keep him interested. With Willis growing up he ought to go to school regularly. I can't go on teaching him much longer. I hope Alf will like it here and I hope you'll like him, Mr. Harcourt."

"If I didn't, I wouldn't have let him have the cottage, Mrs. Wayde," Mr. Harcourt said.

"Now you've mentioned it," Mrs. Wayde said, "it isn't right charging us so little rent, but maybe Alfred got the figure wrong."

Mr. Harcourt placed his napkin on the table.

"It's business, Mrs. Wayde," he said. "Not that I won't be glad to look across the lawn at night and see lights in the cottage. It's to my advantage to have you and your husband contented."

His flat measured voice left no room for argument.

"There are difficulties in running any business. My son Bryson, whom I hope you'll meet later, will take over eventually, but in the meanwhile when the windmill breaks I have to fix it in my own way. Tomorrow I want to talk to you about sending Willis to school, and if there's anything you need, please ask me, Mrs. Wayde."

Willis saw his mother gaze blankly at Mr. Harcourt.

"I'm glad if you appreciate Alf," she said. "A lot of his bosses haven't. All I can say is thank you."

"Don't thank me," Mr. Harcourt said. He pushed back his chair. "Alfred."

"A small explosive charge is better than a big one," Alfred Wayde was saying, "if you're familiar with the conditions, ma'am. Too much power always is a waste."

"Alfred," Mr. Harcourt said again, and Alfred Wayde looked up. "You and I might have our brandy and coffee in the library, and Willis can come with us."

"I ought to get back to unpack," Mrs. Wayde said, looking at Mrs. Blood. "Willis can take me home."

They had all risen from the table, and Mr. Harcourt smiled at Mrs. Blood.

"It's early still," he said. "Ruth, please induce Mrs. Wayde to stay a little longer. You haven't had an opportunity yet to make her feel at home."

"Yes, Henry," Mrs. Blood said. "Please don't leave me alone, Mrs. Wayde."

As Willis followed Mr. Harcourt and his father into the hall, he heard Mrs. Blood speak again.

"Every time I visit my brother," she was saying, "he reminds me more and more of our father. When he speaks in that tone of voice, it's always best to do exactly what he says."

Willis still knew nothing about the Harcourt Mill, but he was already aware of its pervading influence. Ever since he had passed those stark brick buildings that afternoon, their aura had surrounded him. The mill had been with them in the dining room, and it was with them even more obviously in the library. It was a living organism—any factory always was. Mr. Harcourt was its brain and motivating force, but Mr. Harcourt himself was only a part of it, and Alfred Wayde was also part of it, and in consequence so was Willis. Even Mrs. Blood belonged to it. Her pearl necklace and her rings came from the mill, and the same was true of the food that they had eaten. Willis could think of the leather-backed books of the library and its black leather easy chairs and sofa and all its walnut paneling as coming from the mill.

His father followed Mr. Harcourt into the library, walking with his unconsciously careful step, gazing curiously at the books and the moose head over the mantel.

"Sit down," Mr. Harcourt said. "Sit down, Willis. Will you have a cigar, Alfred?"

"Thanks," Alfed Wayde said, "I could do with a cigar."

"It's funny," Mr. Harcourt said, "how few young fellows like you care for a good cigar. I'll get one in my study."

He walked through a narrow doorway, and Willis and his father were alone for a moment in the cool softly lighted room. Alfred Wayde lowered himself into one of the heavy leather chairs.

"How's it going, boy?" he asked.

"Fine," Willis answered.

"Well, take your weight off your feet. This certainly is a soft seat. Different from Klamath Falls, isn't it, boy?"

Willis felt a strong desire to laugh. His father could always make him laugh if he put his mind to it.

"Just take it easy," Alfred Wayde said. "Always take it easy." But they both stood up when Mr. Harcourt came back.

"Here," Mr. Harcourt said, "this is a good light Havana. There's a cutter on the table."

"No need for a cutter, thanks," Alfred Wayde said. He pinched off the end of his cigar and Selwyn came in with a tray of after-dinner coffee and brandy.

"Did everything go all right in Building Three today?" Mr. Harcourt asked.

"It's pretty well cleared out," Alfred Wayde said. "We're going to need some new construction under the vats and a new compressor."

"All right," Mr. Harcourt said. "I'd like to see those blueprints tomorrow morning if they're ready."

"They're ready," Alfred Wayde answered.

"Good!" Mr. Harcourt said. "I should have looked at Number Three myself today, but things were pretty busy in the office. I had Decker in and the lawyers were down from Boston." Mr. Harcourt flicked the ash of his cigar carefully into a brass tray on the table beside him.

"I'm buying those Klaus patents. Bryson isn't going to like it, but I'm going ahead."

Willis's father nodded slowly, without moving his glance from Mr. Harcourt's face.

"You're not going to miss any boats if you do," he said.

Mr. Harcourt sat still for a moment.

"It's difficult when you get to be my age," he said, "to branch into new ideas. Well, Bryson isn't going to like it."

"You won't miss any boats," Alfred Wayde said again. "You've got to get into conveyor belting, and the Klaus patents will put you on the ground floor. You won't ever be the Goodrich Rubber Company, but you'll have a process no one else owns."

"I hope so," Mr. Harcourt said. "We'll have a business talk tomorrow, but let's talk about Willis now. His mother was asking about what he will do for school."

"Oh," Alfred Wayde said. "Yes, Cynthia wants me to stay put somewhere until Willis gets to college."

Willis never forgot that scrap of conversation about the conveyor belts. Later, when he was able to understand its significance, he understood why they were living in the garden house. If it had not been for the Klaus patents, the mill would have lost business all through the twenties and would not have survived the depression, and it was his father who had advised the purchase.

Selwyn tapped softly on the open door of the library.

"Mr. and Mrs. Bryson Harcourt are with the ladies in the drawing room," he said.

The long drawing room with its tall French windows looked over the south terrace. If it represented the late Victorian period of decoration, all its furnishings, down to the useless articles that cluttered the tables, possessed their peculiar relationship. Its two crystal chandeliers from England, its mantel of Italian marble, its groups of chairs and sofas, and its ornate lamps—now converted from kerosene to electricity—were cumbersome taken by themselves, but they all added a personal quality to the room. Somehow they reminded you of the people who had gathered about the grand piano and had walked over the huge wine-colored carpet, which was growing worn. It was one of those rooms that could never be imitated. Even if Willis could have gained possession of all the room's furniture, it would never have been possible to have arranged those component parts into the pattern he remembered. And the people standing near the fireplace, even down to his mother and father, were part of the pattern.

"Mildred," Mr. Harcourt said, "you haven't met Willis Wayde yet, have you? Willis, this is my daughter-in-law, Mrs. Harcourt, and Mr. Harcourt. I'm sorry you didn't bring the children over, Mildred."

He spoke as though Willis were a grown-up guest, but then his manner always was the same with everyone. He had been born with that sort of inner assurance you could never pick up from any book of etiquette.

"Happy to meet you, ma'am," Willis said, and he could hear his own voice from that past balanced awkwardly between childhood and adolescence.

If Mrs. Bryson Harcourt did not look entirely happy to meet him, nevertheless she managed to smile. She was tall and angular in her green silk dress, taller than her husband.

"How do you do?" she said to Willis, and gave his hand a strong quick shake. "I'm sorry I didn't bring Bill and Bess over, Governor. I just didn't think about it."

She always called Mr. Henry Harcourt "Governor."

"Hello, young fellow," Mr. Bryson Harcourt said. In many ways he was a picture of what Mr. Henry Harcourt must have been when he was younger. His clean-shaven face was tanned and he had a trace of the Harcourt lower lip, but his features always seemed less in focus than his father's.

"We can only stay for a minute, Governor," Mrs. Harcourt said. "We just stopped over to see how you were."

"I'm bearing up, Mildred," Mr. Harcourt said. "We had Decker and the lawyers over at the mill today, Bryson."

"I was at Marblehead racing," Mr. Bryson said.

"Of course," Mr. Harcourt answered. "I should have remembered. How did you come out, Bryson?"

"Third," Mrs. Bryson said. "Almost second, Governor."

"Mildred always hates to lose," Mr. Bryson said.

"Of course I do," Mrs. Harcourt said. "Married couples never ought to sail in the same boat. Bryson, didn't you tell the Governor you weren't coming in today?"

"It doesn't make any difference," Mr. Harcourt said, "but see me the first thing tomorrow, won't you, Bryson?"

"All right, Father," Bryson said. "It must have been a hot day for traveling, Mrs. Wayde. I hope everything in the cottage is all right. I wanted to add on to it when we were married but Mildred wanted to build."

"I was right, wasn't I, Governor?" Mrs. Harcourt said.

"Of course Mildred was right," Mrs. Blood said. "A larger house would not have looked well across the lawn."

Those brief snatches of dialogue were a part of the façade with which the Harcourts always contrived to surround themselves. There was good nature and affection in the words and even humor, without a trace of strain and no undertone of disappointment. Only time and perspective lent significance and sadness to anything that was said. It was only after Willis knew what the Klaus patents meant that he recalled that Bryson

Harcourt had been racing at Marblehead on the day they were purchased. There had not been a trace of anger and not a hint of sorrow. The truth was that the Harcourts were all too fond of each other and knew each other too well to betray obvious emotion. Something must have been said, of course. Willis often wondered what words the father and son had spoken when they met in the mill the next morning, but no one had ever heard that conversation and neither of them ever mentioned it.

His mother was the only one who noticed anything at the time. When they were walking home across the lawn to the cottage, she was the first one who spoke.

"Alf," she said, "they're not our kind of people."

"How do you mean, not our kind of people?" his father asked.

The lawn, Willis was thinking, resembled the heavy carpets in the Harcourt hall.

"They're not our kind of people," his mother said again. "Alf, you never notice people."

"My God, Cynthia," Alfred Wayde said. "They were just talking, weren't they?"

"There was something that made Mr. Harcourt angry," Willis's mother said.

"Who? Old Harcourt? He didn't act angry."

"I know he didn't. That's why I say they're not our kind of people."

"Well," Alfred Wayde said, "we got a good feed out of it, and you didn't have to cook it."

"Alf," his mother said, "there's one thing I don't like."

"What don't you like?" his father asked.

"Somehow he makes me feel we're all living here, Alf, on charity."

"Charity?" Alfred Wayde said, and he laughed. "Don't you believe it, Cynthia. I'm earning everything we get."

His mother's voice grew sharp. Willis could not see her face, but he knew that her lips were closed in a tight, disapproving line.

"Then why doesn't he pay you cash instead of giving us things?" she asked.

It was a good question and his father must have known it.

"Because he would rather give than pay," he said. "It makes some people feel better—giving than paying."

That answer of his father's was one of the wisest things that Willis ever heard him say about people. Mr. Henry Harcourt had to be the center of the Harcourt world, and he was a very good one, too, until he died.

Willis often thought that there was always a greater change when darkness gathered over the Harcourt place than there was anywhere else. The darkness was like a rising tide that covered the gardens and the houses, erasing everything as a still sea erased footprints on a beach. The sound of the night, the incessant calling of the crickets, assuming an intensity that never rose or diminished, covered all vanity and striving. A greater, more mysterious world, one that cared nothing for minutiae, covered the world of the Harcourts. In no other place he knew did he have such a strong feeling that small things did not matter, including his own ambitions, as when night engulfed the Harcourt place.

It was always different in the morning, when the mist and the damp of night rolled back before the sun. The complicated values returned with daylight. Willis was awakened the next morning by the whistle from the mill, which always blew at seven. He heard the thump of his father's feet on the floor of the bedroom across the upstairs hall, and then he heard his mother calling him to get up and start the fire in the kitchen. They were all following the familiar routine which had been created by other whistles in other places.

"What am I going to do if you take the Ford, Alf?" his mother asked. "I've got to get downtown and buy some groceries."

Alfred Wayde looked up vaguely from his coffee.

"Someone from the other house will be going," he said. "Call up and ask. They'll give you a ride to town."

"No," his mother said, "I don't want to be obligated, Alf."

"All right," his father said. "I'll be back at five and drive you over."

She said she wanted to get the feel of everything in the house and she could only do that when she was alone. She told Willis to go out and walk around and get used to the lay of the land, and keep away from the big house and not bother anyone.

It was quite a walk that Willis took that morning. The dew was still over everything and there was a smell of fresh-cut grass, where two men were working on the lawn with hand-mowers.

When he walked down the road to the stables, the routine of the place was already starting. Two more men were working in the kitchen garden and another was trimming shrubbery. A stoop-shouldered man with a blank and patient face was spraying roses in the cutting garden and talking to himself.

"God damn them bugs," he was saying.

It was Mr. MacDonald, the head gardener, and Mr. MacDonald was always a dour man. A stout man in blue overalls was standing by the gasoline engine in the pump house. His hands were in his pockets and his face was red and chubby. He took one glance at Willis and then turned away again. It was Mr. Beane, the estate superintendent, who knew every pipe and wire and water conductor on the place. Like Patrick, the people on the place already accepted Willis as a fact, but they did not know where he fitted in any more than Willis knew himself, and they did not want to talk until they knew, but Mr. Harcourt's police dog felt differently. When Benny saw Willis he wagged his tail and ran ahead of him toward the oak woods beyond the house. Benny was the only one that morning who knew where Willis fitted in. Benny was always agreeable to the employees on the place, but he never went for walks with them, not even with Mr. Beane.

The stretches of woodland behind the walls were as disciplined as the paintings of an English park, and like the brook that ran through the southern end of the property they were all units in the landscape plan. Once each year a party of tree surgeons, watched by Mr. Harcourt and Mr. Beane, cut down dead limbs and crowding brush and saplings, so that the large oaks and pines and beeches were allowed to grow unhindered, with the brook winding softly among their shadows. It was possible to walk freely beneath the trees, but for greater convenience the place was interspersed with well-cleared paths called walks, the names of which soon became familiar—the Brook Walk, the Pine Walk, the Hickory Hill, the Azalea, and the Rhododendron Walks. Without knowing its name yet, Willis walked down the Brook Walk with the police dog trotting ahead of him. The shade of the path and the cool sound of the brook could not dispel the heat above them, and bright shafts of sunlight continually fell across the path. He was walking toward the Bryson Harcourts' house and he saw it for the first time when the trees thinned out near the edge of a large field. The house lay at the end of a gradual slope, a newer structure than the big house and almost as large, made of brick in Georgian style, forming a minor principality within the general boundary, with its own lawns, gardens, stable, and tennis court. The unexpected sight of it made Willis feel like a trespasser, and sudden shyness made him turn away.

He was walking back toward a bend of the path near the foot of a large white pine tree when the dog sprang forward suddenly and a girl's voice called, "Down, Benny." For a second Willis felt an acute desire to hide, but instead he walked slowly around the turn and saw a girl somewhat younger than himself, patting the police dog's head.

The girl in front of Willis wore a middy blouse and a blue pleated skirt, and her blond hair was done in a heavy braid. Her face was as freckled as his own and her eyes were critical. He never forgot their color—a sort of greenish-blue.

"How did you get in here?" she asked.

"I was just walking around with the dog," Willis answered.

"Well, he isn't your dog," she said.

"I know he isn't," Willis said.

"Then how did you find him?" she asked.

"He was over by the big house," Willis answered, "and he came along with me for company, I guess."

"Oh," the girl said. "You're one of the people that my grandfather gave the garden house to, aren't you? Beane said there was going to be a boy."

"Yes," Willis said, "that's me, I guess."

"Well, that's all right then," the girl said. "Beane said you were about Bill's age, but you're bigger. I thought you were a town boy. They sneak over the wall sometimes."

"I didn't sneak over any wall," Willis said.

"I didn't say you did," the girl said, "and you needn't act angry. This is my grandfather's place, and it's my place, partly. At least my brother and I are going to own it some day."

"I'm not acting angry," Willis said.

"You don't need to," the girl said again. "And I have a right to ask you questions. You don't know your way around here, do you?"

"No," Willis said. "I was just looking around. He said I could go anywhere."

"Who said?"

"Mr. Harcourt said," he answered.

"All right," she said, "but I guess you don't know who I am, do you?"

"I guess you must be the girl," Willis said.

"What girl?" she asked.

"The girl they were talking about at the big house last night."

"Oh, you were up there, were you?" she said. "Well, my name's Bess Harcourt. What's your name?"

"Willis," he told her, "Willis Wayde."

"Did you know this brook is stocked with trout?"

"No," Willis said.

"He didn't tell you you could fish, did he?"

"No," Willis said.

"You could if I told you. Do you know how to cast?"

"Yes," Willis said.

"I bet you don't," she said. "Where did you learn?"

"Out West," Willis said. "There are a lot of streams better than this out West."

"I've got to study French with Mademoiselle this morning. Do you know French?"

"Not very much," Willis said.

"I didn't think you did, but we can go fishing this afternoon. Maybe I'll bring Bill. Meet me here at three o'clock and put on some old clothes. Where did you get those clothes?"

"In Kansas City," Willis answered.

"I should think you'd take your coat off anyway," she said. "Can you play tennis?"

"No," Willis said.

"Well, maybe Bill's tutor can teach you. Bill has a tutor from Harvard. Can you ride?"

"Yes," Willis said, "everybody can ride out West."

"I don't mean Western riding," she said. "I wish you had a haircut, and you wouldn't look so funny."

"You don't look so hot yourself," Willis said.

"It's none of your business how I look," she answered. "I'm not trying to look any way at all."

"Neither am I," Willis said.

"Oh, yes, you are," she answered. "You're trying to show off. I'll be here at three o'clock, and don't keep me waiting."

"Bess," a boy's voice was calling, "Bess!"

"Oh, all right," Bess called back, "all right."

"Come on so we can do our damned French," the boy's voice called.

Of course it was Bill Harcourt who was calling. A second later Willis saw him, hurrying down the path, a slender, dark-haired boy in white duck trousers.

"It's all right, Bill," Bess said. "He's one of the people in the garden house. His name is Willis Wayde."

"Oh," Bill said. He looked at Willis quickly but not critically like Bess.

"It's nice there's someone else around here," he said. "You've got to come over and see us."

"We're going fishing this afternoon," Bess said.

"You and your fishing," Bill said. "All you want is someone to show off in front of. Come on, Bess."

Everyone had certain functions on the Harcourt place, as Willis learned without resentment. It was part of the order, he began to understand, that Patrick and Mr. Beane and everyone else should address Bill and Bess as Mr. Bill and Miss Bess, when they usually called him Willis. On the other hand, Bill and Bess asked him around quite often to their house, but they hardly ever asked Mr. Beane's son, Granville, there. It was natural, however, that Willis and Granville became best friends, because they went to high school together. When anyone told him, as the town girls and boys frequently did, that Bill and Bess Harcourt were stuck-up kids, Willis knew that this was not so. Bill and Bess were no different from anyone else, when you got to know them. They only led different lives.

The Bryson Harcourts always moved to Boston in the autumn to a life of which Willis knew nothing, and Bess went to a girls' private school there, and Bill went to a boys' boarding school in Milton. Willis was not even curious about what they did, being absorbed in his own problems. They would part casually and without much regret, and when they met they would pick up things where they had left them.

Mr. Harcourt went to Boston, too, in late November, but the big house stayed open, and he or Mr. Bryson were always in it for a night or two every week. The general affairs of the mill were in the hands of Mr. Henry Hewett, the plant manager, who lived with Mrs. Hewett in a square white house just across the street from the mill buildings, but Mr. Harcourt was the one who made the main decisions.

III

ONLY A DAY or two after he had arrived, Willis saw Mr. Harcourt again. It was a lonely time before school opened, with nothing much for him to do except run errands for his mother, who was very busy putting things to rights in their new house. The size of the estate still made him homesick, if you could be that way without having any particular home to be sick for. Yet he must already have begun fitting into the place, because Mr. MacDonald had spoken to him that morning, when Willis had started out on another of his walks. He had stopped at the edge of the vegetable garden, which lay basking in the sun. Its rows of corn, carrots, lettuce, and beets stretched like city streets to the cold frame, and Mr. MacDonald was scowling at the turf edging of the strawberry bed.

"Hello, Willis," Mr. MacDonald said.

"Good morning, sir," Willis said.

"You call me Mr. MacDonald, Willis," Mr. MacDonald said. "But there's no need saying sir. God Almighty, I don't own this garden."

"Excuse me, sir," Willis said. "You talk to older people that way out West."

"Is that so?" Mr. MacDonald said. "You never saw an estate like this in the West, did you?"

"Maybe not so fancy," Willis said, "but there might be something like it in California or Oregon."

"California," Mr. MacDonald said. "Everybody's always blowing about California. I bet you never saw a squash like that in California. It's going to win first prize at the fair, if the judges ain't crooked, and so will my glads and chrysanthemums, by God! Hell, you can raise anything on this ground that they raise in California, only you got to work for it here and not loaf. They don't have the bugs we do in California."

"They've got quite a lot," Willis said.

"Hell," Mr. MacDonald told him. "There's a special bug here that eats everything, and more of them keep coming, because we're civilized. I bet they don't spray their apples five times a year like I do mine."

Mr. MacDonald stopped and rubbed his hands together.

"You've got to know your bugs here and you've got to watch 'em. Like I say, there's some little bastard eating everything—green worms on the tomatoes, and potato bugs of course, and corn borer in the corn, by God, and cutworms underground. Mr. Harcourt don't know what we're up against here. I don't know how it's going to end."

"Well, everything looks pretty good," Willis said.

"You're damned right it looks good, because I make a study of it. You go down there and look at Mr. Bryson's vegetables, or flowers. Hell, that feller Wilkins down there puts on a show, but there's nothing behind it."

"Who is he?" Willis asked.

"Hell, he's Mr. Bryson's gardener," Mr. MacDonald told him. "I don't say anything against anyone, but I've got eyes. You'll see a lot around here if you keep your eyes open, boy, and now you'd better run along. I'm busy."

"Mr. MacDonald," Willis said, "is there anything I could do to help you, for a day or two?"

"For a day or two?" Mr. MacDonald said. "God Almighty, it would take me a year or two before you'd be of any help."

"I've worked summers on my grandfather's farm. In Kansas," Willis said, "out around Topeka."

"God Almighty, this isn't a farm," Mr. MacDonald said. "Why don't you go and feed the swans down in the pond?"

"What swans?" Willis asked.

"God Almighty, haven't you got eyes?" Mr. MacDonald asked. "The swans, down in the pond off the front driveway, for God's sake. Now run along. I'm busy."

Those were the first words Willis had had with anyone on the place, except a few with Patrick. He had seen the pond on the lawn by the front driveway, and sure enough there were three swans down there, floating effortlessly on the smooth water, and there was a little island in the middle of the pond with a small house on it. While Willis stood on the bank, the largest of the birds glided toward him, and Willis called to him encouragingly. He had not the remotest idea of what might happen, until the bird made a hissing sound, flapped its huge wings and half flew and half sprang out of the water. Willis took a startled step backward, but the bird propelled itself toward him, and Willis backed away again.

"Don't run," a voice behind him said. The swan still hissed and spread its wings, and Willis turned around and saw Mr. Harcourt.

"Jupiter always loses his temper if you go too near the edge," Mr. Harcourt said. "Get back in the water with the girls, Jupiter. Behave your-self, behave."

Mr. Harcourt walked briskly toward the swan.

"Get back in the water, Jupiter," Mr. Harcourt said, "and you needn't expect a gratuity every time you see me."

"I didn't mean to stir him up, sir," Willis said.

"The next time you come, throw him a piece of bread," Mr. Harcourt said. "He's like certain members of my own family. He expects something and loses his temper if he doesn't get it. Even the rector is that way if you don't give enough. I've just been talking to Mr. Bowles on the telephone for half an hour about the parish hall. That's why I'm late, and just when I was driving out I saw you." He nodded toward the driveway, and Willis saw that the Locomobile was standing waiting.

"I was just walking around, sir," Willis said. "I was up in the vegetable garden and then I came down here."

"Landing in a place like this must be a little difficult," Mr. Harcourt said. "Of course I'm used to it, having been brought up here. My father always kept swans in the pond. I suppose that's why I do. Was MacDonald in the garden?"

"Yes, sir," Willis said.

"I suppose he talked to you about insects," Mr. Harcourt said. "He always does to me. If you haven't anything to do, why don't you come down with me and see the mill?"

Mr. Harcourt could always put anyone at ease. It was not charm ex-actly. It was his being the same with everyone.

He told Willis not to sit with Patrick but in back with him, because, he said, he wanted the pleasure of his company. It was only a long while later that Willis came to learn that there was a reason for Mr. Harcourt's interest when Mr. Harcourt asked him where he had lived and where he had gone to school. He was really asking about the life of Alfred Wayde, and it was not such a bad way to gather information, as Willis realized later, when he learned the same technique. If you talked to someone, even a boy, there had to be an exchange of confidence, and you had to tell about yourself in return for what you got, and this required a deceptive sort of guile. It was a form of art which very few could master, and Willis never could be the artist that Mr. Harcourt was.

When Mr. Harcourt was a boy, he said, he used to drive with his own father to the mill—in a buggy drawn by a dappled gray. There were more workers' houses along the Sudley Road now, but he had tried to keep to Mr. George Harcourt's plan when new houses were being built during the First World War. A war, Mr. Harcourt said, had always made the factory grow. It was during the Civil War that Mr. Harcourt had started riding down there with his father. It was quite a place in those days, more picturesque than now. The mill had been run by steam instead of electricity, and coal barges were unloaded at the dock by gangs of Irish workmen. The houses made a little village of their own now. There was a general store, and the general manager's house had been built in the eighties just where Mr. Harcourt's father had wanted it to be. Mr. Harcourt touched on these matters casually, as though Willis knew about them already, and that was the best way to learn about the mill, by a sort of osmosis.

The Harcourt Mill was running at full blast that morning. The hum and the clatter that came from its open windows and the pungent smell of rubber from the vats combined to make it into a great machine, and all the people behind the wire fence that surrounded it were moving according to its discipline. That was the best way to envisage any industry.

The machine was running smoothly, as it always did while Mr. Harcourt was alive. When the Locomobile pulled up in front of the mill, the gates swung back, but Mr. Harcourt shook his head.

"No, no," he said to Patrick, and he had to raise his voice above the noise. "I'll walk around for a while, but come back for us at lunchtime, Patrick."

He stepped out of the Locomobile lightly and quickly and nodded to the gateman.

"Stay close behind me, Willis, or you may get lost," he said, and he hurried past the trucks by the loading platform. No one seemed to notice Mr. Harcourt and Willis as they walked by. Mr. Harcourt always prided himself on never interrupting anything, and everyone there accepted his presence as a piece of everyday routine. Mr. Harcourt never stopped, he never gave Willis an explanation, no matter how strange the sights were they encountered, but still a picture of the Harcourt process unrolled scroll-like for Willis as he followed Mr. Harcourt.

The Harcourt process was an accumulation of skills that had begun when the Harcourt Mill itself had started spinning yarn back in 1850. The durability and strength of Harcourt belting had given it a reputation in the trade of which the mill was proud. Though the process was largely mechanical, it was one that demanded care and precision. You talked about workmanship in sales conferences, but the morale of workmanship was something different. Later Willis learned subconsciously to estimate this morale, and he felt its presence on that first walk past the noisily accurate machinery. The labor in the Harcourt Mill was good skilled Yankee labor. Everyone in the Harcourt Mill was as good as everyone else, in his own way. The elderly foremen did not bother to look up as Mr. Harcourt moved past them, and every motion that the men made was lazily casual but at the same time beautifully precise. Mr. Harcourt walked through Sheds 1, 2, and 4 and through the pump shed and through Warehouse No. 1 to the shipping shed and then to the newer brick building, Unit No. 3, where they were installing new machinery. Except for sounds of hammering and the clicking of chain hoists, Unit 3 was quiet. A section of a boiler was being lowered to its foundation, and Willis saw his father in his shirt sleeves standing among the workmen, and for the first time in their walk Mr. Harcourt paused to watch.

"Easy, Joe," Willis heard his father saying. "Hold it." Alfred Wayde raised his voice to a shout. "Did you ever see an elephant set his foot on a man's head in the circus? Well, he's got to put his foot down easy. Good morning, Mr. Harcourt."

"Is it coming down all right?" Mr. Harcourt asked.

"The boys are doing fine," Alfred Wayde said.

"Then don't stop on my account," Mr. Harcourt said. "I brought Willis along with me this morning."

"Oh," Mr. Wayde said, "hello, Willis. Let her down, Joe. . . . Easy, easy."

His father had no time for anything except for the problem in front of him. He was always at his best when he was facing mechanical fact.

"We'd better go to the office now. I don't think we'll be able to help them, Willis," Mr. Harcourt said.

The mill office building had been designed by the Boston architectural firm of Wentworth and Hynde, early in 1916. Representatives from a number of industrial plants had begun to visit the mill at that time, and Mr. Harcourt had been the first to see the sales value of an impressive place in which to receive customers. Though the general spirit of the building was in keeping with the older mill construction, a considerable sum had been spent on nothing but appearance. Its large arched doorway and its small-paned windows with green shutters gave the mill office the appearance of a Federalist dwelling, as it stood by itself at the northwest corner of the plant on a carefully tended plot of lawn. It looked, as Mrs. Blood had once said—because she and some other family stockholders had been opposed to the extravagance—like a headmaster's overgrown house in a boys' school, but at the same time it indicated without words the solidity and prosperity of the whole establishment.

The interior also looked more like a house than an office. There was a fine hallway, and a broad staircase rising to the sales and plan departments. There was a large waiting room with a comfortable open fireplace —almost like a room in a men's club, as Mrs. Blood said—and there were a directors' room and rooms for all the chief executives. Instead of contracting with an office-supply house for the necessary desks, chairs, and tables, Mr. Harcourt had called in an interior decorator, who had furnished the main office with antique reproductions and often with genuine pieces of English Chippendale. The walls of the main hallway were hung with a collection of sailing-ship pictures, and the table in the directors' room was a Duncan Phyfe. As Mr. Harcourt said, the office building was the one place in which he had been allowed ever to express his own taste. If none of it had anything to do with commercial belting, it gave an impression of quality, which was the basis of the Harcourt product.

Mr. Harcourt's mind was on this subject now, as he walked into the main hall with Willis and nodded to Miss Minton, the receptionist, who sat behind a flat Georgian desk.

"How does this strike you, Willis?" he asked. "I've never seen why business should not be conducted in agreeable surroundings or why people should suffer when they talk over costs and figures. Is Mr. Hewett in, Miss Minton?"

"Yes, Mr. Harcourt. He was asking for you," Miss Minton said. "Shall I tell him you're in?"

"Oh, no," Mr. Harcourt said, "I'll stop in and see him."

Mr. Hewett's door was open. It was one of the rules at the Harcourt Mill that every one of the key officers should keep his door open except when he was in a private conference, and also that every officer should be ready to see any employee whatsoever, without appointment; and it was not a bad rule either for a small organization. Except for his neat brown suit and for his age—he was in his sixties then—Mr. Hewett reminded Willis of Mr. Beane at the Harcourt place. He had the same broad heavy shoulders and the same broad face, but unlike Mr. Beane he wore horn-rimmed spectacles. He was seated at his desk reading a report when Mr. Harcourt entered.

"Hello, H.H.," Mr. Harcourt said.

"Hello, H.H.," Mr. Hewett answered.

It was one of the old Harcourt jokes, that they both had the same first name and the same initials.

"This is Willis Wayde," Mr. Harcourt said.

"Oh, he's Alf's son, is he?" Mr. Hewett said. "Mary's been planning to pay a call on Mrs. Wayde, but she said it was only fair to let her get settled first. Well, how do things seem to you, Willis?"

Willis cleared his throat, and his voice broke slightly.

"It's pretty big to get an idea of it all at once," he said.

"Some people around here never do," Mr. Hewett said. "Will you draw up a chair and sit down, H.H.?"

"No, thanks," Mr. Harcourt said. "Is there anything I ought to know about, Henry?"

"Nothing this morning," Mr. Hewett said. "Decker is coming in this afternoon. Do you want me to sit in with you?"

"It might be just as well," Mr. Harcourt said. "Is Bryson in?"

"He's upstairs going over sales," Mr. Hewett said. "Bryson's got a new chart."

"No doubt I'll hear about it later," Mr. Harcourt said. "Henry, Number Five is working all right now, isn't it? At least it sounded right."

"Old Man Avery was sick that you noticed it yesterday," Mr. Hewett said. "He's breaking in two new cutters, you know. Anything else on your mind, H.H.?"

Mr. Harcourt pinched his lower lip gently.

"I saw them testing out that yarn, and I still wouldn't call it long-staple Egyptian. They ought to know better than to send us a shipment like that, and I wish you'd tell them so from me. And the skylight's still out at Unit Three."

"You're right it is," Mr. Hewett said, "but the boys are setting the new glass now."

Willis followed Mr. Harcourt further down the hall, and Mr. Harcourt stopped at another open door.

"Go in, Willis," he said. "This is where I stay when I'm here."

Willis was surprised by the simplicity of Mr. Harcourt's office. It was larger but its appointments were much simpler than those in the room of any other executive, but there was a reason behind everything with which Mr. Harcourt was connected. The battered desk, the old-fashioned carpet, the wooden chairs around a bare pine table, the grate, the tongs and shovel, the coal bucket by the fireplace had all come from the old office of William Harcourt. Then they had been used, with only a few additions, by Mr. George Harcourt, whose portrait, with that of Mr. William—both replicas of the ones in the Harcourt dining room—stared somberly from the walls. The furnishings indicated dramatically that Mr. Harcourt, as the head of the Harcourt Mill, could dispense with elaborate settings.

"These things here," Mr. Harcourt said to Willis, just as though Willis were a distinguished visitor, "were bought by my grandfather when he started the mill in 1850. A lot of business has been done across this desk. Sit down there, won't you, Willis?"

He pointed to a chair beside the desk and sat down himself on the swivel chair behind it, first glancing out of the window behind him and then out of the window to his left. Then he examined some papers in front of him without bothering to put on his spectacles.

"Excuse me just a minute, Willis," he said, and he read the office memoranda with a concentration that made Willis think that an invisible curtain had fallen between them.

"Miss Jackman," he called, "will you come in, please?"

Miss Jackman had been his secretary for twenty years, and she had been in the accounting department for some years previously. She was gray-haired and straight-backed, with steel-rimmed glasses that made her look like a schoolmarm. She opened the door of her own office at the end of the room, strolled across the threadbare carpet and halted in an almost military way in front of Mr. Harcourt's desk. Mr. Harcourt smiled at her, but she did not return his smile.

"You've got me down for a pretty tight schedule this afternoon, Miss Jackman," Mr. Harcourt said. "I'm getting old and I like time to turn around in."

"Yes," Miss Jackman said, "but you haven't got the time today. You should have been in earlier this morning."

"Perhaps I should have," Mr. Harcourt said.

"The bank's called you from Boston," Miss Jackman said. "Will you be at the meeting on Tuesday?"

"Yes," Mr. Harcourt answered, "and I'll have lunch at the club."

"Mr. Bryson wants to see you."

"What does he want now?" Mr. Harcourt asked.

"It's about the sales department."

"Oh dear me," Mr. Harcourt said. "Tell him to see me at the house this evening."

"They have guests for dinner tonight."

"Well," Mr. Harcourt said, "tell him before dinner. Is there anything else?"

"Yes," Miss Jackman said, and Willis thought that she hesitated because he was there.

"Well, what is it?" Mr. Harcourt said.

"Mrs. James telephoned. She's very anxious to have you call her back."

"She called me here at the office? She really shouldn't do that," Mr. Harcourt said. "Well, get her for me in ten minutes. Thank you, Miss Jackman."

Miss Jackman strode back into her own office and closed her door sharply and decisively, and Mr. Harcourt smiled.

"I'm afraid Miss Jackman is displeased with me this morning," he said. "Perhaps I'm too dependent on her, and it never pays to depend too much on anyone. I wonder what you think of the Harcourt Mill, Willis, now you've seen it. It seemed like a big place to me when I saw it first, but it isn't really. Perhaps you'll work here some day. Would you like it if I got you a job next summer in the school vacation?"

"Yes, sir," Willis answered. "I'd like it very much."

Hero worship is always natural in a boy. You were always filled at that age with unfulfilled wishes, and Willis was wishing just then that he could be exactly like Mr. Henry Harcourt, without having the least idea what such a wish entailed.

Mr. Harcourt leaned back in his swivel chair and his lower lip twitched slightly.

"From what I hear," Mr. Harcourt said, "your family moves around a lot. I used to enjoy change once myself. When I was your age I wanted to go to sea. When I was a little older my father had me travel for the mill. I always liked to see new parts of the country and to arrive in a strange town at night and move on next day, but now I'm caught in the mill machinery—not literally but figuratively. I suppose nearly everyone gets caught in some way eventually."

"I guess Pa doesn't want to get caught," Willis said.

"Your father has a creative mind," Mr. Harcourt said. "It's hard for anyone to stay still who has a mind like that."

"The last man Pa worked for," Willis said, "was a man named Mr. Harrod Cash in Denver. He's a pretty rich man, I guess. Maybe you're acquainted with Mr. Cash."

"Yes, I know him," Mr. Harcourt said. "He's a lot richer man than I am, actually."

"Well, he hired Pa to get the water out of a silver mine of his," Willis said, "and after Pa did it Mr. Cash wanted him to run the mine, but Pa said the mine wasn't a problem any longer."

"Your father told me about that," Mr. Harcourt said. "What does your father want you to do, Willis?"

"He wants me to be an engineer, too," Willis said. "He tries to get me to do logarithms and things like that. When there isn't any school around, Pa teaches me geometry and things and Ma teaches me the rest. She taught school once."

"Do you want to be an engineer?" Mr. Harcourt asked.

"No," Willis said. "I like making things, but I can't take machines apart."

"Do you like to read?" Mr. Harcourt asked.

"Yes, sir," Willis answered, "but not scientific books."

"Well," Mr. Harcourt said, "it seems to me it's time you went regularly to school. I'm going to tell you a secret, Willis."

Mr. Harcourt's face wrinkled into a frosty smile.

"It's rather a simple secret. You can repeat it if you want to, though I'd just as soon it remained between you and me. I happen to think your father is very exceptional in many ways. I want to use you to keep him with us, Willis."

"Me, sir?" Willis said.

"Yes," Mr. Harcourt answered. "I'm going to talk to him about your future this afternoon."

"I don't think he thinks much about my future, sir," Willis said. "Pa thinks mostly about machinery."

"Every father thinks about his son," Mr. Harcourt said. "You'll know when you have sons of your own."

He stopped, because the door to Miss Jackman's office had opened.

"Will you speak with Mrs. James now?" Miss Jackman said.

"Oh, yes, all right," Mr. Harcourt said.

There were two telephones on Mr. Harcourt's desk, one for the mill and one for the outside. He lifted up the receiver of the outside telephone.

"Hello, Harriet," he said. "I've been meaning to call you. I'll be in town on Tuesday—the bank meeting. . . . Yes, you can reach me at the club. . . . Why, that sounds delightful, Harriet. Shall we say the usual place at the usual time? . . . I don't really give a damn what Mildred and Bryson think. On Tuesday, then. Good-by, my dear."

Mr. Harcourt hung the receiver back and laughed softly. He glanced in a startled way at Willis.

"Excuse me, Willis," he said. "Miss Jackman!"

Miss Jackman opened the door quickly.

"Will you call up the house in town," Mr. Harcourt said. "Tell them I'll be in town over Tuesday night and if Patrick's waiting I'll go home for luncheon now."

"Mr. Bryson has asked you for dinner Tuesday night," Miss Jackman said.

"Yes," Mr. Harcourt said, "I know. Will you call up Mrs. Bryson and tell her that I'm sorry, I'll be in town, and you might tell her that I'm dining with Mrs. James."

"Wouldn't it be better if you told her that yourself?" Miss Jackman said.

"No, no," Mr. Harcourt said. "Well, Willis, we'd better be leaving now or your mother will think you're lost, and I want to thank you for your company, Willis, and for giving me a very pleasant morning."

IV

CLYDE AS a town had a self-consciousness peculiar to all small towns that have been settled for several centuries. New arrivals were always set apart from everyone else in Clyde. They might live there for years, die there, and leave their children there, but they were never an integral part of the town itself.

When Willis's mother joined the Ladies' Alliance of the Congregational Church, she was always known as Mrs. Wayde from the Harcourt Mill; and his father, when he joined the Clyde Men's Club at Mr. Hewett's invitation, was always known as the Wayde who worked at Harcourt's. It seemed curious to Willis that his own position was slightly different from that of his parents. The difference must have started with high school, where he was always known by the boys as "the guy," and by the girls as "the fellow," who lived at the Harcourt place. He was never the smartest boy in his class or the dullest one either, and he had entered school too late to be identified with any particular group. Yet it was amazing how much people remembered about him when it became worthwhile to remember.

Several of Willis's schoolmates had exchanged photographs with him at graduation time, and were happy to exhibit these pictures in later years. Willis was younger then, of course, but who wasn't? Still, in the school picture he had all the makings of what he was later—fine broad shoulders and a handsome face, in a manly way. It seemed strange, come to think of it, that he hadn't been voted the handsomest boy in the graduating class, instead of its president, Howard Twining. The reason probably was that Willis was still a little gawky and hadn't grown up to himself. He hadn't broadened up to his tallness, and he still was outgrowing his clothes. Even so he was very neat and eagerly agreeable-looking. His hair, though a mite long, was all slicked down and neatly parted, making one recollect that Willis was one of those boys in high school who was careful to carry a pocket comb. The nice thing about that picture was the straight, reliable way in which Willis looked at you

—an honest look and no smirking. His was a face you could trust, a sincere, honest, unpretentious face.

Mr. Bertram Lewis, who retired as principal of the Clyde High School in 1927, even at the age of eighty, distinctly remembered Willis Wayde. It seemed that Mr. Lewis, called Gumshoe Lewis by generations of his pupils, had realized the instant he set eyes on Willis that the young man had a future ahead of him, although Mr. Lewis did not announce his discovery for many, many years. It seemed only yesterday, he used to say, that Willis and his mother had called at the old high-school building on the day before school opened in September, 1922. He was struck immediately by the young man's fine, upstanding appearance. He could tell right away that Willis was exceptional. Often when the winter twilight fell and Mr. Lewis made a final tour before going home, he would find Willis still studying at his desk, and he remembered what Willis said, just as though it were yesterday. "When I work something out by myself," he said, "then I know it, Mr. Lewis."

It was strange when Willis once heard this anecdote repeated that he could not remember a single occasion when he had stayed after school, except once when Miss Minnie Wilson had kept him there after she had caught him passing a note across the aisle to Susan Brown, and it was not his note either. It was a note that Bill Ross, now owner of the Ross Garage, wanted delivered to Susan Brown.

Miss Minnie Wilson, who had taught English and kept Room 3, remembered Willis too. Willis wrote beautiful compositions, the best of which was entitled "The First Snowstorm of Winter." There was one thing about Willis that was very sweet. She thought he was just a little bit in love with her—you know how boys were sometimes. When she kept him after school once for passing the note to that little blond girl, Susan Brown—who was a flirt, if Miss Wilson did say so—she never forgot what Willis had said after they had been alone for a whole hour.

"You won't do it again, will you, Willis?" she had asked him.

"No, Miss Wilson," he had answered.

He had said it looking straight into her eyes. He was really saying that he had no use for any little flirt like Susan Brown and he cared for someone else, and she could tell who that someone was.

As years passed Susan Brown, too, became able to recall more and more about Willis Wayde at school. She had left high school abruptly in the middle of her senior year to marry Gerald Holtz, who was learning to compound prescriptions in Wilson's Drugstore. Since she had been going with a lot of other fellows, including Bill Ross, various individuals began counting on their fingers when their first child was born, but information as to the date of birth was vague, because Susan had been visiting cousins in Keene, New Hampshire, when this happened. By the time the last of the five Holtz children had reached school age, Susan remembered so much about Willis Wayde that she was finally able to reveal that she could have started going with Willis Wayde instead of with Gerald Holtz any time when they were at high school. Her desk was just across the aisle from his in old Minnie Wilson's room, and Willis Wayde was always leaving mash notes in her desk. She could have married Willis just as easily as not, and if she only had, as she frequently told Gerald, she wouldn't be living in any two-family house on Center Street doing all the work, and she would have known all those stuck-up Harcourts too. In fact, Willis had proposed to her four times.

Gerald Holtz only said, that was Susy for you. You got to know who was going with who if you jerked sodas at Wilson's. Willis Wayde never bought a soda for a girl, let alone Susy, except once when he treated Winnie Decker, Steve Decker's sister, to a strawberry nut sundae.

Steve Decker had been in Room 3 with Willis too. They had studied plane geometry and Latin together, taught by old Gumshoe Lewis, and old Gumshoe was always bawling Willis out because Willis was pretty slow. Willis's old man knew his old man out there at Harcourt's. That was why he had Willis over to the house sometimes, and once they were on the debating team together. The subject was "Should Capital Punishment Be Abolished?" Steve also remembered the time when Willis had treated Winnie to a strawberry sundae. Willis had been asked to supper, and after supper Willis had said suddenly:

"How would it be, Winnie, if we went down to the drugstore and I was to buy you a soda?" It was a fact that Willis said "was," not "were," in those days.

Howard Twining, who later started Twining, Inc., Real Estate and Insurance, with offices in the Purdy Block on Dock Street, was president and valedictorian of the high-school class of 1924, and of course he remembered Willis Wayde. He and Willis and Steve Decker were almost inseparable, and Howard Twining himself had seen that Willis was on the committee of the senior-class dance, and Willis had walked in the grand march with Patricia Ryan, who was voted prettiest girl in the class. Frankly, he knew for a fact that Willis was sweet on Winnie Decker, who was in the sophomore class. Willis used to take her to Wilson's Drugstore constantly and buy her sodas. Howard always knew that Willis was the most likely to succeed in the class of '24.

Other people whose names and identities Willis had entirely forgotten began to remember the youth of Willis Wayde. Their insignificant reminiscences were like the calcified remains of coral animalcula, building up the reef of Wayde legend until it rose above the surface of fact and became impervious to the dashing waves of truth.

The truth was that his school career in Clyde left only a vague impression on Willis. He never had the time to appreciate the town or the acquaintances he made there. He must have felt that he was only passing through, like the drummers who spent a night at the hotel. Every morning he would meet Granville Beane at the gate of the Harcourt place and would walk to the car stop at Sudley Road and take the trolley car to town. The personality of Granville was more definite to Willis than that of any other of his schoolmates, because Granville and he took those trips together, walking through the autumn leaves, and through the snow, and later through the slush and mud of early spring.

All his other schoolmates were abstractions to him. The debating tests and the senior dance, and the social evenings in the parish hall of the Congregational Church which his mother made him attend, were only half-remembered interludes which had none of the validity of other aspects of his life. The high school supplied him with no love object, any more than the London streets had supplied one for Kipling's soldier fresh from Mandalay, because he was on a plane far above that of Patricia Ryan or Susy Brown or Winnie Decker. The plane, of course, was Bess Harcourt.

During all the years that his parents lived on the Harcourt place, his mother was always cheerful when October came.

"They'll be going to the city any day now," she used to say, "and we can have everything all to ourselves."

This was what she always said in the autumn, but she must have known that they would never have the place to themselves—except Alfred Wayde, whose obliviousness to surroundings made everything belong to him. In good weather on Saturdays or Sundays when he worked on the engine of the Ford or in the winter when he set up a bench and a metal lathe in the cellar or brought his drawing board into the living room, Alfred Wayde did not care where he was. It was different with Willis's mother, and Willis understood her moods much more clearly than his father's.

When the trees were bare and the gardens were mulched for the winter or when the snow on the lawns made the fir trees and the rhododendrons cold and dark, there were always a few lights in the big house and someone was always waiting there in case Mr. Harcourt should arrive suddenly from town. You never could tell exactly when he might arrive, and the same was true with the Bryson Harcourts, who came to their own house for the school holidays and often unexpectedly for week ends.

The place would be watchful and silent one day and on the next you might hear the voices of strangers everywhere—friends of Mr. and Mrs. Bryson Harcourt's and school friends of Bill's and Bess's. If you walked through the woods by the brook, you never knew exactly whom you might meet on week ends. Sometimes Willis would meet Bess with some other girls from her Boston school, and on these occasions Bess would pass by quickly, simply saying, "Hello, Willis," and he would sometimes hear Bess explaining him to the company.

"He lives on the place," he would hear her say, "in the garden house."

It was different when he met Bill or some of Bill's friends. Bill would often stop and introduce Willis to the company, and sometimes he would ask Willis to join them in whatever they were doing. Willis was never worried that he did not fit into these groups, because when they were by themselves he and Bess and Bill were friends in their own especial way, and they all knew that it was no one's fault that they were separated by circumstances beyond their joint control.

Bess explained the situation to him once that winter in the frank way that a girl of her age would—not that Bess was not always frank. Willis met her one Saturday morning when he had gone to look at the hothouse grapes, which Mr. MacDonald had said he could visit any time as long as he went in and out quickly and always closed the greenhouse door. On that sharp cold morning a fresh fall of powdery snow made everything dazzlingly white under a sunny cloudless sky. He came face to face with Bess just as he left the greenhouse. She was wearing a pleated blue serge skirt, a gray sweater, gray mittens, and a toboggan cap to match.

"Hello," she said. "What are you doing here?"

"I was looking at the hothouse grapes," Willis said.

"Well, don't eat any," she said. "MacDonald can always tell. Where are you going now?"

"Home," he said.

"I'm going up to the pine woods to look for animal tracks in the snow," she said. "Would you like to come along?"

"All right, if you want me to," he said.

"If I didn't, I wouldn't ask you," Bess answered. "Hurry up. I'm cold standing still."

It was hard to find the paths through the woods beneath the snow, but Bess knew them all by heart.

"I always like going places with you, Willis," she said, "when there isn't anyone else around."

"Is that a fact?" Willis said.

[47]

"Don't be silly," Bess said. "When I have friends it isn't the same. They wouldn't like you and you wouldn't like them."

"Is that a fact?" Willis said.

He said it because it was an easy thing to say, and he could afford to be amused. He was older and his age put him in a superior position.

"Don't be silly," Bess said. "I like you when I'm alone."

"All right," Willis said. "I've got my own friends."

It was pleasant in the pine woods. Beneath the trees the snow looked almost blue.

"Have you ever kissed a girl?" Bess asked him.

"Yes, I have," Willis answered.

"Oh," Bess said. "Where was that?"

"Back in Colorado."

"Oh, was she prettier than me?"

"Yes," Willis said, "and she was more grown-up."

"Well," Bess said, "a lot of girls in my class have kissed boys."

"Is that a fact?" Willis said.

"I wish you wouldn't keep saying that thing," Bess said. "I've never kissed a boy. I suppose I'll have to sometime."

"Is that a fact?" Willis said.

"I wish you wouldn't keep saying that thing," Bess said again. "Would you like to kiss me?"

"No," Willis said, "not especially."

"Well," Bess said, "go ahead anyway. I've got to kiss a boy sometime, and I may as well get it over with. Go ahead."

She shut her eyes tight and clenched her fists and turned her face up toward him.

"Well," she said, "that wasn't much."

"No," Willis answered, "it certainly wasn't."

"It's silly, isn't it?" Bess said. "But we can try it again sometime."

The next time he saw Bess was an evening two weeks later, when he and his father and mother were asked quite suddenly by Mr. Harcourt to come to supper at the big house—informally, Mr. Harcourt said—and he apologized for the abruptness of the invitation. Bryson and Mildred and Bill and Bess would be there, he said, and he would appreciate having someone outside the family, if Mrs. Wayde would agree on such short notice. He had seen a great deal of the family lately in Boston, and perhaps there was such a thing as too much unadulterated family.

The big house was always wonderful in winter. Once you were in the hall, with the heavy-framed pictures and Selwyn, there was no sign at all of winter, and there was a summer smell of hothouse flowers. The

Bryson Harcourts had arrived already, and everyone was in the drawing room.

"Mr. Harcourt's expecting you, sir," Selwyn said to Mr. Wayde. "Would you mind finding your way to the drawing room yourself while I hang up the wraps?"

It was Selwyn's way of saying that they were welcome guests. As usual the rugs deadened the sound of footsteps so that no one heard the Waydes when they arrived at the open door of the drawing room, and thus they had an unanticipated glimpse of the Harcourts around the open fire. Mr. Harcourt in his dinner coat was facing the marble mantel, and Mr. Bryson Harcourt, in a brown tweed jacket, stood beside him. Mrs. Harcourt was seated in a light armchair looking up at them with the firelight making an attractive sort of halo around her head. Whatever they had been saying seemed to have caught her full attention and had given her good-natured florid face an anxious look. Bill and Bess were seated side by side on a sofa like two bored spectators who wished they were somewhere else—Bill in a dark blue suit, and Bess in a young girl's dress of English silk.

"I don't mind in the least your being frank, Bryson," Mr. Harcourt was saying.

His voice sounded light and untroubled. It was one of those moments when one did not know whether to interrupt or to stand there listening, and the Waydes paused indecisively at the door of the drawing room.

"I think you should give more consideration to the family point of view, Father," Bryson Harcourt said. "The business is going beautifully and no one sees any need for turning everything inside out."

"No doubt I'll hear all about it at the June meeting," Mr. Harcourt said. "I'm customarily blamed for something there. But just remember this." Mr. Harcourt touched his lip with his forefinger. "The whole lot of you together can't outvote me, can you? I suppose I sound arrogant. I dare say I am."

Then he stopped. His glance had traveled to the drawing-room door. The façade was up again, and the Harcourts were again a united family. Bryson Harcourt hurried across the room to shake hands with Mrs. Wayde, and Mrs. Bryson Harcourt had risen and was smiling. Mr. Harcourt patted Willis on the shoulder.

"Willis," he said, "you're growing all the time. You'll have a Martini, won't you, Alfred?"

"I certainly will," Mr. Wayde answered.

"Hello, Willis," Bill said. "How have you been?" And then Willis shook hands with Bess.

"Hello," she said, and she drew her hand away quickly, looking as though she had never seen him before.

One afternoon in March, in that tedious time of year when you became uncertain whether winter would ever end or not, the word came from Mr. Beane that no one would be on the place for the week end, and there was also a rumor that Mr. Harcourt had gone suddenly to Florida. On Saturday afternoon Willis's father had asked him to get a good hot fire going in the kitchen stove and then to come down cellar to help while he attached an electric motor to a centrifugal machine that he had been working on for several weeks.

"It's about time you learned to use your hands, Willis," his father had said. "My God, I've never seen a boy so clumsy with his hands."

Some time before, Alfred Wayde had brought home a bag of potato chips, of which he was very fond, and, while eating them, he had begun to wonder whether it would not be possible to slice and fry bananas in the same manner. He had found that he could slice bananas and cook them in deep fat and the immediate result was satisfactory, but an hour later the banana chips became limp and spongy. Banana chips, Alfred Wayde had discovered, were deliquescent, and now he was thinking of some way to get the water out of them, and he had put together a centrifugal machine.

The device, which roughly resembled a windmill, and which was to be turned by a small electric motor, was going to get every bit of water and excess grease from the bananas.

"What are you going to do next if it does?" Willis asked his father.

Alfred Wayde looked at Willis impatiently.

"How's that again, son?" he asked.

"What are you going to do if it does work?" Willis asked.

"It doesn't make a damn bit of difference," Alfred Wayde answered. "I only want to see whether it will. What made you ask such a fool question, son?"

"I thought maybe you could patent it and sell it," Willis said.

"Well," Alfred Wayde said, "why should I? I'm only doing this for my personal enjoyment."

"But there might be money in banana chips," Willis said.

"Money in banana chips?" Alfred Wayde answered. "My God, I don't want to go into the banana business. Now hand me the small wrench and the box of nuts, and don't spill them all over the floor."

"If they keep absorbing water out of the air," Willis said, "why does it do any good to get the water out of them?"

"Listen, son," his father said, "I don't give a damn what happens to them later if I can get the water out of them just once, and now you'd better go for a walk and not ask any more fool questions."

It was half past five in the afternoon. The sky outside was leaden gray, but there was still plenty of light because the days were certainly getting longer. There were icicles on the eaves of the big house, which looked more solid than ever behind the swaying limbs of the bare trees around it. The snow along the wood path by the brook was slippery and wet, and as Willis walked along he began thinking what the woods must have been like a hundred years ago, before there was any Harcourt place. Some of the larger trees had been growing then, and he could imagine that they were speaking among themselves of the past, as the wind moved through their tops. He could imagine, too, that he heard voices. He thought that he heard Mr. Harcourt's voice—which he knew was impossible, since Mr. Harcourt was in Florida. He was very much astonished when he suddenly saw Mr. Harcourt walking toward him.

Mr. Harcourt was dressed in the black broadcloth coat with the fur collar that he usually wore when he motored from the city. He was accompanied by a slender, middle-aged lady whose hat and whose fur cape looked more like the city than the country. She was holding Mr. Harcourt's arm.

"Why, hello," Mr. Harcourt said. "I never expected to see anyone out here. Why aren't you in the house like sensible people, Willis?"

"I've been working down cellar with Pa, sir," Willis said. "He's making a machine to get water out of bananas. He's just doing it for fun."

"Well," Mr. Harcourt said, "everyone to his own taste, I suppose. I suppose we're out here for fun ourselves, aren't we, Harriet? This is Willis Wayde, the son of my plant engineer. They're living in the garden house, you know."

"Oh yes, of course," Mrs. James said, and she smiled at Willis and held out a gray-gloved hand.

"Mrs. James and I have been motoring," Mr. Harcourt said, "and I suggested that we might stop for a cup of tea before returning to Boston."

"Yes, sir," Willis said.

Mr. Harcourt touched his lower lip, and suddenly he began to laugh at some private joke of his own.

"I really thought I'd never see anyone at this time of day, but you never can tell, can you? Won't you join Mrs. James and me in a cup of tea?"

"I guess I ought to be getting home, sir," Willis said.

They were acting as though the whole thing were perfectly natural, but Willis was sure it was not.

"Please come with us, Willis," Mrs. James said. "You look as though you need a cup of tea."

"And you can tell us why your father wants to get water out of bananas, Willis," Mr. Harcourt said.

Patrick's wife, who always helped out in the winters, served tea in the library. The ornate silver service, which Willis had seen in the dining room, had been placed on a low table in front of the black marble fireplace, where three lumps of cannel coal were burning. Almost as soon as they arrived, Patrick's wife, in her black dress and stiff starched apron, brought in the silver hot-water kettle, placed it on the rack above the spirit lamp and lighted the wick. It was the first time that Willis had ever seen the conventional serving of tea.

"Nellie," Mr. Harcourt said, "this is Mrs. James. I'm not sure whether you've ever met her before."

"Pleased to meet you, ma'am," Patrick's wife said, "and I hope the tea will be all right."

"If you will bring in the bread and butter and toast, please, Nellie," Mr. Harcourt said, "and some pound cake, if there is any. I'm sure Willis could do with some cake."

No one spoke again until Nellie had left the room.

"Are these Ethel's tea things?" Mrs. James asked.

"Yes," Mr. Harcourt said, "a wedding present. That was quite a while ago. You can tell from looking at Nellie and me."

"Do you want me to pour, Henry?" Mrs. James asked.

"I think so," Mr. Harcourt said, "if you would be so kind, Harriet," and suddenly he laughed.

"What are you laughing at?" Mrs. James asked.

"Only at the general situation," Mr. Harcourt said. Mr. Harcourt looked handsome and younger when he laughed, and somehow Mrs. James looked younger too. Suddenly Willis was sure that she was kinder than Mrs. Blood.

"I wish you didn't have such a sour sense of humor, Henry," Mrs. James said.

"Not sour," Mr. Harcourt answered, "mature, Harriet."

When Patrick's wife came back carrying a peculiar piece of furniture which Willis knew later was called a curate's delight, Mrs. James was seated before the tea table, her hands moving gracefully and quickly, and she measured out tea into the silver pot and poured hot water into the fragile cups to warm them and then poured the water into a silver bowl. Willis never again saw anyone who could pour tea and move all those things about as beautifully as Mrs. James.

"Now just what is it that your father's doing in the cellar?" Mr. Harcourt asked.

Something inexplicable had happened that had made Willis feel perfectly at home. They were interested when he described how he and his father had both fried and baked banana chips and then went on to the centrifugal machine.

"I guess Pa's still down there working," Willis said. "Maybe he won't bother to come up for supper. When he gets working on something, he's like that."

"Yes," Mr. Harcourt said, "the creative mind."

"There's one funny thing about Pa," Willis said. "He doesn't care what's going to happen, if he works it out about those bananas. He just says he doesn't want to be a banana king."

"He's not like me, Willis," Mr. Harcourt said. "He doesn't need to be a king of anything. What would you do if the bananas worked out right?"

"I guess I'd think about starting some kind of factory, sir," Willis said.

"That's what I'd do too," Mr. Harcourt said, "exactly." His head turned quickly to the window, and Willis saw the lights of the Locomobile coming up the drive.

"Dear me," Mr. Harcourt said, and he pulled a gold watch from his waistcoat pocket. "There's Patrick and it's six o'clock. I suppose we'd better leave, Harriet."

"It's been ever so nice seeing you, Willis," Mrs. James said, "and I hope we'll meet again."

"You'll meet again," Mr. Harcourt said. "Willis is going to work for me at the mill this summer, aren't you, Willis?"

"Yes, sir," Willis said.

He felt tremendously happy as he walked down the passage to the front hall. Mr. Harcourt had spoken previously of his working at the mill, but he had never said before that Willis would work for him. You had to have a hero when you were going on sixteen, and Willis would have gladly died for Mr. Harcourt.

Willis was to spend his life in a highly competitive arena in which, in spite of a surface geniality, there was a peculiar lack of mercy once the chips were down. All sorts of small things added themselves together in that competition so that microscopic errors of judgment and careless moments often became momentous in the end. The line that separated success from mediocrity was fascinatingly thin and wavering. That meeting with Mr. Harcourt and Mrs. James he could see later was one of those events which finally put him on a confidential basis with the Harcourt family.

Willis was not surprised at all when the news broke suddenly that Mr. Harcourt and Mrs. James had been married quietly and had gone for a while to Palm Beach in Florida. He could not understand in the least why everyone, including Mr. Beane and Mr. MacDonald, appeared surprised and unsettled. Except for himself, it seemed to Willis that Patrick was the only one who was not surprised, and he should not have been, having driven them in the Locomobile. Willis discovered that Patrick's attitude toward him had changed after that tea party, and incidentally Patrick began to call him Master Willis.

Perhaps Patrick never kept his mouth as tightly shut as he said he did, or perhaps it was Nellie, his wife, who did the talking. At any rate the word must have got around that Willis had known all about Mr. Harcourt and Mrs. James before anyone else, and it gave Willis a new position on the Harcourt place.

He understood more clearly that he had been in the midst of an earth-shaking event the next time he saw Bess Harcourt.

"You say you saw her?" Bess said.

"Yes," Willis answered. "She was at the big house."

"She doesn't look like much, does she?" Bess said. "Just an old lady without any money or anything. I don't know why old people get married and make things hard for everybody."

"I thought she was kind of nice," Willis said.

"That shows how little you know," Bess said. "She wasn't nice to get Grandfather to marry her and get all the money that Daddy would have had, but we're all going to be pleasant to her when she comes here. We mustn't show the way we feel."

"Well, I thought she was sort of nice," Willis said.

"Don't be silly, Willis," Bess said. "You don't understand because you haven't got a single cent of money. Grandfather is a silly old man, and Mummy's making me embroider a pincushion cover for her."

"Maybe I'll make some money some day," Willis said.

"Don't be silly, Willis," Bess said again. "I don't know why I like you when you talk that way."

"I don't care if you don't," Willis said.

"Well," Bess said, "as long as we're here and there's no one else around, don't you want to kiss me, Willis?"

"No, not much," Willis said.

"Now, Willis," Bess said. "We're going to have a dance this spring in the vacation, and Mummy says she's going to ask Steve Decker and Winnie Decker. We have to ask them because their father is the mill's lawyer. And I'll get Mummy to ask you too. I'm going to put my hair up for it. Please kiss me, Willis."

Willis had a happy time at that party, and, in fact, he always did have a good time whenever he was invited to the Bryson Harcourt house. Both Mr. and Mrs. Harcourt had a way with young people, if you wanted to use the term, perhaps because they had remained young in so many ways themselves. Mrs. Harcourt always made an especial effort to talk to him, but her attention never made him self-conscious. Mr. Bryson was kind to him too. Mr. Bryson Harcourt was impulsive and generous, and Bill was very much like him. It made no difference if they remembered you only when they saw you.

It was a very informal party—just two or three girls who were friends of Bess's from Boston and two or three school friends of Bill's, and then Steve and Winnie Decker and Willis. After what Mrs. Harcourt called a pickup supper in the brightly lighted dining room—the Bryson Harcourt house always looked very new and cheerful—they rolled back all the rugs in the big front hall, and Mr. Bryson turned on the phonograph.

Willis always did have trouble learning steps, but Mrs. Bryson Harcourt went out of her way to say that he was doing very well, and those friends of Bess's all tried to teach him, and Bess was very kind herself. She wore her hair up, as she had said she would. She had also, she told him, borrowed two kinds of perfume from her mother's dressing table and, if he would promise not to tell, a little rouge from her best friend, Gertrude Fredericks. Mrs. Harcourt asked him in a low voice to try to be especially kind to Winnie Decker, who was a fattish frightened girl in those days. Willis was sure that he was having a much better time than Steve Decker, who looked tall and sallow and sour.

"Say," Steve Decker said to him, "let's step outside and smoke a cigarette."

Willis had never smoked in his life, but he would have died rather than tell Steve Decker. He was very glad to step outside with him on the driveway.

"What are you coughing for?" Steve asked him. "Haven't you ever smoked a cigarette?"

"Oh yes," Willis answered, "lots of times."

"These parties bore me," Steve said. "Every time the Harcourt kids ask us to one, the old man makes us go. Bill Harcourt isn't so hot either, do you think so?"

"No," Willis said, "no, he isn't so hot."

"And Bess, she isn't so hot either. Say, do you know what?"

"No, what?" Willis asked.

"She asked me to kiss her. She said it was time she learned how to kiss a boy. Say, what do you know about that?"

Willis coughed again.

"What do you know?" he said.

"Say," Steve said, "when's the old man getting back?"

"What old man?" Willis asked, as he coughed again.

"God Almighty," Steve Decker said, and he laughed urbanely. "Old Harcourt and his new wife. Boy, I'd like to have been around when the family got that news. I bet it set old Bryson right on his ass."

Willis could still feel the acrid sting of the cigarette smoke and recall his twinge of fascinated horror at that allusion to Mr. Bryson Harcourt. He could still feel the cool April air on his face with its message of early spring and growth. He could even remember the exact sound of a foot-step behind him on the gravel drive. It was young Bill Harcourt, already taller than his father.

"Hello," Bill said. "What are you two doing out here?"

"Just resting," Steve Decker said, "and taking a drag on a cigarette."

"Oh, boy," Bill Harcourt said, "give me one, will you?"

Bill was always ready to try anything, and his enthusiasm never died. Willis always had a warm spot in his heart for Bill.

The annual meeting of the stockholders of the Harcourt Mill occurred just after high school had closed in June and just before Willis had started to work at the mill. Everybody was back on the place by then— the Henry Harcourts, the Bryson Harcourts, and Bill and Bess. The leaves were all out on the trees except for the catalpas. It was all a time of newness and hope when the stockholders gathered at the Harcourt Mill and then met for luncheon at the big house. The machinery, the offices and Harcourt belting were symbolized at the Harcourt place each June by the fresh edging of the turf along the drive and the flowers of the rhododendrons and the laurels, and by the swans floating on the still waters of their pond.

As the hour approached that marked the end of the meeting at the mill, everyone was too busy to think of Willis Wayde. He wanted to keep out of the way, but curiosity impelled him to stand in the corner of the rose garden, where he could see the automobiles as they came up the drive. That was where Bess Harcourt met him and asked him, as she often did, what he was doing.

"You can see," he said, "I'm not doing anything."

There was no doubt that Bess was growing up. She was no longer the middy-bloused girl that she had been the previous summer. Her braid was doubled up now and tied by a ribbon, and she wore a blue sweater and a red belt around her waist, but she still had her blue serge skirt and her sensible square-toed low shoes.

"Well, I'm not doing anything either," Bess said. "I guess they're fighting down at the mill. It always means they're fighting when they're late."

Willis did not answer, but Bess was still young enough to talk freely.

"They all think Grandfather's spending too much money," Bess said. "Cousin Emily was awful cross this morning. She was in the den with Daddy before they went to the mill, and then Cousin Roger came, and then the Hayward cousins came. Mummy doesn't like the Haywards and I hate them."

The mill problems were all new to Willis then.

"When Cousin Emily's mad her nose gets thin," Bess said. "Do you think my nose looks like hers?"

"I've never seen her nose," Willis answered.

"It's shiny. She never puts on powder."

"Is that a fact?" Willis said.

"Don't keep saying that," Bess told him. "Let's go inside the big house and look around."

"No," Willis said, "we wouldn't have any business being there."

Bess looked at him thoughtfully. It seemed to Willis lately that she was always looking him up and down as though she had never seen him before.

"You haven't but I have," she said. "If anyone catches us I'll say that I invited you, but no one's going to notice."

"I'll stay here," Willis said. "You go if you like."

She took his hand and tried to pull him after her.

"Gosh," she said. "You're twice as strong as Bill. I know a place where we can hide and see them through the banisters, at the head of the stairs. I did it last year."

He was sure he would not have gone if she had not said that he was twice as strong as Bill.

The front door stood open but there was no one in the hall, and there were flowers at the foot of the staircase, banks of flowers, and not a sound except in the kitchen and the dining room. Willis could almost believe they were invisible as they tiptoed through the house.

"Look at the drinks in the library," Bess whispered, "but those are only Grandfather's second-best cigars. He never has his best ones for Cousin Roger and the Haywards. Look at the dining room. All the cut glass is out. When they start eating we can stand here and watch."

The dining-room table was stretched its full length and there were turkeys and whole hams on the serving table beside the pantry door and heavy lace tablecloths and the green Chinese place plates, but the cut glass was what Willis recalled most clearly—that heavy, ornate glass of another age, a tumbler and three wine glasses beside each plate, glittering like ice in that silent room.

"It's handsome," Willis whispered.

"They always have it for the meeting," Bess whispered back. "I was going to have it some day, before he got married again."

Then Bess drew a quick sharp breath.

"Hurry," she whispered. "They're coming," and she reached for his hand. "Hurry."

Then he heard the sound of wheels on the gravel driveway, and he and Bess seemed to be like people in a dream. She was still holding his hand as they ran on tiptoe down the hall.

"The wisteria never looked better," he heard a man's voice say.

"Hurry," Bess whispered. "Upstairs, hurry!"

In a second they reached the balustrade of the upstairs passageway that looked down on the hall below. There was a casement window on the left and a small niche beside the window which gave access to the window and nothing more.

"Here," Bess whispered.

It was not a bad place to hide, affording just room for them to sit close together on the floor and to peer through the banisters.

"This is it," Bess whispered, and she still held his hand.

The whole house had suddenly become alive. Mr. Henry Harcourt had appeared, and Mrs. Harcourt was with him. They were standing near the foot of the staircase, and Willis never knew how they had arrived there so quickly. He could hear Mr. Harcourt's voice.

"Roger," he was saying, "I'm not sure whether you have met your Aunt Harriet."

He was speaking to a stout middle-aged man whose hair was so closely cropped that you could see the pink of his scalp beneath. He was so fat that he should have had the conventional jolly expression, but instead his round face had a petulant look and his voice had a precise and fluty quality.

"No, Uncle Henry," the fat man answered, "I haven't had the pleasure. Welcome to the family, Aunt Harriet."

"That's Cousin Roger," Bess whispered in his ear. "He owns a lot of stock."

"Didn't Catherine come with you?" Mr. Harcourt said. "Oh, here she is. I don't believe you've met your new Aunt Harriet, Catherine. This is Roger's wife, my dear."

A tall lady with bony wrists and gaunt rangy shoulders came into Willis's line of vision.

"I've been looking forward to it," she said, "dear Uncle Henry."

"That's Cousin Catherine," Bess whispered. "She's nasty, and their children are nasty."

"And here's Will Burnham," Mr. Harcourt said. "But you remember Will, don't you, Harriet?"

"He's the president of Grandfather's bank," Bess whispered. "So he doesn't count, and there's old Decker, with spots all over his coat. He doesn't count much either."

The hall was filled with people now, shaking hands with Mr. and Mrs. Henry Harcourt and then moving toward the living room.

"Selwyn has cocktails for us in the library," Mr. Harcourt was saying.

"There come Mummy and Daddy," Bess whispered. "There must have been a fight at the meeting. You can tell because Daddy's laughing too much. And here come the Haywards, sticking together as usual. Grandfather bought most of their stock anyway, but Daddy says they never miss a free meal. Everybody hates the Haywards."

"Doesn't anybody like anybody else?" Willis whispered.

"Of course not," Bess whispered back, "except when they take sides in a fight."

"Hello, Ruth," Mr. Harcourt said, smiling at Mrs. Blood.

"Will there be green-turtle soup for lunch as usual?" Mrs. Blood asked.

If they did not like each other Willis could see that there were bonds which held them together, so that, confronted by a common danger, they would stand together against a stranger. They were proud that they were Harcourts and proud of their dislikes.

The group in the hall was growing smaller.

"Only distant cousins are left now," Bess whispered. "I don't know why Grandfather wastes his time with them."

But Mr. Harcourt was always the same with everyone. He seemed to be having a delightful time. He seemed to be particularly pleased to see each one again.

Finally Mr. and Mrs. Harcourt stood alone near the foot of the stairs, and Mr. Harcourt's glance traveled slowly around the empty front hall.

"Well, my dear," Mr. Harcourt said, "I think that's the lot—the white man's burden, you know—and we won't have to do it again for a year. By the way, Harriet, don't forget that I shall say grace."

"Grace, Henry?" Mrs. Harcourt repeated.

"It's a custom my father started," Mr. Harcourt said. "It won't hurt any of them to remember God and to thank Him that He has allowed me to look after their interests."

"Don't be sacrilegious, Henry," Mrs. Harcourt said.

"I'm not," Mr. Harcourt answered. "There's a bonus check beneath every one of their plates, you know. They can't wait to get in to lunch to see how much it is."

"Henry," Mrs. Harcourt said, "you look tired."

"It's always a strain handling damn fools," Mr. Harcourt said, "particularly one's flesh and blood. Let's go and look at them, Harriet."

They turned and walked away toward the living room, and Willis moved uneasily but Bess shook her head.

"Don't," she whispered, "don't move. Here's Grandfather coming back."

She had seen him before Willis had. He came walking across the empty hall with his quick, deliberate step, holding a cocktail glass. He paused near the open front door for a moment and then he began walking slowly up the stairs.

"He must be going to the bathroom," Bess whispered.

Willis thought that it was a most indelicate remark. They could see him walking up the stairs, but when he reached the upper hall, they could only hear his footsteps moving nearer. Then they heard his voice right beside them.

"You can come out now," he said. "The show is over."

Willis heard Bess give a sharp gasp as he struggled to his feet. Mr. Harcourt was standing just in front of the niche that led to the window.

"It's all right," he said. "I noticed you up there," and then he laughed. "I wished several times that I could be up there with you. Come here and kiss me, Bess. You're getting big enough to kiss."

"Oh, Grandfather, don't be silly," Bess said, and she giggled.

"It was quite a show, wasn't it?" Mr. Harcourt said. "I used to watch it from here myself. In those days they had stovepipe hats and Prince Alberts. Now if I were you two, I'd sneak down to the kitchen and tell Mary to give you some food. If she's cross, tell her it's my orders, Bess."

"Oh, Grandfather," Bess said, "you're awfully sweet."

"Sweet as sugar," Mr. Harcourt said. "Well, Willis."

Mr. Harcourt's lower lip was motionless.

"Yes, sir?" Willis said.

"Well, you've seen the family," Mr. Harcourt said. "It may help you when you come to work for me next Monday. I'm putting you under old Bill Jackson in Building 1. Beginning Monday you and I will both be working for those people."

He laughed and walked away.

"Gosh," Bess said, "I thought that he'd be angry."

Willis had half forgotten Bess, in his realization that he was no longer a stranger but a retainer of the great house. Mr. Harcourt had as good as told him so. He would have followed Mr. Harcourt anywhere, or died for him.

V

IN LATER years, like any other successful man at the head of a growing organization, Willis was naturally sympathetic with people having problems similar to his, and he could hardly help but make all sorts of interesting contacts at conventions and business luncheons, which he cultivated as assiduously as a farmer cultivated his crop, with Christmas cards and notes at suitable intervals. If you had a good secretary, she would tell you, for instance, that it was about time to write to Mr. Charles Bottomly, the president of the Plywood and Binder Company in Wilmington, California.

"Dear Chuck," you would write. "How's it on the Coast? Long time no see. Huey Jenks from the Guaranty was around here yesterday, and he says the job you're doing out there is terrific. Are you coming East to the NAM?

"Please find enclosed a little verse about Truman and the music critic that's going the rounds here, in case you haven't seen it yet. Well, long time no see, but give my regards to Clara and the kids, in which Mrs. Wayde joins me, even if she hasn't had the pleasure of meeting them. Sincerely, as always."

You never could tell when a little bread cast upon the waters might pay off. It never hurt to have too many friends doing the same sort of thing you were. Willis had told many of them a lot about himself over drinks in hotel suites, in corners of clubs and on golf courses, and a lot of them had told Willis a lot about themselves in return—of what they thought about so-and-so, about their yachts, about their hobbies, and their tastes in women and liquor and automobiles. This sort of thing was the currency of business friendship.

There was one thing Willis always noticed about all these friends. When they touched on their own careers and their own adventures in free enterprise, they usually began to deal in vague generalities. It was not that these people had anything to conceal. It was only that the average business life—one's hours and years in plants and offices and conference rooms—was too personal to be explained fully. None of these events were dull to one who lived them but none had much value for anyone else. At least Willis knew that this was true with him.

He was almost seventeen the first summer he worked at the Harcourt Mill, and his days behind the fence had nothing much to do with his leisure time. He was only tired at night and very hungry. He was there to learn and he had learned better than the average. He worked with some others of his schoolmates that summer as a helper in Building 1, and then as an assistant checker in the warehouse. Steve Decker had started with him that summer, because Steve's father had wanted him to learn the business too, but Steve had developed a bad cough and had to quit after a month of it. Willis was never good with machinery but he learned how to work with the rest of the repair gang and by the end of summer he knew the whole process in Building 1 pretty thoroughly. The next summer, after he graduated from high school, he went through Buildings 2 and 3, and later, when Mr. Hewett put him in to help in the sales office, Willis had a good knowledge of the whole plant, or a base, at any rate, on which his experience could build. He always possessed an instinct which enabled him to see the whole in spite of all the complicated parts. He could even see that the finished product of the Harcourt Mill was itself only a part of something larger.

He had begun to learn, even when he was a worker in Building 1, that it was possible to hire someone to do almost anything, and that no one could do everything himself. The secret was to know enough to understand what specialists must do, and some people could never learn that secret. Mr. Hewett, for example, knew only part of it, and Mr. Edward Briggs, the sales manager, knew only another part, but someone like Mr. Harcourt could hold it all together. Very few people seemed to learn that the whole was greater than any of its parts. Minds stopped in the Harcourt Mill, lost at some stage in the process, and if your mind once stopped you stayed right where you were—in Building 1 or Building 2, or in the outer office. It may have been luck or it may have been ability that made Willis move further forward.

If his detailed knowledge of belting and the part that belting might play in an industrial plant finally impressed a good many other people, he knew now that he could thank his father for this familiarity. By the time that Willis began working summers at the Harcourt Mill, Alfred Wayde knew every shaft and machine by heart. Moreover he was able to put his finger on the basic problems and the critical spots. In fact the Harcourt plant had grown so simple to Alfred Wayde that he was beginning to become bored with it, and his mind was constantly occupied in theoretical devices for cutting down on labor. Men made mistakes, he used to say, but machinery never. He was ashamed that a boy of his was not as smart as he was with machinery. He used to say, by God, that he would ram a little practical sense into Willis if it took ten years. He didn't want the shop foremen to laugh at his son. He was always ready to go over and over with Willis the basic principles and the details of the machinery. Willis could still remember his father's voice shouting simple facts about cogs and gears above the noise of machines. There was a relentless pressure about Alfred Wayde that finally made it impossible not to learn something, and Willis felt deep gratitude after a lapse of years.

He never expressed this gratitude to his father until a long while afterwards, not until the year 1948, to be accurate, when Alfred Wayde was retired and living in Southern California. Willis had gone to the Coast on a quick business trip by air, and his friend Ralph Schultz, vice president of Hocking Aircraft, with whom Willis had been doing some business, had asked him up to his house for dinner. When Willis had told Ralph that he could not make it because he had arranged to have supper with his father and mother, who were living in one of those new developments near San Bernardino, Ralph had insisted that Willis take a company car and a driver. It was late afternoon when Willis got to the development, called Canyon del Oro.

Canyon del Oro was one of those groups of ranch-type dwellings that kept springing up like mushrooms in California, each house on a lawn with its garage attached. The air was dry and the mountains behind were brown, as they were in summer, and the surroundings made Willis wonder why his father and mother had ever picked California. It took some time to find his parents' house because it was indistinguishable from other redwood, picture-windowed, wide-eaved dwellings. Its number, thirty-seven, was on the gatepost and there was a newly planted hibiscus hedge in front and an old olive tree on the lawn. His mother, wearing dungarees and sneakers, was watching a lawn sprinkler when the car stopped outside the gate. Her hair was white but she moved as fast as ever.

"Willis," she said, "isn't it a lovely home? It's just what I've always dreamed of."

"Yes," Willis said, "it looks swell, Mom."

"It'll look better," she said, "when the vines get growing. Do you want the young man driving the car to stay for supper?"

"No," Willis said, "he can get something to eat in San Bernardino."

"All right," she said. "We're having steak. Your father's taking the car apart again." She raised her voice to a commanding shout. "Alf, Willis is here."

His father appeared holding a monkey wrench. He had put on weight and he was puffing slightly.

"Hello, Willis," he said. "How's tricks? Cynthia, you get supper, and Willis and I will sit in the breezeway and have a drink."

It was hot in the breezeway, and Willis took off his coat and unbuttoned the soft collar of his shirt.

"You're all pressed up like a knife, aren't you, boy?" Alfred Wayde said, when he came out of the house with a tray and glasses. "These God-damned aluminum chairs. I always think they'll break."

It was like old times, because nothing ever changed his father. As they sat there watching the sun drop to the west, Willis thought of the summers at the Harcourt place when Alfred Wayde and he came home from the mill together.

"It's a long way since that damned Harcourt Mill," Alfred Wayde said.

Alfred Wayde had seen plenty of other plants since Harcourt's, but somehow the Harcourt Mill seemed clearer to them both than anything else, particularly to Willis.

"Now old Harcourt was always a good Joe," Alfred Wayde said. "But Bryson—Jesus! How's Bryson now?"

"He isn't around much," Willis said. "He does a lot of sailing."

Alfred Wayde rattled the ice cubes in his glass.

"How's Bill?" he asked.

"He isn't around much either," Willis said, looking at the cloudless sky and the burnt-orange grass in the distance. "He has a place in Marion now, but Bill's all right."

He always did have a warm spot in his heart for Bill. But Alfred Wayde's mind was still on the Harcourt Mill. He still spoke of it as though he had been there yesterday.

"You taught me all I know about the mill," Willis said.

"You're damned well right I did," Alfred Wayde said. "God, you were a dumb kid."

He must have been dumb from Alfred Wayde's point of view.

"You never could have got through Tech," Alfred Wayde said, "not even with me on your neck. It's just as well you went to Boston University. Do you remember something?"

"What?" Willis asked.

"You asked me the dumbest question once. I guess it was the first summer, when I was trying to knock some sense into you about that mill."

"What question?" Willis asked.

Alfred Wayde rattled the ice cubes in his glass again.

"Your mother always says I drink too much," he said. "Hell, alcohol's never made me a failure, and I don't set myself down for one."

"What question did I ask you?" Willis asked.

"Oh yes," Alfred Wayde said. "You asked me if I knew so much about that Harcourt Mill, why didn't I want to run it?"

Willis did not answer but it was a question he still asked himself when he thought about his father.

"Boy," Alfred Wayde said, "I've never wanted to run anything except machines. A good internal-combustion engine is better than a man."

You could buy people who fiddled with machines, and the price of people who fiddled with men came higher, but Willis did not tell the old man that.

"Old H.H. was always monkeying with people," his father said. "He couldn't keep his hands off. I saved his bacon when I got him into conveyor belts, but old Harcourt was a good Joe."

"I owe a lot to him," Willis said.

Alfred Wayde laughed suddenly.

"Still on the same beam, aren't you?" he said. "Listen, boy. I've told you we don't owe them one God-damned thing any more than the engine in my Buick owes anything to me."

There was such a thing as loyalty, but Willis did not bring it up. His mother was calling them in to supper, and he had not known that his father owned a Buick. He never would have owned one if Willis had not been more like Mr. Henry Harcourt than Alfred Wayde.

If Mr. Harcourt had taken an interest in Willis he had always known where to draw the line between interest and partiality. There were never any favorites or white-haired boys when Mr. Harcourt ran the mill. No one was rewarded for anything but merit. Mr. Harcourt never forgot the faces or the characters of his employees, and he knew their wives and children, and he always asked kindly questions when there was illness or trouble. If anyone was in trouble, even the lowest man on the wage scale, he could always see Mr. Harcourt at the office or at six o'clock at the big house, where Mr. Harcourt always kept an hour open before dinner.

Mr. Harcourt treated Willis the same way he treated everyone else, and when Bill Harcourt worked there for a month there was no way of telling that Bill was his grandson, except that Mr. Harcourt expressly told the foremen in Building 3 that Bill was lazy and not to let him get away with anything. If Bill did not like it he could always leave like anybody else, and Bill took it very well too, because he was always good-natured about everything.

When Mr. Harcourt used to meet Willis on the Harcourt place, he hardly ever alluded to the mill, but he often asked Willis about his high-school studies. When Willis took his college-board examinations, Mr. Harcourt asked about his marks, and seemed relieved that Willis had not done badly. Willis had got eighties in physics, mathematics and elementary French, and Mr. Harcourt did not take the dim view that Alfred Wayde took.

Alfred Wayde had never thought that a son of his would get a low seventy in geometry, and a sixty-eight in trigonometry. After all the work he had done with Willis on wintry evenings, it simply did not seem possible.

"He ought to have been allowed to study last summer," Mrs. Wayde said, "instead of working in that mill. It's what comes of us always moving around, Alfred. Willis has never had the chance."

They were still talking about his marks when he walked out of the house feeling hurt and angry. It was the beginning of summer again, a gray and chilly day for June, and the weather was as unsettled as his thoughts.

There was never a time in life when you took things harder than when you were seventeen. Willis wanted to be alone and he was thinking of the pine woods on the hill beyond the brook. The last person he wanted to see was Mr. Henry Harcourt, but there he was, in the vegetable garden.

"Hello, Willis," he called. "Have you heard from your examinations yet?"

"Yes, sir," Willis said. "The marks came in the other day. I passed but they weren't much good. Maybe I'm just dumb."

Mr. Harcourt glanced at him in a quick, hard way.

"Oh no, Willis," he said, "you're not dumb."

Willis often thought that this was the kindest thing Mr. Harcourt ever said to him. His voice was soft and casual, as it always was, but the words had a complete validity.

Willis knew very little about colleges. The question that mattered most was how you could buy a college education on the most reasonable terms, because the Waydes had not been able to lay aside much in the way of savings. There was Technology, but Willis had no head for mathematics. There was Mass. Aggy, where Granville Beane was going. Then there was Harvard, where Bill and Steve Decker were going. The other schools, like Amherst and Brown and Dartmouth, were only names, and they were too far away, his mother said. She wanted Willis somewhere near so that he could come home for Sunday. That was how Boston University entered into the discussion, being a good school, as she said, right in the middle of Boston, without too many rich boys going to it. Willis had no fixed idea one way or the other, and the chances were he might not have gone to B.U. at all if Mr. Harcourt had not called from the big house on the telephone the Sunday morning after Willis had told him about his marks.

Mr. Harcourt called to ask if he might drop in after church to talk over a matter to which he had been giving some thought. They were having a boiled dinner that day, and the living room was filled with the aroma of cabbages and turnips, but Mr. Harcourt had said there was nothing so good as a good boiled dinner. As he sat in the living room, his church clothes—his striped trousers, his black coat, his stiff collar, and his severe gray tie—made all the rest of them look very simple.

"Say, Mr. Harcourt," Alfred Wayde said, "how about a little rye and ginger ale?"

"Not at the moment, thank you, Alfred," Mr. Harcourt said, "but don't let me stop you."

"You sit down, Alf," Mrs. Wayde said. "Mr. Harcourt says he wants to talk to us about something."

Alfred Wayde sat down heavily, and Mr. Harcourt smiled.

"It won't take more than a minute, Alf," he said. "I only wanted to say a few words about Willis."

"Oh," Mrs. Wayde said, "has Willis done anything?"

"No, no," Mr. Harcourt said. "This isn't anything about what Willis has done. I hope you're planning to send Willis to college."

Willis saw his mother straighten herself in her stiff-backed chair, and he was thinking that she never leaned against anything when she was talking to Mr. Harcourt.

"Why, yes," she said, "we are hoping to, Mr. Harcourt."

"I'm delighted to hear it," Mr. Harcourt said. "I hope you're going to send him to Harvard. Bill's going there next year."

"Well," Mrs. Wayde said, "Alfred and I think it's too expensive a school for Willis."

"Oh, I would hardly say that," Mr. Harcourt said. "There will be expense anywhere." He touched his lower lip with his forefinger. "It occurred to me last night that I might be of some help along those lines. I'm sending Granville Beane to Massachusetts State. It would give me great pleasure—a selfish sort of pleasure—to help send Willis to Harvard, Mrs. Wayde."

There was a moment's silence and Alfred Wayde pulled a bag of tobacco and some cigarette papers out of his coat pocket, but he did not speak. He and Willis both looked at Mrs. Wayde.

"That's very kind and thoughtful of you, Mr. Harcourt," she said, and she folded her hands carefully in her lap. "I guess Alfred and I are independent people. It will mean more to us if we can do this without help, and more to Willis, I'm very, very sure, and Willis has his own savings, working summers."

Mr. Harcourt nodded.

"Well," he said, "I respect your point of view. As long as Willis is going somewhere to college. Where are you thinking of sending him, Mrs. Wayde?"

"We haven't made up our minds yet," Mrs. Wayde said, "but we're thinking about Boston University."

"My God, Cynthia," his father said, after Mr. Harcourt had gone, "why shouldn't old Harcourt have sent the boy to college?"

"Because it wouldn't have been right, Alf," she said. "I wish he wouldn't always be trying to do things. We're obligated enough to the Harcourts, living here, and I don't want Willis to be weak."

During that summer, whenever Willis saw Bill and Bess, their relationships were the same as they always had been. The Bryson Harcourts asked him twice to supper, and he had been over to play tennis sometimes on Sunday afternoons. On Sundays after church he had fallen into the habit of walking by the brook, and it generally happened that he would meet Bess there, although neither of them had ever made open plans. Then, one Sunday in October, just after he had started college, everything changed.

He saw Bess coming toward him, and in the distance she looked the same as she always had, but not when she came nearer. All of a sudden Bess was all grown-up, unapproachable and unattainable. Her tawny hair was pinned up in a knot, and she had powder on her nose, which looked more like the noses in the Harcourt portraits than it ever had before.

"Why, Willis," she said, "you look like someone else. You look all grown-up."

"Well, so do you," he said.

"Why shouldn't I?" she asked. "I'm going to the junior dances now."

"Are you really?" he asked.

"Anyway," she said, "you don't say, 'Is that a fact?' any more. That's something."

"Yes," he said, "that's something."

She stood looking at him critically.

"You've got a new suit of clothes, haven't you?" she said. "Where did you get it?"

"Downtown," he told her.

"Well," she said, "it looks it. Well, how do you like Boston University?"

"It's all right, I guess," he said.

She swayed slightly, from one foot to the other, moving her head as though she heard distant music.

"You were an awful fool," she said, "not to go to Harvard when Grandfather offered to send you."

"Harvard isn't so hot," he said.

"Don't be silly," she said. "Nobody goes to Boston University."

"That's all you know about it," Willis told her.

"You wouldn't look so bad if you had a different suit," she said. "Do you remember when I used to let you kiss me? It seems ages ago, doesn't it?"

"You didn't let me, you asked me to," he said, "and you asked Steve Decker too."

"Oh, Willis," she said, "don't be perfectly ridiculous. Anyway, it was ages ago."

"It isn't as long as that," he said.

"But it seems like ages ago. We must have been awful fools. If I did it now, you might think you'd want to marry me or something."

"I don't want to marry anybody," Willis said.

She smiled and her body swayed to that inaudible music.

"All you think about is working, don't you?" she said. "Well, I suppose you have to. Well, you can work for us at the mill when you get through with Boston University."

"There are a lot of other places to work," Willis told her.

"We'd like to have you," she said, "and Grandfather says we need new people."

"What about Bill?" he asked.

"Oh, Bill," she answered, and she laughed. "It has to be someone who has to work. Willis, you still look nice when you're in the woods. You want to kiss me now, don't you?"

"No," he said.

"Anyway," she said, and she moved a step nearer to him, "you do. I can tell you do."

It made him angry that she could tell, and he put his arm around her roughly.

"Oh, no," she said. "Willis, no." But she leaned close against him. It was different from those other times he had kissed her.

"I don't know why I'm such a fool," she said, "but it's all right here, as long as it's only here."

He did not answer, but they stood there for a while close together.

"You see we both belong in other places," she said, "and we can't help that, can we?"

[69]

Perhaps this was the wisest thing that Bess Harcourt ever said to him. Bess always had a lot of common sense, more than he ever had, perhaps.

Willis always had a warm spot in his heart for old B.U., as he often called it later, though he could not say that the personalized side of it had meant much to him. He had no time for extra-curricular activities, because he completed the requisite work for his degree in three years, and besides he had to be careful of every cent he spent. There was not much time, either, for outside intellectual enthusiasms, due to the number of courses he was taking, and because he lacked the solid groundwork of a consistent secondary education.

During the three winters he spent at old B.U., he lived throughout the week in a hall bedroom that his mother had found on Beacon Hill in a Pinckney Street lodging house. He ate his breakfast and his supper each weekday in a boardinghouse on Joy Street, patronized by office workers and a few law-school students. Boston was a fine old town with its historic monuments and its art museums, but he did not have the cash to buy a good meal at a restaurant or to attend the theater, except now and then in the second balcony. Anyway he was obliged to spend his evenings working.

If he had learned any refinements of life from observing his surroundings, he had learned them at the Harcourt place and not at old B.U. Mr. Harcourt was a model worth copying, and Willis never forgot what Bess had said about his clothes the autumn he had started off to college. He observed the dress and behavior of Bill and his friends, and he hit upon the idea of going to Harvard Square in Cambridge and buying clothing secondhand. There was always a time before the holidays when students who were short of funds disposed of clothes that were almost new, and Willis found a tailor down on Anderson Street who made alterations cheaply. By the end of his third winter, he owned a tuxedo, two good suits, one shabby one, and two pairs of white flannel trousers. He also owned a few books from Everyman's Library and a typewriter. He never forgot that B.U. gave him a college education, and he always had a warm spot in his heart for Boston University.

He only realized later how much else he must have been learning. He knew a great deal about the mill and a lot about the Harcourts by the time he had finished college. He saw the Harcourts often during the week ends, and they always asked him at least once to some party during the holidays. He never blamed them if they seemed to forget in the winters that he was living in Boston too. It did not strike him as strange at all, until much later, that he had never been inside Mr. Henry Harcourt's house on Commonwealth Avenue until March of his last year at B.U.

Mr. Harcourt expressed some surprise about it one Sunday when the Waydes had been asked to lunch at the big house, as they were about once a month. Willis never forgot the pattern of those Sunday luncheons—the standing rib of roast beef and the vanilla ice cream made of real cream from the farm, with the chocolate sauce in the silver gravy boats, and the hot black coffee in the library in the small blue rice-pattern cups.

"When do you go back to Boston, Willis?" Mr. Harcourt had asked.

Willis took an early train every Monday morning, he said, in time to get to a nine o'clock lecture.

"I don't know why I've never thought of it before," Mr. Harcourt said. "If you want a ride back on a Sunday evening, let me know any time, Willis. And there's another curious thing. We never see you in Boston, do we? We'll be at home on Tuesday night. Why don't you come around at seven o'clock for dinner?"

"Thank you, sir," Willis said. "I'd like to very much."

"That's a very nice suit of clothes you have on, Willis," Mr. Harcourt said. "I always like a well-cut coat." He hesitated for an instant. "Don't bother to dress on Tuesday, Willis. I will because I always do."

Willis checked himself from saying that he owned a tuxedo now, but nothing could have stopped him from wearing it that evening.

When Willis walked that Tuesday evening over melting snowbanks on his way to Commonwealth Avenue, the brick houses of Beacon Hill, with their curving Bulfinch fronts and the warm vague light from their shaded windows, spoke of a life around him of which he had no part. When he got on Commonwealth Avenue the street lights, cutting yellowish spheres in the dark, made all the houses seem unnaturally large, and Mr. Henry Harcourt's was as large as any of them. Its glass doors, protected by an iron grill, opened into a vestibule paved with squares of marble. Through a second glass door he could see a broad marble-paved hallway and French mirrors.

"Good evening, Mr. Willis," Selwyn said. "I'm afraid Mr. and Mrs. Harcourt aren't down yet, but if you'll wait upstairs I'm sure they'll be with you in a few minutes."

"Whereabouts upstairs?" Willis asked.

"I'd forgotten you didn't know your way," Selwyn said. "Your tie is a trifle crooked. Would you care to have me straighten it?"

"I guess I'm not very good at tying a bow tie," Willis told him.

"It will come with practice," Selwyn said. "You look well in evening clothes. Not everybody does. May I make one suggestion, Mr. Willis?"

"Is anything wrong?" Willis asked.

"I wouldn't say wrong," Selwyn said. "But I wouldn't wear a handkerchief jutting out of my breast pocket. Mr. Harcourt never does and neither does Mr. Bill. Mr. Bill and Miss Bess will be with us tonight—just the family. This way, Mr. Willis."

There was another broad hall upstairs, with the dining room to the left and a large sitting room to the right. The sitting-room walls and woodwork were freshly painted in dull green, and yellow curtains of heavy silk were drawn across the windows, and all the upholstery on the furniture was fresh and new.

"They'll be down in a minute, sir," Selwyn said. "There's the bell, I think. That will be Miss Bess and Mr. Bill."

Then Willis heard their voices in the downstairs hall.

"Hi, Selwyn," he heard Bill call. "How's it going?"

"Hello, Selwyn," he heard Bess say.

"Gosh," Willis heard Bill say, "the old man's done the whole place over."

Then he heard them running up the stairs.

"Hi, Willis," Bill said.

"Oh, Willis," Bess said, "let me look at you. You don't look like yourself at all."

Neither did Bess, for that matter. Her dress was a brilliant blue, and her shoulders were bare and her face was fresh and warm from the cold outside.

"I wouldn't know you either," Willis said. "That's quite a dress."

"What there is of it," Bill said, and he laughed.

"Oh, stop it, Bill," Bess said. "They're coming downstairs."

Now that Willis was old enough himself to appreciate the beauties of youth, he could imagine that the three of them had delighted Mr. and Mrs. Harcourt. He and Bill and Bess had emerged from the chrysalis of adolescence, and the corrosion of time had not touched them yet. In Willis's memory Bess Harcourt was never quite so beautiful again.

"How nice you three young people look," Mrs. Harcourt said, and Mr. Harcourt looked at them as though he were examining a newly acquired picture.

"Yes," Mr. Harcourt said, "you're quite right, Harriet. Bess, will you kiss your old grandfather? Willis, it's nice to see you in Boston, and, Bill, I was afraid they might need you at the club tonight."

"I'm afraid I'll have to leave right after dinner, sir," Bill said.

"Well, well," Mr. Harcourt said. "I haven't told you I was delighted by the news, not that it was unexpected."

Willis did not know what they were talking about, but Bess smiled at him as though of course he knew. Mr. Harcourt rubbed his hands together.

"A pleasant ending for a busy day," he said. "I went down to Cohasset to see your Cousin Eldridge this afternoon, Bess, and then I had a most rewarding tea party on the way home with your Cousin Lillian."

"I thought you didn't like them," Bess said.

"Well," Mr. Harcourt said. "Can't you guess why I called on them then?"

"Did you want to buy their stock?" Bill asked.

Mr. Harcourt's face wrinkled into one of his broadest smiles.

"Exactly," he said, "exactly."

"What do you want it for?" Bill asked. "Haven't we got enough?"

"Perhaps," Mr. Harcourt said, "but your Cousin Roger wanted it, and if Roger wants something . . ." Mr. Harcourt left his thought unfinished. "Here's Selwyn. You're old enough to have sherry now, aren't you, Bess?"

Willis was surprised to find that Mr. Harcourt was looking at him and not at Bess when he asked the question, but almost immediately his glance moved on. Willis was proud that he had been allowed to hear this family gossip and he knew that he had been deliberately allowed. Mr. Henry Harcourt never forgot anything when he handled people.

Bill excused himself directly after dinner, because he had to go back to Cambridge. He said that he was particularly glad to see Willis. Bill even went so far as to ask him to come out to Cambridge to see him some time. When Bill and he shook hands, Willis saw that Mr. Harcourt was watching them both with a half sad expression, and he did not speak until the front door closed.

"Everything always comes easy for Bill," he said. "It's hard on anyone when everything comes easily."

"You mean we've been born with silver spoons?" Bess said. She moved her head impatiently, and Willis could see her profile, thin and eager, resembling Mr. Harcourt's. "Well, don't blame us. It isn't our fault, is it?"

"Oh no," Mr. Harcourt answered, "it isn't your fault, Bess."

"Besides," Bess said, "you were born with a spoon yourself, weren't you?"

"Why, yes," Mr. Harcourt said. "It's something I've always tried to remember, and see you don't forget it either, Bess."

"All right," Bess said, "but I'm tired of being told about advantages."

Mr. Harcourt took a cigar cutter from the low coffee table and snipped the end from his cigar.

"This is a hard world, Bess," he said, "with a great many ruthless people in it. It's always useful to remember what you are. It's easy to pretend that you're something else. At least I've always found it so."

The Bryson Harcourts lived only a few blocks away on the water side of Beacon Street. When Bess said it was time for her to go home, it was only natural for Willis to ask if he might not walk home with her. When he said good-by to Mrs. Harcourt, she told him he must be sure to come again, and that at any rate she would see him soon in the country.

"I'm afraid perhaps we haven't acted as though you were company," Mr. Harcourt said, "but then perhaps you aren't."

"Of course Willis isn't company," Bess said.

She wore a gray squirrel coat, and when they were on the street with the glass and iron doors closed behind them, Bess was like a stranger until she abruptly put her arm through his.

"It's funny seeing you here," she said. "You really look very nice in Boston."

"How did you think I was going to look?" Willis asked.

"I don't know," she answered. "Worse than you do, I suppose. How did you think I was going to look?"

"I didn't think," Willis said, "because I didn't know you'd be there."

"We always have to go there when we're asked," she said. "You never can tell what my grandfather's going to say, can you? It makes me feel creepy the way he watches everyone. He was watching you tonight."

"Was he?" Willis asked.

"Of course he was," she said. "You know he was."

Willis did not answer.

"I was glad to see you. I didn't think I would be. Were you glad to see me?" she asked.

"Yes, I guess I was," he said.

"Of course you were," she said. "You kept looking at me. You're not the way you are in the country."

"Well, you aren't either," Willis said.

"Of course I'm not," she answered. "Why should I be? Bill's been taken into the A.D. Club, you know. That was what they were talking about tonight."

"What's the A.D. Club?" Willis asked.

"That shows you don't know anything," she said, "but you look as though you did. What do you do in Boston, Willis?"

"I go to B.U. and I study," he said.

"But you must know some girls."

"I haven't time to know any girls," Willis said.

"That isn't so," she said. "You have time to see Winnie Decker week ends."

"Who told you that?" Willis asked.

"Steve Decker, of course. I see him at the dances. He's on the list."

"What's the list?" Willis asked.

"Oh, never mind," she said. "You must be hard up if there's only Winnie Decker."

It was only a short walk through that dark night, along Commonwealth Avenue and right on Clarendon Street and across Marlborough and then up Beacon Street, where the wind was beginning to blow hard across the Charles.

"Well, here we are," she said.

She stopped at the steps of one of those brownstone houses that still impressed Willis as more aloof and forbidding than any houses in any other city he had known.

"You might as well come in for a minute," she said. "Nobody's at home."

The hall lights were on and she turned on the lights in a small downstairs room that must have been called the reception room at the time the house was built.

"Thanks for seeing me home," she said.

Then, perhaps before either of them knew it, or before they thought of it, they were in each other's arms.

"I'm an awful fool," she whispered. "Oh dear, I wish that things were different."

VI

WILLIS ALWAYS admitted that his characteristics of aggressiveness matured in him later than they did in some young men. He had qualities of patience and a sort of modesty that combined to keep him from pushing ahead in any annoying manner.

This slow development of Willis Wayde probably explained why he had never attracted great attention during the summers he worked at the mill, but later all sorts of people remembered him. Both of his contemporaries, Bill Harcourt and Steve Decker, who had been sent to learn the business when Willis Wayde was there, had their own pictures of Willis. Mr. Henry Hewett, after he was retired, added more to the portrait, as did Mr. Briggs, but then Mr. Briggs was bitter after Mr. Bryson Harcourt had accepted his resignation.

It was the business of Miss Minton, the receptionist, to remember everyone, and Willis was tall and handsome, with nice blond hair that always needed cutting, and there were girls in the office who used to say that they would like to muss up Willis's hair. Willis was popular but he was never fresh, the way Mr. Bill Harcourt sometimes was.

Mr. Hewett often said that he could have told plenty, if tact had not prevented him, about the goings on at the mill in those days.

Henry Harcourt was having his troubles with Bryson, and Roger Harcourt was trying to shoot holes in everything and waiting for Henry to die so he could muscle in on the management; and Bill had no serious interest in the plant. Mr. Hewett had been surprised when H.H. once told him that if Willis had a few more years on him he'd be management material. Old H.H. was always making plans, but Mr. Hewett could not see what old H.H. saw in Willis. Willis was a hard-working boy and a nice boy with manners, but Willis lacked in push and aggressiveness in those days.

Mr. Briggs, being closer to the firing line in those days as sales manager, saw more of old H.H. in his last years than he had at any time previously. In spite of his age, H.H. had a mind that was twice as young as

Bryson's. He was constantly playing with ideas for enlarging the Harcourt line and he was never afraid to spend money on experiment in spite of the rest of the family. He saw that if you stood still you were lost, in an expanding era like the twenties. He was constantly calling Mr. Briggs into conferences with Alf Wayde. Alf Wayde might not have looked like much, but he had made his own refinements in the Klaus patents, and he had perfected the Harcourt interwoven joint and the machines that made six different Harcourt carcasses. Harcourt Mill was beginning to develop a line that could answer any industrial requirement, and time was all that interfered. If they had only followed the plans of expansion which were already in the works, Harcourt's would have been the sweetest piece of property in the business. Alfred Wayde certainly knew his belting, but no one could have guessed in those days that Alf's son Willis was good for much.

Willis was not aware of any of the upper-level stuff that was going on at Harcourt's in the summer after he had graduated from Boston University. He and Bill Harcourt and Steve Decker did odd jobs in the sales department and ran all sorts of errands, and Mr. Henry and Mr. Bryson Harcourt and Mr. Hewett and Mr. Briggs were distant figures. Yet everyone knew that there was a cleavage of ideas, and that before old H.H. began planning expansion, the mill had been a comfortable family business that paid excellent dividends. Mr. Bryson never saw why it should not have been kept that way and Willis had one clear glimpse of that difference of opinion between Mr. Henry and Mr. Bryson.

During July both he and Bill were in the sales department helping one of the new assistants, a Mr. Harrow, prepare a sales folder with photographs and cross sections of the new Harcourt belting. Mr. Harrow, who had recently been imported from New York, was engaged that afternoon in writing brief descriptions of different Harcourt belts, and Willis and Bill Harcourt were preparing rough drafts for Mr. Harrow to put into final form. They sat in their shirt sleeves side by side at a table upstairs in the sales department.

"Say," Bill was saying, "here's a new one."

"Which one?" Willis asked.

"Harcourt Oak-Heart," Bill said. "I never heard of that one."

"Oh," Willis said, "that's the general-purpose white belting."

It seemed to Willis that Bill should have known by that time that Harcourt Oak-Heart was one of the most stable features in the line. The binder threads in Oak-Heart were interwoven in such a way that ply separation was entirely eliminated.

"What's ply separation?" Bill asked.

It was difficult to do his own work and Bill's at the same time, but

Willis knew a lot about Harcourt Oak-Heart, and he was starting to explain the whole thing to Bill when Mr. Briggs opened the door of his corner office. Mr. Briggs was in his shirt sleeves too, and his starched collar was wilted. He was holding a sales form covered with figures.

"Willis," he asked, "can you drop what you're doing?"

Mr. Briggs's belt made a crease around his middle, and as usual he was in a hurry and as usual he spoke in the ringing tones that he used when he was addressing his salesmen.

"Yes, sir," Willis said.

"Take this down to Mr. Harcourt's office, will you?" Mr. Briggs said, and then he saw Bill Harcourt and his voice grew more cordial. "You don't mind my taking Willis away from you for a minute or two, do you, Bill?"

Bill folded his hands behind his head and smiled.

"Oh no," Bill said, "just as long as he comes back."

Mr. Briggs laughed heartily.

"That's fine," he said. "That's fine. Right up to your ears in it today, aren't you, Bill?"

"Over my head and treading water," Bill said.

Mr. Briggs laughed again. "Well," he said, "that's fine. Mr. Harrow showed me the piece you wrote about Harcourt Vulcanoid. It had a real punch to it. Take this and get going, Willis."

The office building, which had once seemed overambitious, was beginning to grow cramped and inadequate. The inventory department had been moved outside, and the engineering department now occupied the vacant room. Carpenters were putting up temporary partitions for the two engineers whom his father had hired recently, and Willis had a glimpse of Alfred Wayde smoking his pipe and bending over his drawing table, oblivious to the carpenters' pounding. Things were quieter when Willis descended to the lower floor. There the illusion of the Federalist mansion still existed, and the door to Mr. Harcourt's office was open as usual. Although Mr. Harcourt always wore his coat, he contrived to look cool in summer. He was seated in his swivel chair and the light of the window behind him, from where Willis stood, made his features shadowy, until he pivoted slightly sideways. Mr. Bryson Harcourt was seated near the corner of the desk, with the light directly on his face.

"I only wish you'd tell me," Mr. Bryson was saying, "what on earth you think is going to happen here eventually?"

The chair springs squeaked discordantly as Mr. Harcourt leaned back.

"We've been over that before," he said. "It will have to be your problem eventually."

"Father," Mr. Bryson began, "I wish you'd try to see this from my point of view."

"Excuse me, sir," Willis said. "Mr. Briggs sent this down to you."

"All right," Mr. Harcourt said. "Thank you, Willis."

As Willis crossed the room and laid the paper on the desk, they were both looking at him uncomfortably.

"Well, Willis," Mr. Bryson said, "how's Bill getting along upstairs?" His voice was friendly. The façade was back in place.

"He's doing fine, sir," Willis said.

It was one of those things that one remembered only in view of what happened later. It was not Mr. Bryson's fault that he had not inherited the ability of Mr. Henry Harcourt. A part of old H.H. was as antiquated as the Locomobile that Patrick drove, but if he were alive today, Willis was sure that Mr. Henry Harcourt would have done very well indeed.

When the five o'clock whistle blew that afternoon, his father asked him if he wanted a ride back home. He was still driving a T-model Ford. Its fenders were battered and its chassis creaked, but its engine ran like clockwork.

"It's a damn funny thing," his father said, when they reached the driveway of the Harcourt place, "to be driving this can in these surroundings, but it runs all right."

"It ought to," Willis told him. "You take it apart and put it together enough."

"Say," Willis's father said, "you're working up there with young Bill. Is he any good?"

"He's all right," Willis answered.

"You know damn well he isn't," his father said. "Not that he isn't a nice enough kid. I wish you wouldn't play around with those Harcourts so much, Willis. It seems to me that you're getting big ideas."

"What sort of ideas?" Willis asked.

Alfred Wayde laughed harshly.

"Like marrying the boss's daughter, and you don't want to marry any boss's daughter."

Willis felt his face redden. The Ford had stopped in the road by the garden house, but Alfred Wayde still sat with his hands on the wheel.

"I don't see how you got that idea in your head," Willis told him. "I'm not thinking of marrying anyone."

Alfred Wayde breathed deeply through his nose.

"Don't act like I've been spying on you, boy," he said. "It's only that there's some things about you that worry me, Willis. Now listen. No man ever thinks seriously about marrying. It just comes over him when he reaches a certain age. But, God—I don't want to give you a lecture.

[79]

When I was a young fellow your age, I always liked girls. Sometimes I had four or five at once, but I never went seriously with anyone until I saw your mother in Topeka, and then it came over me the way I say. But, hell, I don't want to deliver a lecture."

There were beads of perspiration on Alfred Wayde's forehead and he rubbed his sleeve across his face.

"I wish you'd take a few drinks sometimes, Willis, and hell around and see some girls—in your own group, I mean—not girls like Bess."

Willis cleared his throat.

"What girls, for instance, Pa?" he asked.

"Hell," Alfred Wayde said, "it isn't my function to pick out girls for you. What I mean are reciprocating girls."

"Reciprocating girls?" Willis repeated after him.

"Now, Willis," Alfred Wayde said, "I'm using a mechanical term, but I mean girls who are able to give you back the same that you give them. Not girls like pack rats. You remember the pack rats in Arizona?"

"I remember them," Willis said, "but I don't see what they have to do with it."

Alfred Wayde rubbed his face with his sleeve again.

"Sometimes I wish to God we'd stayed in Arizona, and you'd be different, son. A pack rat always leaves you something, but once one of them in Arizona ran off with a five-dollar gold piece of mine and left me a piece of horse manure. Reciprocating girls do better than that. You don't want to end up with a cow chip, Willis."

Willis laughed, but he was sorry that he had when he saw his father's face.

"I'm no good at giving a lecture," Alfred Wayde said. "All I mean is you ought to go around with some girls made out of the same ply as you. Instead, you run over and see Bess and those Boston girls and press your pants in the kitchen. You ought to go downtown and have a few drinks and see some real girls."

"But what girls?" Willis asked. It was hot in the Ford and the locusts in the trees made a buzzing noise like tea kettles.

"Well, for a starter, why not take Mazie Minton from the reception desk to the pictures? She's a pretty girl."

"She's too old," Willis said.

"Well, then, some of those kids you went to high school with," his father said. "The town is full of pretty girls."

"Look," Willis said. "I understand what you mean, partly, but I don't have much time."

Alfred Wayde turned his head slowly and stared at him. He was wearing a blue work shirt without a tie. His trousers were baggy and spotted, and no amount of machinist's soap ever completely removed the ingrained grease from his hands.

"How do you mean you don't have much time?"

Willis was suddenly acutely aware of his own neat coat and tie.

"I've been working pretty hard," he said. "I got through college in three years, you know, and I've been working every summer."

"Hell," Alfred Wayde said, "I used to work twelve hours firing a donkey engine college vacations, but I was always full of piss and vinegar at night. The thing with me was I never gave a damn. I'll tell you what the trouble with you is."

Alfred Wayde snorted and looked through the windshield as though he were driving the stationary car.

"You're trying to be something you aren't," he said. "You watch it, Willis. You keep on trying to be something you aren't, and you'll end up a son of a bitch. You can't help being, if you live off other people."

"I don't get your point. I honestly don't," Willis said.

Alfred Wayde shifted his weight and leaned his elbows on the wooden steering wheel.

"Listen, boy," he said. "People are divided into two parts—people who do things and the rest, who live off those who do things. Now I may not amount to much, but I've had a pretty happy time, because I can turn out something. I can do anything in that damn mill that anyone else can do, and they all know it, boy. Well, maybe you'll spend your life living off other people's doings, but if you have to, don't fool yourself. Maybe you'll end up like Harcourt. I don't know. But you'll never *be* like Harcourt."

There was a good deal in what his father had said, and Willis realized it even then. He was listening to the age-old definition of management and labor, to a description of the chasm that always divided the creator and the entrepreneur, and of course his father had been right, but Willis could only put his thoughts in a single awkward question.

"But you like Mr. Harcourt, don't you?" Willis asked.

"Hell, yes," Alfred Wayde said. "All his moving parts are greased. He knows what he is, and we get along, but he lives off me just the same."

"Well, you live off him, too, don't you?" Willis said.

"All right," Alfred Wayde answered, "all right. There always has to be a boss in the front office. I only say, don't try too hard, Willis, or else you'll end up a son of a bitch."

Alfred Wayde was a realist who always told the truth. He was simplifying the Harcourts in exactly the same way he could simplify the explanations of a complicated process.

"Sometimes," Alfred Wayde said, "I wish I'd never brought you here.

By God, I should have stayed out West. It's time we started moving, but now, by God, old Harcourt's got us, and he isn't going to live forever either."

Alfred Wayde pushed himself away from the wheel and kicked open the door of the Ford.

"Well, I guess that's about all I've got to say, Willis, and now I'm going in to get a rye and ginger ale and you better have one too, but just remember what I said. Look around for some reciprocating girls."

Cynthia Wayde opened the door of the garden house just as they were getting out of the car.

"What have you two been talking about," she asked, "out there in the sun?"

"I've just been telling Willis a few facts," Alfred Wayde said, "and now I'm going to give him a drink."

"Oh, Alf," Mrs. Wayde said, "you know Willis hardly ever takes anything."

"It's time he started," Alfred Wayde said.

"Well, Willis isn't like you, Alf," Mrs. Wayde said, and she stood in front of Willis in the parlor while Alfred Wayde went to get the glasses and ginger ale. "Willis, I wish you knew some nice girls."

"Gosh," Willis said, "do you wish that too? Reciprocating girls, not pack-rat girls?"

But he was not obliged to explain what reciprocating girls meant, because the telephone rang in the hall.

"I'll go," he said, and it was Bess Harcourt calling.

"Is that you, Willis?" she said. "How about coming over after you've had your supper. The family's gone away to the shore, all except me, and Daddy forgot and left the liquor closet open. We can have some Scotch if you come over."

"Why, thanks," Willis said, and in spite of everything he did not feel tired at all. "I'd like to very much."

Perhaps in some ways Bess was a reciprocating girl.

Bess was waiting for him on the driveway outside the Bryson Harcourt house. The brick Georgian house which Bryson Harcourt had built was still untrammeled by tradition and it always looked to Willis rather like a country club, with its tennis court and its swimming pool. The last of the evening light was still in the sky that evening, and the scene remained in his memory as a sort of dream of wish fulfillment.

Like the house, Bess in her cool silk summer dress was a part of that dream, but he was familiar with her too. In fact they knew each other better, perhaps, than either of them knew anybody else. Nevertheless he could never tell when he met her whether she would have good manners or none at all. She seemed almost shy that night.

"I feel awfully lonely tonight," she said. "It's too hot in the house. Let's go and sit by the swimming pool. It's awfully nice of you to come over, Willis."

"I always do, when you ask me," Willis said.

"Yes," she said, "I know."

The pool was near the woods, and its water reflected the dying light in the sky. The pool was far enough away from the house so that no one could see them, and both of them must have known that this was their reason for going there.

"If you're lonely," Willis asked her, "why didn't you go to the shore with your family?"

"You know why perfectly well," Bess said, and she laughed. "Don't you miss me sometimes?"

"Yes," he told her, "sometimes."

"It's nice to have a secret sin," Bess said, "and you're my secret sin. Well, what are you waiting for?" She had stopped in front of the pergola at the end of the pool, where the reclining chairs were. There was no reason to wait any longer, and of course he kissed her.

"I'm awfully glad you're here," she said, "even if it isn't sensible. I've been in and out of the water all day, but I'll watch you if you want to swim."

"No thanks," Willis answered. "It's getting pretty cool."

"All right," she said. "I've sneaked out the soda and the ice and everything. You can pour me a small drink if you want to. . . . Bill says it's time I learned to drink a little, and it's part of the secret sin."

"That's just what my father was saying," Willis answered, "that I ought to take a drink occasionally."

"It tastes horrid, doesn't it?" she said, and Willis silently agreed with her. "Your father's a funny man. Sometimes I think he never notices me."

"Everybody always notices you," Willis said.

She sat down on one of the reclining chairs.

"Move over close to me," she said. "I wish I didn't always like it when you're with me, and we can't go on like this indefinitely, can we? Or people will begin to talk."

"Yes, I guess that's so," Willis said, "but then, you asked me over, didn't you?"

She reached out her hand toward his.

"You wanted to come, didn't you?"

"Oh yes," he said, "I wanted to."

"All right, as long as you wanted to," and she held his hand tighter. "I wish you could always be around when I want you."

He did not answer.

"Willis," she said, "I've felt queer all day. I've felt awfully old."

"Why do you feel queer?" he asked.

"I don't know why," she said, "and I don't know why I can talk to you better than anyone else. Maybe I love you. But that would be awfully silly."

His common sense made him agree with her. Both he and Bess Harcourt always had the gift of knowing exactly where they were.

"I've been wondering all day what's going to happen to us all," she said. "Daddy's nice but he's a rather stupid man, don't you think so? Willis, I have the queerest feeling." Her voice choked suddenly. "Promise me you won't go away."

"You don't want me around," Willis said, "not really."

"I half want you," she said, and then her voice dropped lower, almost to a whisper. "There's got to be someone to look after us, Willis."

It was a preposterous remark, and his own answer was equally preposterous.

"You know I love you, Bess," he said.

"All right," she told him, "I wanted you to say that, but it's utterly ridiculous." She stood up suddenly. The afterglow had left the sky and the stars were out.

"I know you can't change anything any more than I can," she said. "If we have to be ridiculous, let's go walking in the woods."

Willis was sure that something serious was facing him when he received a typewritten memorandum brought up by one of Miss Jackman's typists to the sales department late one afternoon a few days after his evening with Bess. The name of the girl who brought it was Nellie Bailey, he remembered. She had been in the class ahead of him at high school, not that that detail mattered, except to show that he still recollected every circumstance surrounding that message.

"Mr. Harcourt," the memorandum read, "wishes to know if it is possible for you to call on him at the House at eight o'clock this evening. Please answer by bearer. Edith Jackman. Confidential."

The memorandum was characteristic of Miss Jackman's style, even down to spelling house with a capital. Willis picked up a pencil immediately and wrote, "Yes," on the square piece of paper and handed it back to Nellie Bailey. Then he had a physical sensation that bordered on nausea. He was almost sure that the summons had something to do with Bess, because in the end Mr. Harcourt always heard and noticed everything. There was one thing he did not want and this was for his father and his mother to see that he was worried. Lately he suspected that his parents had been discussing him, and his mother had brought up the subject of nice girls several times.

"Willis," she said, as soon as he got home, "is anything the matter?"

"Why, no. What makes you think so?" Willis asked.

"Because you don't look happy."

"I'm perfectly happy," he told her.

"No," she said. "You look drawn around the eyes. Can't you tell your mother what's the matter?"

"It isn't anything, Mom," he said, "except Mr. Harcourt wants to see me at the big house at eight o'clock."

"Alf," she called. "Alfred, come in here out of the kitchen."

His father came from the kitchen holding a Stillson wrench.

"You told me to fix the sink trap, didn't you?" he said. "What is it, Cynthia?"

"Mr. Harcourt wants to see Willis at the big house." She spoke slowly and carefully, as though he might find the statement difficult to understand.

"Is that so?" Alfred Wayde said. "I told you we ought to have moved out of here before this, Cynthia."

"I hope he isn't going to try to do something for Willis," she said.

"Willis is working for him, isn't he?" Alfred Wayde said. "Just the same as I am."

"I know," she said. "I don't know why it should bother me when Mr. Harcourt gets talking about Willis, but it's sort of as though he owned him."

"He owns everybody," Alfred Wayde said.

"Well, he doesn't own me," Cynthia Wayde said. "It isn't as though he isn't very kind, but I hope he isn't going to do too much for Willis. If he wants to do anything, he could raise your pay, Alf."

"I could make him easy enough," Alfred Wayde said, "if I wasn't too much obliged to him."

"There," she said, "there! That's exactly what I mean."

Willis later often gave talks to chosen young men in his office on the subject of the successful interview. Actually there were only two things to remember, and the rest would look out for itself. You had to bear constantly in mind exactly where you stood and where the other person stood. It helped to think of yourself as playing a hand of bridge. When the dummy was on the table, you could judge with fair accuracy what your opponents held, if you recalled the bidding and the conventions. It was even easier when there was only one opponent.

When Willis walked from the garden house to the big house to call on Mr. Harcourt, he had already developed some adroitness. It was Stevenson, he believed, who once had said that a young writer must learn to play the sedulous ape, and the same thing was true with a young man who tried to get on in business. Willis had never been wholly sedulous but he was proud of the model he had chosen, and he liked to think that evening that he had been a little like Mr. Harcourt. He had brushed his hair carefully and had put on his best suit and he had shined his shoes down cellar, but he had been careful to wrinkle his coat slightly and also to disturb the slickness of his hair with his fingers. No matter what happened he was going to be as much as he could like Mr. Harcourt and in a smaller way like Bill.

"Good evening, Mr. Willis," Selwyn said. "Mr. Harcourt's waiting for you in his study off the library."

Willis felt a pulse beating in his throat.

"Selwyn," he said, and he smiled. "Do you notice anything about me?"

"No, Mr. Willis," Selwyn said.

"No handkerchief in my breast pocket."

"No one has to tell you anything twice," Selwyn said, "as I heard Mr. Harcourt say this evening, Mr. Willis."

It was the way Selwyn might have spoken to Bill. There was no wonder that he always had a warm spot in his heart for Selwyn.

Mr. Harcourt was in his small study with piles of papers in front of him.

"Oh here you are, Willis," Mr. Harcourt said. "I hope this does not keep you from some more agreeable engagement."

Willis could not be sure, but it seemed to him that Mr. Harcourt had underlined the last phrase slightly.

"Sit down," Mr. Harcourt said, "but close the door first."

Willis crossed the small room while Mr. Harcourt was speaking and seated himself in the caller's chair facing Mr. Harcourt, trying neither to slouch nor to sit too stiffly. The single casement window of the study was closed when he came in, and with the door closed the study was cool and so quiet that he could hear the ticking of Mr. Harcourt's gold watch in his waistcoat pocket. Mr. Harcourt looked smaller and frailer than usual and his face looked paler and the lines deeper, but the silent room continued to exaggerate his careful detachment and the slow, deliberate motions of his hands.

"I've been intending for some time to speak to you frankly, Willis," Mr. Harcourt said, and his voice was measured and soft, but in the closed room it had a resonant, chimelike quality. Then Mr. Harcourt smiled one of his quick formal smiles that only went so far as to curve his mouth and immediately disappear.

"In a way I am going to throw myself on your discretion and say one or two things of a highly personal nature, which I shall rely on you not to repeat."

"Yes, sir," Willis said.

"You see, I have to rely on people," Mr. Harcourt said, "and I haven't gone wrong often. Hand me that box of cigars, please, Willis, and the cutter."

Mr. Harcourt selected a cigar and the cold snip from the cutter sounded so unnaturally loud that Willis felt his muscles tense.

"Well," Mr. Harcourt said, "I was speaking about you to Bess the other evening. Hand me the matchbox please, Willis."

Willis reached quickly for the silver box that stood at the end of Mr. Harcourt's work table, but his fingers closed on it clumsily.

"Thanks," Mr. Harcourt said. "I wish she were a boy. She has the family ability, I think, and Bill hasn't got it. Do you agree?"

"I don't know, sir," Willis said.

"Of course you know," Mr. Harcourt said. "Some people have a commercial instinct and some haven't. Bill's like his father—not that I'm not fond of them. They're loyal to me."

He paused as though he expected Willis to say something.

"Commercial instinct may not be the proper phrase. It's something I have and something they haven't. It isn't only an ability to make money—that's an incidental part. At any rate I think you have it."

Mr. Harcourt paused again, and Willis felt a strange tingling in his spine.

"Well," Mr. Harcourt said, "if the family hasn't got the instinct, we must find it elsewhere, Willis. Henry Hewett's a good man, but he's too old for any long-term planning. Briggs is all right in sales, but he's too nervous to take on anything else. It's a mistake to think you're going to live forever. Well . . . I'm calling in a management firm—Beakney-Graham in New York. I'm asking them to go over the office setup and to make general recommendations. You don't know why I'm telling you this, do you?"

"No, sir," Willis said, "I don't."

Mr. Harcourt stared at him for a moment without speaking.

"Because I'm thinking of taking you into my office as a sort of assistant, Willis. I'm going to need someone in about two years who is loyal and who knows me and knows the family. Bill is going to the Harvard Business School in the fall. I want to send you there too."

Mr. Harcourt's measured voice stopped, and probably it was time. At any rate Willis needed time to put what Mr. Harcourt had said into any sort of order.

"Well, sir," Willis began.

"Just a minute," Mr. Harcourt said. "I haven't finished yet. I want you to meet customers who come to see me. You must get to know the stockholders and learn to get me information when I want it. Before you can be what I'm thinking of, I want your rough edges smoothed off. Bill can teach you a little. I know you've been watching him, and I can help you myself, but most of it is going to be up to you. I hope you see what I mean."

Willis cleared his throat, but his voice was still hoarse when he answered.

"I see what you mean, sir," he said, "but I don't know as I'd be able to do it."

Mr. Harcourt tapped his finger several times against the end of his cigar.

"Maybe you won't," he said. "I'll have to see."

"You're being mighty kind to me, sir," Willis began, but Mr. Harcourt stopped him.

"No," he said, "I haven't the slightest intention of being kind to you."

He stopped and still kept his glance on Willis.

"Have you talked to my father about this, sir?" Willis asked him.

"Why under the sun should I?" Mr. Harcourt said.

"He wouldn't like it, sir," Willis said, "and he wouldn't send me to any business school."

Mr. Harcourt coughed gently.

"He isn't going to," he said. "I'm paying for this party, Willis."

There was something arrogant in the way he said it that Willis did not like even then.

"No," Willis said, "I couldn't do that, sir."

At least for once he had looked Mr. Harcourt in the eye and had laid it on the line.

"All right," Mr. Harcourt said. "All right, if that's the way you want it, Willis."

Willis pushed back his chair and stood up.

"But thank you very much for offering this to me," he said.

Mr. Harcourt placed his cigar on his ash tray.

"Sit down," he said. "We haven't finished yet. Suppose we put it this way. It takes two years to go through the Harvard Business School. I am prepared to lend you three thousand dollars for your expenses, Willis, and you can give me your note for it at six per cent. You'll be working in the summer. I'll have it amortized out of your salary. I'm taking a calculated risk, but I do that every day. Do you like that better, Willis?"

"Yes, sir," Willis said. "But it's a lot of money."

"I suppose it is, from your point of view, but these things are always relative," Mr. Harcourt said. "Will you do it, Willis?"

It was the first decision that Willis Wayde had ever been obliged to make, and he liked to think that he did it rather well.

"Yes, sir," he said, "I'll do it, and thank you very much," and then he cleared his throat again, "and I'll always try to do the best I can, Mr. Harcourt."

He meant every word of it, and it was easier to be nice in those days than it was later. Mr. Harcourt laughed softly.

"You'd be a damn fool if you didn't," he said, "and I've never set you down as one. Well, that finishes our conversation. Let's go out and join the ladies, Willis."

His first instinct was to thank Mr. Harcourt and to say he should be going home, but instead Willis followed him down the hall to the living room. Even on that short walk he began to be vaguely aware that he had lost some sort of freedom which he could not name exactly and which he had not valued until he lost it.

He was not surprised when he saw Mrs. Harcourt and Bess seated on the living-room sofa, and it was a suitable ending for that evening.

"Well, Harriet," Mr. Harcourt said, "Willis is going to the Harvard Business School."

He was surprised, although it did not seem unnatural, that Mrs. Harcourt took his hand in both of hers.

"Oh, Willis," she said, "I'm so glad for you, and I'm glad for us. I know you're going to be a great help to Mr. Harcourt."

There was a great deal more to her words than met the ear. She seemed relieved and happy, and Bess seemed happy too.

"I'm glad too," Bess said, "but you certainly took an awfully long time talking about it."

"Not so long," Mr. Harcourt said. "There'll be some more details tomorrow, Willis. I want to see you and Bill at the office at ten o'clock."

"I'd better be going home now," Bess said, and she smiled in a quick way like her grandfather. "You'll walk home with me, won't you, Willis?"

It was more like an order than a question.

"Yes, of course, Bess," Willis said.

"He says it just like a yes man, doesn't he?" Bess said, and everybody laughed.

"Willis, dear," Mrs. Harcourt said, and he was startled. It was the first time she had ever called him "dear." "We want you to feel that you are a part of the family now, don't we, Henry?"

Mr. Harcourt put his hand on Willis's arm.

"He knows that already," he said, "or he ought to, Harriet."

Willis knew that it was true. In some way, without the words being spoken, he had sworn some sort of allegiance in Mr. Harcourt's study. He had traveled a long way since he had stepped off the train with his suitcases and his Stetson hat one summer afternoon, and he was sure that Mr. Harcourt had planned it. Mr. Harcourt had always planned everything.

VII

WHAT HAD the world been like when Willis had attended the Harvard Business School? He could explain it in terms of graphs and curves. He knew on paper many pertinent details of that time, but when he had lived it he had, of course, been too young for any balanced appreciation. He had only lived through it emotionally and it was still a part of his youth.

What had he been like in those days? He could not tell exactly, any more than he could recall the facts and theories he had absorbed under the famous Case System. He could only recall a sense of general excitement and well-being. He had suddenly become a bright boy at the Harvard Business School. He had begun to absorb a picture there which he had never lost of the broad forces behind trade and organization. He had even gained, perhaps, the beginnings of a philosophy, yet he could not for the life of him remember much about himself. He had begun to gain an assurance with the high marks they gave him. He was brighter than most of the young men around him, and he had ceased to be afraid of money and he had begun to learn its uses. There was no wonder that he had a warm spot in his heart for the Harvard School of Business Administration in spite of some of the confusions of its theories.

This was the only picture he could give of himself or of his attitudes when Bill Harcourt had introduced him to a girl named Sylvia Hodges and her family in his final year at the Business School. He was not impressed by this event at the time, which indicated, of course, that he had developed a rudimentary sort of social life. There were not only the usual smokers and get-together teas, but several members of the faculty had asked him to tea or supper. After all, he was presentable. He had learned to return hospitality in a small way by taking several girls to tea dances at the Copley-Plaza in Boston and occasionally to the theater. Also, Mr. Harcourt had asked him to dinner several times and so had the Bryson Harcourts, and he saw Bess occasionally, but never as often as he saw her in the summer. Thus he was not surprised when Bill asked him to go with him to see the Hodgeses on Craigie Street.

It had been on a Friday, when he was helping Bill with a course on marketing, that Bill brought up the subject. Willis could still see Bill's room with his photographs and his neckties and his framed club invitations from his undergraduate days and his evening clothes flung over a chair waiting for the valet service and the small wine keg in the closet in which Bill was endeavoring to manufacture claret. Willis could still see the papers on Bill's desk, always in disorder, and he could see Bill himself in his gray slacks and his soft shirt.

"You know I did the damnedest thing the other night," Bill said. "I went to one of those dances in Brattle Hall. Honestly, I thought I'd outgrown that sort of thing."

"Why did you go if you didn't want to?" Willis asked.

"There was a dinner," Bill said, "and the family wanted me to go. I haven't any character. I'm always nice to everybody."

Bill stretched his arms above his head. Whenever he had to study, he always wanted to put the moment off.

"Some day I'm going to stop being nice," Bill said. "Now take the other night. I was introduced to a girl and I was stuck with her for about an hour. She's somebody Steve Decker knows, and now she's written me a note."

He rustled through the papers on his desk and handed Willis a letter written in a girl's precise, small hand.

Dear Mr. Harcourt,
    I remember your saying the other evening, though perhaps you have forgotten it, that you never can find much to do on Sundays. We always have a pickup supper every Sunday night and we play pencil-and-paper games, or something like that. Steve Decker, who says he knows you, is coming next Sunday, and I hope you can come too, at half past six o'clock, and bring a friend, if you would care to. It's just an informal family pickup supper, but it will give you something to do on Sunday.
                                      Sincerely,
                                        Sylvia Hodges

Sometimes it seemed to Willis that he had been born with an instinctive faculty for recognizing and respecting the motives of other people. When Bill Harcourt invited him to call on the Hodges family in Cambridge that Sunday afternoon, Willis knew very well that Bill would not have asked one of his closer friends to share in this ordeal, but it pleased him that Bill had asked him, because it indicated that Bill thought him adequate.

In fact Bill was disarmingly grateful when they walked along the wintry sidewalks of Brattle Street. There was something about Cambridge people, especially professors, Bill said—and this girl's father was a professor—that made him nervous. He had taken a course in geology under this Professor Hodges. It had been highly recommended as impossible to fail in and had consisted of a series of lectures supplemented by several trips to nearby places in the country to look at rocks. Old Man Hodges had given him a "C," and the professor even had a sort of a sense of humor. Nevertheless, in Bill's opinion professors and their families were hard to understand.

Without ever having been to the Hodgeses', Bill knew what it would be like. Mr. and Mrs. Hodges would be trying to have their daughters meet some nice young people, and he and Willis were elected. The other guests would be Radcliffe girls and graduate students that no one had ever heard of.

The Hodgeses lived in a beige-colored Victorian house that stood on a small lawn dotted with spindly bushes. It was cold inside because the hot-air furnace was giving trouble. There were a lot of young people in the large Victorian parlor and in the dining room behind it. As Mrs. Hodges said, the latchstring was always out on Sunday evening for the children's friends, and Cambridge, if it was nothing else, was a town of young people. The hall was full of overshoes and rubbers, and the umbrella stand and the chairs beside it were piled with overcoats. Mr. and Mrs. Hodges seemed ill at ease with the young people. They stood in front of the parlor fireplace with Sylvia's sister, Laura, a pale girl of about sixteen, who also looked uneasy.

Sylvia had answered the doorbell herself. She wore an inexpensive dark-red velvet dress which gave the impression of being too large for her, and her straight dark hair was unbecomingly bobbed. Willis remembered that Bill had mentioned being stuck with Sylvia at a dance, and he could understand the reason. He had not the experience, in those days, to perceive what a well-cut dress and a more sympathetic hairdo might have done for her.

"Oh, hello, Mr. Harcourt," Sylvia said to Bill. "I was beginning to be afraid you'd found something better to do."

"Oh no," Bill said, "and I've brought a friend from Business School—Willis Wayde."

"That's awfully nice," Sylvia said. "Mother was hoping you'd bring someone. How do you do, Mr. Wayde. Is Business School fun?"

Sylvia spoke so rapidly that she gave Willis no time to tell her whether Business School was fun or not.

"Leave your galoshes and coats anywhere," she said. "It's funny I've never met anyone from Business School except Mr. Harcourt, but, oh—" Sylvia pivoted around nervously—"here's someone who says he knows you. You know Steve Decker, don't you? He's second-year Law, you know."

Then Willis saw that Steve Decker was standing behind Sylvia, and they must have been talking together in the hall when the doorbell had rung.

"Hello, Bill," Steve said. "Hi, Willis."

"Oh," Sylvia said, "do you know Mr. Wayde too?"

There had to be a time when you first became interested in someone. Though Willis could not say that he was interested in Sylvia at the moment, he felt sorry for her, because she was trying so hard to make things go, as her mother would have expressed it.

"Yes," Steve Decker said. "Willis and I are schoolmates. We wear the old school tie."

"That's right," Willis said, but he resented the way Steve smiled at him.

"Then you must tell me all about Steve," Sylvia said. "Steve and I took a long walk this afternoon. Steve was hard to keep up with but it was fun slopping through the slush, wasn't it, Steve?"

"Yes," Steve Decker said, "there was a lot of slush."

It was strange how one could sometimes guess things immediately. Nothing more needed to be said for Willis to be absolutely sure that Sylvia Hodges was crazy about Steve Decker.

"And now come in and meet the family," Sylvia said. "I'll be back in just a minute, Steve, and maybe you won't mind helping me bring the salad from the kitchen."

"All right," Steve Decker said, "I'll be right there, Sylvia."

Steve Decker's words were polite, but there was something patient in them, something condescending.

Willis was not personally impressed by Sylvia Hodges. She was too thin and too intense for his taste. It never occurred to him that she was the sort of girl who might grow prettier as she grew older. But suddenly he wanted to be kind to her if only because Steve Decker was not. He found himself hoping that he was the only one who could tell what was happening.

He remembered that he spoke to Sylvia as he walked with her to the parlor.

"My mother says I'm pretty handy around the house," he said, "if there's anything I could do to help."

"Oh no," Sylvia said, "you're company. Mother, this is Mr. Harcourt and this is Mr. Wayde."

If Mrs. Hodges had thought more about her clothes, she would have been handsome in her middle age. Her face and figure were fuller than Sylvia's. Her eyes were deep brown like Sylvia's and her features were composed. If he had looked more closely at Mrs. Hodges he might have seen that Sylvia possessed many possibilities.

"Homer," Mrs. Hodges said, "this is a friend of Sylvia's. Oh dear, I'm very bad at names."

"It's Wayde," Mr. Hodges said. "In my classes I always begin to forget when I get down to the W's myself."

Mr. Hodges looked at Willis with the expression of someone who has seen too many young male faces. He was a thin man, and his gray mustache, slightly stained by tobacco, concealed the corners of his mouth.

"Did you ever take my introductory course, Mr. Wayde?"

"No sir," Willis answered, "I went to Boston University."

"Dear, dear," Mr. Hodges said, "I attended the University of Chicago myself once, but I finally contrived to live it down. Don't you think so, Martha?"

"No, Homer," Mrs. Hodges said. "You've never lived down anything."

"You see," Mr. Hodges said, "Mrs. Hodges is a Cambridge girl herself. What are you doing now, Mr. Wayde?"

"I'm at the Harvard Business School, sir," Willis said.

"Dear, dear," Mr. Hodges said, "that model village across the river that has the answer to everything?"

"Oh, Father!" Sylvia said. "Here's Mr. Harcourt, Father. He says he was in your course."

"Well, well," Mr. Hodges said, and his expression brightened. "If it isn't my old friend Harcourt. Fancy meeting you here, with your taste for geology."

Bill Harcourt began to laugh.

"I had a fine time, sir," he said, "and anyway I got a 'C.'"

"Yes," Mr. Hodges said. "I was going to give you a 'D' but I couldn't when I remembered your necktie. You see, Mr. Wayde, mine is what is sometimes called a necktie course."

"Oh, Father," Sylvia began.

"Be at ease, Sylvia," Mr. Hodges said. "In just a moment your mother and I will go to my study and eat our chicken salad. But we understand each other, don't we, Harcourt?"

"Yes, sir," Bill said, "I guess we do."

"There's nothing like a necktie course," Mr. Hodges said, "or at least nothing exactly like it."

But Sylvia was speaking quickly again, because Steve Decker was in the hall.

"I wish Father wouldn't tease everyone," she said. "Every boy—I mean man—I ever ask around here has to go through with it, but you really mustn't mind him."

"I don't," Willis said, because he was anxious to say something pleasant. "I think he's wonderful."

As Bill said afterwards, it was one of the damnedest evenings he had ever spent, what with old Hodges and the pencil-and-paper games. But Willis had meant what he said that night. He never did get to understand Mr. Hodges, because they were poles apart, but there really had been something wonderful about him. Whenever Willis thought about him, he always admitted that Mr. Hodges had something that he would never have, and he was sure that Sylvia understood this, although she very seldom mentioned it.

"Laura," Sylvia said to her younger sister, "will you please take Mr. Harcourt and Mr. Wayde around and see that they meet everybody?"

Laura Hodges gave them a panic-stricken look.

"Can't you do it, Sylvia?" she asked. "You know everybody better than I do."

"No, I can't," Sylvia answered. "I have a lot of things I have to attend to."

"I know what you have to attend to," Laura said.

"Laura," Sylvia said. "You do what I say or I'll speak to Mother."

"Don't worry about us," Bill said. "We'll get along all right."

Sylvia had left them while Bill was still speaking, and Laura blushed unbecomingly.

"I didn't mean it that way," she said, "but Sylvia's always bossy."

"That's all right," Bill Harcourt told her. "Big sisters always are."

"She knows I don't like introducing people," Laura said, "but we'll have to do it now, or Sylvia will find out later."

It interested Willis to remember that it was Sylvia's younger sister, and not Sylvia, who introduced him to that new world of Craigie Street. Though Willis became well acquainted with most of them later, he always thought that those people who came to Craigie Street on Sunday evenings were a peculiar crowd, but he was always grateful for the contacts, because it was an education to meet people out of the ordinary run. In memory, he could still hear Laura's strained voice as she led them around the room.

"This is my brother Tom," Laura said, and there was Tom Hodges, who always did strange things, like voting for Henry Wallace.

"This is Henry Halstead," Laura said. She could never introduce people gracefully. Instead she pointed them out like books on a library shelf. And there was Henry Halstead, an instructor in one of Mr. Hodges's courses who later became an oil geologist.

"This is Norma Ritchie," Laura was saying, and there was Sylvia's Radcliffe classmate Norma, the girl with acne, who was studying social sciences and who later had something to do with the United Nations and who sent Christmas cards of little-known saints from odd corners of French cathedrals.

"This is Hunter Baxter." And there was Hunter Baxter, the poet, who never used rhymes and who later lectured to women's clubs and was investigated by the Un-American Activities Committee.

"This is Simeon Flyrood," Laura was saying, and there was Tom's Law School classmate Simeon Flyrood, who liked to have his friends call him "Red" because of his ginger hair and freckles. He was the same Simeon Flyrood who later had something to do with the National Labor Relations Board, until he got mixed up with Communism in China.

"This is Elsie O'Donnell." And there was Sylvia's Radcliffe classmate Elsie O'Donnell, whose hair never looked washed, no matter how often she washed it, and who became a script girl in Hollywood and finally did very well writing the Jack and Josie Breakfast Series on the radio, a daily drama of married life—although Elsie never did marry anyone.

"This is Claude Little," Laura was saying, and there was Claude Little, who was the syndicated columnist today, a very interesting man and a good contact in Washington.

There must have been a dozen others—graduate students working for their doctorates and others in the Law and Medical Schools. There was Roy Fitzroy, for instance, who later became an authority on nutrition, and Hank Parkinson, who ended up in the Manhattan Project. They all looked uneasily at Willis when they heard he came from the Harvard Business School, but they were very interesting contacts, and it paid to know how to get on with this type of person.

"Supper's ready," he heard Sylvia calling.

There was chicken salad and cocoa and prune soufflé in the dining room, and everyone seemed hungry except Bill Harcourt.

After supper everyone drew lots for a team to do the dishes. Willis was on the team with Bill Harcourt and Hunter Baxter and Laura. Although Willis was not used to the routine, he was good at doing dishes, and everyone began looking at him approvingly.

While the team worked, Willis could hear calls from the parlor for Red Flyrood to get out his guitar and sing some Western songs, and Red sang "Home on the Range" and "Bury Me Not on the Lone Prairie" in a voice loud enough to be clearly heard at the kitchen sink. When he began to sing about the caissons rolling along, Laura asked Willis if he would mind going to her father's study across the hall to get the dishes there. Mr. and Mrs. Hodges always had their supper alone in the study.

"Well, well," Mr. Hodges said. He was sitting behind his desk with a pile of manuscript in front of him. "Would you mind closing the door so I won't have to hear Mr. Flyrood quite so clearly?"

"Now, Homer," Mrs. Hodges said, "the young people are having a good time, and it's very sweet of Mr. Wayde to enter in."

"Yes," Mr. Hodges said. "Yes, Martha. Did you ever take a course in geology, Mr. Wayde?"

"No, sir," Willis told him.

"It's a pity," Mr. Hodges said. "It's very good for the soul."

"Homer," Mrs. Hodges said, "Mr. Wayde is busy with the dishes."

"Yes, Martha," Mr. Hodges said. "On an evening like this it's pleasant to think of geological time. It's reassuring, to me at least, to realize that our lives are only a fraction of a second in that scale. I wish we lived back in the Devonian era with the ganoids."

"Homer," Mrs. Hodges said, "Mr. Wayde isn't interested. Sylvia tells me you went to school with Mr. Decker, Mr. Wayde."

"Yes, that's so, Mrs. Hodges," Willis said.

Mrs. Hodges smoothed her dress.

"I'm sure Stephen was very popular," she said.

"Who's popular?" Mr. Hodges asked.

"Stephen Decker, Homer. He went to school with Mr. Wayde."

"I really can't see what Sylvia . . ." Mr. Hodges began, but Mrs. Hodges raised her voice.

"We mustn't keep Mr. Wayde any longer," she said. "They're waiting for him in the kitchen."

It was surprising how quickly they got the dishes done, and when they were all back in the parlor Simeon Flyrood wanted to sing "Danny Dever" but Sylvia stopped him.

"We're going to choose teams now," Sylvia said. "I'll take one team and Tom will take the other. I choose Steve Decker. Pass the pencils and papers, Laura." Willis, too, was on Sylvia's team, and the first thing they did was to write down in two minutes all the rivers they could remember beginning with the letter "M." It was still pleasant for Willis to recall that he had turned up with the largest number and that he had also come up with the longest list of Roman emperors in their proper chronological order.

You could not help but feel a warm glow of satisfaction when you did well at anything. Sylvia really noticed him when he remembered all the emperors, and she looked sorry when Bill Harcourt said they really had to go. He didn't want to break anything up. They were having a wonderful time, but he did have a lot of studying to do. Sylvia went with them to the hall and stood talking to them while they looked for their overshoes and coats.

"You must be sure to come back again," she said, "and thanks for winning with the emperors, Mr. Wayde."

She looked at him questioningly, and he knew she was asking him whether he had not had a good time, and he knew that she hoped he had.

"And thanks for helping with the dishes," Sylvia said. "I told you it was just an informal pickup supper. Now be sure to come again."

"Oh, Jesus," Bill Harcourt said, when they were outside on Craigie Street, "I really didn't know I was getting you into anything like that. I guess the old man's right when he says you know how to get on with people."

There was no reason for Bill Harcourt to apologize. If Willis had said that he had enjoyed the party, he knew that Bill would not have believed him, and perhaps Willis had not actually enjoyed it, and he was not sure that Sylvia had really enjoyed the party either. He was not sure that she had even liked the pencil-and-paper games, but she had wanted him to come back again and she had known that Bill Harcourt never would. Willis never ventured to tell Bill that he went back to Craigie Street again the next Sunday.

During the winter and spring when they first met, Sylvia had been very obviously in love with Steve Decker, and all she had wanted of Willis was to talk about Steve in an awkward sort of way. Willis would never have gone for walks with Sylvia around Fresh Pond or have been Sylvia's harmless confidant if Bess Harcourt had been different, but then she had not been. One sad thing about being young was that you did not have the sense developed by later experience, and when you finally did gain that sense and understood a few principles regarding the workings of a woman's mind, it was too late to use them, because you had been caught years before in the emotional meshes of natural selection. You could listen to the advice of your elders—and sometimes, perhaps, basically approve, but the only way you could acquire experience was by experience itself. Willis had listened to what his father had told him about reciprocating girls and about playing around with girls in one's own group and had only thought that the old man was a lovable but deluded old character. Now he could see of course that the old man had been perfectly right—now that it was all too late. He could only blame his own ambition that had always made him interested in girls from the right side of the tracks, not that he did not detest the expression.

VIII

THE SUMMER preceding the winter that Willis had met Sylvia had
been one of the happiest of his life. He had completed his first year at
the Harvard School of Business Administration as one of the top men
of his class. He was being trained as an executive assistant to Mr. Henry
Harcourt, a new position created with the approval of the managerial
firm of Beakney-Graham, who were making recommendations for the
personnel reorganization of the Harcourt Mill; and he had been as-
signed a private room adjoining Mr. Harcourt's office, with a buzzer
on his table so that Mr. Harcourt could call him.

It had been a busy summer at the Harcourt Mill, and an uncertain
one for many people, a summer of hiring and firing that bewildered
many older employees. Mr. Bryson Harcourt was one of those who could
not understand the reason for so many radical changes, but Willis had
always got on well with Mr. Bryson.

"I'll say one thing," Mr. Bryson had told him. "Frankly I was appalled when Father told me about the plans he had for you, but you've
made good, Willis. I know you're going to be a great help to Father and
the rest of us. You're a friend of the family now, and I know you're
loyal, Willis."

As far as warmheartedness and generosity went, there never was anything wrong about Mr. Bryson Harcourt. There were a lot of intangibles
one could buy, such as technical skill, but loyalty was a commodity
that varied with each individual. The Harcourts did not need to buy
Willis's loyalty.

When he had come under Mr. Henry Harcourt's personal supervision,
Willis could not help but see that he was regarded in a new light by
everyone in the plant. The workmen he had always known were as
friendly to him as ever. Labor, he was to learn later, seldom could be
made to take an interest in management; but it was different in the office, where people he had known through many summers now gave him
appraising, suspicious looks. Willis could sympathize, because he had

been pushed forward above the heads of many who had been working there for years. He knew that Mr. Briggs in the sales department disapproved of his promotion. Mr. Briggs had told him that he had worked at Harcourt for fifteen years before he had been pulled off the road to be assistant sales manager. You worked your way up from the bottom in those days, and the way to learn business was doing business, instead of studying at some school. Mr. Hewett had a more generous attitude, perhaps because he knew that his days at the mill were almost over. Mr. Hewett often told Willis to watch this or that, because Willis might be in his shoes some day. He spoke only half seriously, and Willis was under no illusions, since it would obviously be years before he could ever manage Harcourt's.

His father's attitude was what disturbed Willis most.

"Son," his father said one evening, "I had a friend once, out in San Francisco. We'd been working together building dams for Pacific Gas and Electric, and then he joined up with Standard Oil. I remember when he took the boat to China. We had quite a lot of drinks the night before, telling each other what we were going to do, because we were pretty young then, and kids all want to be American heroes. Now I suppose you want to be one too, but I don't any more. It's hard enough to try to be what you are. Well, anyway, I stood on the pier seeing Bill off, and I had quite a head that morning. I was there quite a while watching the ship pull out, seeing it get smaller, and I knew Bill was going somewhere I wasn't ever. Well, it's the same with you. Only just remember this one thing. Every now and then take a look at yourself, and try to be sure where the hell you're going. I can't tell you because I wouldn't know."

Willis always remembered that expression, and he often quoted it afterwards—take a look at yourself and be sure where you're going. It might have been a good thing if he had taken more of a look at himself that summer, but when you're young, you simply go.

His mother felt, too, that she was standing on a pier watching him move away. Alfred Wayde had been working on the model of a new impregnating machine that summer, the patents for which eventually became the property of the Harcourt Mill and were a projection of the Klaus patents and the Klaus methods. He was constructing his small working model in the cellar, where he had installed a formidable line of machine tools, some borrowed from the mill machine shop and some bought with his own savings. It was his habit that summer to go down cellar directly after supper and work for several hours, so that when Willis and his mother sat in the upstairs parlor, they could hear the whirring of the lathe and Alfred Wayde's footsteps on the concrete floor and occasionally the muffled sound of swearing. His mother, while she darned the socks and sewed buttons on the shirts, often said she was sure that she did not know what Willis's father was doing, but it was all to the good, because he was never restless when he was working on machinery. She hoped that Willis would always remember that his father was a sort of genius like Eli Whitney, or Mr. Henry Ford. She knew that Alfred could have invented a horseless buggy himself, if that sort of thing had ever interested him. His one trouble was that he was restless.

It was hard for her sometimes to think that Willis was all grown-up and was doing so well. She only wished that Willis had time to see more young people, but she knew he was working very hard. She wished that Willis would not see so much of Bess and Bill Harcourt, or not quite so much, although she did not mean that Bess was not a nice young girl, but sometimes she was afraid the Harcourts were making use of Willis.

She hoped that Willis remembered the old days, when he was five or six or ten. Did he remember the winter they had spent in Steamboat Springs in Colorado? She wished the air here in Massachusetts were more like Colorado. Did Willis remember the little Navajo Indian boy he had played with in New Mexico? And the adobe schoolhouse where he had gone one winter? Did Willis remember the summers they had spent at Grandfather's farm in Kansas and what a fine man his grandfather was? Did he remember his aunt and his cousins and those Sunday dinners when everyone had too much to eat? Of course Willis did remember. He remembered the summer heat that everyone always said was so good for growing corn, and he remembered the white-faced steers being fattened for the market, and his grandfather carrying buckets to the pigpen, but it was all a very long while ago. His childhood seemed longer than a lifetime.

Well, Willis was all grown-up now, his mother said. He was all through college now, and she was proud that Mr. Harcourt thought so much of him. She had been very worried when Willis had accepted that loan from Mr. Harcourt to go to the Harvard Business School, but now she could see that Willis had been right. After all, that three thousand dollars had been a loan, and she knew that Willis would not forget it. It was fortunate, perhaps, that her father had died during Willis's first year in Business School. When the farm was sold in Kansas, she had planned to give Willis some of her share of the money to pay off the loan, and this was exactly what she did, and it was something to remember that he had paid off every cent of that loan to Mr. Harcourt before he died, with interest at six per cent.

There was certainly no reason for his mother to have worried about Bess that summer. Bess had come out the winter before at a large ball at the Copley-Plaza, and though Willis had been invited, he had not gone, and that summer she had nearly always been away somewhere. Thus Willis had only an occasional glimpse of her, and even then Bess was always with other friends, playing tennis or sitting around the swimming pool. She was a debutante, she said, and for a few months everyone rushed you and invited you to so many parties that you were a physical wreck. Willis must realize to look at her that being a debutante was terrible—no sleep, big dinners and whirls around the dance floor with all sorts of men about whom you cared nothing at all but to whom you had to be especially nice or else they would not dance with you. Then you were a faded, broken blossom after a year of it and the stag line paid no attention to you any more, and Bess could not wait until she was a broken blossom. Then she and Willis would see as much of each other as they had before—and everything. She knew that Willis understood and she was glad that he was so understanding.

Her activities did not matter very much to Willis that summer, because he was going through a critical part of his development. He was emerging from the stage of taking orders to giving them, or at least of transmitting some of Mr. Harcourt's orders and seeing that they were carried out; and it was necessary to do this tactfully, without offense.

Actually Bess had hardly any time to see him for more than a moment until late in August. He never expected she would call him at the mill, and he still recalled the intense pleasure he felt when the telephone on his table rang and he heard her voice. It was just after four o'clock one Saturday, and the office building was already deserted and everything was quiet outside because the machines had stopped at noon. Mr. Harcourt had left at noon himself and had told Willis to leave as soon as he had finished his work.

"I am feeling my age today," Mr. Harcourt had said. "I'm going to look at the swans and take a walk along the brook, and then do nothing all Sunday except lunch with Mrs. Harcourt. Just finish that digest on Vultex. I'll need it the first thing on Monday morning. The Meader people are sending over a man from Providence."

Harcourt Vultex, which Willis had helped Mr. Harcourt to christen, was a new addition to the Harcourt line. It was a conveyor belt designed by the engineering department to meet demands of food-processing factories, and it had only the week before been placed in full production. The sales department had been asked for a popularized description and Mr. Harcourt had wanted something shorter and less florid than the one Mr. Briggs had offered. Willis had finished his final draft by four o'clock that Saturday. It was ready for Miss Jackman to type, when the telephone on his table rang and he heard Bess Harcourt's voice.

"Willis," she said, "whatever are you doing?"

"I'm just here at the old salt mine," Willis said. He was getting good at little jokes like that. "What are you doing?"

"Oh," Bess said, "I'm not doing much of anything."

"Well, that's quite a novelty, isn't it?" Willis asked.

"Yes," she said. "Willis, can't you come over and play some tennis and have a swim?"

"You know I'm not much good at tennis," Willis said.

"It doesn't matter," Bess said. "It will just be comedy tennis."

"Is anyone else over there?" Willis asked.

There was a short pause and then he heard Bess laugh.

"No," she said, "not really. There's just another boy here, but he's going home in a little while. Please come over, Willis. I haven't seen you for simply ages."

Willis had a mortifying memory of his haste to get home and to prepare himself fittingly for a late afternoon of tennis at the Bryson Harcourts', and he was ashamed of his naïve pride in having the right things for the occasion, all except a tennis racquet. At home Willis planned his appearance in accordance with the illustrations he had seen in current magazines. He took a bath and put on clean B.V.D.'s, the conventional underwear of the period. He also selected a clean white shirt, but not a new one, because he was going to play tennis, and no tie of course, and he left the soft collar open at the neck of course, and then slicked down his hair and brushed it carefully. Then he put on the white flannels that he had purchased that spring at the Harvard Co-operative Society. His sneakers were immaculate and he had a light pullover sweater resembling one that Bill wore, of natural wool and imported from England. When he saw all he could see of himself in the mirror above his bureau, he was satisfied that he did not look badly—careless, athletic, and accustomed to that sort of thing. Then he took a briefcase from his closet, a new and rather polished acquisition, in which he packed a new set of underwear and another clean shirt to put on after swimming, and one of his newer ties with stripes.

"Where under the sun are you going, Willis?" his mother asked.

"Oh," he said, "just over to the Harcourts' to play tennis and have a swim."

"Well," his mother said, "why don't you wear your old gray trousers and not use up your new white ones?"

Afterwards whenever Willis saw a tennis court, he used the court on the Harcourt place as a standard of comparison, and when he finally built a court of his own, he wanted a grass terrace, with chairs and tables near the net exactly like the Harcourts' that were always put away at night in the small house behind the court, and he wanted honeysuckle on the back and side fences. Only honeysuckle would do, because he could still remember the smell of the blossoms on that hot, still afternoon.

A young man Willis had never seen before was sitting in one of the wicker chairs close beside Bess. The visitor must have been saying something that amused her, because he heard Bess laugh her lightest, gayest laugh. She was wearing a cotton print dress with little flowers on it— simple but not so simple as it looked. Her hair, which always had a spun-gold look, was tied back with a ribbon.

"Oh, hello, Willis," she said, and she held out her hand. "This is Willis Wayde, Ed. I don't believe you've ever met Edward Ewing, have you, Willis?"

She was right. Willis's memory, already cultivated for names and faces, told him that the young man, who had arisen quickly, had not been among the friends of Bill's and Bess's whom he had met occasionally, although he had the same qualities that Willis associated with the others. From the interested way he looked at Willis, it was clear that Bess had been discussing him, but his look was not inquisitive, simply the look of someone who was meeting a stranger from another group to which he was not entirely accustomed.

"How do you do?" he said to Willis.

"How do you do?" Willis said. "I'm glad to meet you, Mr. Ewing." Willis had already learned the trick of mentioning a name so you would not forget it. "It's a nice day for loafing around a tennis court, isn't it?"

The name was Ewing, not difficult to remember. He was dark with a longish face, brown eyes and closely cropped brown hair, a Harvard man, a club man, and an athletic type, like all those fellows who went to prep school and had learned to play all sorts of games. He was shorter than Willis and more delicately made, but not a student type. He was likable, with a nice smile. He was wearing white duck trousers, not flannels. He had a heavy coat of tan. The name was Edward Ewing, and he wore a ribbon belt with stripes on it.

Somehow the tan made Willis conscious of his own yellow hair and comparative paleness, inescapably indicating that he had been working indoors. He found himself wishing for a frantic second that he had brought his pocket comb with him in case his hair got mussed up playing. Then he told himself that this worry was ridiculous. He was bigger and stronger than Ewing and he was well set up too. Frankly, Willis knew that he looked just as well as Ewing and that his manners were just as good and that he was much better equipped to get ahead in the world.

"I'm sorry if I'm late, Bess," Willis said, "but things are pretty hectic these days at the office."

"Willis works at the mill," Bess said to Edward Ewing. "Everything here revolves around the mill—even me."

"You haven't been revolving here much lately," Willis said, and he laughed easily, "but whatever you've been doing seems to have done you good."

"Why, Willis," Bess said, "I didn't know you'd been developing a line. Willis goes with Bill to the Harvard Business School, Ed."

"Oh, do you?" Edward Ewing said. "I hear it's quite a place."

Willis laughed again easily.

"Quite an institution," he said.

"You see, he even has a briefcase," Bess said. "What have you got in it, Willis?"

"Oh, just a change," Willis said, "in case we play tennis, if we do play tennis."

"You certainly look as though you wanted a game," Bess said. "It's too hot and I won't play. You go ahead and play, Ed, but hurry so we can have a swim."

"Well, just one set," Ed Ewing said, and he picked up a racquet from the wicker table. "It's pretty late and I've got to get back to the shore, Bess."

"I'm not much good," Willis said.

"Oh, I'm no good either," Edward Ewing said.

"All right," Willis said, "if it doesn't bore you, but I haven't played all summer."

"Don't talk so much about it," Bess said. "Here's Bill's racquet, Willis."

Willis could still remember, particularly when he tried not to, each detail of that tennis set, and when he did, he always felt the weight of his humiliation. He could see himself in his tennis flannels—too white, too new—on one side of the net, and across from him Edward Ewing— careless, graceful, and oblivious. It did no good for Willis to tell himself again and again that it had only been a friendly game and that there was no reason to have been ashamed of his maladroitness. He could tell himself that he would have been the better player if he could have had the practice of his opponent across the net, since he had been taller, and stronger, with good coordination of hand and eye. Given the opportunity to have learned the strokes from childhood, he would have been the better player, but as it was he had come from another world. There was always a net between himself and anyone like that friend of Bess

Harcourt's. Sometimes the net might be invisible, but it had been there always.

"Do you want to rally for a minute before we start?" Edward Ewing asked.

"Well, thanks," Willis answered, and he laughed. "Not that it will improve me any."

It was perfectly clear how the game would go, the moment Edward Ewing hit a ball to him. Willis could still remember the expert smacking sound of the racquet and his own clumsy stroke when he drove the ball into the net.

"Oh," he said, "sorry. Shoot me over another, will you?"

He was desperately anxious to make a good appearance, but the painful thing about it was that the harder he tried the tenser he became. He was aware of a dull anger rising in him that was only anger at himself, since it was just a game. He served rather well, because his strength partially compensated for the awkward half-swing he had developed. He found himself fighting for every point in a desperate, breathless way.

"Oh, nice," he would hear Edward Ewing say. "Good shot!"

Nevertheless none of his shots were good, and of course Edward Ewing knew it. The worst of it was that Willis was almost sure that his opponent across the net was growing so sorry for him that occasionally he returned the ball with deliberate easiness and even missed intentionally.

"Oh, nice," Ewing kept saying. "Good shot!"

The worst of it was that he was sure that Edward Ewing threw away two games just to make things look better. The worst of it was that Willis was wringing wet with perspiration and half blinded by the sweat in his eyes when the set was over, but Edward Ewing looked as cool as he had when they had started.

"Thanks a lot," Willis said. "I'm sorry I couldn't give you a better game."

"It was fine," Edward Ewing said, and there was something horrible about his forced enthusiasm. "It was exactly the sort of workout I needed."

Bess had not said a word, and Willis half hated her for her silence. She knew perfectly well how poor he was at tennis.

"You ought not to have put me in there with a champ," Willis told her, and he tried to laugh but his voice sounded hoarse and unnatural.

"Why, Willis," she said, "don't be so serious. It was only a game."

The worst of it was he could not control his mood, or pass it off lightly, as he should have.

"Well, let's have a swim," Bess said. "It will cool you off anyway, Willis."

Willis looked straight at her before he answered, and she gazed back at him innocently.

"Yes," he said, "I guess I need cooling off."

Bess ran ahead of them to the girls' dressing room while Willis walked to the men's bathhouse with Edward Ewing.

"Nothing like a swim after tennis," Edward Ewing said.

"That's right," Willis answered. "Nothing like a plunge."

"Bess tells me you live on the place here," Edward Ewing said.

"That's right," Willis answered. "We live in the garden cottage."

"It's quite a place, isn't it?"

"Yes," Willis said. "It's quite a place."

It was beautiful to see Edward Ewing do the Australian crawl up and down the pool and then do a swan and next a jackknife dive. When Bess asked him, Willis said that Edward Ewing certainly was a good swimmer. It was beautiful to see Edward Ewing when he stepped out of the bathhouse ready to leave, dressed in a neat gray flannel suit and carrying a tennis racquet and a small suitcase.

"I'll see you tomorrow evening, won't I, Bess?" he said.

"Oh, yes," Bess said, "and I'll see you off, Ed. Don't hurry away, Willis. I'll be right back."

It seemed like hours before Bess came back, and somehow waiting for her did not help his mood. When he saw her walking toward him across the lawn to the pool, he noticed that she did not hurry.

"Willis," she asked him, "what's the matter?"

"Nothing, Bess," he said.

"Willis," she asked him, "are you cross about anything?"

"Of course I'm not cross about anything," he answered.

"Oh, yes, you are," she said. "I didn't know you'd get cross about a game."

"I'm not cross about any game or anything," he said.

"I wish you wouldn't try so hard about everything," she said.

"How do you mean?" he asked.

"Oh," she said. "You're always trying to be so smart about everything lately."

"I don't mean to try to be smart," he said.

"You've changed," she said. "You're not the way you used to be."

"Well, you've changed too," he said.

"Maybe we both have," she said. "Would you like to walk up to the pine woods before supper? There's still time."

"It's pretty late now, isn't it?" Willis asked her.

"Oh, Willis," she said, "I wish . . . well, never mind."

"What do you wish?" he asked her.

"Oh never mind," she said. "Wishing never gets you anywhere."

Willis could occasionally convince himself that there had never been anything serious between him and Bess Harcourt and that he had always possessed a strain of hard common sense which prevented his indulging, like a lot of young fellows, in impossible dreams about the future. He also took pride in thinking that he was not the type of man who married the boss's daughter. In fact he always despised the men who did. These individuals—and he had to cope with plenty of them in his industrial career—were invariably either conceited or unsure. They were flies that had fallen into a pot of honey, and they were self-conscious always, acutely aware that they had not got where they were because of their own efforts. Willis was proud to think that he had paddled his own canoe, even when he had been up the creek with the paddle broken. He was not the type who married the boss's daughter, and that was all there was to it.

By the Monday after the tennis game, there were plenty of other things to think about. The mill was undergoing a thorough process of reorganization, too long delayed, perhaps, but it was remarkable how Mr. Harcourt had handled it, considering his age. Mr. Harcourt's problem was primarily one of new personnel, and it was a liberal education to Willis, in view of his courses at the Business School, to observe the changes which were taking place. Mr. Hewett had a new assistant, for one thing, a man in his late thirties named Norman Percival, who came from Toledo and was being groomed for Mr. Hewett's job. It was a good lesson to Willis to see how quickly someone like Percival could step into harness. Then there was Bill Sobol, a new assistant for Mr. Briggs in sales, and Tom Powderman from DuPont's, who was made production manager, working under Norman Percival, a position hitherto unknown at Harcourt's. And half a dozen new salesmen were on hand, not to mention the new engineers. The truth was that Harcourt's, that summer, was ceasing to be a small-town New England mill.

The changes were made under the advice of the Beakney-Graham Management Company, with head offices in New York, and Willis was never to lose his respect for the capacities of that organization. After they had made their preliminary survey, they had sent down one of their chief executives, Mr. Joe McKitterick, to stay awhile at the plant until the gears were meshed, and to recommend new personnel. McKitterick was a topflight man, as Willis knew even then. Somehow you got the feel of a topflight man just as soon as you saw him, and Willis could never forget the first time he saw Mr. McKitterick.

About a week after Willis had begun his summer work at the mill

Mr. Harcourt had called Willis to his office, on a fine clear morning, the sort that put you on your toes.

"Come in, Willis," Mr. Harcourt said, and Willis noticed that Mr. Harcourt was wearing a white carnation in his buttonhole. "I want you to meet Mr. McKitterick, who comes to us from Beakney-Graham."

Mr. McKitterick, seated in one of the old wooden chairs beside Mr. Harcourt's desk, seemed to fit perfectly into the atmosphere. His hair was grizzled and a lock of it kept falling untidily over his forehead. He had on a wrinkled blue serge suit and a blue shirt with a soft collar, and he wore heavy horn-rimmed spectacles. His face was leathery and square and his eyebrows were very thick. When Mr. Harcourt introduced Willis, Mr. McKitterick pushed himself slowly out of his chair, and Willis saw that he was six feet tall, just about his own height.

"This is Willis Wayde," Mr. Harcourt said in his soft voice, which could always carry above the sounds of the machinery from the open windows. "Take Mr. McKitterick around the plant, Willis, and I want you to answer any questions he asks, no matter what—even about me, Willis."

Willis could not understand why he had been selected for this job. It did not occur to him until later that Mr. McKitterick had examined him as closely as the mill.

"If you're ready, let's go," Mr. McKitterick said, and they walked through the hallway of the office building, with its handsome antique furniture. They did not speak until Mr. McKitterick stopped in front of the tall clock.

"That's a nice piece," he said. "Made by Godfrey in London, I take it."

"Yes, sir," Willis answered. "It's a Godfrey."

"How did you know?" Mr. McKitterick asked.

Willis had learned it from the office inventory of the English furniture and he explained that Mr. Harcourt took a personal interest in the antique furniture of the office building.

"How much did he pay for it?" Mr. McKitterick asked.

"A hundred and seventy-five pounds, sir," Willis said. "Mr. Harcourt says that antiques don't depreciate like new furniture."

"That's so," Mr. McKitterick said. "If they're good. How much did those chairs cost, I wonder?"

"Two hundred and seventy-five pounds," Willis said.

"Say," Mr. McKitterick said, "you've got a pretty good memory, haven't you?"

"Yes, sir," Willis answered. "I can remember figures pretty well."

"This whole plant is quite a period piece, when you come to think of it," Mr. McKitterick said. "Do you know its history?"

Until Willis had begun to answer those questions, he had not realized how thoroughly he knew the Harcourt Mill, because it was the sort of knowledge that had come to him gradually, and because for years the Harcourts and the mill had been the center of his interest.

"Who's the man over there by that compressor?" Mr. McKitterick asked. They were in Building 3 and he had to speak loudly. "He looks like a pretty good man."

"Yes, sir," Willis told him, "he's good. He's Wesley Bryan. He's been here for twenty-five years."

"Do you know all these other people?" Mr. McKitterick asked.

"Yes, sir," Willis said, "of course I do."

"How do you get on with them?" Mr. McKitterick asked.

"Why, I get on all right," Willis said. "You see, I've known most of them ever since I was a kid."

"Well," Mr. McKitterick said, "you certainly know this place. How much do you get paid a week?"

"Thirty-five dollars, sir," Willis answered.

"You ought to get more," Mr. McKitterick said, "but it's not a bad place to start. What do you think of Mr. Harcourt?"

Willis was not sure whether or not he ought to answer until he remembered Mr. Harcourt's orders.

"I think he's twice as good as anyone else here," Willis said.

"What do you think's wrong with him?" Mr. McKitterick asked. "There's something wrong with everybody."

"There isn't much wrong with him that I know of," Willis said, "except that he never lets anything go."

"Well," Mr. McKitterick said, "if he ever lets you go, I wish you'd let me know."

"Thanks," Willis told him, "but I don't want another job as long as Mr. Harcourt wants me."

"All right," Mr. McKitterick said, "let's get out of here now. I haven't finished with you yet."

Mr. McKitterick had finished by four in the afternoon, and Mr. Harcourt called for Willis about half an hour later.

"Well," Mr. Harcourt asked, "did you show him everything?"

"I showed him everything I could," Willis said. "He certainly asked a lot of questions."

Mr. Harcourt was silent for a moment, and then he looked at the two portraits on the wall, and then his glance moved to Willis. He could not tell whether Mr. Harcourt was thinking of him or of something else, until his glance grew sharper.

"It's his business to ask questions," Mr. Harcourt said. "What did you think of him, Willis?"

"I never saw anyone just like him," Willis said, "but I guess he knows what he's doing. Anyway he knew who made the tall clock in the hall."

Mr. Harcourt's lower lip twitched and he touched it lightly with his forefinger.

"Showing off," he said. "I wouldn't say it was necessary. When he was on the subject of antiques, did he ask about me, Willis?"

"Yes, sir, he did," Willis said, "and I didn't like it much."

"Never mind what you like," Mr. Harcourt said. "Just tell me what he asked."

Willis was standing in front of Mr. Harcourt's desk because Mr. Harcourt had not asked him to sit down, and he shifted his weight uneasily from one foot to the other.

"He wanted to know how good I thought you were."

"Well, well," Mr. Harcourt said. "Those people are always showing off. I'm better than he is, Willis—at least I think I am. I wonder if he offered you a job."

"He spoke about it, sir," Willis said.

"Well, I'd have done the same thing myself," Mr. Harcourt said, "and I suppose he knows how much I'm paying you?"

"Yes, sir," Willis said. "You told me to tell him everything."

Mr. Harcourt leaned back in his swivel chair.

"I know I did," he said. "You see, Mr. McKitterick and I understand each other, Willis. He's here on a consulting fee of a thousand dollars a week, and I think he's going to be worth it. The next time you see him I wish you'd let him know I told you how much I'm paying him."

"Why, sir?" Willis asked.

Mr. Harcourt smiled.

"Because I'd like him to know where you stand with me," Mr. Harcourt said. "I'd like him to know I don't have to buy you, Willis." His chair creaked as he leaned forward and he looked younger than he had all day. "I'm glad you've had a chance to see Mr. McKitterick. You made quite an impression on him."

That last remark of Mr. Harcourt's made Willis realize that Mr. McKitterick had been asked to make a report on him among his other reports.

"I thought you knew me well enough yourself, sir," he said, "not to need anything like that."

Mr. Harcourt raised his eyebrows slightly.

"Anything like what?" he asked.

Willis looked straight back at him. He was glad to remember that he respected but that he had never been afraid of Mr. Harcourt.

"I mean you didn't need to have anyone check on me," he said.

Mr. Harcourt nodded slowly.

"I guess you're right," he said. "I didn't know you were learning so fast. I hadn't thought the idea would occur to you."

Mr. Harcourt paused, but Willis did not speak, because it seemed to him that it was better not to say too much.

"I'm making no apology. Do you understand?" Mr. Harcourt said.

"Yes," Willis said. "I wouldn't have expected you to apologize."

He felt a strange elation when he spoke. Just then he was on equal terms with Mr. Harcourt, and all sorts of inhibitions evaporated. It would not have been like that a year ago. Mr. Harcourt picked up a pencil and tapped it gently on his desk.

"Some day when you have people working for you," he said, "you'll find they're quite an investment, in time and money and trouble. It's always wise to have a confirmation of your personal judgments, if you can get one. For instance, I always have an expert check my securities, although I think I'm a rather good investor. Of course I had Mr. Mc-Kitterick check on you. It's what he's here for."

Mr. Harcourt paused and tapped again on his desk with his pencil, but this sound was lost in the noise of the mill outside. They were both a part of that machinery, and you could never be wholly yourself when you were working for a company. You had to share some of the relentlessness of the machinery.

"I don't believe in flattery," Mr. Harcourt said. "I will say, though, that I think you have quality, and I like quality, even if I don't know exactly what it means. You're going to amount to something. I don't know exactly what, because everyone has defects."

Mr. Harcourt looked at the two portraits on the wall. Perhaps he was thinking that he too would be hanging on that wall some day beside his father and his grandfather.

"That's right," he said, "don't interrupt me, Willis. Perhaps I'm growing garrulous, but I won't keep you standing there much longer. Most people who work for you are commodities, up to a certain point. Mr. Mc-Kitterick is a very able man, but I can buy everything he has to offer because brains are always for sale. Mr. Decker is a commodity. He charges me a legal fee. But there are other people in a different category, and you can't buy them with money. I'll tell you something, Willis, but don't let it spoil you."

Mr. Harcourt stood up abruptly and walked slowly around the desk.

"You and I aren't in the same age group," he said, "but we're head and shoulders above anyone else around here, Willis—at least in a business way. I can't buy you with money."

Willis cleared his throat. It was curious that he had felt no surprise. "You've bought me already," he said. "I guess you know it, sir."

"I got you rather cheap," Mr. Harcourt said. "I wouldn't like to have to buy you later on."

IX

In April of his last year in the Harvard Business School, Willis had felt older than most of his contemporaries. Only a very few of them knew as much as he about the practical side of manufacturing and not many of them had his head for figures or his ability to visualize tables of organization. Yet you could not grow up all at once and be mature in every department. He was still absurdly young and Bess Harcourt was too, when he called her up in April, 1929.

He called her from a pay telephone in a Harvard Square drugstore and he remembered standing in the constricted booth in the back of the store and looking out on a display of soaps and cosmetics as he gave the number.

"Hello," he said to the maid who answered. "Is Miss Harcourt at home? This is Mr. Willis Wayde."

He waited, rehearsing exactly what he was going to say, until he heard Bess Harcourt's voice.

"Hello, Bess," he said. "How are you? It's been a long while since I've seen you."

"I know," she answered. "It's been simply ages, Willis. Why haven't you been around?"

"Well," he said, "I wasn't sure whether you'd have time to see me."

"Oh, don't be silly, Willis." Her voice sounded light and warm. "You know I'd love to see you."

"Bill says you're pretty busy," he told her, and then he heard her laugh.

"I'm never as busy as Bill," she said.

"Well, what are you doing Friday night?" he asked her.

There was a pause, and pauses always meant more over the telephone than anywhere else.

"Let's see. Why, I'm not doing anything Friday night."

Willis drew a deep breath, but he did his best to sound casual.

"I hear there's a good musical show at the Colonial," he said. "I don't know whether you've seen it or not."

"Why, no," she said, "I haven't seen it."

"Well then we might go to it," Willis said, "and have dinner somewhere first—say at the Ritz."

"Why, Willis. At the Ritz?" she said.

"Why not?" he asked. "What's the matter with the Ritz?"

There was another slight pause.

"Why, Willis," she said, "I think it's awfully sweet of you. I think it would be lovely. What time?"

"I'll call for you at a quarter before seven," he said. "Now don't forget."

"Why, Willis," she said, "of course I won't forget."

Often when he thought of that Friday evening he also thought of the vast succession of later times when he had entertained socially in business, either on an expense account or as a deductible item from his income tax. Willis was at home now with the headwaiters and the captains. He knew just when to bestow a firm glance and the exact psychological moment to hand out a bill accompanied by a friendly handclasp, and he could say without any effort whatsoever, "Good evening, Louis. It's a long time since I've seen you," or else he could say if he did not know the place, "Captain, can't you put us somewhere else where it's not so noisy?" As the years went on his voice carried increased authority. You were judged by the way you handled yourself at the Stork or Twenty-one. It was business entertainment. As time went on you learned how to be at home in hotel suites and how to handle room-service waiters and bellboys and clerks and managers. Each individual required a slightly different technique, but it was not difficult, when they knew you required good service and were willing to pay for it generously. You had to realize that all these people had their problems and you had to know how to make allowances up to a certain limit, because in a great democracy all men were brothers. It cost money and time to learn to do these things in the right way, but most of it was business expense.

He often thought how much his world had changed, since he had asked Bess Harcourt out. There was no office in those days to attend to the arrangements. He made them all himself, late on Wednesday afternoon, riding on the subway to Boylston Street and buying the tickets at the Colonial Theater and thence walking to the Ritz to reserve a table. He could not decide on Friday whether or not to wear evening clothes and he finally compromised on his best blue suit. He did not look as badly as he might have. Though he was still thin, his weight was catching up to his height. He had twenty-five dollars in his wallet, and the theater tickets in his inside pocket.

Willis had already learned promptness by the spring of 1929. He changed from the Harvard Square subway at Park Street to a car which took him to Copley Square. Then he walked to the Bryson Harcourts' house on Beacon Street, not hurriedly, because he wanted to arrive there at exactly a quarter before seven, and he did so, to the minute. When the maid opened the door—it was Tillie, the Bryson Harcourts' waitress —he saw that the dining-room doors were open and that the table was not set, which meant that Mr. and Mrs. Bryson Harcourt were dining out, and their absence made the house seem large and lonely.

"I'm calling for Miss Bess, Tillie," he said, and he tried to sound like Mr. Henry Harcourt. "I'll wait here for her, if you'll let her know."

"Miss Bess is in the upstairs sitting room," Tillie said. "She asked if you would please go up."

Willis had been at the Bryson Harcourts' often enough to know where the upstairs sitting room was, a pleasant Beacon Street parlor where Bess and Bill entertained their friends while Mr. and Mrs. Bryson Harcourt used the library. He ran up the stairs quickly, and there was Bess, ready and waiting, standing in the center of a blue Chinese rug. She wore a black velvet dress and she had pinned on it the white gold and diamond clip that her parents had given her on her last birthday. He had never seen Bess look better and it made him happy that Bess had gone to so much trouble.

"Why, Bess," he said, "you look wonderful."

She did not smile, nor did she hold out her hand. She stood in the center of the blue Chinese rug, and he could still recall its pattern of yellow dragons.

"Oh, Willis," Bess said, "I'm glad you came on time."

"Of course I came on time," he told her. "I wouldn't have missed a minute of it."

"Oh, Willis," Bess said, "I'm terribly embarrassed, but I know you'll understand, because we're such old friends. There's something I want to explain. It's dreadful but I simply can't go out with you tonight."

"You can't?" he heard himself repeating after her. "Why, what's the trouble, Bess?"

"Willis," she said, "I'm so glad it's you. I have another engagement to-night and I simply forgot about it. There wasn't time to get hold of you or anything."

She spoke faster than usual, like a child reciting from memory, and for some reason Willis groped over her words clumsily before he could get them into sequence.

"You have another engagement?" he repeated. "You mean you're go-ing out with someone else?"

"I know it's dreadful, Willis," Bess said, "and I'll promise not to let it happen again. I just forgot completely until he called me up this after-noon."

"What made you forget?" Willis asked. "Don't you write things down?"

She shook her head.

"I should have," she said. "Don't look so upset, Willis. We can go out some other time—any time at all."

It was unfortunate that she used that phrase "any time at all." It went through his mind like a glowing spark. He had an even temper and he usually could keep his emotions under control up to a certain point. If he passed that point it must have had something to do with the taken-for-granted quality of her speech, which indicated that he was Willis Wayde and that she could do anything she wanted with Willis Wayde.

"That's right," he answered slowly, "any time at all."

He never did forget the relief that lighted up her face.

"Oh, Willis," she said, "I knew you'd be nice about it."

"All right," he said, and his speech sounded rougher than he had meant it to. "All right, I'll be nice, Bess."

"Thanks, Willis. Thanks ever so much," she said.

"You don't have to thank me," he answered, "but next time let me know sooner when you find something you'd rather do."

He was glad he had looked straight at her.

"Willis," she said, "that isn't so—not really."

"Listen," Willis said. "I'm not as dumb as all that, Bess."

"Willis," she said, "you needn't look like that. Sometimes I hate you."

Willis felt his lips curve into a smile.

"Other times you don't," he said.

"Oh, God," she said, "I don't know how I feel about you. I wish I'd never known you."

"You needn't lie," he said. "You're standing me up, aren't you?"

"I didn't know it would be like this," she said. "Willis, don't be angry. Please," and her voice dropped to a whisper. "*Please.*"

While the sound of her whisper was still in his ears, Bess Harcourt's eyes had widened and she was looking in panic at the open door. The front doorbell must have rung and neither of them had heard it, and now there was a sound of brisk footsteps on the stairs. He saw Bess swallow quickly.

"Oh," she said, "hello, Ed."

It was the Edward Ewing with whom he had played tennis, and Edward Ewing, unlike himself, was in a dinner coat.

"Edward," Bess said, and her voice sounded choked, "you remember Willis Wayde, don't you?"

"Of course I do," Edward Ewing said. "How's everything going?"

"Fine," Willis answered. "I'm glad to see you again."

"I'm awfully sorry, Bess," Edward Ewing said. "I wasn't able to get anything at the Colonial. The time was just too short, I guess, but we can go to a movie anyway."

Willis smiled again, though his face still had an ironlike feeling, and he reached in his pocket and drew out a small envelope.

"It's a funny thing," he said. "I have a couple of tickets for tonight for that show at the Colonial. I just stopped in to ask Bess if she didn't want them, because I have to write a report. It's due first thing tomorrow morning. The Harvard Business School, you know."

All at once he felt completely easy, and he was amused by Edward Ewing's puzzled look.

"Why that's awfully nice . . ." Edward Ewing began, and Bess Harcourt interrupted him.

"Isn't that the queerest thing, Edward," she said, "to have Willis come around with those two tickets?"

"Yes," Edward Ewing said slowly. "Yes, it's pretty queer."

It was the first time that Willis ever recognized his ability to control a situation, and it was something worth remembering.

"It's what we call coincidence, I guess," he said. "I'm glad you showed up just now and I hope you'll use them. I hear it's quite a show. I wish I didn't have to miss it."

"Of course I can mail you a check in the morning, but are you sure you don't want them?" Edward Ewing asked.

"Yes," Willis said, and he laughed. "Absolutely sure."

"I was taking Bess out to dinner," Edward Ewing said. "Why don't you have dinner with us before you go out to Cambridge?"

"That's very kind of you," Willis said, "but I've really got to get back. Bess wouldn't like it if I stayed," and he laughed before Bess could interrupt. "You see, her grandfather is helping me through Business School, and I've got to get good marks."

"Oh, Willis," Bess said, "why can't we all have dinner? It's such a good idea."

"Good-by, Bess," he said, and he held out his hand.

He had walked to Central Square before he was in the least aware of anything around him. He could never forget his sense of his own inadequacy. He knew that Bess Harcourt's attitude toward him was his fault as much as hers. He had always felt inferior to her, and his inferiority had always fed her arrogance. He told himself that night that he was through with Bess and that he would never see her again, and yet all the while he knew as sure as fate that Bess only needed to call him back.

Two days later she sent him a letter, and he must have been expecting it because he felt a great relief when he saw the envelope addressed in her bold slanting handwriting. Its sentences were still clear in his memory.

Dear Willis,

I am ashamed of what I did the other night and I have been wretched ever since. I don't know why it is that I sometimes want to hurt you. I don't behave that way with other people, and I promise never to do it again. Please forgive me, and please—I'll be in the country on Saturday and until Sunday afternoon—please come and see me. It's always better when we are alone together.

With love,
Bess

Although he made up his mind not to, of course he saw her that Saturday, but if you were hurt once, you were instinctively careful not to be hurt that way again.

X

WILLIS NEVER could have explained to anyone else exactly what it had meant to him when Mr. Harcourt had invited him to attend the stockholders' luncheon at the big house in June, 1929.

"Oh, by the way, Willis," he had said, "I have been meaning to give you a little present. Here are five shares of common stock in the Harcourt Mill made out in your name. Don't thank me too much for them. Their par value is negligible."

It was the gesture that counted, and Willis still had that original certificate, framed and hanging on the wall of his study. It was more important to him than his diplomas and other mementos, and when he looked at it he could always remember Mr. Harcourt.

"Besides," Mr. Harcourt said, "it is a necessary gesture, because I want you to attend the stockholders' meeting and to be at the house for the customary luncheon. It's time you met some of the more remote members of the family."

It had been a long time since Willis and Bess Harcourt had looked down from the second floor upon the stockholders of the Harcourt Mill. Things were subtly different now, because Willis had a feeling of being part of the house itself. If the sensation was slightly feudal, it still was real. It seemed to him that day that he was almost like Bill Harcourt or something that Bill Harcourt should have been. He wondered sometimes why Bill Harcourt had not been acutely jealous of him, but it was not in Bill's nature to be jealous, and perhaps he had always thought of Willis as relieving him of responsibilities.

In fact Bill Harcourt had expressed some of these thoughts himself on the afternoon of the luncheon. He was often surprisingly frank in the things he said. Bill was standing on the flagstone porch by the front door smoking a cigarette.

"Thank God you're here," he said. "It takes a great weight off my mind."

"What sort of weight?" Willis asked.

"I mean I won't have to make an ass of myself," Bill said, "trying to answer a lot of questions. You can do all the talking for me. I always hate these parties. Thank God there's someone bright around the house."

Willis laughed. It was always easy to laugh at Bill and still feel loyal to him, and the truth was that Bill had never cared about the Harcourt Mill and knew that he was not obliged to care, except in a superficial manner.

"All right, Bill," he said, "but you're not as dumb as all that, you know."

"I know exactly how dumb I am," Bill said. "I wish I didn't have to keep pretending I'm something that I'm not."

"That's a fine way to talk," Willis said, "when you'll be the boss here some day."

"Hell," Bill told him, "I don't want to be the boss of anything."

Willis laughed again. It was true that the place belonged partly to Bill, but Willis was part of it too. He was more aware than he ever had been of his position when he and Bill walked into the front hall. Mr. and Mrs. Henry Harcourt were already there, waiting to receive the guests.

"Hello, boys," Mr. Harcourt said, just as though Willis were a member of the family. "There's punch in the living room, and Bill, I'd like you to see that Willis meets everyone."

Physically Mr. Harcourt had changed very little. He had always looked small and slightly frail and old, but not too old. He always had a bright alertness. He was always carefully dressed. Though his hair may have grown grayer and his motions a trifle slower, he looked about the same to Willis as when Willis had seen him first. He had reached a static, timeless period like the house in which he lived, and the same was true with Mrs. Henry Harcourt. Her hands still looked as delicate as they had over the tea tray on that winter afternoon in the library.

"Willis, dear," she said, "I want to talk to you for a minute after the guests have left. You and I are the only outsiders here—not that we're really outsiders."

"Harriet means that she's thinking of you as my keeper, Willis," Mr. Harcourt said. "She's going to talk to you about my general health and ask that I don't overdo."

"Henry," Mrs. Harcourt said, "I wish you'd remember what Dr. Blair said in Boston."

"Harriet, dear," Mr. Harcourt said, "I remember very well what Dr. Blair said. Anyway, I'm not dead yet, Harriet, though I dare say several people here would like me to be."

"Now, Henry," Mrs. Harcourt said. "Who would like to see you dead?"

"Probably my nephew Roger," Mr. Harcourt said. "There's always a lot of solid hatred in a well-regulated family, Harriet. Willis, I want you to be especially pleasant to Roger if he should ask you about anything. Now, Bill, you and Willis go into the living room and have some punch. It's very weak."

In the long dark hall leading to the living room Bill grasped Willis by the arm so hard that Willis remembered he was startled.

"What's that about Dr. Blair seeing Grandfather?" he asked.

Willis could see that he was genuinely concerned and that something Bill had always counted on was threatened, and Bill had always hated change. Willis could only answer that it was the first time that he had ever heard of any doctor.

"Blair's a heart specialist," Bill said. "I don't believe anyone's told Father."

Willis knew that he was representing Mr. Harcourt in a way. He knew that it would be wrong for the news to get around suddenly and he told Bill exactly that.

Then they were in the living room among the people around the punch bowl, and Willis was speaking to Mr. and Mrs. Bryson Harcourt. Mrs. Harcourt said it was wonderful that Willis was doing so well. She had heard so much about Willis lately.

"Willis is all right," Mr. Bryson Harcourt said, "and Willis has always been all right. How do you think Father's looking, Willis?"

Obviously Mr. Bryson Harcourt had heard something.

"I think he's looking fine, sir," Willis said.

"He is," Mr. Harcourt answered. "Just what I was thinking, and we've had a fine year but we've got to keep Father from overdoing. I know you'll help me out on this, Willis."

Then Willis shook hands very formally with Bess Harcourt and Bess laughed.

"It's funny to see you here," Bess said. "You might almost be Bill."

"Oh no," Willis answered. "I'm just the handyman."

"Then don't look so superior," she said. "This isn't such a great occasion. Don't look so highly honored."

"I didn't know I looked that way," he told her, "but maybe it's a greater occasion for me than it is for you."

"Don't sound humble like Uriah Heep," she said. "Maybe you are Uriah Heep."

"Not that I know of," Willis answered.

Bess looked straight at him, and her greenish-blue eyes were wide.

"You're always part way humble, and I hate that side of you," she said.

"Maybe it's because I have to get along with all of you," he told her, and he felt his face flush. "Maybe I'm just a poor boy trying to get on."

Bess shook her head impatiently.

"Well, don't have it on your mind so much. Do you know Grandfather says I ought to have been Bill?"

"Well," Willis said, "you're not."

"No," she said, "I'm not. That's why I'm glad you're here. I'm glad we have some brains around."

Then Bill Harcourt interrupted them.

"Who says I haven't any brains?" he asked.

"I did, stupid," Bess said.

"All right," Bill said, "but never mind it now. Cousin Roger wants to meet Willis. I'm sure I don't know why. He just expressed the desire."

"You never know about anything," Bess said. "You never try to know."

"What's the matter?" Bill asked. "What are you mad about now?"

"I'm mad at you," Bess said, "and when I'm not mad at you, I'm mad at Willis."

Bill began to laugh.

"Now, Bess," he said, "don't keep trying to run the mill."

Willis may have been too humble and too anxious to please in those days, but it was an insult to be compared with Uriah Heep, and Bess Harcourt's words had been like an unexpected dash of water on his face that reddened it and challenged his self-control. His nerves were still on edge when he followed Bill across the worn carpet of the living room to where Mr. Roger Harcourt was standing a pace or two away from old Mrs. Blood and Eldridge Harcourt and the Haywards.

It was the first time that Willis had ever spoken to Mr. Roger Harcourt, although he had seen him several times. Roger Harcourt was utterly unlike his first cousin, Mr. Bryson, with none of Mr. Bryson's outdoor look and none of Mr. Bryson's guilelessness. He was ponderous and fat. His face was a soft pinkish white, and it had a petulantly childish expression.

"So this is Uncle Henry's factotum, is it?" Mr. Roger Harcourt said, in a voice that was incongruously thin for his weight. His cheeks creased into difficult dimples as he smiled. "I've heard a lot about you from Bryson and everyone. You don't mind if I call you Willis, do you, since you seem such a part of the family around here?"

"No, sir," Willis said, "of course not."

"I'm just a family stockholder," Roger Harcourt said, "but I like to think I'm an interested one. Uncle Henry put you through Business School, didn't he?"

"He lent me the money," Willis said, "but it's been paid back."

"I'm sure Uncle Henry didn't expect it," Roger Harcourt said, and he leaned back on his heels, but his glance never moved from Willis's face. "Uncle Henry really isn't in need of funds, you know."

Willis looked straight back at him and smiled.

"No, sir," he said, "I don't suppose he is."

"I've a great admiration for Uncle Henry," Roger Harcourt said, "even if he has occasional whims that I don't agree with. You do seem rather young."

"Yes, sir," Willis answered, "I guess I'm pretty young."

"But that will cure itself in time," Roger Harcourt said. "Time has a way of fixing everything."

"Yes, sir," Willis said. "Maybe I'm too young to know."

"I don't like to make quick judgments," Roger Harcourt said. "I've always been predisposed against boy wonders, but I've a feeling that you and I might get on quite well together, given time."

"I'm glad if you think so, sir," Willis told him.

"Some day before too long," Roger Harcourt said, "I want to devote a day to the mill. I'd like to have you take me around, if Uncle Henry can spare you."

"I'd be very glad to," Willis answered.

"This firm of experts we've been hearing about in the meeting—" Roger Harcourt removed his right hand from his trousers pocket and rubbed the back of his neck softly—"these smart New Yorkers—Beakney and Graham—who've been pulling and hauling things around. Do you think they're any good?"

"Mr. Harcourt thinks they are," Willis said.

"Now let me ask you another question." Roger Harcourt put his hand back in his pocket. "Did you ever hear of a firm called Simcoe Rubber Hose and Belting?"

"Yes, sir," Willis said, "I've heard of them."

"You know they're a very large company, don't you?"

"Yes, I know that, sir," Willis said.

Of course Willis had to know about competitors. Roger Harcourt was gazing at him fixedly, as though he were trying to read some secret.

"There's a rumor"—Roger lowered his voice—"there's a rumor that they're prepared to buy us out. Have you heard it?"

It was the second surprising thing that Willis had heard that day. "No, sir," he said. "I haven't heard a word of it."

Roger Harcourt laughed, but he looked as though he had learned something.

"Uncle Henry said he hadn't heard either," he said. "Do you mind if I ask you one more question?"

"No, of course not," Willis said.

"I know you see Mr. Harcourt every day. How would you say he's feeling? I mean his general health?"

"I would say he's feeling fine," Willis said. He hoped he did not speak too quickly, but he was not sure. He did not like Roger Harcourt, but he felt a reluctant respect for him.

"I'm relieved to hear that," Roger Harcourt said. "I'd hate to have anything happen to Uncle Henry, but time will march on."

Roger Harcourt smiled faintly, nodded, and moved away slowly across the living room. It had been what you might call an exchange of information, guarded and watchful. If Mr. Roger Harcourt had learned anything, Willis had learned something too, and he only wished he knew whether or not Roger Harcourt had intended him to learn it, but there was no time to think this over at the moment, because Mr. Decker was speaking to him. Willis had seen Mr. Decker often at the mill lately, and Mr. Decker had been kind to him ever since he was at high school.

"Well, well, Willis," Mr. Decker said, "so you're a stockholder now, aren't you?"

"Five shares," Willis said, "but I'm here for lunch."

Mr. Decker was wearing his old pepper-and-salt suit. Sometimes Willis thought that Mr. Decker tried deliberately to look like a small-town country lawyer.

"I saw Roger putting you on the stand," Mr. Decker said. "Well, well, Roger does that to everyone. Have you seen Steve lately?"

"No, sir," Willis said, "not lately."

"Steve says he sees you around Cambridge sometimes. You both know some people named Hodges. He's a geology professor, isn't he?"

"Yes, sir," Willis said.

"And there's a girl named Sylvia, isn't there? It's funny to think of you and Steve running after the same girl."

"I'm not running after her," Willis said.

"Well," Mr. Decker said, "maybe she's just running after Steve. Now it looks as though lunch is ready. Mr. Harcourt will make a speech, I guess. I always like his speeches."

The family and the stockholders made a strange group in the dining room. There was a veneer of good-fellowship and good manners, but there were murmurings beneath it, and Willis was sensitive enough to feel the small tensions. He and Bill and Bess were the only young people there and they sat far down the table, but he could see Mr. Harcourt talking easily while his glance moved swiftly from face to face, and he knew Mr. Harcourt was enjoying himself. He was a captain guiding a ship through a troubled sea. The stockholders were all connections of the family, except a few like Mr. Decker. It was all a picture of another age, something that never repeated itself in that manner any more.

Nearly everyone Willis knew in later years seemed to share the belief that a great deal could be accomplished if a group of conflicting and often uncongenial personalities could only eat or drink together. Willis had attended dozens of steak and fish fries and office picnics with field sports on someone's large estate, and formal dinners in the private dining rooms of country clubs and city clubs, punctuated by jokes and with set speeches at some point in the proceedings. They had to be dull; they began with a few good stories, and it was just as well to have your secretary keep a file of good stories. These were followed by a few remarks on the joy derived from being in such a fine group. What was business without the lasting friendships that one made on such occasions? Willis could accept the truth that good businessmen were seldom good orators, although they always thought they were. Their words were as tasteless as the florist's table decorations, mixed like the cocktails in a wholesale way, as perfunctory and polite as the hired waiters who served them.

None of these gatherings was ever like the old Harcourt luncheons. The very best of the old china and silver was set on the Venetian lace tablecloths, and the champagne was always properly chilled. The food may have been simple but it was always hot and good. There was a sense of hospitality that was decorous, measured, and calm, because it was part of a tradition, solid as the sideboard and the family portraits. There was strawberry ice cream for dessert, made of strawberries from the garden and cream from the farm. There was black coffee in rice-pattern cups and no smoking in the dining room. Anyone who wanted cigars or cigarettes or brandy later would find them in the library.

When the coffee appeared, Mr. Harcourt tapped on his glass, softly as though he were in no hurry. Yet the gentle tinkling sound rose above the scraps of luncheon conversation until no one spoke, and then Mr. Harcourt rose from his chair and glanced slowly up and down the dining room.

"It is a pleasure to welcome you all here today," he said, "as I have for so many years in the past and as my father did before me. This house is a part of the Harcourt Mill and it has always extended its hospitality to those who own the Harcourt Mill, and I hope it will continue to do so."

He stopped, but he was not groping for any words.

"Most of us here are related and are only too well accustomed to this small ceremony. The Harcourt Mill has always been a family business whose shares have never been widely distributed. We have lived from the Harcourt Mill"—he tapped his lower lip softly—"for nearly eighty years."

Mr. Harcourt stopped again.

"I think we have had a very successful year. I've already thanked you for your continued support, and I am glad to welcome a new face on the board—that of my nephew, Roger Harcourt, who should, perhaps, have been with us long before, considering the size of his interest."

Mr. Harcourt coughed and smiled and there was a slight stirring about the table. He waited until it subsided.

"Some of these words may sound hollow to those of you who know only too well that my branch of the family is in control. Yet I hope I have always listened to suggestions. My office door is always open, but I know very well I'm like the King of France who said, 'I am the state.' Well, in a way I suppose I am, but though times have been changing, your dividends have gone up. I think we are all in a pretty sound position. I do not want to say, like another monarch, 'After me the deluge.'"

He stopped again and raised his champagne glass.

"Perhaps I've been here too long, but I know very well I can't be here forever. There won't be any deluge, if you hang together and try not to hang yourselves separately. And now I want to give you our customary toast—the Harcourt Mill."

Willis often wished later that he could make a speech as unpretentious and one that said as much. Some of its undertones had been ironical, but it had all been true, and when Mr. Harcourt had finished everyone stood up together, but when someone started to clap he raised his hand.

"Don't," he said. "There's no need for applause. If everyone is finished, brandy and cigars are in the library, and if anyone likes they can see the grounds and flowers, but the swans are nesting. Don't go too near the swans."

It was time for everyone to go, or almost time, and then Willis remembered that Mrs. Harcourt had asked to see him.

"Come out on the porch, Willis, dear," she said, "for just a minute."

They stood on the porch that looked over the fields and trees to the river, and Willis remembered it was where he first met Mr. Harcourt and Mrs. Blood, but it was early summer now and the hayfields were all green.

"Didn't you think it was a nice speech?" Mrs. Harcourt asked. "He always says the right thing, doesn't he? And he didn't look tired at all. Willis, if you see him looking tired, please call me from the office."

Willis said that of course he would and that he liked the speech himself.

"I wish he hadn't said that about the deluge," Mrs. Harcourt said.

"I can't bear to think of being here alone. You know I depend on you, Willis."

"Do you mind if I say something?" Willis said. "I didn't know that Mr. Harcourt wasn't well. I don't believe he wants anyone to know it."

Then the veranda door opened and there was Mr. Harcourt.

"I saw you coming out here," he said. "Were you talking to Willis about the doctor, Harriet?"

"Henry," Mrs. Harcourt said, "I simply had to talk to someone."

"I suppose everyone has to know eventually," Mr. Harcourt said. "What was Roger talking to you about, Willis?"

"He wanted to know how your health was, sir," Willis said. "I said you were feeling fine."

"Do you think he believed it?" Mr. Harcourt asked.

"No," Willis said, "I don't think so."

Mr. Harcourt smiled his thinnest smile.

"Well," he said, "I guess he understood that bit about the deluge. What else did Roger ask you?"

Willis hesitated for a second.

"Whether I'd heard that Simcoe Rubber Hose and Belting is going to buy us out," he said.

"I thought he might ask that," Mr. Harcourt said. "I hope you looked surprised."

"Why, Henry," Mrs. Harcourt said. "You never told me about that."

"There wasn't any need to bother you about it, Harriet," Mr. Harcourt said. "Roger's always hoping I'll sell out. What did you think of Roger, Willis?"

"I think he's pretty clever, sir," Willis said.

"He's clever but he's timid," Mr. Harcourt said. "I don't like clever, timid people. I shouldn't have pleased Bryson by putting Roger on the board."

"Henry," Mrs. Harcourt said, "don't you think you ought to take a rest after the meeting and the lunch and everything?"

"No, no," Mr. Harcourt said, "and we've been out here too long. Willis, you'd better come with me. There's brandy in the library."

Then Mr. Harcourt smiled at him.

"Willis," he said, "do you remember when I told you I didn't think that you were dumb?"

The realization that Mr. Harcourt's health was failing made Willis feel for the first time in his career that solid ground was slipping from beneath his feet. He was still too young to realize that no ground is ever solid. He had possessed a youthful belief in permanence and an illusion that one's elders would live forever, but now everything about the Harcourt place seemed as unsubstantial as a cloud in the sunset. He had never been obliged to deal with setting suns.

By sheer accident no one was in the library when he and Mr. Harcourt got there.

"Well, well," Mr. Harcourt said. "I guess everyone's gone outside, but they'll be back to say good-by. Would you like some brandy, Willis? It's my father's brandy."

"No, thank you, sir," Willis said.

"Are you sure?" Mr. Harcourt asked him. "I think I'll try a little. What's the matter, Willis?"

"You're not going to sell the mill, are you, sir?" Willis asked him.

It was an indication of his own distress that he had ever ventured to put such a question to Mr. Harcourt, and as soon as he spoke he knew that he should not have asked. Mr. Harcourt had poured out a sip or two of brandy and he revolved it slowly in his glass.

"Well," Mr. Harcourt said, "do you think we ought to sell out, Willis? Prices are high right now."

"I guess I've said too much already," Willis said.

"That's quite all right," Mr. Harcourt answered. "I've always made it a practice to entertain any reasonable proposition, and I'd do the same thing if I were you."

Willis could think of no reply to make, and in fact there was nothing much he could have said. Mr. Harcourt took another sip of brandy.

"You're familiar with my investment list," Mr. Harcourt said. "The mill here has been only a plaything for me for quite a while."

His head turned suddenly and his words trailed off into silence. There was a discreet knock on the panel of the open door, and Willis saw that Selwyn was standing there.

"Sir," Selwyn said, "the gentleman has come."

"What?" Mr. Harcourt asked. "What gentleman?"

"The gentleman who you said was coming for dinner and for the night," Selwyn said. "Mr. Nagel, sir."

"Good God Almighty!" Mr. Harcourt said. "It's only half past three."

"Yes, sir," Selwyn said.

"Good God Almighty!" Mr. Harcourt said again. "Get him in here as quick as you can, Selwyn, and send his car away and don't take out his luggage."

It was almost the first time that Willis had heard Mr. Harcourt swear.

"Good God Almighty!" Mr. Harcourt said. "Couldn't he come when he's invited? You'd better go. . . . No, stay here with me, Willis."

Selwyn was back a second later with a heavy, thickset man in his middle forties who looked like a football player, except for his immaculately pressed brown double-breasted suit.

"Well, hello, Henry," he said. "Have I barged into a garden party or something?"

"Hello, Percy," Mr. Harcourt said. "Selwyn, wait outside and say I'm busy."

"What the hell's wrong?" the stranger asked. "I just drove out in a rented Cadillac. I thought we might have time to see the works."

"Damn it," Mr. Harcourt said. "It's the stockholders' annual luncheon."

"Oh my God," the stranger said.

"Willis," Mr. Harcourt said, "this is my old friend and competitor Mr. Nagel, of the Simcoe Rubber Hose and Belting Company. Take him into the study and lock the door and don't come out till I knock. I'm dreadfully sorry, Percy."

"Call me a son of a bitch," Mr. Nagel said—"a lot of people do— but not Percy."

"Take Mr. Nagel into the study, Willis," Mr. Harcourt said, "and you'd better take the brandy with you."

It was like being thrown suddenly into a prison cell with Mr. Nagel, once they were in Mr. Harcourt's small study. Mr. Nagel moved restively around the shadowy room, glancing out of the narrow lead-paned windows, examining the glass-enclosed shelves that contained Mr. Harcourt's collection of antique firearms and the old-fashioned safe that had Mr. Harcourt's father's name painted on it. His eyes had a watchful glint and his florid face wore the puzzled expression that Willis had observed on the features of some other customers who had visited the Harcourt place. Finally he drew an immaculate white handkerchief from the breast pocket of his double-breasted suit and passed it gently over his forehead.

"I picked up a cold on the Century," he said. "I thought I could sweat it out in a Turkish bath in New York but it only opened up all my pores." Mr. Nagel blew his nose. He smelled strongly of bath salts and nose drops.

"Maybe you would like a little brandy, sir," Willis said.

"Say," Mr. Nagel said, "pour me out a slug, will you?" He sat down in the chair behind Mr. Harcourt's table and tossed off the drink in a single gulp. "Oh, boy," he said, "I'd like to contact the bootlegger who sells this stuff."

"It's been in the family," Willis said. "It's Mr. Harcourt's father's brandy."

Mr. Nagel laughed in an affable, reminiscent way.

"My old man didn't pass me on any heirlooms," he said. "I assume you're Mr. Harcourt's grandson, aren't you?"

"No, sir," Willis said. "I work in the mill office."

"Is that so?" Mr. Nagel said. "What did you say your name was, son?"

"Wayde," Willis said, "Willis Wayde."

"Then you'll be old Alf Wayde's boy, won't you?" Mr. Nagel said. "Old Alf is the best damned engineer in the belting business. I want to see Alf before I get out of here."

"I didn't know you knew him," Willis said.

"Hell," Mr. Nagel said, "everybody in belting knows Alf. Say, if you're ever in Chicago, look me up. I'm still young enough to know what young fellows like, and I've got a lot of good addresses."

"Thanks very much, sir," Willis said.

He did not know anything about traveling then, but he was flattered that Mr. Nagel thought he knew.

"We've got a fine crowd of young fellows in the office," Mr. Nagel said, "and I'll see personally they show you the town. This is quite a setup they've got here, isn't it?"

"I guess it is," Willis said. "It's the only one I know. We came here when I was fifteen."

"Well," Mr. Nagel said, "I've seen some of these family setups in my time. I know Mr. Henry Harcourt and I say this from the bottom of my heart. He's a very lovely gentleman."

"Yes, sir," Willis said, "I guess he is."

"It's a lovely home," Mr. Nagel said, "and Mr. Harcourt is a lovely old sweetheart. He ought not to have to monkey with any old mill."

"Would you like some more brandy, sir?" Willis asked.

"No, but thank you very kindly, son," Mr. Nagel said. "I have a way of dreaming dreams. They call me P.L. in the office. They say, 'Old P.L. is dreaming out loud.'"

Willis did not answer, and Mr. Nagel sighed.

"I guess you've got a mother that you think the world of. Well, I had a mother myself. Mother taught me to dream dreams." Mr. Nagel blew his nose again. "Always be good to your mother."

But Mr. Nagel did not have a chance to continue, because there was a knock on the study door.

"I guess that's Mr. Harcourt, sir," Willis said, and when he opened the door he was surprised to see that Mr. Harcourt was not alone. Mr. Bryson Harcourt and Mr. Roger Harcourt were with him.

"You can come out now," Mr. Harcourt said. "I'm sorry to have kept you so long, Percy, but the guests were leaving. This is my son Bryson and this is my nephew Roger, but I understand you've met them already."

"Hello, fellas," Mr. Nagel said.

"Let's all sit down," Mr. Harcourt said. "I don't think we'll be disturbed in here," and he waved toward the library chairs and sat down on the sofa. "It occurred to me that we might have our conference now, Percy, and I thought it might be a good idea for Bryson and Roger to sit in on our talk."

If one had not known Mr. Harcourt well, it would have been impossible to detect any difference in his manner, but Willis felt a rising excitement.

"You won't want me any longer, will you, sir?" Willis asked.

He spoke because he thought that Mr. Harcourt had forgotten him. He should have known that Mr. Harcourt never forgot.

"I think I'd like to have you stay, Willis," Mr. Harcourt said. "It might not be a bad idea to have someone outside the family hear this conversation. Willis, pass the cigars."

There was a heavy silence and no one but Mr. Harcourt took a cigar.

"We all know why Mr. Nagel is here," Mr. Harcourt said. "Percy, stop me if I say anything wrong or inaccurate."

Mr. Harcourt lighted his cigar carefully.

"I suppose there have been rumors," he said, "and that is why I've asked you here, Roger. I want you to know that Mr. Nagel has made an offer for the Harcourt Mill, and he's given me some excellent reasons why it might be well to take it. I think it's a startlingly generous offer."

Mr. Harcourt drew on his cigar and watched the smoke rise slowly toward the ceiling.

"The transaction would be an exchange of stock—one share of ours for two of Simcoe's. The cash value at the present time would amount roughly to five million dollars."

He mentioned the sum in an offhand way, still watching the smoke from his cigar.

"What's that?" Roger Harcourt asked. "Five million?"

Mr. Harcourt nodded.

"It does seem high, doesn't it, Roger?" he said. "But then it isn't the mill that Mr. Nagel wants so much as the Klaus patents and some of our other processes."

Willis sat rigidly, fascinated by the evenness of Mr. Harcourt's voice.

"I've been over this in some detail with Bryson. What do you think of the offer, Roger?"

Roger Harcourt's thin, high voice held everyone's attention.

"I imagine you know what I think already, Uncle Henry," he said. "It will be a great relief for you not to bother any longer with a difficult business and a credit to you if you can sell at such a price. I think we ought to take it before Mr. Nagel changes his mind."

"I'm not changing my mind," Mr. Nagel said. "It's been one of my dreams to get this settled, personally."

Mr. Harcourt nodded and gazed at the end of his cigar.

"Perhaps you're right, Roger," he said. "I've given this serious thought and I dare say you are right. Incidentally I want to thank Mr. Nagel for his thoughtfulness and for coming here prepared to make final negotiations. Furthermore he's been generous in other ways. He will undertake to manage the mill as it stands for three years and to do what he can for our key personnel after that, thus avoiding any sudden change. I think logically we ought to take the offer. It's hard to see how we can ever do better."

Mr. Harcourt's expression had not changed and it seemed to Willis that Bryson Harcourt looked startled, but anyone could see that Roger Harcourt and Mr. Nagel were relieved.

"If it's that way, Henry," Mr. Nagel said, "maybe I'd better get on the phone and let them know in Chicago."

"Just a minute," Mr. Harcourt said, and his voice was sharper. "I'm afraid you misunderstand me, Percy. I've been thanking you, but we're not selling."

Mr. Harcourt pushed himself up from his seat on the leather-covered sofa.

"I've made enough speeches today. I know I ought to sell but I'm not going to. This mill has made money for a long time and it's supported a lot of people here. I have an obligation to them, and I'm proud to say my son feels as I do. You agree with me, don't you, Bryson?"

"Yes," Bryson Harcourt said. "I'm right with you, Father."

"It's old-fashioned, I know," Mr. Harcourt said, "but I'm glad my son's old-fashioned too. It would be easier to take our money and run, but you see, we've always belonged here. You don't understand me, do you, Percy?"

"That's right, I don't," Mr. Nagel said. "I think you're crazy, Henry."

Mr. Harcourt tapped his lower lip gently.

"Yes," he said. "Yes, I think perhaps I am."

"Don't make a snap decision," Mr. Nagel said. "Let's go over the figures again tonight."

"Oh no, Percy," Mr. Harcourt said. "This hasn't got anything to do with figures."

"Uncle Henry," Roger Harcourt said, "there are a lot of people in the family . . ."

Mr. Harcourt raised his hand and Roger Harcourt stopped.

"I know, Roger," he said. "There'll be broken hearts tomorrow, but there are a lot more people working in the mill. Willis, ring for Selwyn, will you? Mr. Nagel might like to see his room, and then I'd like to take you for a walk, Percy, before it's dark."

XI

WHEN WILLIS walked through the place the next morning, he saw Mr. MacDonald and Mr. Beane standing by the vegetable garden.

"What's your hurry?" Mr. Beane called. "Come over here a minute, Willis." Mr. Beane was now the only one there who did not call him Mr. Willis, and it was an accurate indication of his own and of Mr. Beane's position.

"Willis," Mr. Beane asked, "have you heard the news up at the house?"

"No," Willis said, "what news?"

"I guess you know what I mean," Mr. Beane said. "That party from Chicago. You were in the library with him and Mr. Harcourt and Mr. Bryson and Mr. Roger, weren't you?"

"Yes," Willis said, "I was there for a little while."

"They say that this party from Chicago tried to buy the mill." Mr. Beane spoke slowly and Willis understood that Mr. Beane and Mr. MacDonald were accepting him, like themselves, as part of the place.

"Who says so?" Willis asked.

"I know it isn't your place to talk," Mr. Beane said, "but I wish I had been there with you in that library. I'd like to have seen Mr. Harcourt take the skin off him."

"What makes you think he did?" Willis asked.

"Because he wouldn't have done anything else," Mr. Beane said. "By God, Mr. Harcourt's a grand old man."

Then Willis understood that Mr. Beane had only called him over so that all three of them might share the warmth and loyalty they felt. It was a June morning. He could hear the robins and the orioles singing, and the air was being warmed by the summer-morning sun. Though they never mentioned it, they must have all known that Mr. Harcourt's sun was setting, but there was no doubt that Mr. Harcourt was a grand old man.

That morning Mr. Harcourt went over his investment list. He was planning to sell his common stocks, Willis remembered, and to convert into Government bonds, and Willis had been with him when he had called his brokers in Boston. Then in the afternoon there had been some problem in Building 2, the details of which Willis had forgotten, but Mr. Harcourt had visited Building 2 himself and he had asked Willis to go with him. Building 2 was always noisy. When they stepped inside and began walking down the broad center aisle, somebody raised a cheer that rose above the sound of the machinery and that made Mr. Harcourt stop for an instant. Then he walked straight on, as though he had not noticed, and he did not speak until they were out of the building and in the yard.

"That was peculiar, wasn't it?" he said. "Some people in there must have heard the news."

When a salesman in Chicago was taken ill with appendicitis, Willis was sent to call on the Haverford people there, a milling firm that was one of Harcourt's best accounts; Mr. Harcourt had insisted that Willis should go out to finish the sale. Mr. Briggs had objected, and Willis had not blamed him much, seeing that Willis had never sold anything in his life, but Mr. Harcourt had insisted. It was time that Willis began to move around, he said, and see the country. It was something to remember —your first trip for any firm, and your first expense account. He was to stop at the Hotel Blackstone, Mr. Harcourt had said, and Willis always had a warm spot in his heart for the Hotel Blackstone.

You could never tell, until you tried, whether you could sell or not, and Willis immediately enjoyed the arts of logical persuasion and the elation that finally came with writing down an order and finishing a deal. It was always a new adventure—the contacts with new people and the feeling that the firm's reputation depended on your judgment and behavior. Any executive, he always thought, should have sales ability, because you could never tell when an emergency might arise when this ability might be required. Things were moving very fast, although Willis did not know it then.

Later Willis realized that Mr. Harcourt knew very well that his time was short, and Willis saw others who faced that same eventuality. You only had to read the papers to realize that the business world was full of sudden death. After you had reached a certain age, and even though you were still young and active, you had to face the unpleasant fact that extermination might catch up with you at home or in the office, on the golf links or in the street, and if you were a good executive you were always ready for it, because things would have to run without you.

Mr. Harcourt was one of the best long-term planners Willis had ever met. There was no dramatic sense of haste and no small farewell speeches.

In fact there was no appreciable change in Mr. Harcourt, who acted to all outward appearances as though he had years ahead of him, and all his decisions reflected this belief. If he had more conferences than usual with Mr. Decker and his Boston lawyers, the times were uncertain. He had been ready for the crash of October, 1929. He had even begun cutting down the mill inventory that summer in case there should be a business slump. The truth was that anyone of Mr. Harcourt's ability was able to face anything, and death was no exception.

Willis believed that he was one of the few people who knew that Mr. Harcourt was facing it, not that Mr. Harcourt had ever mentioned the prospect. Willis had only a single glimpse of Mr. Harcourt's thoughts, and this occurred on the day he returned from that trip to Chicago, and it was only a glimpse, a veiled reference and nothing more. Willis arrived in Clyde from Chicago at a quarter before two, and the station looked exactly as it had when he had seen it first, except that it seemed dingier and smaller. He reached the mill office at half past two, carrying his new leather suitcase. Perhaps he should have reported to Mr. Briggs first, since Mr. Briggs was the head of sales, but instead he stopped in to see Mr. Harcourt. His office door was open, as it always was, and Mr. Harcourt sat at his battered desk with a pile of legal papers in front of him.

"Why, hello, Willis," Mr. Harcourt said. He spoke just as though Willis had never been away, but at the same time Willis had a feeling that Mr. Harcourt was very glad to see him. "I'm glad to be here to see you back."

Willis only remembered this remark later. It did not strike him as peculiar at the time.

"Put down your bag and sit down," Mr. Harcourt told him. "That's a very nice suit you have, Willis. You always wear clothes well. I was talking to Jess Haverford on the telephone this morning. You seem to have made a happy impression."

"I'm glad if things went all right, sir," Willis said.

"I thought you'd like traveling," Mr. Harcourt told him. "When I was young there was nothing I liked better than moving around and going places, but now I hate the idea of moving. I hear you took Mr. Judson from the purchasing department out to dinner. And you gave him that bottle of Scotch from me, I hope."

"Yes, sir," Willis said. "He's going to write you a note. We had a drink of it up in my room before dinner."

"It's funny, this drinking in a hotel bedroom," Mr. Harcourt said. "I've never been able to get used to it. You gave Jess Haverford those cigars, I hope."

"Yes, sir," Willis said.

"Jess is a good judge of cigars," Mr. Harcourt said.

"He asked particularly how you were, sir," Willis said.

"I hope you told him I'm feeling fine." Mr. Harcourt spoke more rapidly than usual. "I always liked Chicago." The springs in his chair creaked as he leaned back. "It's always living in the future, something I'm less and less inclined to, I'm afraid. I'm getting surprisingly fond of the present. Well, I mustn't keep you, Willis. You ought to be seeing Mr. Briggs now."

Willis rose but Mr. Harcourt raised his hand.

"I want to hear more about Chicago. I'd like you for dinner at the house tonight." He paused a moment. "Bess is coming, and no one else. Make it half past six, so we'll have time to sit on the west veranda. I thought you'd like it if I asked Bess for you."

Of course he liked it, but he was surprised that Mr. Harcourt should have mentioned Bess.

"She's looking very pretty these days, isn't she?" Mr. Harcourt said. "And she's getting very direct. She said she'd love to come over if you were there."

You were always living in some fool's paradise or other when you were twenty-two. Although he liked to think that he had discounted a great deal, he could not blame himself for the things he thought that day. When he was talking to Mr. Briggs in the sales department about the Hartex conveyor belting that Haverford had ordered, a part of his mind was still concentrated on what Mr. Harcourt had just said. Why, Willis kept asking himself, had Mr. Harcourt said that Bess was looking very pretty? Why had he mentioned that Bess was glad to come that evening if he would be there too? Then his mind moved further, on the supposition that what he thought was true. He could see himself married to Bess Harcourt, living in a house of their own on the Harcourt place, a part of the Harcourt family, as Mr. Bryson's son-in-law, assisting Mr. Bryson at the plant. He could never blame himself for indulging in this fantasy. You always lived in some sort of fool's paradise or other when you were twenty-two.

There was something down to earth about driving back with his father to the garden house and washing up before dinner.

"I do think, Willis," his mother said, "that Mr. Harcourt might not have invited you tonight, the very first moment that you got back home."

"Now listen, Cynthia," his father said, "Willis is a big boy now. He's a management boy. Look at the crease in his pants."

"I don't mind if he looks nice, Alf," his mother said, "but I do wish

Mr. Harcourt wouldn't act as if he owned Willis. I think he might have asked us too. Don't you think so, Alf?"

"It's a hot night, Cynthia," Alfred Wayde said, "and I'd rather get up a sweat at home. I wish we were in the mountains. Say, Cynthia, we haven't been away from here for years. Remember how cool it used to be at the mine?"

"Don't start getting restless, Alf," she said. "Who else is going to be there, Willis?"

"No one," Willis told her, "only Mrs. Harcourt and Bess."

"Oh dear," Mrs. Wayde said, "I thought you weren't seeing so much of Bess."

"I'm not seeing much of her," Willis said. "She's just going to be there."

"Oh dear," she said. "I don't mean she isn't a very nice girl, but she isn't your kind of girl, Willis."

He wished his mother would not keep saying that Bess was not his kind of girl. The repetition always broke the continuity of his thoughts.

The Harcourts were all on the west veranda.

"Oh, Willis, dear," Mrs. Harcourt said, "we're all so glad you're back, aren't we, Bess?"

"Yes," Bess said, "we're pretty glad right now."

Bess was looking very pretty. It was a sort of beauty that had nothing to do with her features, and made you forget their irregularity. There was a glow in her tan cheeks, and the tan made her yellow hair seem lighter and brought out the greenish-blue color of her eyes.

"Willis," Mr. Harcourt said, "when you come here there isn't any need for you always to ring the front doorbell. Bess and Bill don't and you needn't either. It only bothers Selwyn."

"I can't see Willis not ringing a bell," Bess said. "I always think of him as ringing bells."

"It's all right," Willis said, "as long as I ring a bell with you, Bess."

"Well," Bess said, "this must be what comes of going to Chicago."

There was no sharpness at all in the way she said it. She seemed to know as well as Willis that Mr. Harcourt was watching them, but she did not appear to mind, and when Willis drank the Martini that Mr. Harcourt gave him, anything seemed possible.

It was the same at dinner—anything seemed possible—and Mr. Harcourt had asked Selwyn for champagne.

"Well, Willis," Mr. Harcourt said, "tell us about your trip."

"Well," Willis began, "it's quite a place, Chicago. You know, I hadn't been there since my mother and I passed through it when we first came here."

Then curiously, without his having intended to do so, he began talking about the only other time he had been in Chicago and not about this trip at all. He told about visiting the farm in Kansas on the way to Chicago, and then about the mine and the luncheon in Denver at the home of Mr. Harrod Cash. He had never realized that he could recall those details so clearly, although he had a feeling that he was talking about someone else.

"Why haven't you ever told us any of this before, Willis?" Mr. Harcourt asked.

"I don't know," he said. "It was quite a while ago."

It was quite a while ago. He had not realized how far he had traveled from those memories or how little they mingled with the present, and he never forgot one thing that Bess said to him after dinner.

"When you were talking," Bess said, "you sounded like what you're really like. You made me feel I knew you."

He could not blame himself for being puzzled, but it still struck him as a strange remark.

"You ought to know me by now," he said.

"I guess I do," she told him, "but you sounded natural."

At half past nine o'clock Mr. Harcourt said he was sorry to break up such a pleasant evening but it was time for him to go upstairs.

"Harriet's been signaling to me," he said. "All right, I'll go to bed now, Harriet, and we might bring *Gulliver's Travels* up with us. It's queer, my mother used to read it to me when I was a child, and now Harriet's reading it to me. Eventually everything ends up in a sort of circle. Good night, Bess dear. You'll see her home, won't you, Willis?"

There was only starlight, but both of them knew the place by heart, and if it had been pitch dark they could have found their way to any part of it. They walked down the drive to the third large beech tree, which rose in front of them like a still cloud, and then diagonally across the lawn toward the woods and the path by the brook.

"Willis," Bess said, "I do wish I understood you better. I want to try. I really do."

"I'm not much of a puzzle," he told her. "You ought to know that by now."

"Then put your arm around me," she said. "It always helps when **you** do that."

When he put his arm around her, he remembered the other times when they had been alone at night together, but they had never seemed to be so alone as they were then.

"Willis, tell me what you want," she said. "Everybody must want something and you've never told me—never."

"Well," he said, "it's pretty hard to say it all at once. I guess I want to get along. Maybe that's what everybody wants, but you don't have to want it as much as I do, I suppose."

"That's a stupid thing to want." Her voice was very low and so close to him that it sounded like his thoughts as her hair brushed against his cheek. "Do you ever think about me, Willis?" Her hair brushed against his cheek again.

"Yes," he said. "Of course I do."

"I think about you, too," she said, "all sorts of times when I don't expect it."

She leaned her head against his shoulder. "I wish I weren't so afraid," she said.

He held her closer to him. "Afraid of what?" he asked.

"Of what's going to happen to all of us, but I've told you that before. You remember, don't you?"

"Yes," he said, "I remember, but there's nothing to be afraid of, Bess."

"Willis"—her voice was almost a whisper—"did Grandfather say anything about me today?"

"Yes," he said, "a little."

"Well, what?" she asked him. "What?"

"He said you were looking very pretty."

They did not speak for a while but their thoughts were very close together.

"I think he'd like to have us get married," she said. Everything inside Willis seemed to stop. "It would be awfully queer, wouldn't it?"

"Why would it be?" he asked.

"I don't know," she said. "It just would be. . . . Willis?"

"Yes?" he said. "What is it, Bess?"

"I'm awfully glad you're here, and I don't want you to go away. You mustn't go away."

"I won't if you don't want me to," he told her. "I love you. Do you love me, Bess?"

"I don't know," she said. "Oh, Willis, I don't know."

"Don't you know at all?" he asked.

"Yes," she said, "sometimes. I do right now, but let's not talk about it now, as long as I know you're here."

Then he saw the lights of the Bryson Harcourt house in front of him. There were cars on the driveway, and there were people. He could hear their voices on the terrace.

"Willis," she said, "let's not go in right now."

He called up Bess the next morning from the mill and her mother answered the telephone. Bess had left that morning, she told him, to visit her school friend Mary Adams, at Seal Harbor. She would be away for a week. Hadn't Bess told him she was going? He could almost believe that none of it had happened when he saw Bess again.

"Willis," she said when she saw him again, "let's not talk about it now. You know there's lots of time."

Of course he thought there was, when summer changed to autumn in 1929. He was behind the bulwark of the Harcourts then, protected from the financial repercussions of that autumn, too young to understand their significance, just as Mr. Harcourt was perhaps too old. The Harcourt Mill had lived through other grim readjustments, beginning with the great depression that had followed the Civil War. Besides, there was an upturn after the initial market crash, and although there was a slackening of business, as Mr. Harcourt had foreseen, there was no demoralizing slide. Willis never realized until everything was over that he and the Harcourts and all the fabric of life around them had been moving through a period of catastrophic change, because everything had seemed to be going on a fixed and even course. Yet when everything around him had appeared most tangible, the Harcourt Mill and the Harcourt place had been losing substance. He was like someone in the cabin of a ship, absorbed in the immediacy of pressing business while the ship was leaving land. The Willis Wayde who had known Bess Harcourt was back there in the distance, and suddenly he was alone and the Harcourt place was gone.

XII

MR. HENRY HARCOURT died on the eighth of April, 1930. Willis could never forget his incredulity when he heard the news, and he saw the reflection of his own surprise on the faces of everyone else. It was a surprise that rose in one slowly, like high tide. Selwyn had called the garden house at half past seven in the morning, and Willis had answered the telephone himself. Mr. Harcourt had passed away quietly in his sleep. Mr. Bryson and Mr. Bill were already at the house, and Mr. Bryson wanted Mr. Willis to come over as soon as possible.

The weather that day was more like early March than April—damp and cold and misty. The mist had made his face wet and drops of water were falling from the bare wisteria vines on the porch of the big house. It was his imagination, of course, that there was an emptiness in the big house which had never been there before—something that was palpable and startlingly impressive. He rang the doorbell, but when he did so he remembered that Mr. Harcourt had told him that there was never any need to ring it, and a lump rose in his throat. It was a dark morning, and the hall lights were on, giving the impression that it was still night outside.

"Mrs. Harcourt is upstairs, sir," Selwyn said. "It is a shock to Madam, and he was so well yesterday."

Mr. Bryson and Bill were in the drawing room. Willis had never seen Bill look so pale and he had never seen Mr. Bryson so upset. When Mr. Bryson spoke, his voice choked and he had to stop and begin his speech again.

"I loved him," he said, "and I know you loved him too. I don't know what we'll do without him."

Mr. Bryson was the head of the family now, but he had a bewildered look.

"There's a lot we've got to do," he said, "and I don't know where to begin. You've got to help us, Willis."

He did not sound like Mr. Henry Harcourt, but then he never had, and Willis could not help thinking that Mr. Harcourt would have been amused. He could almost see Mr. Harcourt touching his lower lip when Mr. Bryson had said he did not know where to begin.

"Is the doctor here?" Willis asked.

"The doctor?" Mr. Bryson said. "Yes, Selwyn called Dr. Carter at once. I can't understand why he isn't here now."

"He'll be here, Father," Bill said. "He was out on a call and they're trying to reach him."

"Yes, that's right," Mr. Bryson said. "I remember now. I don't suppose there's much to do until he comes. Let me see. Where's your mother, Bill?"

"She's upstairs, Father," Bill said, "with Grandmother Harriet."

"Have you called Mr. Decker, sir?" Willis asked.

"Decker?" Mr. Bryson said. "Why, no, and of course I should have called him. Bill, go and call up Mr. Decker."

"Yes, Father," Bill said.

"Ask him to come as soon as he can. There'll be all the arrangements, and the press should be notified, shouldn't it? But Decker can help us with that. I'm sorry I can't seem to keep things straight at the moment. What else ought we to do?"

"Perhaps I ought to go down to the mill, sir," Willis said. "Perhaps there ought to be some sort of notice posted."

"That's true," Mr. Bryson said. "Thank you, Willis. Tell Mr. Hewett, and wait for me in Father's office."

"Yes, sir," Willis said.

"My car's outside. Have it take you down," Mr. Bryson said, "and then send it back. I'll join you there, Willis, with Mr. Decker." He stopped and his voice choked. "I keep thinking how much better Father would do all this."

The news had reached the mill before Willis arrived there. Old Pete Sullivan, the day watchman, was wiping his eyes with a blue bandanna handkerchief. Miss Minton, at the reception desk, was crying, and there was nothing that Willis could say to comfort her. Miss Jackman was in tears too, and her tears wilted her like a melting candle.

"And he was right here yesterday," she kept saying. "He was so well yesterday."

In fact Mr. Harcourt's office looked as though he might be arriving at any moment, with a coal fire burning in the grate, and all the papers on his desk in order, and his appointments for the day written on his calendar. For a moment Willis stood irresolutely in Mr. Harcourt's office, trying to face the facts, and he was aware that he was in a peculiar position. He was only Mr. Harcourt's assistant, but at the same time he represented the Harcourt family until Mr. Bryson should arrive, and until that time he was obliged to give directions in Mr. Bryson's name.

"Perhaps you'd better tell Mr. Hewett that Mr. Bryson will be here in a few minutes," he said, "and ask him if he'd mind coming up here now. Then open the safe and bring in Mr. Harcourt's private files."

It was the first time in his life that he had ever deliberately assumed authority. For a few minutes, at least, he was the head of the Harcourt Mill, and he knew better than Mr. Hewett what Mr. Harcourt would have wanted. He was glad that Mr. Hewett did not resent his being sent for.

"Mr. Bryson wanted us all to meet up here," Willis said, "instead of in your office, sir."

"All right, Willis," Mr. Hewett said. "This is a shock for everyone. Poor old H.H. I've never worked for anyone but old H.H."

Neither of them spoke for a moment and both of them must have had a vision of Mr. Bryson sitting in Mr. Harcourt's chair.

"How's Bryson taking it?" Mr. Hewett asked.

"He's very much upset, sir," Willis said. "Of course it was very sudden."

"I wish this hadn't happened when business was sliding off," Mr. Hewett said. "Bryson's pretty out of touch with things. Well, we've all got to help him."

"Yes, sir," Willis said.

"I've always told old H.H. that he ought to use Bryson more," Mr. Hewett said, and he seemed to forget Willis's age at the moment. "There's no one to take over except me, and I've never been in the front office. We ought to get Briggs down, and we've got to get your father down. Miss Jackman, send for Mr. Briggs and Mr. Wayde. Let's see, what else ought we to do?"

Willis was not used to indecision, because it had not existed in Mr. Harcourt's time.

"Perhaps we'd better get a notice ready," he said. "I'll try to dictate one, sir, and we should prepare telegrams to the stockholders and the family. Then Mr. Harcourt had customers coming up from Providence this morning."

"You'd better see them," Mr. Hewett said. "Bryson won't want to and he won't know anything about it. There ought to be some telegram signed by Bryson, and I suppose there'll have to be a stockholders' meeting."

The mill's balance and equilibrium were lost already, and it seemed to Willis that he, and not Mr. Hewett, was doing the thinking. Mr. Briggs was of very little help.

"All right, boy wonder," Mr. Briggs kept saying. "Let the boy wonder do it."

Willis had never got on well with Mr. Briggs and he had never been so aware of Mr. Briggs's limitations. He was glad when his father intervened.

"Oh, shut up, Briggs," he said. "The boy's doing the best he can. Maybe it's lucky we've got somebody—even a boy wonder."

"Well, it's a damned funny situation," Mr. Briggs said. "I always told H.H. he should have got somebody older."

"Yes, it's a damned funny situation," Alfred Wayde said, "but Hewett and I can run the works for the time being, and maybe you'd better try to sell belts for the time being. I haven't seen you selling any lately."

"What do you mean 'for the time being'?" Mr. Briggs asked.

"Exactly what I say," Mr. Wayde answered. "I mean this is purely temporary."

"Now, boys," Mr. Hewett said. "Now, boys, we've got to pull together."

Everything was under reasonable control when Mr. Bryson finally arrived with Mr. Decker. Mr. Hewett outlined the various steps they had been taking, and Mr. Bryson sat in his father's chair and gazed at the portraits on the wall.

"Alfred," he said, "I'd just as soon you wouldn't smoke that pipe in here. Father always hated pipes."

"I'm sorry," Alfred Wayde said, "he never told me so. Well, I'd better be going now. The crane's broken down in Number Three."

"We've all got to pull together," Mr. Bryson said, "and I hope we'll make a good team, but I haven't got much mind for details today, what with all the—the arrangements."

"That's all right, Bryson," Mr. Decker said. "We'll take care of everything. I guess I'd better see your father's papers."

Then Mr. Briggs said that he had better go upstairs, and Mr. Hewett said that he had better be going but he would be on hand when he was needed. Mr. Decker was the one who gave a final O.K. on the notices and telegrams while Mr. Bryson sat doing almost nothing.

"You know," Mr. Bryson said, "I'm not good for much here today. Willis, you know better than anyone what Father was doing. I authorize you to run the office today just the way he would have run it. Just let me know if anything important comes up. Mr. Decker and I will be very busy."

It was obviously a great relief to everyone when Mr. Harcourt's sister, Mrs. Blood, drove out from Boston. She had Mr. Harcourt's lightness of touch, and his air of arrogant indestructibility, but instead of his kindness she had a cold, impersonal compassion. She was like one of the

Fates in Greek mythology, the lady with the shears who cut the thread, or she might have been like Penelope, who was always making a tapestry in the daytime and destroying it at night. At any rate Willis remembered what Mr. Bryson had said when he heard that Mrs. Blood was at the house.

"Thank God," he had said, "Aunt Ruth is here. She'll know where everybody ought to sit in the church."

Fifteen minutes after Mr. Bryson had expressed his relief Miss Jackman came in to say that Mrs. Blood wanted him on the telephone and Mr. Bryson asked if she could not call later, because he had to deal with a number of immediate business matters; but Mrs. Blood wanted to speak to him at once, and Willis still remembered the telephone conversation.

"Yes, Aunt Ruth," Mr. Bryson had said. "Yes, Aunt Ruth . . . Well, can't Mildred help you about that? . . . Then why don't you ask Bill? . . . Or Bess, or somebody else? . . . No, Aunt Ruth, I can't let you have Willis now. I'm very busy here. There are a great many things that Father hasn't told me. . . . I said I want Willis to help me here. . . . Well, all right, if you put it that way, Aunt Ruth, but I want him back in half an hour. There are some people coming from Providence."

Mr. Bryson's face was red when he hung up the receiver.

"Mrs. Blood wants you at the house for a few minutes, Willis," he said, "but don't stay any longer than necessary."

Mr. Jethro, the undertaker from Clyde, and two younger assistants were waiting in the hall of the big house. One of them was Mr. Jethro's son, Cliff, who had attended high school with Willis.

"Do you know, Willis," Mr. Jethro asked, "who is going to select the casket?"

Willis could only tell him that he would ask Mrs. Blood.

Mrs. Blood was in the library, sitting straight in a stiff-backed chair. In all the years Willis had known her he had never said much to Mrs. Blood, but at some point in their acquaintance Mrs. Blood must have made up her mind about him, and now she seemed to take him as much for granted as though he were Mr. Decker.

"Well, Willis," she said, "how is Bryson doing?"

"I think he's rather upset, Mrs. Blood," Willis answered.

"Confused, you mean," Mrs. Blood said. "Bryson's always confused when anything unexpected happens. Henry always wanted to do everything about everything ever since he was a boy, and now see where we are. Henry should have sold the mill, of course, to that horrid man. What was his name?"

"His name was Mr. Nagel," Willis said.

It was amazing to hear Mrs. Blood speak so freely, just as though they were relatives and contemporaries, but then everyone was unstrung that day.

"Yes," she said, "Mr. Nagel. Henry always kept his hand on everything, but he might have realized he couldn't run his own funeral. Did he leave a list of pallbearers with Mr. Decker?"

"No," Willis answered. "Mr. Decker was just speaking of it."

Mrs. Blood sighed in an exasperated way.

"It isn't like Henry not to have expressed a few wishes, but then Henry always did ignore facts if they didn't interest him. Well, I've made out a list." Mrs. Blood picked up a piece of note paper from the table beside her. "You'll find your name on it, Willis. Do you own a cutaway coat?"

"No, Mrs. Blood," he said.

"Then that man Mr. Jethro will have to get one for you, and I want you to have this list typed and all the people notified."

"Yes, Mrs. Blood."

"Then I want you to call up the obituary editor of the *Boston Evening Transcript*. They will have an obituary of Henry already prepared, I'm sure. I want you to ask him to give the details to the Associated Press. Bryson would only forget about it if I were to ask him. That Mr. Jethro is waiting outside, isn't he?"

"Yes, he's outside, Mrs. Blood," Willis said.

"I suppose Henry knew I'd be here," Mrs. Blood said. "Well, I am, and Bill has gone to get the clergyman. Mr. Bowles, isn't it? I hate the way he reads the service. I want Mr. Swithin up from Boston. I want you to call Mr. Swithin."

"Yes, Mrs. Blood," Willis said, "I'll telephone him right away."

"I don't know why Harriet should be so upset," Mrs. Blood said. "She's buried one husband already, and these things have to happen. Mildred and Bess are upstairs with her now. Tell Selwyn I want to see Bess, please, and that will be all for the moment. You'd better get back to Bryson now, and I'll want you this afternoon to help me with the seating at the church."

Then suddenly Mrs. Blood burst into tears, and it was the last thing that Willis would have expected. It was as though the whole Harcourt place were crumbling when Mrs. Blood began to cry.

Willis met Bess in the passageway just as he left the library, and they both stopped and looked at each other, and then she threw her arms around him.

"Oh, Willis," she said, "thank God you're here."

The funeral was held at two o'clock on Thursday at Saint John's Church in Clyde. Willis stood by the door with Mr. Roger Harcourt and Bill and two of the Haywards, in his rented cutaway that was tight underneath his arms. He had memorized the arrangements and he was the one who had whispered to the others where the family and friends should sit and pointed out the foremen from the mill and employees of over twenty years' standing. He had never before heard the words of the Episcopal service—"I am the resurrection and the life" and "In my father's house are many mansions"—words that were like a wave that finally covered Mr. Harcourt and all his life. He followed the casket again into the April daylight and finally stood by the open grave gazing at the granite stones of the other Harcourts. Afterwards he was asked with the other ushers and the family to the house, and he remembered the gathering in the living room, which Mr. Harcourt would have enjoyed, especially because everyone was obviously thinking of the provisions of the will.

Actually the will had been surprisingly simple, since Mr. Harcourt had made provision for his issue long ago, and had transferred large blocks of the mill stock to Mr. Bryson, Bill and Bess. After a series of bequests to charities and to the servants, the remainder of his estate, including his house on the Harcourt place, was left to his widow under trust for her lifetime. There was only one provision that was peculiar. Mr. Harcourt's remaining holdings in the mill were left to her outright.

Willis imagined that Mr. Bryson and the other members of the family must have been surprised by this, but Mr. Bryson never showed it. The mill, as Mr. Bryson stated in a letter to the stockholders, would continue under his direction in accordance with tradition and with his father's expressed wish.

"Willis," he said, "I want you to be in the same position with me that you were with Father. I've been rather out of touch with things, but you'll back me up, won't you?"

"Yes, sir," Willis said. "I'll do the best I can."

"I'm going to try to induce Mr. Roger Harcourt to advise me with the management," Mr. Bryson said. "Roger has a very good head for business."

Willis knew even then that it was a ridiculous way to divide authority. If he had been thirty-five or even thirty, he could have told Mr. Bryson what he thought, but not when he was in his early twenties.

"You're the boss, Mr. Harcourt," he said.

Mr. Bryson slapped him on the back.

"Don't say it that way, Willis," he said. "You and I are old friends. If you were only older, I'd ask you instead of Roger to help me out, but you can help us both."

"Yes, sir," Willis said. "I'll do anything I can."

That ensuing year at the Harcourt Mill was a history of confusion and diminishing profits, and all sense of security was gone. In June, the week before the stockholders' meeting, Mrs. Harcourt asked Willis up to tea.

"Willis," she asked, "how do you think Bryson is doing?"

Of course Willis could not give her a true answer.

"I'm so confused," she said. "Roger was here yesterday and he was so depressing about Bryson. He says we ought to sell the mill. Bryson won't hear of it, but Roger says with his stock and mine we can make him. What do you think, Willis?"

He told her that business was bad—not only at the mill but everywhere else—but the mill was a modern, well-coordinated plant which controlled patents whose value would increase rather than diminish. There might be a cut in the dividend this year, as a purely precautionary measure, but there was a large cash surplus, and ample working capital placed the mill in a strong position in case of future crises.

"Willis, dear," Mrs. Harcourt had said, "it's such a comfort to hear you say this. It's just what Bryson told me."

Of course it was what Mr. Bryson had told her, because it was what Willis had told Mr. Bryson, and it was just what Mr. Harcourt would have said if he had been alive.

Summer moved into autumn and business still grew worse. Autumn moved into winter, and because of falling orders the mill was operating at half-time, and there was a cut in the office force in January. Any organization, as Willis knew now, should have its second team ready to take over in case of sudden change, but there were simply no substitutes at the Harcourt Mill ready to move in and close the ranks, because Mr. Harcourt's efforts to infuse new blood had come too late and Mr. Bryson and Mr. Roger had been utterly unprepared. There was only one thing that saved the situation. Mr. Henry Harcourt had always been conservative in paying dividends, and thus for years some of the earnings had gone into surplus. As the Harcourt Mill entered the depression, its cash reserve was so large that its directors could have voted dividends for several years if the mill had not earned a cent. The surplus had been large enough to carry subsequent loss, but watching Mr. Bryson in the office was like watching an unskilled artist endeavoring to finish the canvas of a master, and Willis winced at every bungling stroke. In February Mr. Bryson lost the Haverford account. In February Mr. Hewett announced that he was retiring, and a week later Mr. Briggs quarreled with Mr. Bryson and handed in his resignation. It was all right, Mr.

Bryson said. He never could control Briggs, but the trouble was that Mr. Bryson never could assume leadership.

On March 2, 1931—a date that Willis never forgot—he found a letter from Bess Harcourt on his desk with the other morning mail. He remembered that he had wished to open it at once but he had no opportunity to open it until a quarter before nine, and he remembered glancing into Mr. Harcourt's office first, to see whether Mr. Bryson had arrived yet, but Mr. Bryson had not come in. Willis was pleased to see that it was a longish letter.

> Dear Willis,
>
> It's been quite a long while since we've seen each other, hasn't it? So much has been happening that I want to talk to you about, and Mother has been so busy with plans that we haven't been down to the country for ages. Willis, dear, I know I ought to say this to you instead of writing but I do want you to hear my news first instead of learning it from someone else. This is a sort of a hard letter to write, Willis, dear. I don't seem to understand how this all happened myself, because it happened so suddenly that it's left me all of a heap. I keep trying to think how to say it. Well, I guess I'll have to say it in any old way.
>
> Willis, dear, I'm going to get married, and there it is. Edward Ewing asked me to marry him yesterday. I wonder whether this surprises you as much as it did me. Of course I've seen a lot of Edward but somehow I never really expected it. If I had, I promise you I would have told you. I never knew until he asked me that it must have been what I always wanted. Anyway, it's the answer to everything for me. I never thought that I could be so happy.
>
> I'm so happy that I want everybody else to be, particularly you. I seem to care more about you than I ever did, but in a different way. I know nothing would have worked with you and me, and maybe you'll understand what I mean. I want us both to be happy. It isn't going to be announced until next week. Edward and I are coming down then and we both want to see you. Edward likes you very much—he really does. . . .

Willis put the letter in his pocket, meaning to read the rest of it later, but he never got around to it. He felt no immediate sense of shock; he felt perfectly cool and self-possessed but at the same time he was no longer a part of the Harcourt Mill, and he did not seem to feel either glad or sorry. He was aware of no particular resentment. He only knew that he was not the same person that he had been before he read that letter.

It was strange how everything sometimes happened all at once. What occurred was sheer coincidence but the result would have been the same in any case. Willis had put Bess Harcourt's letter in his pocket, and just then his desk telephone rang. It was his father calling.

"Say, Willis," his father said, "has Bryson come in yet?"

"No, not yet," Willis said.

"Have you got his engagement calendar? I'd like to have ten minutes with him. Maybe I won't need as much as that."

"Yes," Willis said, "I've got it here. You can see him at ten-fifteen."

"That'll do," Alfred Wayde said. "Have you got a minute, Willis?"

"Yes," he said, "I've got plenty of time."

"Then come up here," Alfred Wayde said. "I want to see you."

His father was sitting in his office in the engineering department, which, except for a draftsman, was empty, since the bright young engineers from Technology had been discharged several months ago because of declining business. Alfred Wayde had never wanted a private office, but Mr. Henry Harcourt had insisted on it, and he was sitting alone in it now in front of his bare drawing table, gazing at a projection he had drawn of Building 3 that was tacked on the wall in front of him. He was in his shirt sleeves as usual, smoking his briar pipe.

"Well, sit down, boy," Alfred Wayde said, "but before you do, open the upper lefthand drawer of my desk. You'll find a bottle of prescription rye in there. I keep it for visitors usually, but I'll have a little myself right now."

The bottle was nearly full, and Willis handed it to his father without speaking.

"Willis," he said, "when I see you in your God-damned pressed pants, it makes me pleased that I haven't always lived right. I don't suppose you'd like a pull off of this, would you? Bryson might smell it on your breath."

Willis laughed without his ever having intended to.

"I don't mind if I do right now," he said.

"Why, God Almighty, boy!" Alfred Wayde said. "Somebody might come in."

"Oh, I doubt it," Willis said, and he picked up the bottle and pulled out the cork. It was one of the most surprising and pleasantest things he had ever done, to take a pull of straight rye whisky at nine o'clock in the morning. He was certainly not the same person that he had been before he received Bess Harcourt's letter. There was no compulsion to be careful any longer with his manners or his speech, no compulsion any longer to try to model himself after other people. The truth was that he did not give a damn that morning. He could not say that he was happy, but he did have a sense of intense relief and self-assurance that he had never felt before.

"Have you got a cold or something coming on, Willis?" his father asked.

"No," he said, "I'm feeling fine," and in a way he was. "What do you want to see the boss about?"

"That's what I wanted to tell you," Alfred Wayde said. "I'm fed to the teeth with all this and I'm going to put your mother and me and the suitcases in the car and light out for the West Coast. God damn, I never could stand Bryson. I've had enough of him and that horse's ass Roger monkeying with my department."

"Is that so?" Willis said. "When did this come over you?"

"It's been growing on me, boy," Alfred Wayde said. "God damn, I don't know why I've hung around here so long."

"I suppose you did on account of me," Willis said.

"Oh, yes," Alfred Wayde said, "I had to go steady so you could get an education. Well, by God, you've got it, son."

Alfred Wayde filled his pipe and lighted it.

"Of course there was old H.H.," Alfred Wayde said. "He could always talk me around whenever I got ready to quit. God knows why I worked for him so long, except that he got attached to my back like a sheep tick. Every God-damned invention of mine is owned by this company. I don't mind. I like ideas, but what the hell has it got me?—no more than five or six thousand dollars in the bank and a secondhand jalopy. By God, old Harcourt's rolled me like a drunken sailor, son."

"How do you mean, he's rolled you?" Willis asked.

Alfred Wayde's voice grew louder, and an hour ago Willis would have been afraid that someone might overhear him.

"Just who the hell was old Harcourt?" Alfred Wayde was saying. "What the hell did he ever do except make use of other people, and by God, that's what he's taught you to do. Frankly I'd rather use a monkey wrench and a book of logarithms. To hell with it! That's all I'm saying."

"Yes, Pa," Willis said, "you certainly are saying it."

"And you act as though you understood me for once," Alfred Wayde said. "Maybe you haven't had all the sense sucked out of you. I don't owe these Harcourts a God-damned thing, and you don't either. And just who the hell is Bryson Harcourt?"

"All right, Pa," Willis said, "just who the hell is he?"

"I rather like your attitude today, son," Alfred Wayde said. "Maybe you'd amount to something if you could play around with the boys. I'll tell you what Bryson Harcourt is."

"Maybe you don't have to," Willis said.

"No, no," Alfred Wayde said, "I want to tell you. He's only a bastard without his father's brains. I always liked his father's brains. Well, anyway, I'm getting through. There'll be something on the West Coast."

"Are you sure you are?" Willis asked him.

"Yes," Alfred Wayde said, "God-damn right I'm sure."

You could usually listen to people talk, and agree with them intellectually, without having a single word they said change your preconceived opinion. Willis's father, that morning, was one of those rare exceptions. Somehow Willis believed what he was saying as implicitly as though he had thought of those words himself, and they evoked an instantaneous picture of his past, a slavish undignified picture of assiduity and worry. What had he been doing all those years, he was thinking? Nothing but trying to make himself into something he never was, and he knew he would never again be just the same as he had been. He had stepped across a line, and life was a series of lines, like cracks in a pavement.

"Well, Pa," he said, "I guess I'm quitting too."

"By God," Alfred Wayde said, "I thought they'd sucked the guts right out of you."

"Well," Willis said, "I guess they haven't."

It was a moment in his life of which he was always proud, because he had learned something about the quality of decision then which he had never forgotten. It was advisable to weigh the consequences before you made a decision, but once you were going to act, to hell with compunction and consequence.

"Do you mind if I use your telephone a minute?" he asked.

Miss Ballou, who ran the mill switchboard, answered as soon as he picked up the receiver, and he knew that she would listen, but he did not give a damn.

"Good morning, Miss Ballou," he said. "This is Willis Wayde."

"Oh, Mr. Wayde," he heard her say, "I've been trying to reach you everywhere. Mr. Harcourt wants you right away."

"I'll be there in a minute," Willis said. He remembered wondering what Mr. Harcourt would say, but anything that Mr. Harcourt might say would not be of importance. "I want you to make a call for me, Miss Ballou, and charge it to me because it's personal—to New York City." His words were distinct and unhurried. "To the Beakney-Graham Management Company. I want to speak to Mr. McKitterick personally. If he isn't there, find out where I can reach him. Call me when you get him, please. I'll be in the engineering office at Mr. Wayde's extension."

Willis never expected to see Bess Harcourt before he left, and it was only due to Bess that they did meet. He had written her a note on the same day he had received hers, which he tried very carefully to make agreeable, because any display of pique or bitterness would have made him appear ridiculous; and besides, there was a sense of finality in all his thoughts which he could not possibly escape. Curiously enough, this finality seemed to rob him of his indignation, for everything between Bess and him was like the ending of a book which never should have been written.

Dear Bess,

It was more than kind of you to have told me your good news so soon. I do not need to say that I am delighted in your happiness, and I shall, of course, write Edward Ewing to congratulate him. I hope you won't mind my saying also that I shall always cherish the memory of the good times we have had together, and of the kindnesses that you and Bill and your father and mother have always shown me. I am particularly aware of these now since, as you may have heard, in the next two weeks we shall all be leaving the garden house where we have lived so happily for so long—my father and mother for the West Coast, and I for New York. But wherever I shall be, I shall always remember the Harcourt place, and the old mill, and all the Harcourts, with deep affection.

Again, with all best wishes for your happiness, most sincerely your friend,

Willis

He knew that everything was over as soon as he had mailed the letter—the Harcourt place, and his days at the Harcourt Mill, and every episode with Bess. They were already on one side of the line and he was on the other, when he saw Bess again, just the afternoon of the day before he left the Harcourt place for good. Willis had wanted that afternoon to walk around parts of the place again, in order to keep them firmly in his memory, since he was not in the least sure he would ever come back. There was a strange coincidence in his meeting Bess, because they met face to face, unexpectedly, on the same path by the brook where he had first seen her years before. The surroundings had changed so little that he and Bess were incongruously different, and of course there was no police dog named Benvenuto, nor was their interview any longer a scene suitable for the pages in a back number of the old *St. Nicholas Magazine*. He and Bess were both dressed for the city, Bess having come up just for the day from Boston, and he had packed nearly everything an hour or so before. Even though they knew each other very well there was the moment of surprise in their encounter, combined with a vivid sort of curiosity, but he was not embarrassed.

"Willis," she said. And he was acutely aware of her greenish-blue eyes and of the windblown look of her tawny hair. "I was hoping I might meet you here."

"Why, hello, Bess," he said.

"Willis," she asked. "Were you thinking of me, on this path?"

Her asking such a question was a good example of her arrogance. It annoyed him that she should still think she was the center of all his thoughts, but he knew it was no time to show annoyance. However, there was no reason not to be frank, now that he no longer owed the Harcourts anything.

"I don't know what you want to see me for," he said.

"Oh, Willis," she said, "I wish there was something we could do about everything. I just wanted to have a talk with you."

"I don't know what you want to have a talk about," Willis answered.

"Oh, I don't know either," Bess said, "except that I want you to have some sort of kind feeling about me, Willis, even if you think I've been rotten to you, and of course I have."

"Why, Bess," Willis said, "you needn't worry about anything like that. I have the kindest feelings about you."

"You know you haven't," Bess said. "You're just trying to have. Oh, God—don't you see I couldn't help it, Willis?"

"Of course you can't help it, Bess," Willis said, "and I'm sure you're doing the right thing."

"Oh, Willis," Bess said, "I wish you wouldn't be so complacent, just as though you never liked me. That's one of the things that put me off you—your complacency. Oh, Willis, let's go up to the pine woods just this once."

Willis could not remember whether he had been shocked by this suggestion or surprised, but it was exactly like Bess Harcourt to have made it.

"And don't say it wouldn't be right," Bess said. "To hell with its being right."

"Bess," Willis said, and he was able to laugh at her for once, "it would not only not be right, but it wouldn't do any good."

"At least we'd feel more kindly toward each other," Bess said, "and more human, and it would be a good way of saying good-by. I wish you were more human, Willis."

"Now, Bess," Willis told her, "I still don't think it would be a good idea—and you won't have to worry about my personality defects any longer."

"I don't want to get into an argument," Bess said. "I just feel miserable about everything. Willis, do you really have to go away?"

"Oh now, Bess," Willis said, "of course I ought to go away, and you know it. Besides, from a purely personal point of view it's time I had some new business experience. You always get in a rut, you know, if you work in the same place too long."

"You know Father doesn't want you to leave, don't you?" Bess said. "He feels very upset about it. In fact he wants me to try to dissuade you, Willis."

"Your father said a great many very kind things to me," Willis said, "but you know it's better that I leave." And then for just a second he was angry. "What can you expect? What do you think I'm made of, Bess?"

"I know," Bess said, "but I don't see what we're going to do without you."

It was like them all, he was thinking, to expect him to stay because they couldn't do without him.

"The mill's going to get along," Willis said. "No one's indispensable, particularly me." And then he was able to laugh again. "You haven't found me indispensable."

"Oh God," Bess said, "the trouble is I don't know *what* I've ever found in you."

Then she must have known just as he did that nothing could be gained by talking any further.

"Well," she said, "good-by, Willis."

"Good-by, Bess," he said, "and once again, all sorts of good luck."

"Oh, Willis," she said, "aren't you going to kiss me good-by—after—after everything?"

He could always think of that moment as belonging entirely to Bess and him, and it never was anybody else's business.

"Why, yes, Bess," he said, "if you want me to."

"Damn it," Bess said, "why should I have asked you to, if I didn't?"

But he was no longer a follower of the Harcourts when he kissed her.

"Oh God," Bess said, "I wish we'd gone up into the pine woods." And then she began to cry.

"Now, Bess," he told her, and her tears did not move him very much, "there's nothing to cry about. You'll forget me an hour from now, and you know it."

But still, it was always something to remember, that Bess Harcourt had cried when he had said good-by to her.

XIII

ONE SATURDAY afternoon in mid-May, 1936, Willis Wayde met Sylvia Hodges on Fifth Avenue in New York near the southwest corner of Fifty-fifth Street. He had not seen her since he had left Cambridge about seven years previously, and they would have passed each other without speaking at all, if he had not possessed an excellent memory for names and faces.

Mr. Beakney had been giving a private luncheon at the University Club for Mr. Nat Hawley of the Hawley Pneumatic Tool Company of Cleveland and two others of the Hawley crowd. Mr. Beakney had asked Joe McKitterick and Willis Wayde to attend this small get-together, because Mr. McKitterick and Willis would probably end up by going to Cleveland to survey the setup there, and Willis's special task was to make the stay of Mr. Hawley and the Hawley crowd a happy one while they were in New York. Willis had checked up that morning on their accommodations at the Waldorf, and that evening it was his duty to take the whole Hawley bunch to a dinner at Twenty-one and then to the theater to see the musical comedy *Red, Hot and Blue,* which Willis had already seen seven times with other clients. Afterwards they would make the rounds of three or four night clubs. Mr. Beakney was too old for that sort of thing and so was Mr. Joe McKitterick, but Willis was to see that they all had a happy time. Then on Sunday morning he was to accompany the Hawley crowd by motor to Mr. Beakney's home on the Sound near Darien, Connecticut, where they could relax and exchange a few more general thoughts before the Monday conference.

The luncheon at the University Club had been a warm, informal affair. Mr. Hawley had said several times that he had never realized he was going to encounter so many lovely human beings, and there was no doubt he was being sold on the Beakney-Graham service.

"Now, Nat," Mr. Beakney had said to Mr. Hawley, "I'm putting you all in Willis's hands tonight. Being just a youngster, Willis knows all the hot spots. If he doesn't get you what you want, I'll spank him personally."

Mr. Hawley had put his arm around Willis's shoulders.

"I know a lovely human being when I see one," Mr. Hawley said. "And I know that Willis won't ever in this world make me do anything that Mrs. Hawley wouldn't like."

Mr. Beakney swallowed a digestive tablet, but no one noticed except Willis.

"I'll tell you something, Nat," Mr. Beakney said. "Willis is a Harvard man, but you wouldn't know it."

It was pleasant sometimes to be considered a Harvard man, as long as no one perceived it, and Willis could always say that the Harvard Business School did not make him a Harvard man.

It was half past three in the afternoon when Willis left the luncheon group, and there was nothing for him to do between then and six forty-five except to go to his apartment and bathe. It was so warm and sunny that you could smell the asphalt on the Avenue; and the clear sky and the fine buildings, and the shiny cars and the green busses and the yellow taxicabs and the pretty girls who walked past him, all fitted his mood. When everything was going right, a fine spring day on Fifth Avenue always made Willis think of the future, which unrolled in front of him like the thoroughfare. He did not covet the motor cars that moved past him, because he knew that he would own one himself some day. In fact he could buy a small one immediately if he wanted. It was great to be successful and good to be alive.

Even if it did not matter where he was going that afternoon, he must have had some idea of taking a quick walk in the Park, because he had turned uptown. When his glance fell on a tall girl walking toward him, he did not remember her at first. It may have been her quick, easy pace or the awkward cut of her tweed suit, or her gray hat—he never could remember what it was that first attracted his attention. Then he found himself looking at her pale face and her mouth that had hardly a trace of lipstick, and somehow the unkempt look of her dark brown hair made her seem distinguished. Then he had a sense of having seen her somewhere else at some other time or place, and his pace must have slowed automatically. Then he thought of Craigie Street and of Cambridge winters, and he remembered it was Sylvia Hodges.

"Why, hello," he said, and there was a cordial lift of his voice that made him sound like Mr. Beakney. "Why, hello, Sylvia Hodges."

This was a technique that he had learned recently, of using the full name in greeting someone when you were not sure whether the first name might not be too informal. He could see that she did not remember

[160]

him immediately, and there was no reason why she should have, but she did remember before he could tell her who he was.

"Why," she said, "you're Willis Wayde," and he was amused by the surprised way she said it.

"You guessed it the first time," Willis said, and he laughed.

"Why, to think of seeing you here in New York," she said. It was just what he would have expected her to say, and her voice still had its old nervous and insecure quality.

"Well, here we are," Willis said. "Are you down here for long?"

Her brown eyes had a surprised look, as though she saw something new and strange in him.

"Oh, yes," she said. "I'm working at Columbia, on some research there."

"Columbia," he said. "Well, that's fine. I'm working here myself but not at Columbia. It's funny, running into you."

"Why, yes," she said, "it's been such a long time, hasn't it?"

"What are you doing now?" he asked.

"Why," she said, "I'm doing some research in sociology for Professor Gilchrist there."

"I mean what are you doing now?" Willis asked.

"Oh, I just came downtown to look at the shops," she said. "Gilchrist doesn't work on Saturday."

"Well, if you're just out for a walk," Willis said, and he felt relaxed and friendly, "how about walking over and having a cup of tea at the Plaza?"

"The Plaza?" she repeated after him. "I've never been to the Plaza." The way she said it indicated that the Plaza was something she had always wanted to see.

"Well, it's time you went there then," he said. After all, it was always pleasant to be able to do some small kind deed for someone. "The Plaza is a bit of old New York, you know, like the horses and the cabbies waiting near it to take you through the Park. I always like the Oak Room there for an after-the-theater snack, and you can't help liking the palm court and the fountain and the little tables. It's rather French, you know, but still it's old New York."

"Well," she said, "thank you. It would be nice to go there with someone who knows so much about it."

"Oh, I don't know so much," he said, "but I do go there occasionally. No one can ever learn *all* about New York, but I've been here long enough to learn a little. For instance here's Bergdorf Goodman's, which stands on the site of the old Vanderbilt mansion. They always have wonderful window displays. Those are nice summer dresses, aren't they?"

They both stopped to look at the pallidly slender figures in chiffon gowns grouped on an abstract summer terrace.

"I hate to think what those things must cost," Sylvia said, and Willis laughed easily.

"So do I," he answered. "So do I." It was very pleasant to be able to be kind to Sylvia, and he could extend his kindness in imagination.

"I'd like to see you in that—er—green gown," he said, and he hesitated because he didn't know whether or not "gown" was the word for it.

"So would I," she answered.

It was a useless thought, of course, but it had the quality of Cinderella and the coach, and it blended with all the sights and sounds on the Avenue.

"There's never any harm in wishing," he said. "Very frankly it's an idea of mine that if you wish for something hard enough and often enough, it might come true sometime."

"Do you really think so?" she asked him. She looked at him, and then she looked back at the dresses in the window.

"Yes," he said, "at least that's my theory at present."

"All right," she said, "all right, I'm wishing."

He was glad that he had thought of the spacious, decorous order of the Plaza. There were very few people in the palm court, and the music had not started yet, so that you could hear the gentle splash of water from the fountain. Although he did not know the captain, Willis greeted him as though he did.

"I think the lady would like to sit a little nearer the fountain, if you could manage it," he said. "Will it be tea or would you rather have something to drink, Sylvia?"

"Oh, tea, thanks," Sylvia said, "and an English muffin and marmalade, if they have it."

He watched her take off her gloves and fold them carefully.

"This is great fun," she said. "And it's so civilized to think of tea. Everyone's always drinking cocktails at Columbia."

"I agree with you about tea," Willis said. "I don't mind a drink before dinner, but not in the middle of the afternoon. I hope everything's all right in Cambridge."

"Oh, Cambridge," Sylvia said. "It's the same old place, but there comes a time when you want to be independent, don't you think so?" She looked at him with a quick, rather timid smile.

"I've always thought it must be difficult for a girl at home after she's finished with college and everything," Willis said. "I hope your mother and father are well."

"Oh, yes," she said, "they're doing splendidly. Father was made president of the Geological Institute last year. He makes fun of it, but secretly he's pleased, and his book—did you know he had finished his book on the Devonian ganoids?"

"No," Willis said. "Well, that's fine. Personally I don't seem to get much chance to read, but I have bought Dr. Eliot's Five-Foot Shelf of Books. Fifteen minutes' reading a day, you know," and he laughed.

Sylvia's forehead wrinkled.

"Oh, yes," she said, "I've seen advertisements of it. The family used to know President Eliot. I used to be rather frightened of him. How do you like your tea?"

"Just as it comes," Willis said, "and two lumps of sugar and lemon. How's your sister?"

"Oh, Laura," Sylvia said. "Well, Laura's all through with Radcliffe, and she's teaching Latin in a very snooty girls' school in Connecticut, and Tom's in a law office in Boston. He's engaged to Mary Smythe. Did you ever know Mary Smythe in Cambridge?"

"No, I don't think so," Willis said. "I never got around much when I was in Cambridge."

"Well, let's just forget about Cambridge and remember that we're here," Sylvia said. "I really thought for a minute you were a handsome stranger trying to pick me up. Tell me all about yourself and what you're doing and everything."

It was a conversation that anyone might have conducted who had suddenly met a girl after a considerable lapse of years. Each of them was building up a separate picture behind those brittle words, of what each would like to be.

"Oh, there isn't much that's interesting about me," Willis said. "I'd rather hear about Cambridge and what you're doing."

"Oh, no," she said, "everything I do is very plain and dull."

"Well," Willis said, "I'm working in an office—Beakney-Graham and Company. It's a management concern and it sounds dull to everyone but me."

It was very much like a pencil-and-paper game that they used to play at the Hodgeses'. Sylvia Hodges looked at him with bright attention, like a girl in a college lecture.

"I suppose I ought to know," she said. "What is a management concern?"

"Well," he said, "frankly, it's sort of like an industrial doctor's office. If someone is having trouble running his business or his factory, he comes around to us for advice and assistance, and we tinker with the organization, and it's a real industrial education, but I'm afraid it all sounds boring."

"Oh, no," she said, "but I still don't see exactly what you do."

"That's the fascinating part about it," Willis said, "because we do almost everything. Personally, I'm assisting one of the big shots, Mr. Joe McKitterick, and I go with him on jobs all over the country. A while ago we were down South with a fertilizer company, and before that we were up in Minnesota with a pulp mill, and when we're not doing things like that I'm writing reports or entertaining clients."

"I don't see why you say it sounds boring," Sylvia said.

"I mean it doesn't sound interesting unless you know about it," Willis said. "Oh, excuse me, I should have asked you before. Would you care for a cigarette?"

"Oh, thank you," Sylvia said, "I would, if you happen to have one with you."

"Certainly," Willis said, and he pulled a silver cigarette case from his inside pocket and snapped its lid open. "Excuse me, I should have asked you long ago."

He held a lighted match for her and that little pause seemed to break the current of their thoughts.

"You certainly look as though you were doing well," she told him. It was the first personal thing she had said, and he laughed.

"You have to look that way if you work in Beakney-Graham," he said. "You have to look as though you knew all the answers in the book."

"You're certainly different from what you were in Cambridge," she said.

"I guess I was pretty provincial when I was in Cambridge," Willis said, "but I don't think I've changed much, basically."

"Oh," she said, "maybe it's because you have to know the answers. I wish I knew the answers to anything."

"That's funny," Willis told her, "I always thought you did."

"Oh, no," she said. "I must have been terrible when I knew you in Cambridge. You see, I was in love. A girl is always terrible when she's in love."

Willis felt a slight twinge of embarrassment when he remembered the indifference of Steve Decker.

"Why, I never thought you were terrible," he said.

"I don't suppose you did," she answered, "because you never really thought of me at all. Would you like another cup of tea?"

"Thanks," Willis said, "I would enjoy another cup," and his mind moved awkwardly as he tried to think of something else to say. "It's a good thing, getting over being in love with someone. It clears the decks, doesn't it?"

"Yes," Sylvia Hodges said, "it sort of clears the decks. Let's talk about something else."

"All right," Willis answered, "anything at all."

The orchestra had begun to play as they were talking, but Willis had not been aware of the music until then. It was true he had never thought of Sylvia Hodges. This was the first time he had thought of her seriously as a person separate from her environment.

"Suppose you tell me what you really want, I mean out of life and everything," she said.

"Out of life?" Willis repeated after her.

"I know it's a silly question," Sylvia said, "and probably it shows why I'm not good at talking to men."

"How do you mean," he asked her, "that you can't talk to men?"

"Oh," she said, "I always say something like that and it drives them off."

"Well," Willis said, "personally I always like a good serious talk. I guess everybody tries to figure what he wants out of life. I know I've given it serious thought personally, but I don't want to bore you."

"It won't," Sylvia said. "I know it's fresh of me but just looking at you makes me curious, because you look so happy and so sure of everything."

"I'm glad you think I look happy," Willis said, "but I wouldn't say I am, entirely. Actually—to draw an inventory—I want to be successful, to get ahead, and eventually to be my own boss, with a business of my own some day and a home of my own of course, and a family. But my main problem just at present is to get ahead, and that's quite a game in this town." He had forgotten about Sylvia, being lost for a second in his own imagination, but he was acutely aware of her when he paused. She was leaning toward him listening, and it was the first time he had ever thought of her as good-looking. "Well, that's my picture and now it's your turn. If you had a wish what would you wish, Sylvia?"

He saw her hesitate but the light had not left her face.

"I'd like about what you want," she said, "but a girl can't get any of those things by herself, you know. I'm awfully tired of being poor and bright." She gave her head a quick shake. "I'm tired of being just me. If I were to tell you what I want just now, you'd think I was an awful fool."

"Oh, no," Willis said. "Go ahead and tell me."

"All right," she told him, "I want that green dress in Bergdorf Goodman's. I always want something I can't get."

The Plaza was not a bad place for wishes, he often thought afterward. The voices and the music made Willis gay and reckless.

"Personally," he said, "I've been wanting to buy an automobile all day, and drive to the country with the top down."

"Have you?" she asked him. "Really?"

Nothing that he was thinking made much sense. He could never analyze the reason behind the decision that he made, and he never cared to try to explain it.

"Listen," he said, "if you want that dress we'll go over and buy it."

"Don't be silly. Of course I can't do that," she said.

"You can if you want to," he told her. "We'll buy the dress and then we'll buy a car. It might be a very good idea if you and I did what we wanted for once."

"Willis," she said, "don't be ridiculous. Of course I couldn't do anything like that."

He smiled at her. He had often considered large sums of money in the abstract, but he had never realized so definitely and concretely exactly what money meant.

"Sylvia," he asked her, "what's the matter? Are you afraid?"

"No," she said, "of course I'm not afraid, only—what would people say?"

"No one needs to know," he said, and he nodded to the waiter and asked him for the check.

He was Willis Wayde again as soon as they were out of the Plaza, and Sylvia Hodges, though she did have a good figure, looked plain and rather pale. She would have looked much better if she had worn more lipstick. She was Sylvia Hodges again, the girl whom he used to know in Cambridge.

"You know I can't let you buy me a dress," Sylvia said, and it no longer seemed possible now they were out of the Plaza.

"I don't suppose you can," Willis said, "but just the same I'm glad I asked you."

"I never thought that you and I could be so much alike," she said.

"I guess we're both tired of what we are, aren't we?"

"Yes," he said, "I guess so."

"Well," she said, "it's been awfully nice seeing you, and thanks for the tea. I really ought to be going now."

"But you haven't told me where you live," Willis said. "Can't I come up and call on you sometime?"

"Oh, I live in an apartment with another girl," she said. "You don't want to see me again, do you?"

"Yes," he said, "seriously, I want to," and he got out his notebook and pencil, and she gave him her address and telephone number. "But I am going to buy an automobile today, even if it's a Ford."

"Then I'll go with you," she said. "I'd like to see what it's like to buy one."

Willis's five years in New York with Beakney-Graham and Company had molded him into the man he became. He had risen by gradual steps from an ordinary employee in the office to a first-rate junior executive, and he had started from the bottom in the worst years of the depression. It was confusing to him that Sylvia Hodges should have disturbed his assurance that afternoon.

There was always a reaction to everything, and reaction swept over him when he went to his apartment on West Tenth Street in order to bathe and change before meeting those clients at the Waldorf. Willis lived at that time on the third floor of one of those old brick dwellings that he liked to call "mansions" which still existed on Tenth Street. His room might have been the owner's bedroom before the house was remodeled into apartments. Its proportions reminded him occasionally of the Harcourt house, and the Harcourt house was always the standard of his tastes. This must have been in his mind when he had shopped around for secondhand furniture and rugs, at a time when it was still possible to pick up Victorian chairs and tables at a reasonable price. His studio couch and typewriter were all that gave his room a modern touch. His clothes were in a black walnut wardrobe which he had purchased for fifteen dollars. The rugs, though worn, were good Persian carpets. He had bought a mirror and two steel engravings for the wall, and a Morris chair and a General Grant desk and a revolving bookcase. If acquaintances from the office asked why he didn't buy some new stuff now that he could afford it, Willis always answered that he liked it as it was. He always felt at home whenever he reached his apartment, but its quiet was like a rebuke on that May evening.

He felt foolish and uncertain of himself, once he was inside the room and the door was closed. He had bought a runabout and he had written his personal check for it in the showroom and had agreed to take delivery late Monday afternoon. He did not mind the expense as much as not knowing exactly why he had made the purchase, but he did know that he would never have taken such a sudden step if he had not met Sylvia Hodges. He had done it on account of her, but now that she was gone the episode was like a daydream.

At the same time a trace of his elation still was in him. Without his being in love with Sylvia Hodges, for a while their minds and desires had blended together, and they had defied together things that held them. They had both wanted the power of money, and they had felt its power. It had expressed itself in the glittering showroom with its friendly salesmen and in the red paint and leather of the car. They had also shared an identical sense of guilt. He remembered she had told him in a frightened whisper that he really ought not to do it.

"It's just as though I had done it myself," she said. "I never thought you'd be so crazy," but she was really saying he was not crazy, that she admired him for the act and that she understood his motives.

When he selected a new tie and looked at himself in the mirror, his features and his light hair were the same as they had been that morning. It might be just as well not to see Sylvia Hodges again. She was plain and awkward and yet she would have looked well in that green dress.

When his telephone rang, Willis was so deep in his imagination that the sound made him start guiltily.

"Hello, Willis," a girl's voice said.

"Oh," he answered, "hello, darling."

It was Lydia Hembird calling, who had an apartment in the Village in order to get away from her parents' home in Montclair, New Jersey, and who was studying at the Art Students League.

"Darling," Lydia said, "have you got a girl up there looking at etchings, or have you got a cold or something?"

"Oh, no," Willis said. "Why?"

"I'll bet someone *is* there," Lydia said. "Your voice sounds so devious. I'll bet you've got someone in bed with you this minute."

"Oh, no," Willis said, "not this minute, darling."

"You're too cute to be trusted around the corner," Lydia said. "Willis, how about coming to dinner, and then, the way it was the other Saturday? You haven't forgotten, have you?"

"Of course I haven't, darling," Willis said.

He had to leave to keep his appointment at the Waldorf, but at the same time he had an alluring mental picture of Lydia.

"Look, Lydia," he said, "you don't know how much I wish I could, but I've got to go right out. Business entertainment. It's a crowd from Cleveland and I've got to see *Red, Hot and Blue* again."

"You poor darling," Lydia said. "You promised you were going to call me up this afternoon, you know."

He had completely forgotten that he was going to call up Lydia. Nothing ever seemed to end with Lydia.

"I know it, darling," he said, "but I've been tied up with these people all afternoon."

"Oh, Willis," she said, "you know you could have taken a minute off to call me. It's awfully thoughtless of you when I've been waiting around for hours."

Of course he should have called her and of course he should have remembered.

"I never dreamed you'd be waiting around all this time just to hear from me," he said.

"But I told you I was going to," she told him. "Haven't you had me on your mind at all? You said you were always thinking about me. You told me so the other night."

"Of course I've been thinking about you, darling," Willis said, "but there are lots of other things."

He found himself pacing nervously back and forth before his writing desk, but he was tied by the cord of the telephone, which also tied him to Lydia Hembird.

"What sort of other things?" she asked.

"Business," he said, "and it looks as though I've got to go out to Cleveland next week."

"I'll bet it wasn't all business this afternoon," she said. "I'll bet you were out with some other girl."

"Lydia," he told her, "I've really got to be going now. I'm sorry I was thoughtless, Lydia."

"Then if you can't come over tonight," she said, "come over for breakfast in the morning."

He was still tied there by the telephone cord to Lydia.

"I wish I could," he said, "but I have to take those people out to Darien in the morning."

He waited for her to answer, but there was nothing but unbelieving silence. It was a relief at last to be able to feel honestly indignant.

"If you don't believe me," he said, "get up tomorrow morning and stand by the Park Avenue entrance of the Waldorf. I'm going out to Darien with Mr. Hawley from Cleveland."

"Darling," Lydia said, "you can come around on Sunday night, can't you?"

"Why, yes, I'd love to, Lydia," he said, "and good-by until then, darling, and I'll tell you a secret, but I didn't mean to tell you until Sunday night."

He could not understand what made him say those last placating words, except it was unkind to leave her with the feeling that he was not enthusiastic. "I've bought a Ford runabout with red leather upholstery. I bought it this afternoon."

"Oh, darling," she said, "was that why you didn't call me?"

"Yes," he said, "of course it was."

"Darling," she said, "I can't wait. I'm awfully sorry I was mean to you."

Willis had a feeling of temporary relief when he hung up the telephone, and it was a greater relief to think about Sylvia Hodges. She was

[169]

different, he was thinking, from any girl he had ever known, shy and aloof and proud, and even her plainness was appealing. Sylvia Hodges would never seduce him in an off moment. Sylvia would never bother him on the telephone.

It was also a relief to meet Mr. Nat Hawley in his suite at the Waldorf, because there Willis was dealing with a familiar personality. Industrial executives, Willis was beginning to learn, were different from Mr. Henry Harcourt, who was an older model, but they were all pounded and battered and then smoothed on a sort of universal production line.

Mr. Hawley's suite was in disorder. There was an array of bottles on the table, and ice and soda and an untouched plate of sandwiches and even two individual bottles of milk. The contents of a briefcase were scattered over another table, and coats were draped over the backs of chairs. Mr. Hawley was pacing back and forth in his shirt sleeves, holding a highball glass. Pete Judkins, second vice president of Hawley Pneumatic Tool, was pouring himself a drink, and Art Rose, assistant sales manager, in his undershirt, with his face covered with shaving cream, stood in a bedroom doorway.

"Damn it," Mr. Hawley was saying, "after you've made a sale take your hat and get the hell out. You can tell all the boys that from me personally, Art."

When he saw Willis, Mr. Hawley gave a loud, happy cry. He was a heavy-jowled man with black eyebrows, and he clasped Willis by the hand and at the same time held him by the elbow.

"Well, well, if it isn't our host for the evening," he said. "We've just been sort of washing up and having a little *skitch* and soda before we get on the road. Help yourself to skitch, unless you want some bourbon."

"Thanks, I could certainly do with a touch, Mr. Hawley," Willis answered heartily. It was always best to pretend that you liked liquor, and yet he knew that Mr. Hawley's hard brown eyes were watching how he handled it.

"You call me Chief," Mr. Hawley said. "You're working for Pneumatic Tool tonight, isn't he, boys?"

"He sure is, Chief," Pete Judkins said.

"Okay, Chief," Willis said. "Hello, Pete. Hello, Art."

He had not forgotten that they had reached a first-name basis at the University Club. It paid never to forget.

"You go wash your face, Artie," Mr. Hawley said. "We've got to get on the road and see *Red, Hot and Blue*. What's the plot of it? Am I right in believing that a girl sits on a waffle iron?"

"That's right, a waffle iron," Willis said. "There are really some good bits in the show."

"That's a pretty hot one, a waffle iron," Mr. Hawley said.

"It was a pretty hot iron for her too," Willis answered.

"Oh, boy," Mr. Hawley said, "did you get that one, Pete? I've got to remember that one at the Orono Club." He cleared his throat. "That's in Cleveland. I get in twice a week to grab a bite of lunch at the Orono."

"How about another short snort, Chief?" Pete Judkins asked.

Mr. Hawley frowned and handed the second vice president his glass. "Just a light one, Pete. Say, Willis, do you know what I always tell my boys?"

Willis laughed. You always had to get into the spirit of the moment.

"I'd really like to know, Chief," he said.

"Come here, Pete," Mr. Hawley said. "Willis, you take a good look at Pete."

Willis laughed again and took a good look at Mr. Judkins.

"I'll tell you something about Pete confidentially," Mr. Hawley said, and he lowered his voice elaborately. "Pete's all right except when it comes to women. I practically wet-nursed you, didn't I, Pete, and look where you are today."

"Still with the old chain gang, Chief," Mr. Judkins said, and he smiled to indicate it was all good clean fun.

"You know," Mr. Hawley said, "I've got the finest, most loyal crowd around me that there is in any God-damn organization in this whole beautiful country. My boys make me proud, and seriously, just a little humble too. We're all for one and one for all in Pneumatic Tool, and —well, here's what I tell the boys. Work hard and play hard."

It was amazing how clearly Willis could remember the scene. He already knew that you should never underestimate anyone like Mr. Hawley. If he sounded fatuous and silly, it was well to remember that he wasn't. None of them were. They were all lions in the cage.

"Personally," Mr. Hawley said, "I believe in having a lot of fun."

"Say, Chief," Mr. Judkins said, "don't you think we ought to be going?"

"Yes," Mr. Hawley said, "but let me make my point."

Mr. Rose had returned from the bathroom, and they all waited for Mr. Hawley to make his point, and this was somewhat difficult, because Mr. Hawley appeared to have forgotten just what point he was making.

"Personally," Mr. Hawley said, "I used to be quite a playboy, but I have to watch the skitches now."

Everyone laughed sympathetically, and Mr. Hawley cleared his throat.

"The greatest playboy I ever knew in business," he said, "happens to have one of the finest organizational minds I know, and he is a very dear close personal friend of mine. I don't know how he still keeps it up at his age. His name is Percy L. Nagel, and P.L. is a sweetheart."

There was a moment's respectful silence. The name came out of the past, but Willis was always good at names.

"Is that Mr. Nagel of Simcoe Rubber Hose and Belting?" Willis asked.

"It certainly is," Mr. Hawley said. "Were you ever acquainted with P. L. Nagel?"

It all went to prove that it paid to remember names and faces.

"I only just met him," Willis said. "It was when I was working in a small plant in Massachusetts—the Harcourt Mill. Mr. Nagel wanted to buy the mill."

"Son," Mr. Hawley said, "you can shake hands with me again. Any friend of P.L.'s is always a friend of mine."

"I just happened to meet him," Willis said. "There isn't any reason why he should remember me."

"Don't you fool yourself, son," Mr. Hawley said. "P.L. remembers like an elephant and he's a very dear friend of mine."

"Say, Chief," Mr. Judkins began.

Mr. Hawley waved his hand.

"Don't crowd me, boys," he said. "Let me make my point. I believe in fun, but life isn't all fun either. There are finer things in life."

Mr. Hawley looked around him sharply, but everyone was listening.

"Life isn't all play," he said, "and it isn't all work. A well-rounded man makes all sorts of contacts. I like queer people. I like preachers except on Sunday."

Everyone laughed heartily, but Mr. Hawley raised his hand. "Just a minute, fellows," he said. "Just a minute—let me make my point. I suppose you think I'm a silly old crock, don't you?"

Everyone laughed gaily.

"Now, for instance," Mr. Hawley said, "about three years ago we were selling some drills to Rothstein Mining and Development. You remember sitting around the table with those people, don't you, Pete?"

"Yes, Chief, I certainly do," Mr. Judkins said.

"It was a real experience," Mr. Hawley said. "Everything's a real experience, even down to the socialist sons of bitches in Washington."

Everyone laughed, but Mr. Hawley raised his hand.

"There were all sorts of experts around that table—mining engineers and geologists and things like that—among whom was a college professor."

Mr. Hawley cleared his throat again. "I don't recall why the Rothstein people had retained that professor, but he was a real contact. He knew about fishes and red sandstone, and he wrote a book which he presented me with, personally inscribed. His name was Hodges. He's a professor of geology from Harvard University."

"Chief," Mr. Judkins said, "we really ought to be going."

"All right, Pete," Mr. Hawley said, "but let me make my point. My point is that my acquaintance with this Professor Hodges was a real experience. Get my coat, will you, Rosey?"

It was strange how the name had come up out of nowhere. For a moment Willis was undecided whether or not to say anything, but finally he spoke.

"The fishes were called ganoids, weren't they?"

"Say," Mr. Hawley asked him, "how the hell did you know that?"

"Why, I happened to know Professor Hodges myself in Cambridge quite a while ago," Willis answered. It was strange to think that Professor Hodges could be useful to him in a business way.

"Say," Mr. Hawley said, "I forgot you were a Harvard man." He looked at Willis suspiciously, and Willis felt out of the group for a moment.

"Not really a Harvard man," he said quickly, "only Harvard Business School," and the tension around him relaxed.

"Say," Mr. Hawley said, "when did you see the old prof last?"

"Oh, not for quite a while," Willis answered, and he still spoke easily, "but I happened to have tea with his daughter just this afternoon at the Plaza."

"Well, son," Mr. Hawley said, "that's a fascinating coincidence. Those contacts never do anyone a bit of harm. That's exactly the point I've been trying to make. Now what was that one about the girl sitting on the waffle iron?"

For a moment Willis could not imagine how he could go through a whole evening with Mr. Hawley and his two employees. He was sure that he was a better man than Mr. Hawley ever had been in his best days. He hoped that he would never be as boring after two drinks as Mr. Nat Hawley. There were, as Mr. Hawley had said, finer things in life, and Willis had a sudden sharp desire for them, and this may have been why his mind went back to Sylvia Hodges.

When they were on the street waiting for the doorman to call a taxi, Mr. Judkins squeezed his arm affectionately.

"The chief is in quite a mood tonight," Mr. Judkins said. "You made a real hit with the chief upstairs."

"Thanks," Willis said. "That makes me very happy."

It made him happy, but not in the way that he implied. It was dangerous to underestimate anyone, but Willis believed that he could handle anyone like Mr. Hawley. All at once he knew as sure as fate that he could strike Mr. Beakney for a raise to ten thousand dollars a year—and get it—because those unpalatable minutes in that hotel suite had made him harder and shrewder. As a matter of fact he asked Mr. Beakney for exactly that increase in salary on Monday afternoon, after the contract with Hawley Pneumatic Tool was signed.

You never knew that you had been changing until after you had changed. He did not know how much five years in New York had influenced him until he found himself facing Mr. Robert Beakney without nervousness or apprehension, and this would not have been possible a year before. The truth was that he was beginning to know Mr. Beakney rather well, and when you knew someone, your respect might grow, but you were bound to lose your awe.

Willis had been told, and he believed it, that he had a future in Beakney-Graham. He had worked his way from the outer office to the row of cubicles in the inner office set aside for junior executives, and recently he had become one of five who worked across the corridor from the partners. He did not rate a leather-upholstered couch as yet, but his name was on his door as large as the names of the other four men who had space beside him. His office came first, and next to him was Hal Towle, graduate of Cal Tech, next Cliff Schirmer, who handled legal problems, and then came Bud Reed, who had been hired from DuPont, and finally Milton Rouse, who had gained his training with International Paper and Power. Beakney-Graham depended on personality, so that all those juniors were hand-picked for ability and presentable exterior. Though competition was so keen that you learned not to trust anyone completely, still there was a spirit of companionship in the inner offices. As Mr. Beakney had pointed out to Willis when he had been moved there—there were always tempting offers from other firms, and Beakney-Graham must count on loyalty. Ability came first but loyalty was second. There were always young men waiting for your place, but if you stayed, as Mr. Beakney said, there was a real future. Actually Willis had seen two men leave Beakney-Graham in the past year, but he had no desire to follow them, because he was grateful to the firm and devoted to Joe McKitterick, who had placed him where he was. Of course he spoke to Mr. McKitterick first, being careful to explain that he was perfectly happy, with no complaint about anything.

"It only seems to me that I'm worth more than I'm getting," he said, "but stop me if you don't agree."

Mr. McKitterick looked pained, of course, as anyone would who had to deal with such requests.

"All right," he said, "go in and see Beakney, but Bob isn't going to like it. I thought you were perfectly happy."

"I am," Willis said, "perfectly happy, Joe."

"Then who's been making you unhappy?" Mr. McKitterick asked.

"No one, Joe," Willis said. "I just feel I'm worth more than I'm getting."

Mr. McKitterick drummed his fingers on his desk.

"Willis," he said, "there's such a thing as pushing too hard."

"If that's what you really think," Willis said, "I won't push this any more."

"No," Mr. McKitterick said. "Frankly, I told Beakney the other day he ought to do something about you. I don't want you walking out of here just when I've got you into shape. Go ahead in and see him. He's alone right now."

There was no wonder that Willis had a warm spot in his heart for Joe McKitterick, because Willis never could forget that Joe McKitterick got him in there at the beginning of the depression, but at the same time it was due to his own ability that he had stayed.

"Well, thanks, Joe," he said, "I guess I will go in and see him," and was surprised at the matter-of-fact way he said it.

"You've certainly moved on since I saw you there in Massachusetts," Mr. McKitterick said. "I never thought you'd get hard to handle."

"Don't say that, Joe," Willis told him. "You know I'd do anything for you."

"I didn't mean it that way," Mr. McKitterick said. "Actually I'm rather proud you're getting hard to handle."

In his own thoughts, the few yards Willis walked to Mr. Beakney's corner office was a highly symbolic journey. Willis remembered his curiosity and confusion when he had first been called to Mr. Beakney's office with a set of organizational blueprints, but now he was near the end of that long walk. Miss Harrison was typing in the small reception room. The typewriter had the sound of rustling leaves stirred by a gentle wind.

"Hello, May," Willis said, because he could call her May now. "Do you think the boss could see me for a minute?"

She pressed a button on the interoffice telephone. "Mr. Wayde," she said, "wonders if you might give him a few moments, Mr. Beakney." Then she smiled at Willis. "Yes, you can go right in."

Mr. Beakney's corner office afforded a fine view of the Hudson and the Jersey shore. An office, Mr. Beakney often said, should be a place for thought and work, and the man who occupied it ought to be man enough to stand out by himself without the assistance of interior decoration. At any rate, in Willis's opinion Mr. Beakney was one of the best salesmen he had ever known. Mr. Beakney, when you came to think of it, was manipulating a collection of brains he had gathered around him, and also such invisible things as integrity, confidence, and experience. You had to be good to explain those to a customer, and they all had to be inherent in yourself as an individual, expressed and subtly emphasized. On entering his office you had an impression of the hazy city and then of two or three college diplomas, one of them honorary, which were the only decorations. You always saw Mr. Beakney first, a carefully tailored man, gray at the temples, with aquiline, mobile features, who without the slightest effort could shift himself from mood to mood. Like other young men in the office, Willis must have unconsciously imitated parts of Mr. Beakney's manner until he had become proficient.

"Well, well, Willis," Mr. Beakney said, "the day is nearly over and night is drawing nigh. Sit down and let's look at the view. It's a city of stone and steel, isn't it?"

"Yes, sir," Willis said, "it looks beautiful from here."

"Stone and steel," Mr. Beakney said. "That was a phrase I used when I was addressing the chemists' convention the other night. Have you seen a copy of my speech yet?"

"Yes, sir," Willis said, "I read it."

He saw that Mr. Beakney was watching him closely.

"Yes," Mr. Beakney said, "but you didn't come here to speak about my oratory, did you?"

His mood was no longer mellow; he was the quick, incisive Mr. Beakney.

"No, sir," Willis said, and he made his mood change too.

"Well, get it off your chest," Mr. Beakney said. "I have to go to the club and dress for dinner."

"All right, sir," Willis said. "I want to know if you don't think I'm worth ten thousand dollars a year."

Mr. Beakney gazed at the view for an appreciable length of time without giving any answer, and Willis knew the pause was deliberate and designed to disconcert him.

"I don't like this sort of thing," he said, "at the end of a hard day. It's not the custom here for my people to ask for raises."

Instead of being crushed, as he would have been a short time ago, Willis kept his wits about him. Watching Mr. Beakney was enough to tell Willis that he was in danger. Willis had only to say the wrong thing once, and Mr. Beakney's cool expression told him that it would be very easy to say it.

"Mr. McKitterick said you wouldn't like it," Willis said.

Mr. Beakney looked again at the Hudson River.

"Just what in hell"—Mr. Beakney's voice had risen to a cool, hard note—"makes you think you're worth ten thousand a year?"

"I didn't say I thought I was," Willis answered. "I only asked you if you thought so."

"So that's it," Mr. Beakney said. "Hawley's been getting after you, has he? I rather thought he would."

It was a question of whether to answer or to remain silent, and there was only a second in which to make the choice.

"I wasn't especially attracted by Mr. Hawley," Willis said.

You could always tell when you had said the right thing, and all at once the tension was broken.

"You wouldn't get on with him at all," Mr. Beakney said. "Personally, I disliked every moment I spent with him. You're happy with us here, aren't you?"

"Yes, sir," Willis said, "very happy."

"I'm glad to have you say so," Mr. Beakney said. "You've been making a real place for yourself here, but I guess we'd better change your plans a little." Suddenly Mr. Beakney laughed, and slapped Willis affectionately on the knee. "I guess we'd better send Hal Towle with Joe to Cleveland. I wouldn't want to see you in Hawley Pneumatic Tool."

"I woudn't want to be there," Willis said.

"Now, Willis," Mr. Beakney said, "if two thousand dollars more a year makes you happy, why, what's two thousand dollars? It won't mean anything to you in a while at the rate you're developing, but after this, you let me make the raises. It's annoying, being asked."

"I'm sorry, sir," Willis said.

"Don't say you're sorry," Mr. Beakney said. "I was young myself once. I know what it's like when someone like Hawley puts on pressure. I wish I knew what he offered you, for purely academic reasons. I'll bet it was more than ten thousand, but I won't ask."

"Thank you, sir," Willis said.

"I get this in a better perspective now," Mr. Beakney said. "It was loyal of you to come to me first. I won't say I would have matched him, but it was loyal. Ability is first here, but loyalty is a close second."

Mr. Beakney slapped his knee again and stood up.

"Just the same," he said, "I guess you'd better not go to Cleveland. I've got another problem that came to us yesterday. The Rahway Belt Company wants a survey done. It's a small outfit—not promising—but it's a chance for you to develop, and you worked at Harcourt. Have you forgotten about belting?"

"No, sir," Willis said.

"Well," Mr. Beakney said, "clear up what you're doing around here.

Next week we'll send you down to Rahway. I wonder what you want that two thousand for. You're not thinking of getting married, are you, Willis?"

"No, sir," Willis said, and he meant every word of it. "It's the last thing I've been thinking of."

Until then Willis had been in the ranks of bright nice boys who attempted to achieve success by pleasing. He had spent years like a trained terrier in a vaudeville act, jumping through hoops and turning complicated somersaults in order to earn commendation. He had never snarled or bitten or dreamed of turning on his trainer. It would not be accurate to say that he had finally snarled at Mr. Beakney, but he had, for once, met a superior face to face. He had never realized, until it was over, that he could be capable of meeting successfuly anyone of Mr. Beakney's caliber. What still puzzled him was what had ever made him dare, at that particular time, when he had been doing very well indeed, to face up to Mr. Beakney? His salary would have taken care of itself automatically if he had continued jumping through the hoops. There was some other, deeper, cause for restiveness.

After leaving the office he went straight to his apartment on Tenth Street and sat for quite a long while thinking. He had succeeded with Mr. Beakney, he knew now, by giving himself a value which did not exist. Mr. Beakney had thought erroneously that Willis had received a tempting offer from another source, and Willis's conscience stirred uneasily, because he had allowed Mr. Beakney to think it, but then it had all been Mr. Beakney's own idea. Mr. Beakney was astute enough to look out for himself, and if he had fallen into a trap of his own contriving, there were fine dramatic precedents. If Willis had asked for an even larger raise, he realized that he could have got it. He had missed his opportunity, but he understood that there would be other opportunities. The point was that he was as good as someone in Mr. Beakney's class.

Then he was lonely and he wanted to share his thoughts with someone, which explained why he had pulled out his pocket address book and a moment later he was dialing Sylvia Hodges's number.

"Hello, Sylvia," he said, "this is Willis Wayde. How would you feel about having a bite of supper? I'll pick up the car and we might run out to Long Island somewhere."

What would have happened, he often wondered, if Sylvia had not been at home? As sure as fate he would have called up Lydia Hembird. He was in a mood where he had to call someone.

XIV

Occasionally it seemed to Willis Wayde that his was only the progress of any successful American who had started as a poor boy and had used the opportunities offered in what was called the American way. It was only when one began to search the mechanisms behind this pattern that there were complications, negligible in themselves and even laughable, like the problems in a soap opera, but these were different for every individual. Everyone seemed to deal in a slightly different way with conscience and obligation and everyone had his own concept of happiness and justice as well as his own fears. This may have been why everyone's life, beyond a few fixed points, was somewhat fluid.

For this reason, perhaps, there were plenty of people who set themselves up as authorities on instability, like priests and doctors and social anthropologists. These individuals wrote books about chronic dyspepsia, insomnia, posture, introversion, sex in marriage, and occupational therapy, and how to make friends and influence people. You could read these works, you could attend lectures, but in the end it always seemed to Willis that you were still alone. In the watches of the night at least, you were always you.

In an autobiography that he had once written for a subscription volume entitled *Industrial Leaders of America,* Willis believed that he had adequately covered the high points of his career. "In late May, 1936," he had written, "I was sent by the management company Beakney-Graham to make an industrial study of the Rahway Belting Company."

On the morning Willis first visited the Rahway Belting Company he drove there in his new car. He was dressed so conservatively and carefully that he looked like a picture of a consultant in an industrial advertisement. He had read, of course, all the available material on the Rahway Belting Company. He knew it was a small plant that had suffered badly in the depression—that its working capital was low, that its preferred stock had passed its dividends for three years, that the control of the company rested in the hands of Mr. Manley Jacoby, and that the other principal owners were Mr. John Hingham, a banker in Orange, and a garage owner by the name of Henry Peters, and a Mr. Jack Meister, a businessman who was also interested in a small machine-tool shop. He also knew that what had saved Rahway Belt in the depression and what was all that kept it running still was its product, the Planeroid high-speed belt made by a patented process. Willis had heard Planeroid spoken of when he was at the Harcourt Mill as a type of belting that offered high durability at low cost. Besides the Planeroid line, he knew that Rahway Belting manufactured rubber hose and also a variety of V-belts.

Willis had visited enough industrial plants since he had been with Beakney-Graham to know that exterior conditions were no criteria of efficiency. There were few factories along the tracks between New York and Philadelphia that were objects of aesthetic beauty. Although windows might be broken and paint peeling, a place could still give the impression of order and morale, but his acquired sense of appraisal told him Rahway Belting was a dying duck, with no future and not much of a past. Only a few shabby cars stood in its paper-littered parking lot, and the elderly gatekeeper showed no trace of interest when Willis Wayde approached, but sat slumped in his gatehouse carving a slice of tobacco from a plug.

The yard was as dirty as the parking place, and the wooden steps leading to the office were shaky. The waiting space for callers had not been swept, and the girl at an antiquated switchboard behind the rail knew nothing about his visit. Mr. Jacoby was in, she said, and nodded toward a plain board door. The room where Mr. Jacoby sat reminded Willis of the waiting room in a country railroad station. Although it was late in May, a fire was burning in a hot-air stove, and Mr. Jacoby in his shirt sleeves, seated at a golden-oak roll-top desk, looked exactly like a rural stationmaster. He was fussing with a pile of invoices and he pushed his steel-rimmed reading glasses up over his narrow high forehead.

"Good morning," Willis said. "Am I speaking to Mr. Jacoby?"

Mr. Jacoby pulled a soiled handkerchief from his pocket and wiped the corners of his eyes.

"Yes, young fellow, that's my name," he said, "and it wasn't my idea to get you here."

It wasn't his idea, Mr. Jacoby said, but the bank's idea, and that was the trouble with getting mixed up with banks. Once you started dealing with them you were like a fly on sticky paper. As Willis sat in an uncomfortable chair listening to Mr. Jacoby, he felt like a doctor hearing the complaints of a chronic patient. It was clear that Mr. Jacoby, and Rahway Belting with him, had been on flypaper for a long time. Even while Mr. Jacoby's querulous voice rang in his ears, Willis was beginning to see the picture of Rahway Belt, and he knew right from the beginning that Mr. Jacoby was the key to the puzzle.

Willis could see him still, a tired old man in his middle sixties who was constantly trying to fit the past impossibly into the present. He was only a shadow of what he had been once, and he was running down like Rahway Belt, but Willis could see behind the shadow, because it never paid to underestimate anyone, and traces of shrewdness and vestiges of skill enlarged themselves in various ways as Mr. Jacoby talked.

"Say," Mr. Jacoby said, "you know something about belting, don't you?"

They wouldn't have sent him down if he didn't, Willis told him, and then he mentioned the Harcourt Mill.

"By God," Mr. Jacoby said, "that used to be a nice concern."

Willis often thought that the saying no love is like your first love applied to business as well as sentiment. When the Harcourt Mill was mentioned, old loyalties came over him and old habits of thought that unexpectedly fused into creative desire. He had thought in the first minutes of his interview that there was only one honest recommendation he could make—to put the factory up for sale and to dispose separately of its Planeroid patents. But now he revised that estimate because an old and inefficient man was talking of the Harcourt Mill. It used to be a great place once, Mr. Jacoby was saying, a finely managed property, and he had made a tour of it some years ago. Before he got arthritis—and that was why he had to keep the room dry and hot, on account of his arthritis—he had made a practice of traveling around and getting new ideas. That was why he had invested in the Planeroid patents and had bought into the Rahway Belt—because he liked new ideas. Planeroid was a low-cost process, and there was still a Planeroid market, if anyone had the guts to build it, but since the depression, everything was different, but if he had twenty years off him he could show them. But to get back to the Harcourt Mill—their Oak-Heart line was a fine seller, and Mr. Henry Harcourt was a grand gentleman. Mr. Jacoby wondered, now that Mr. Harcourt was dead and gone and things weren't going so well up there, what had happened to the Harcourt place.

"I guess it's still right there," Willis told him, "but I haven't seen it for quite a while."

Willis had deliberately put the Harcourt place out of his mind for a long while, but now he found himself thinking how it would look with the pear and tulip trees about to start their bloom. He could almost smell the New England spring again, and he could almost feel that Mr. Henry Harcourt was beside him as he talked to Mr. Jacoby. He could even think later that the ghost of Mr. Harcourt must have given him advice and warned him not to miss an opportunity. At any rate Willis grasped the vital fact that the Planeroid process was a very good one. Even before he inspected the plant and the books, he had a good picture of the Rahway problem. The whole answer lay in cutting costs and concentrating first on a single line.

"I'd like to have a look at the Planeroid division if I might," Willis said, and he had been right. It was the only part of the plant that mattered.

It was an opportunity and Willis had been ready for it. He already had a warm spot in his heart for Mr. Jacoby and a protective feeling that was close to loyalty. It was no wonder when little Al was christened that Willis asked Mr. Jacoby to be a godfather. Mr. Jacoby's mind was working too, and it was pleasant for Willis to remember that Mr. Jacoby had trusted him right from the very start.

"What I need," Mr. Jacoby had told him late that afternoon, "is a young fellow who knows this business."

"Well," Willis said, "we've got to look around for someone."

"How about you?" Mr. Jacoby asked.

"Oh," Willis said, "I'm unfortunately working for Beakney-Graham. I'm only here to get things started on the right track, you know, but I do think we can put this property on a paying basis."

"You think so?" Mr. Jacoby asked.

It never paid to be too eager.

"Yes," Willis said, "I think so. I may have a few rather radical ideas, but I hope you'll give us a chance, Mr. Jacoby."

"You show me how we can pay dividends on the preferred," Mr. Jacoby said, "and you can do anything you want. I can handle my associates."

It had been as simple as that, but then after a certain point most negotiations were simple. If anyone wanted something you had to offer badly enough, you could always make him pay.

From the very beginning Willis realized that it was necessary to move carefully. The Rahway Belting Company was a series of fragments that had to be welded together. The personnel and the stockholders and the sales policy were some of these fragments that he must combine without any serious mistake. He would have to use tact and persuasion and ruthlessness. Luck, of course, entered into his handling of Rahway Belt, but his own capacity was always the most important asset.

He wanted very much to talk to someone who would listen as he thought out loud. This was why he called up Sylvia Hodges and asked her to dinner when he reached New York that night—and not because he wanted her advice or applause. He must have understood from the time he had spoken to Sylvia of that green dress in Bergdorf's window that Sylvia was as tired as he was of the small contrivings of mediocrity. He knew that she would have been perfectly happy if he had taken her to some small restaurant in the vicinity of Washington Square, but he took her to dine instead at 21 West 52nd Street, where he had often entertained for the company. Even in those days Twenty-one was already, according to his rather limited knowledge, one of the most interesting restaurants in New York. You always saw personalities there who impressed out-of-town clients—people in the Social Register, individuals whose names were in the gossip columns, actors, Hollywood producers, and sometimes authors and playwrights.

"I sort of thought you'd like to see this place," he told Sylvia. "It's rather interesting, you know. We'll have dinner upstairs, but we might order it at the bar and have a cocktail there while we're waiting. Would you like a Martini, Sylvia? They make very good Martinis."

"Why, yes," Sylvia said, "I'd like one, but you don't have to do these elaborate things for me, you know."

"I know I don't," he said, "but just the same, I like to."

"Well," she said, "I like it more than I ought to, I guess."

It pleased him to observe that people were looking at Sylvia curiously. In Twenty-one people always looked curiously at everyone else, since you could never be sure what stranger might be important. Sylvia was never embarrassed by the plainness of her clothes, and Willis was almost sure that they thought she was too well-known to bother about being elaborately dressed.

"Robert Benchley comes here quite often," Willis said. "You know, Robert Benchley, the humorist."

"Oh," Sylvia said. "He was on the *Lampoon* at Harvard, wasn't he?"

"Yes, I think perhaps he was," Willis said, "but I'm not sure."

It was pleasant to hear Sylvia mention Harvard, and it was pleasant to see that people were trying to catch a snatch of their conversation. It made him feel that he was almost a personal friend of Mr. Benchley, the humorist.

"Have you read his new book, *My Ten Years in a Quandary?*" Sylvia asked.

"In a what?" Willis said.

" 'In a Quandary,' " Sylvia said.

"Oh," Willis said, "I get it now. No. I haven't had much time to read lately, except for fifteen minutes with Dr. Eliot's Five-Foot Shelf before breakfast."

"Do you really do that every morning?" Sylvia asked.

"Of course I do," Willis said. "I try to finish anything I start."

"But, Willis," she said, "it will take you years and years."

"All right," Willis said, "but it's just as well to read something worthwhile, and it's only fifteen minutes a day."

"I wonder why they picked out fifteen minutes," Sylvia said, "instead of twenty-five or thirty minutes."

"Because it sounds easier," Willis said. "It's like the pricing of merchandise. I'm reading Montaigne right now. He's quite a boy, Montaigne."

"But I don't see how you can get much out of Montaigne in fifteen minutes," Sylvia said, and her forehead wrinkled. "Don't you forget what you've read the day before?"

"It was tough at first," Willis said, "but I'm getting the hang of it now. Would you like another Martini, Sylvia?"

"Are you going to have another?" Sylvia asked.

"I don't usually," Willis said, "but I think I will. I've had quite a day today."

He did not mind if Sylvia laughed at him about the Five-Foot Shelf of Books, because he could see the humor in it too, and he knew that Sylvia was not laughing at him seriously.

"Why did you have quite a day?" she asked.

"That's just what I want to tell you," he said, "and I don't know anyone else I want to tell."

Her eyes were bright and there was more color in her cheeks. He had never seen Sylvia look so attractive.

"I guess everybody's always waiting for his chance," he said, "and I have a hunch mine came along today. You see this morning I was sent out to see a plant in Rahway."

He did not have time to go ahead just then because a waiter interrupted him.

"Your dinner is ready, Mr. Wayde, sir," the waiter said. They remembered him, of course, because he brought Beakney-Graham clients there often.

Sylvia listened just the way he hoped she would when he told her about Mr. Jacoby and the Rahway Belting Company, and the way her glance met his when he was talking made everything he said sound like a tale of adventure. If there was one thing he knew, he told her, it was the belting business, and here was his chance right in front of him to put a company on its feet. He was not sure of all the details yet, but he had a general plan, already.

"You wait," he said. "A year from now I'll have the Rahway Belting Company making money."

It was not a heroic statement but his enthusiasm gave it a ringing sound, and Sylvia must have felt its contagion.

"Oh, Willis," she said, "do you really think so?"

All words had a different ring when one was young.

"They've got the Planeroid patents," he said. "Nobody else can make Planeroid."

From the very beginning he was the only one who saw the full potential value of those Planeroid patents.

"Sylvia," he said, and he put his hand over hers without knowing he was doing it, "just wait till you see a sample of Planeroid."

Then Sylvia laughed, but he did not mind, because she did not know what Planeroid was.

"We'll sell the Ford and get a Cadillac before we're through," he said.

He did not realize until the words were out that he had included Sylvia in his vision of the future. In fact he did not realize, until that moment, that he was in love with Sylvia Hodges. It was strange how unexpectedly it had all happened and how naturally they had both accepted it. If it was not all serious, it was partly so, or she would not have said what she said next.

"Willis," she said, "I'm going to spend my vacation with the family. They have a cottage on Lake Sunapee in New Hampshire. I know they'd love to see you, if you'd like to go there too."

He had passed through the preliminaries of courtship without his having known it. Without his ever having kissed her or said a word of love, he knew he was as good as engaged to Sylvia Hodges.

In a busy life it was impossible to recall all dates and sequences, but Willis believed that it was in the summer of 1950 that he had participated in a very worthwhile discussion on the subject of love and marriage. The event had occurred up in Mr. P. L. Nagel's room, where three or four congenial people had gathered, just by accident, just to get away from the noise downstairs during an especially large machine-tool convention at White Sulphur Springs. It must have been August, 1950, because there had been several speeches on the Korean War and it had been a big year for conveyor belts. At any rate there were three or four congenial people up in old P.L.'s room—not a suite due to an error of the management's. Consequently they were sitting around on the twin beds with their coats off, relaxing, and old P.L. had a fine display of bottled goods on his bureau. They were just talking about this and that

—home and kids and golf and gardens—in order to get away from business, when P.L. happened to tell how he had first met Mrs. Nagel.

Willis loved old P.L. by then, and he realized that P.L. had a lot of mellow wisdom, no matter how much bourbon he consumed. He had a glass of it in his hand right then, and he had taken off his shirt. P.L. had met Mrs. Nagel up in the Pinckney office on the seventeenth floor of the Pinckney Building in Chicago, when he had called as a junior executive to carry a message to Jeff Pinckney the year before old Jeff had died of Bright's disease—a tough old rooster and a good old sport, who owned about all the pulpwood in Ontario.

Mrs. Nagel had been the receptionist out in the vestibule, and frankly she had looked like a lot of other receptionists P.L. had met. He had said, "Hello, dearie," to her, not meaning anything at all by it, and she had said he ought to take twenty pounds off before he called anyone "dearie," and one thing led to another, just horsing around waiting for old Pinckney, until he had asked her out to dinner, and that was all there was to it. Mrs. Nagel had been a lovely wife and now she needed to take some pounds off herself. Myrtle's photograph was right there, on the bureau behind the bottles, and he had never regretted for a minute marrying Myrtle. Somehow in business circles if a marriage did not end in divorce no one ever appeared to regret the step.

"And she's a lovely hostess," P.L. said. "If you want a lovely hostess, marry a receptionist. Isn't she a lovely hostess, Cal?"

He was speaking to Cal Biggers, president of Biggers Link and Forging, with whom Willis had been teamed in a foursome that afternoon.

"She isn't any better than Eugenia," Cal Biggers said, "and Eugenia wasn't any receptionist."

"You don't mean Mrs. Biggers?" P.L. said, and he winked to Willis.

"Who the hell else should I mean?" Cal Biggers said.

"I thought Mrs. Biggers's name was Ginny," P.L. said. "I never knew it was Eugenia."

"Ginny's short for Eugenia," Cal Biggers said. "Mrs. Biggers doesn't like the name Eugenia."

Mr. Nagel threw his arm over Mr. Biggers's shoulders.

"Cal, you old sweetheart," he said, "nobody can grill steaks like Ginny, but that isn't my point."

"What the hell is your point?" Mr. Biggers asked.

P. L. Nagel got up, crossed over to the bureau, and poured himself another bourbon.

"Fellas," he said, "I love everybody in this room like my own brother, not that I ever had a brother."

P.L. was a real wit, and it was really pleasant to be up there informally, because he didn't invite just anybody.

"My only point is," P.L. said, "that marriage is an accident. You don't know when you're going to get into it and you really don't know why. If I hadn't gone up to the seventeenth floor of the Pinckney Building, there would have been a different Mrs. Nagel. You don't know what you're getting into until it's over. In fact I didn't really know Mrs. Nagel well until after we were married, and she's developed into a very lovely character."

That was how it was, Willis thought, with him and Sylvia. He had just started going around with her, and finally neither he nor she was going around with anybody else.

Perhaps it was impossible to understand character until after you were married, no matter how much two people had seen of each other before—and he had certainly seen quite a lot of Sylvia the summer he had been working on the reorganization of Rahway Belt. They had fallen into the habit of having a bite to eat together every evening after Willis returned from Rahway—usually at Tony's Italian Restaurant on Bleecker Street—and afterwards they had got in the habit of sitting around awhile in Willis's apartment on Tenth Street, never for very long because Willis had figures to organize and work over every evening. His ideas about the Planeroid process, which did so much to influence his whole career, were already assuming a definite shape. Although Planeroid was designed as power belting, he already believed that some changes in the manufacturing technique could adapt the economical carcass of Planeroid into conveyor belting which would be cheap enough to enter the competitive field.

It was this idea, of course, that finally made Rahway Belt the company that it turned out to be and which helped to make his own industrial reputation. He must have already been thinking of the name that pulled sales promotion together—the Planeroid Carry-All line—but of course all his creative plans were then only in the thought stage. When you had an idea as big as Planeroid Carry-All, you needed to dream dreams. You had to reach the point where you knew those dreams had essential validity before you cut them down to size and began playing with finance and organization. It was a pleasure to tell Sylvia about what he wanted to do, although for some reason he was reticent regarding his earlier days on the Harcourt place, and even at the Harcourt Mill.

Though Sylvia's childhood was different from his, Willis could understand intellectually a lot of the things she had faced. Her parents had never cared about money, but they had cared deeply about education.

Sylvia, as she admitted herself, had always had an ambition to excel in school and college. She had been obliged to face the hard fact that she was not popular at dancing school or dances. She had developed a contempt for clothes and lipstick, and she had carried those ideas to Radcliffe. She had managed to graduate with a *cum laude,* as her father had wanted, but what did it amount to now? It had only taught her that there were a lot of people far brighter than she would ever be, and the last thing that she really wanted was to marry some university instructor and to live the life her mother had. She wanted to have a little fun out of life for once, she said, like having dinner at a place like Twenty-one, and not have to worry about how much it cost. That was one of the wonderful things about Willis, she said—that he never appeared to worry. She wanted to go abroad—not tourist class—and she wanted to stay at hotels instead of pensions. She had seen enough churches and picture galleries to last her all her life, and pensions where girls learned French, like the one she had spent a winter in once on the rue de l'Université.

The first time Willis had ever kissed her was when she told him one June evening at Tenth Street what she really wanted to do in Paris. She made him feel how wonderful Paris was, and even made him forget the Planeroid process for a while.

"Not any stuffy pension in the rue de l'Université," Sylvia was saying, "and not any back seat in the Comédie listening to Racine. I want to go to Foyot's and then to the Folies Bergère."

"Would you like me to take you there?" Willis asked.

"Yes," she said, "on the *Mauretania.*"

"All right," he said, "I'll take you some day, Sylvia."

"I wish we were going tonight," she said. "They always sail at midnight." Then she laughed. She must have been thinking of the crowds and the farewell messages and orchids and champagne and the voices of the room and deck stewards calling out that it was time to go ashore.

"Where's the best place to buy dresses in Paris?" he asked.

"I'd rather go to Worth's than any other," she said.

"Don't worry. I'll take you there," he told her.

It had seemed natural to kiss her then, and she had clung to him, and then she hid her face on his shoulder.

"This doesn't have to mean anything unless you want it to," she said.

Willis had never really known Sylvia until they were married, but he did gain a faint impression of that later Sylvia and a preview of future problems when he went to visit the Hodges family that summer at their cottage on Lake Sunapee.

XV

THE COLUMBIA sociologist for whom Sylvia was working left for a six weeks' trip on the first of July to study the burial, marriage, and other habits of the Zuni Indians, and Sylvia went to stay with her parents at Lake Sunapee until he should return. Although she wrote Willis three or four times a week, letters were not the same as Sylvia. It was fortunate for Willis that complications at Rahway occupied nearly all his waking hours.

There were many later periods of crisis and negotiation in his career which were as arduous and crucial, but he had gained confidence by then so that he never again worked under such strain and pressure as he had in those six weeks. He had to show an external confidence and a serene belief in his judgments which he often did not feel. He had to demonstrate that he knew the belting business, and his comparative youth rendered this most difficult. He had to be a salesman and a promoter and a technical expert all in one, and after he had succeeded in selling the Rahway crowd, he had to go to New York and begin all over again with Beakney-Graham. He always admitted that he could never have handled the Rahway situation without the fine support that Beakney-Graham had given him, especially Joe McKitterick, and there was no wonder he always had a warm spot in his heart for that fine group. Nevertheless, as he once said facetiously later, he was like someone in the circus all that summer, riding a bicycle on a wire and carrying chairs and tables upon both shoulders.

It was all very well to think of Sylvia near a cool lake in New Hampshire, but Willis could not seem to make her understand that he could not dash away for a visit with things going as they were. Nevertheless toward the end of July Willis finally did take three days off, making reservations on the night train Thursday, with return reservations on Sunday. Without ever having been to Lake Sunapee, he had a good idea what it would be like, because he had spent a vacation at Lake Placid once and another near the base of Mt. Washington. He took his golf clubs with him, in case there was an opportunity to shoot a little golf, and his black evening trousers, a cummerbund, and one of those white linen mess jackets which were popular at the time, in case there should be a dance at the country club. He also packed his tennis clothes, because you never knew what you would run into on a three days' vacation. It was a pleasure to watch the porter carrying his golf clubs, his tennis racquet and his new pigskin suitcase when he boarded the evening train.

He arrived at the junction bright and early the next morning, and Sylvia was there to meet him in the Hodgeses' four-year-old Ford runabout. When you were away from someone for some time, perhaps you always built pictures, and somehow Willis had thought that Sylvia would be wearing some sort of print dress. Instead she had on slacks, a man's shirt with a frayed soft collar, and sneakers, and he never forgot her expression when she saw the golf clubs.

"Oh, Willis," she said, "there isn't any golf."

"Oh, that's all right," he said. "I just brought the clubs along in case."

"And there isn't any tennis either," she said. "I don't know why I should have thought you'd know."

"Oh, that's all right," he said. "I'm not any good at tennis anyway."

But she still looked at him doubtfully as he put his suitcase and golf clubs into the rumble seat of the old Ford.

"I don't know why I never described things to you," she said. "We're just here camping out, you know, doing our own work, and I'm afraid you thought there would be a butler."

Of course he had not thought there would be a butler but Sylvia made him feel out of place, even at the junction.

"Well, that's fine," he said. "I've always liked camping out." He did like camping out, although he had never done any of it since he was fifteen, and he was used to housework too, and Sylvia should have known it.

"Willis," she asked, "didn't you bring any old clothes?"

If she had only told him, he could have bought some khaki trousers and sneakers at Abercrombie & Fitch. He could have bought a pocket flashlight too, which he found he needed badly after he discovered that the Hodgeses had no plumbing.

"Well, I haven't got anything exactly old," he said, "just some tennis clothes and bathing trunks, but I'll get along all right."

Sylvia looked relieved when he mentioned bathing trunks.

"You can wear those most of the time and a shirt on top," she said. "Mother always insists on a shirt when we're on the porch."

"Well, that's fine, if it isn't cold," he said.

"It won't be too cold except at night," she told him, "but there are gnats sometimes. Maybe you'd better buy a pair of khaki trousers before we start."

It was a fine idea, and he told her so.

"You pick them out, Sylvia," he told her. "I really do like camping out."

Then in a helpless way she said, "Oh dear, I don't mean to laugh but you keep wanting to buy me ball gowns, and I'm going to buy you a pair of khaki trousers—a present from me to you. Don't you see it's funny?"

It had been a long time since he had seen a small-town men's toggery, but he was able to get into the spirit of it, and it annoyed him that Sylvia seemed to think he couldn't. He was just as good at camping out as she was, he told her, and he liked to fish, he told her. Nothing was more fun than going fishing.

The only trouble was that he had never camped out with any people like the Hodgeses, and that place at Lake Sunapee was different from anything he had ever known. The Hodgeses lived in a shingled cottage on the edge of the lake in a pine grove a long way from anywhere.

"Father bought it for almost nothing during the depression," Sylvia told him, when she tried to explain things while the Ford jolted over a very rough country road.

"Oh dear," Sylvia said, "there's something else I should have told you. Father's against drinking at the cottage, but we could have bought a bottle of something. Maybe Tom has some. He does sometimes."

"You know I don't drink much, Sylvia," Willis said. "It doesn't matter at all." But frequently that week end he would have been less nervous if he could have had a drink.

Once, shortly after Willis had met Lydia Hembird, Lydia had invited him to visit her family in Montclair for a week end, and this had been Willis's only previous experience as an eligible young man. He had not forgotten the embarrassment caused him by the covert watchfulness and elaborately careless questions of Lydia's parents. Yet somehow it had never occurred to Willis until his arrival at Sunapee that his visit to the Hodgeses would offer a similar ordeal. He should have known, of course, from Sylvia's nervousness, and from the moment he saw the family all waiting for him on the front porch, that his visit had an obvious implication. They were a welcoming delegation there to meet him, and he was sure they had been discussing him ever since Sylvia had driven to the station, and, since there were only board partitions between the rooms, Willis heard his name coupled with Sylvia's frequently during his stay, although in tactful whispers.

"They won't be around after supper," he heard them whisper. "Sylvia will want to take him out in the canoe."

"He's really very nice," he heard them whisper. "It isn't his fault that he thought we were living on a golf course."

This last remark had been made by Mr. Hodges, hardly in a whisper. No matter what you might say, Mr. Hodges was a broad-gauged man who knew his way around, even if he seldom went anywhere.

As Willis told Sylvia later, he had been there on approval, like a new vacuum cleaner that could be sent back if it didn't work, not that there were any electric outlets in the cottage. In fact they cooked on a wood stove and went to bed by lamplight, and as Mrs. Hodges said right away, he was a member of the family. Mrs. Hodges, who looked more like a frontierswoman than a professor's wife, shook hands with him warmly and understandingly.

"Of course I remember Willis, dear," she said to Sylvia, "and now you'd better go and peel the potatoes for lunch. You can bring them out on the porch here, dear, and perhaps Willis would like to help you after he puts on some camp clothes, and we can all go on talking about Hitler and the Rhineland and whatever is going to become of it."

"Yes, yes, Sylvia," Mr. Hodges said, "my memory isn't so dim that I don't recall your young gentleman." Mr. Hodges had not shaved that morning, and he wore khaki shorts and a sleeveless undershirt. "There's only one rule around here, Wayde. We wear shirts when we're on the porch. For some reason Mrs. Hodges objects to bare torsos. You'd better strip down, Wayde, and excuse my legs. I admit I have varicose veins."

"I understand they have something they can inject into them now, sir," Willis said.

"Yes," Mr. Hodges said, "silicate, I believe, but I'll leave mine just the way they are. You remember Laura, don't you?"

Of course Willis remembered Laura. Laura was wearing slacks like Sylvia and she looked frankly and adjustedly ugly.

"I choose you for my team if we play games tonight," she said. It touched Willis that Laura remembered that he had been good at pencil-and-paper games.

"Mary, dear," Mrs. Hodges said, "I don't believe you've ever met Sylvia's young man, have you? This is Tom's wife, Willis."

Mary Hodges was a stocky, red-faced girl in shorts. It seemed to Willis that girls with ugly legs always wanted to show them off.

"Hi," she said, and she shook hands aggressively. "You're sleeping in the guest coop."

The guest coop, Willis found out later, was a remodeled brooder house that Tom had purchased from a nearby farm. Tom was always working on what he called "improvement projects."

"Hi, Willis," Tom said. His shirt and bathing trunks and bare arms were caked with clay. "You look as though you've been battening off the workers down there in New York."

Willis felt his face redden. Sylvia had told him that Tom was interested in the CIO, and he certainly did not want to get into a labor argument.

"The way I feel, Tom," he said, "is that the workers are feeding off management just at present. At least that's the way it is down at my belting company."

He should not theoretically have called it his company, but he felt that he had to make some sort of impression.

"You come with me," Tom said, "and you'll see what labor means. Mary and I are laying a new pipe from the spring to the kitchen."

Willis must have looked startled. Sylvia might have warned him about the absence of plumbing, and Tom burst into a roar of laughter.

"There's no private bath, no telephone—and no water if we don't get busy. Come on, Mary, or we'll have to haul it in buckets."

Willis did not mind about the plumbing, but he had never dreamed there would not be a telephone, and he had some notes in his pocket for a call he wished to make to Rahway.

"Don't worry, Willis," Sylvia said, "there's a telephone half a mile down the road and I can run you there any time."

"No you can't," Laura said. "It's my turn for the Ford."

"Then we can walk," Sylvia said. "Willis likes to walk."

"The thing for you to remember, Wayde," Mr. Hodges said, "is that we are only living for a split second geologically. This present interglacial epoch is only fifteen or twenty minutes old geologically. I often find comfort in this fact, and maybe you will too before you return to city life."

"Don't discourage him, Father," Sylvia said. "I'll take him to the guest coop now."

Willis had never thought of Sylvia in this environment; she seemed surprisingly adjusted to it. When they were in the guest coop, she kissed him. It was not much of a kiss because he struck his head against a two-by-four on the roof.

"Just remember," Sylvia whispered, "it's only a split second geologically."

Willis always prided himself on being able to get along with people even if their interests were quite different from his own. He liked to

[193]

think that he had succeeded with the Hodgeses in a measure. But he had never been in a group in which he had felt so inadequate. He would not have minded the simple life if it had been simple, but the Hodgeses neglected the advantages of simplicity and the small creature comforts understood by practical campers. Not one of them knew how to split kindling for the stove properly or how to keep the stove going once it was lighted, and what was more, they honestly did not care. Hardly a breath of air stirred in the pine grove, the sun's reflection glared at them from the glassy surface of the lake, but the Hodgeses did not heed the heat or the gnats.

All the Hodgeses cared about were ideas and talk. One minute they were telling jokes in French and next they were lapsing into German. Then suddenly they would be discussing the immoralities of the Emperor Tiberius and early Christianity in the Roman Empire, which led to the subject of Byzantine influence. The minds of the Hodgeses darted from point to point, like the dragonflies above the lake. They all talked at once—Mrs. Hodges, Sylvia, Mary, Laura, and Tom. It seemed to Willis that Mr. Hodges was the only one who listened, but he too enjoyed every minute of it, and he too would occasionally leap into the discussion. Admitting it was all worthwhile, Willis could find no ending and no beginning.

It seemed that Laura and Tom and Mary had just returned from Europe and they had stayed, as the Hodgeses always had, at a small pension in the rue de l'Université. Remembering what Sylvia had said about this place, Willis glanced at her sympathetically, but Sylvia seemed to have forgotten that she had complained of it. She was listening to Tom give what she called a "free lecture." Instead of being bored by it, Sylvia exhibited a deep respect for Tom.

The inevitable conflict was starting already, Tom was saying, between Nazism and Communism. A decadent capitalistic system inevitably turned to Nazism as a last resort, like the Franco forces in Spain and the Hitler rule in Germany.

"You agree with that, Willis," Tom said, "don't you? Intellectually if not emotionally?"

It was very hot, and Willis kept wishing they would go for a swim but no one suggested it.

"I guess this is all a little over my head," Willis said. "I only know what I read in the papers, like Will Rogers." He laughed and everyone laughed too, briefly and sympathetically.

It was a great relief when Sylvia finally asked him to go for a walk. It had suddenly dawned on her that Willis had not seen anything of the lake, and this fact seemed to dawn on everyone else too at the same instant.

"Why, Willis has just been sitting here, hasn't he?" Mrs. Hodges said.

"I hate to miss any of this wonderful talk," Willis said, "but I would like to take a walk."

Almost the only time the Hodgeses were silent during his visit was when he and Sylvia walked down to the lake path. It was very hot and he stumbled occasionally over pine roots.

"You have to watch where you're going," Sylvia said. "This is an awfully rough path."

"You get a beautiful view from it," Willis said.

"Willis, dear, I'm so proud of you," Sylvia said. "Everyone thinks you're wonderful. Mother and Laura have said so already, and Mary wishes Tom could be more like you. You're having a good time, aren't you?"

"Yes," Willis said, "it's great to get away from the city and get some new ideas."

"Can't you stay for a day or two more and not go back Sunday night?"

"I wish I could," Willis said, and he stumbled over another pine root. "It's been quite a while since I've been walking in the woods."

"You have to get used to it," Sylvia said. "Father's very interested in you."

"I suppose he is," Willis said. "I guess I can't blame him much."

"Oh, dear," Sylvia said, "I didn't mean it in that way, but he probably will try to draw you out. You don't mind if he draws you out, do you?"

Of course he and Mr. Hodges would have to have a little talk sometime, but Mr. Hodges did nothing about it until Sunday afternoon, and then it happened unexpectedly.

"Say, Wayde," Mr. Hodges said, "are you any good in a canoe?"

Willis's father had taught him to paddle, one summer when he had been working for paper interests in Ontario, but once you learned a thing like that, you never wholly forgot it. There was another of those silences while Willis and Mr. Hodges stepped off the porch and pushed the Hodgeses' canoe into the water. Willis was feeling tired by then, because he had not slept well in the guest coop, and his muscles were stiff from walking and swimming. You could tell from the moment anyone picked up a paddle whether or not he knew about canoes, and Mr. Hodges must have learned somewhere besides Lake Sunapee.

"You've been with Indians sometime, haven't you?" Mr. Hodges said.

"Yes, sir," Willis answered, "with my father once in Ontario."

"You must have watched them," Mr. Hodges said. "You can always tell. I made quite a study of Indian paddling in Minnesota once."

Willis was not surprised, because it seemed to him that Mr. Hodges knew something of everything.

"If Horace could ever have been in a canoe, he would have liked it," Mr. Hodges said.

"Horace, sir?" Willis said. He thought that he must have missed a name somewhere and that perhaps Mr. Hodges had a brother named Horace.

"The Latin poet," Mr. Hodges said.

"Oh yes," Willis said, "Horace. I don't know much about him, I'm afraid."

"Don't be," Mr. Hodges said. "Never be afraid of Horace. Sylvia tells me you're making ten thousand dollars a year. Do you hope to make some more?"

"Yes, sir," Willis said. "And I think I will, if what I'm doing turns out right."

"Sylvia says you have something to do with machine belts."

Seated as he was in the bow of the canoe, Willis could only hear Mr. Hodges without seeing him.

"Yes, sir," he said, "it's the only thing I really know about. At least I hope I do."

"I don't," Mr. Hodges said. "My mind's a blank when it comes to belts."

"Well, sir," Willis said, "frankly mine's a blank when it comes to Horace."

"Dear me," Mr. Hodges said, "there have to be zeros somewhere. Four zeros in ten thousand dollars, and more in a million. That's the trouble with money, there must be a lot of zeros."

Willis wished he knew whether Mr. Hodges was being funny or serious, but it was a good remark and one Willis always remembered. Mr. Hodges had been right. You had to sacrifice a lot of things if you made money.

"Last May, sir," he said, "I met a friend of yours in New York—Mr. Hawley, president of the Hawley Pneumatic Tool."

"Hawley," Mr. Hodges said, "Hawley—oh yes. I didn't like him very much."

"I didn't like him much either," Willis said, "but I wouldn't like to have him know it."

"Well," Mr. Hodges said, "I'm glad you didn't. Sylvia tells me you're reading the Five-Foot Shelf of Books—fifteen minutes a day. Why?"

Willis could not turn around. He hoped that he would never again have a serious conversation with anyone when he paddled bow in a canoe.

"I wonder," Mr. Hodges said before Willis could answer, "if you're doing that to please Sylvia. I wouldn't if I were you. Women are intellectual snobs, but I wouldn't let that worry me."

"No, sir," Willis answered, "I'm doing it for myself."

"Well," Mr. Hodges said, "I confess it shows initiative."

Neither of them spoke for a while, and Willis was glad to listen to the dipping of the paddles in the water.

"I'm afraid," Mr. Hodges said, "you've taken quite a beating this week end. Do you still like Sylvia?"

"Yes, sir," Willis said. "It's been very interesting here."

"I've been interested too," Mr. Hodges said, "but then you'd expect me to be, wouldn't you, in my position? Sylvia's always been an independent girl, and perhaps she needs some zeros." He laughed so unexpectedly that Willis missed a stroke. "Perhaps I could do with a few myself. I wouldn't mind some electric light and some water here, within limits. If I may say so, if I were you I wouldn't try too hard to be something that I'm not. Perhaps we'd better turn back now, or Sylvia will be wondering where you are."

That was almost the only serious conversation that Willis ever had with Mr. Hodges, and he always felt that Mr. Hodges had learned more about him than most people did—too much, perhaps. He was glad that he had been able to fix up that camp for the Hodgeses eventually, with electricity and running water, with an electric stove, a refrigerator and a dishwasher and even with a small inboard motorboat, and chairs that you could sit on without pain; yet Willis was never positive that Mr. Hodges had liked these improvements. The last time that Willis ever saw the lake was when he went there with Sylvia, who was settling the estate. It had seemed to him that Mr. Hodges had been watching, and Willis remembered his short laugh when he had spoken about zeros.

The last time Willis Wayde had seen the Hodgeses' house on Craigie Street was when he took Sylvia and their eldest son, Alfred, to the Harvard-Yale game in late November, 1950. The idea had been Sylvia's more than his. He had a business meeting in New York about five days ahead of the game date, and since he was in New York he had planned to stop in Boston to talk over some refinancing ideas with his friend Jerry Harwood, president of the Shawmut Insurance and Accident. They might say he was crazy in Chicago, but he still liked doing business with the Boston crowd.

Then, just when his plans were shaping up, Sylvia had suggested the Harvard-Yale game. She had pointed out that Alfred had started in at Middlesex that autumn and that it would be nice for Willis to show him the Harvard buildings and to let him hear the songs and cheering. It was time for Alfred to get used to the idea that he might be going to Harvard. Also it might be that Tom and Mary and their children would be going to the game too, and Tom and Mary might be able to put them up in Brookline.

Willis had drawn the line at Brookline. At least he could be comfortable when he was making a business trip, and be able to relax between conferences. However, he did want to see Alfred, and he certainly understood how Sylvia felt about Cambridge. He was delighted to have Sylvia make the trip with him and he set up the schedule accordingly. He was able to get a suite for the week end at the Ritz in Boston, and Hank Knowlton, the New England representative, got three good seats on the Harvard side and a Cadillac with a good driver, even though Sylvia had suggested a Drive-Urself car.

The only complication was a small company cocktail party arranged by Hank in the sitting room for late Saturday afternoon so that he could meet a few people whom he really had to see. Otherwise his time belonged to Sylvia and Al, who would stay with them from Saturday noon on through Sunday. He had even agreed with Sylvia to have Sunday lunch with Tom and Mary and their children in Brookline, as long as they drove there comfortably in the rented Cadillac.

He had been in conference for two hours with Jerry Harwood on Saturday morning, and he was feeling pretty tired when he got back to the sitting room at the Ritz and found that Al had already arrived.

"Well, hello, Al," he said. "How's tricks?"

Al looked as neat as a pin, because Sylvia had given him a good going over in the bathroom. He wore gray slacks and a brown tweed jacket, and he looked like a miniature college boy already.

"Hey, Pops," Al shouted—he could never keep his voice down when he was excited, "when do we eat?"

"Right here and now," Willis said. "Lunch is coming right up, and we've got to eat it quick."

"Jeepers creepers," Al shouted, "do we have to eat in this dump? Can't we grab a hot dog somewhere?"

"We're going to eat right here," Willis said, "and the car's coming to take us to Cambridge in half an hour."

"Jeepers creepers," Al shouted, "you don't mean we're going to the game in some old Cadillac?"

"Don't shout," Willis said. "I can hear you perfectly. What other means of transportation would you suggest?"

"Can't we go in the subway," Al asked, "and push along with the crowd?"

"The subway would take us right to the Larz Anderson Bridge," Sylvia said.

Willis sighed and sat down.

"Even if it's a hardship we're going in a car," he said.

As a matter of fact, due to traffic congestion it was advisable to leave the car and to push along with the crowd down Boylston Street and over the Larz Anderson Bridge. Willis felt unusually happy being there with Sylvia and Al. He was particularly glad that Sylvia was wearing her coat of wild mink. It was better-looking than any other coat he observed in the crowd around them.

As they approached the Charles River the landmarks were partly familiar and partly new. On his left the magnificent blocks of brick houses, the gift of the late Mr. Harkness, had become an integral part of the scene. The buildings of the Harvard Business School across the river, which had been aggressively new when he had been there, had been softened by the winters.

It looked as though it would rain during the second half of the Yale game, but fortunately the rain held off. Willis had not been caught by the contagion of the crowd. Instead he had been trying to follow his old footsteps made over twenty years ago. He was the Willis Wayde of the present, and it was time to find the Cadillac, which would be waiting for them on Massachusetts Avenue as near as possible to the subway station at Harvard Square. They could reach the Cadillac in ten minutes if they hurried, and fortunately all the football crowd was now in a hurry to get somewhere. There was that little gathering of a few associates for cocktails in the suite at the Ritz. You could not be casual about such things, and you were always judged by the way they were handled. Sylvia and Al would give it a pleasant homelike touch—people were always pleased when you introduced them to the family.

It was later than he thought by the time they found their Cadillac, and it was a great relief to be sitting beside Sylvia and Al, out of the crowd at last.

"Willis," Sylvia said, "before we go back can't we drive down Craigie Street?"

"Now, Sylvia," he told her, and he found himself speaking carefully, "it's in just the opposite direction and we really should be at the Ritz on time."

"It's only a few minutes out of the way," Sylvia said, "and Al has never seen it."

"Hasn't he?" Willis asked.

"Come on," Al said, "let's go, Pops."

"All right," Willis said. "I thought of course he'd seen it at some time or other." And he told the driver to drive slowly when they finally reached Craigie Street. Except for the traffic, Brattle and Craigie Streets had not changed much.

"There used to be a drinking fountain for horses here," Sylvia said. "Do you remember?"

"No," Willis answered. "What drinking fountain?"

"Perhaps it wasn't here when you were," Sylvia said.

Somehow you always thought of Cambridge in autumn and winter without leaves on the trees. The street lights were on and the early dark of late autumn was beginning to obscure the outlines, but Craigie Street looked about the same and the old Hodges house had not changed at all. It seemed to Willis, when he saw it through the plate glass of the Cadillac side-window, that he was gazing at an exhibit in a museum case. It was still that durable beige color, the same sodden tint as the dead grass on its little square of lawn, and the same bare syringa bushes grew by the front steps.

"Well," Willis said, "there it is, Al. That's where your mother used to live."

"Gosh," Alfred said, "did Mommy used to live in that old shack?"

His young voice startled Willis.

"That's no way to talk, son," he said. "That's where your grandfather wrote his book. You've seen it in the library, haven't you?"

"I'll bet you've never read it, Pops," Al said. "It's all about old sandstone."

"I haven't read it all, son," Willis said, "but that's because I'm not bright enough." The car was moving down Craigie Street. They would reach Concord Avenue in a moment, but the memory of the house seen through the plate glass was still there.

"Well, I guess he didn't make much money," Alfred said, "or he wouldn't have lived in a shack like that."

Willis wished that Sylvia were not there.

"Money isn't everything, son," Willis said. "Your grandfather was a professor. Professors aren't expected to make money."

"I guess he wasn't as much of a success as you, Pops," Alfred said.

Willis felt his cheeks grow hot.

"That isn't so, son," he said. "Your grandfather was more of a success than I'll ever be. Maybe I've made more money, but money isn't everything."

It was curious to be facing truth on Craigie Street and to be telling it to his and Sylvia's son. All at once Sylvia put her hand over his and he was very glad she did not speak.

"Sylvia," he said, "I wish we could have done more for them."

[200]

"You did all you could, dear," Sylvia said, and this was true.

"Sylvia," he said, "is my mother's photograph in my suitcase?"

"Yes, dear," Sylvia said.

"That's fine," Willis said. "I was afraid that maybe I'd left it in the St. Regis. We've got to get it out as soon as we get back." He pressed the button that automatically opened the window behind the driver. "And now take us to the Ritz," Willis said.

It was almost impossible to believe that Sylvia and Al and he had driven down Craigie Street in a Cadillac, even if it was not his own, and he had a sense of uneasiness. He could not call it discontent. There were too many things to think about that had nothing to do with the Ritz.

"Sylvia," he said, "Jerry Harwood's dropping in. I don't think you've ever met old Jerry, but he isn't hard to talk to. He has a son in Harvard, and he's president of the Shawmut Insurance and Accident. We had a very interesting talk this morning."

Exactly what was success, he was wondering. Perhaps it was nothing tangible but rather a state of mind that made you content within the frame where life had placed you.

XVI

THE YEARS immediately preceding the entry of the United States into the Second World War formed the most critical and important period in the entire business career of Willis Wayde. Willis became increasingly aware that he had traveled during all that time along the narrow line that always divides business success from failure, and the wavering thinness of that demarcation still filled him with amazement. He could think of a dozen separate occasions when any deviation from his course would have led him to disaster, and a number of individuals would have rejoiced at his defeat. You could not be loved by everybody when you reorganized a firm like Rahway Belt. All you could do was recognize your enemies without being influenced by emotion and select them with thoughtful care, because it was important to select enemies as carefully as friends.

It was strange, when Willis looked backward, that the business turmoil of those years—the reorganizing of Rahway Belt, his leaving Beakney-Graham, the new plant construction with its financial problems, and the promotion of the Planeroid line—all frequently seemed simpler than many aspects of his private life. It was all very well to say, as so many men he knew kept saying, that business and home should never mix. They invariably did. They always ran together blurring outlines, no matter how carefully you might try to separate them. Although nothing was really settled after that week end at Lake Sunapee, Willis discovered that Sylvia thought a great deal had been. Shortly after this visit she bought several books on cooking and began making out his laundry list and going over his shirts and his socks whenever she visited his apartment. Thus the idea of imminent marriage came over them by degrees, making another problem on top of all his others.

There was also the problem of Lydia Hembird, who finally telephoned one evening when Sylvia was at Tenth Street. There was nothing serious about Lydia at all, which explained why Willis had never mentioned her to Sylvia. Sylvia had come up with him to the apartment after dining at Tony's, and she had been reading a cook book to herself. He had told her that he had to go over the refinancing report on Rahway Belt. He was right in the middle of the proposed common-stock setup, which demanded more close thinking than anything else (because even if the common stock had never paid a dividend, it was the key point in any future situation), when the telephone on the writing table rang, and it was Lydia Hembird.

"Hello, Willis, darling," Lydia said, "are you up there all alone?"

"Oh, hello," he said, "hello."

"Why have you gone completely out of my life, darling?" Lydia said.

"Well," he said, "I've been pretty busy lately."

He saw that Sylvia had closed the cook book, and he smiled at her reassuringly, but Lydia was still speaking.

"Darling, why don't you come up here right now?" she said.

"I've got to hang up," Willis said. "I can't talk to you right now."

There was a frigid silence when he set down the telephone.

"I'm sorry, Sylvia," he said. "It was only someone I used to know before I knew you were in New York."

Sylvia was white and tense and her voice was lightly brittle.

"Why didn't you ever tell me about her?" she asked. "I'm sure I don't want to interfere with anything."

"Listen, Sylvia," he said. "There isn't anything to tell about her. She's just someone I used to know."

Sylvia drew a sharp, quick breath.

"Willis," she said, "I wish you'd tell me when you think we can get married."

Willis squared his shoulders. The subject was up again and he knew that he had been avoiding it unconsciously.

"Now, Sylvia, dear," he said, "I'm glad you brought this up, because it's been on my mind as much as yours."

He could not understand why he felt so nervous, except that he was dealing with a long-term future and life and love and all sorts of other things that were hard to express.

"I'm glad I brought it up too," Sylvia said. "It's awfully hard for a girl to be so indefinite. You do love me, don't you, Willis?"

"Of course I love you," Willis said.

"Then sit here and hold my hand," Sylvia said, "and don't look so worried, Willis. You want us to get married, don't you?"

It was not the way, he was thinking, to conduct a serious conversation.

"Why, of course I want us to get married, honey," he said, and he smiled at her and patted her hand, "but I do have a lot of other things on my mind right now."

"But, Willis," she said, "don't you think that this is more important?"

Willis found himself patting her hand again.

"Absolutely, honey," he said. "It's the most important thing in the world, and because it is, I want things to be set."

"But aren't they?" Sylvia said. "I don't see why we can't get married any time."

"Well, naturally," he said, "of course we could, Sylvia, but for example, I'd like to wait until we know whether I'll be working for Beakney-Graham or whether I'll end up out in Rahway."

"Why, Willis," Sylvia said, "I didn't know you were having any trouble with Beakney-Graham. Didn't they just give you a raise of two thousand dollars?"

"Sylvia, sweetness," Willis said—it was always harder to explain business to a woman than to a man—"if the Rahway Belting Company would make me an offer and give me some common stock, I'd leave Beakney-Graham, because there would be a better future in Rahway."

He could not understand why Sylvia should look troubled, but then perhaps a woman's mind always worked differently from a man's.

"But they sent you there to Rahway Belt," she said.

"Of course they sent me there," Willis answered, and he tried to keep any trace of impatience out of his voice, "but I want you and me to have a future, dear. I don't have to stay with Beakney-Graham."

"But, Willis," she asked him, "do you think that's being loyal?"

He did not intend to be impatient, but she should have seen that loyalty had nothing whatsoever to do with the situation. It simply showed that Sylvia did not know where loyalty began or ended.

"You wouldn't say that," he said, "if you understood the picture, Sylvia. I'm earning every cent that Beakney-Graham is paying me, and more besides. I can't help it, can I, if I'm making a place for myself in Rahway? That's the way the world is, and it hasn't got anything to do with loyalty."

He did not mean to get excited but her whole point of view was preposterous.

"You've got to let me attend to these things, dear," he said, "and let me decide what's loyal and what isn't. What are you crying for, Sylvia?"

There was no reason whatsoever for Sylvia to sit sobbing, with tears rolling down her cheeks, when he was trying to carry on a sensible conversation.

"Oh, Willis," she sobbed. "I didn't mean to make you angry. It's only that I'm so proud of you that I don't want—I don't want—"

"Now, there, Sylvia," he said, and he took her in his arms. "Just let me do the worrying. Don't forget it's a pretty tough world, honey. Everything's going to be all right. Old Jacoby wants to have a talk with me. He's asked me to his house to lunch next week. Everything's going to be wonderful."

"Oh, Willis," she sobbed, "of course you're loyal."

Loyalty was the damnedest thing. It was something that kept cropping up in business at eccentric intervals, and it kept requiring a different definition. At any rate, he had made his point and he had never had to argue in just that way with Sylvia about loyalty again. You had to do the best you could with loyalty. She had stopped crying, and he gave her a clean pocket handkerchief.

It was always significant when a business acquaintance asked you to his home instead of some restaurant. At the very least it meant that he considered you socially suitable to meet the family, and it might also be a gesture that marked the end of mere acquaintance. It signified a decline in watchfulness and a lowering of barriers. It was a time of trial and testing for both guest and host.

In spite of the months that Willis had been working closely in Rahway with Mr. Manley Jacoby, Mr. Jacoby had never invited him to his home. Mr. Jacoby had been slightly apologetic when he finally invited Willis. He had been meaning, Mr. Jacoby said, to ask Willis up to the house for quite a while, and he was sorry that he was asking him home for the first time in order to have a business talk, but things always got around the plant, and he had a few words to say to Willis which were confidential.

"I guess you know already what they are," Mr. Jacoby said, "but at the same time I'm inviting you as a friend."

It had sounded rather like one of Mr. Henry Harcourt's invitations long ago.

"It's very kind of you, sir," Willis said. "Thank you very much."

"Mrs. Jacoby wants especially to meet you," Mr. Jacoby said, "and I want her to sit in on the conference."

Willis knew by then that Mrs. Jacoby was the daughter of the late Mr. Seth Wilfred, a financier whose name was still very well known around the Oranges, and that she had inherited a very considerable sum of money at her father's death, so much in fact that Mr. Jacoby could have retired at any time he wanted during the last few years. Willis also knew that the Jacobys had two married daughters, one living in Chicago and the other in Philadelphia. There was no reason for Mr. Jacoby to make any explanations but it was like him to have done so.

Promptly at half past twelve Mr. Jacoby put on his black alpaca coat and climbed behind the wheel of his old Buick.

"Get in, Willis," he said. "Mrs. Jacoby thinks I ought to have a chauffeur, but I guess I'm independent in some ways. You have to be with anybody like Mrs. Jacoby. I suppose you've heard she's pretty rich."

"Yes, sir," Willis said. "You can't help hearing things like that."

"That's right," Mr. Jacoby said. "I suppose that Jack Meister or Peters told you, and since we're going home to lunch I'd just as soon you'd call me Manley."

It was hard for Willis to call old men by their first names, and to stay respectful and at the same time familiar.

"Mrs. Jacoby—Edie, that is—makes me pretty comfortable," Mr. Jacoby said. "We live in the old Wilfred house, you know, built in 1900 out of field stone sort of like a pudding. Maybe you can guess what it's named."

Willis tried to laugh easily. There was a purpose, he knew, behind Mr. Jacoby's confidence, and he wanted to be particularly careful.

"You'd better tell me, Manley," he said. The first name sounded so awkward that he was afraid he had used it too soon. "I'm no good at guessing."

"The name is Rock Crest," Mr. Jacoby said, and he laughed, too.

"The great thing about a stone house is that it's always warm in winter and cool in summer," Willis said.

"Yes, that's a fact," Mr. Jacoby answered, "and we have quite a view from it."

It was a grim house, standing on a lawn decorated by canna lilies on the ridge of basalt that rose behind the Oranges. Even its porte-cochere was built of lumpy field stone, but the view was magnificent. It was a warm hazy day in mid-September, and you could see the buildings of downtown New York miles away across the marshes, rising dreamily through the mist.

"It rolls out like an Axminster carpet, doesn't it?" Mr. Jacoby said as he climbed out of the car. "I told you it was a view."

It was all different from anything that Willis had imagined. After the plainness of Rahway Belt, he could not help but be surprised when a manservant opened the door.

"Hello," Mr. Jacoby said, and he looked like a small-town visitor in his black alpaca coat. "Is Mrs. Jacoby downstairs yet?"

"Madam is in the east room," the houseman said.

Willis saw many other houses like Rock Crest later. They were too large to live in now but so firmly built that they withstood destruction. They were survivals of the hopeful income-taxless age at the turn of the century, an age which apparently had produced thousands of successful individuals who thought that the mode of life they knew would remain unchanged for centuries. It was startling now to observe the remnants of their culture, now that no one was sure how long he would live anywhere.

The past and the ambitions of the late Mr. Seth Wilfred were preserved with embarrassing clarity in the rooms and furnishings of Rock Crest. His desire for display must have exceeded that of most of his contemporaries. He must have been an arrogant, self-made man of a species which could not exist today, for no self-made man that Willis had ever met would have dared to express his personality so flamboyantly. The east room, as it was called, took up two stories and must have been intended to represent a baronial hall. There was a balcony at one end which was occupied by musicians, as Mrs. Jacoby told him once, when her father had receptions for the directors of the Erie Railroad. There was also an immense pipe organ that no longer worked and a huge fieldstone fireplace. There were some heads of African animals on the walls and some sentimental pictures of cows and sheep and another of French aristocrats going to the guillotine. The floors were covered with Oriental carpets and the furniture was imitation French.

"Quite a little room, isn't it?" Mr. Jacoby said. "I thought it would surprise you. I guess you never pictured me coming home to anything like this."

"It certainly is remarkable," Willis told him.

"You get used to it," Mr. Jacoby said. "But I remember the first time Edie brought me in here to meet the old man. He was in a wheel chair but I was scared. Edie—oh, there you are."

Mrs. Jacoby was seated on a sofa by the fireplace, and her lacy beige dress gave her almost a protective coloring. Her face, which was pale and distinguished, reminded him more of an old man's than a woman's. Her hair was snow white, but her eyebrows were black and bushy, and her eyes were deep brown. She spoke in a precise, almost English way, because, as she told Willis later, she had been taught at a convent school in France.

"I'm delighted to meet you, Willis," she said. "I'm calling you Willis because Manley has told me so much about you."

"It's a great pleasure, Mrs. Jacoby," Willis said, and he tried to act as though he were not astonished by anything around him. It all went to show that no matter how well you knew someone in business, you could not tell how he lived until he took you home.

"You mustn't blame Mr. Jacoby for any of this," Mrs. Jacoby said.

"He married into it quite late in life, and what could we have done except tear the whole thing down?"

"I see what you mean," Willis said, "but everything's very interesting."

"Manley," Mrs. Jacoby said, "if I send Henry upstairs for something else, will you take off that black alpaca coat? Look how nice Willis looks."

"He's a new model," Mr. Jacoby said. "You know I like this coat."

"Manley never wants to forget he's a small-town boy," Mrs. Jacoby said, and she looked unblinkingly at Willis. "Perhaps you've noticed that Manley has an independent streak. That's why he insists on holding onto that one-horse factory. He doesn't need to, but he likes to be independent and he can't keep on being, with his arthritis. That's why I asked him to bring you up here—so I could look at you."

Willis was partially adjusted to the surroundings by then. For a short while the experience had been like falling by mistake into cold water, but now he had reached the surface. He was thinking that Mrs. Jacoby reminded him of someone in the past. He could not remember who until he thought of Mrs. Blood, but Mrs. Jacoby was more masterful. He could not help wondering why she had ever married Mr. Jacoby, who, as she said, was a small-town boy, and what accident had brought them together or what spirit of revolt had made her seek him out, but then perhaps Mr. Jacoby had been young and attractive once.

"How would it be if we had cocktails, Edie?" Mr. Jacoby said. "It might help us all to break the ice and you'd get to know Willis better."

"Not for me, thank you," Willis said quickly. "I don't usually drink in the middle of a business day, Mrs. Jacoby."

"Well, I'm going to ring for Henry, Edie," Mr. Jacoby said. "I'm going to have a Scotch and soda."

"As long as you take your medicine with it, Manley," Mrs. Jacoby said. "Go ahead and have your Scotch and soda. I want to talk to Willis."

Mrs. Jacoby walked over to a mother-of-pearl-inlaid table and picked up a sheaf of papers bound in a handsome morocco cover and Willis gave a slight start. It was the final report and recommendations by Beakney-Graham for the Rahway Belting Company.

"Now," Mrs. Jacoby said. "We may as well sit down and we can start going over this before lunch is served. Manley tells me that you wrote most of it."

"Yes, most of it," Willis said, "but I was helped by other members of my company, and of course we had engineering and technical assistance."

Mrs. Jacoby picked up a pair of heavy horn-rimmed glasses.

"I read this with great interest," she said. "It's a well-organized report. I told Manley to employ Beakney-Graham."

The light from Mrs. Jacoby's glasses glittered disconcertingly as Willis tried to think of a suitable answer.

"I had an idea that the bank had suggested our company," he said.

Mr. Jacoby laughed in a brief and rather mournful way.

"They did," he said, "but Edie suggested it to the bank. She wears the pants around here, or at least she tries to."

"I wish you wouldn't get off these tiresome jokes, Manley," Mrs. Jacoby said. "I've always let you play around with that factory of yours and I've never interfered, except when it's been absolutely necessary."

Willis was glad to see that the houseman was walking toward them across that enormous room, carrying a silver tray and a decanter and tumblers, all of heavy cut glass, because the interruption gave him a moment to think over the situation.

"Manley," Mrs. Jacoby said, "be sure to take your medicine first, and I'll have some Scotch too. Are you sure you won't change your mind, Mr. Wayde—I mean Willis?"

"If you'll forgive me, I'd rather not," Willis said. "I'm afraid a lot of that report must have been dull reading, Mrs. Jacoby."

He was interested to see that Mrs. Jacoby drank her Scotch neat, following it by a little water as a chaser.

"I wouldn't say that any reports are light reading," Mrs. Jacoby said, "but my father trained me to manage my own affairs. Oh, I know what you're thinking."

"I wasn't thinking anything, Mrs. Jacoby," Willis said, and he tried to look through the reflection on her glasses.

"You needn't be polite," Mrs. Jacoby answered. "I know just what men think when old women say they handle their own affairs. They think they're being silly. Well, I'm not silly."

"I'm sure you're not, Mrs. Jacoby," Willis said quickly. "I'm sorry you thought I was thinking any such thing."

"Maybe you weren't, then," Mrs. Jacoby said. "Manley says you're very quick."

"That's right," Mr. Jacoby said. "He's smart. Don't underrate him, Edie."

"My father—that's Mr. Seth Wilfred, you know—always said never underrate anyone until you knew him," Mrs. Jacoby said, "and I don't know you well enough to underrate you yet. I want this first meeting of ours to be frank. I've personally managed all my father's interests since his death. I got out of the market in August, 1929. I got back in again in the summer of '32. I have my own offices upstairs."

"That's right," Mr. Jacoby said. "Edie's a very able woman, Willis."

"Now, Manley," Mrs. Jacoby said, "I wish you'd step outside for a minute, but as long as you won't you'll have to let me do the talking."

Mr. Jacoby laughed again, in a short, resigned way.

"I brought the young man here," he said, "for you to talk to him, didn't I?"

Since his days at the Harcourt Mill, Willis had seen a good many rich men, and he was beginning to judge their abilities and weaknesses, but he was not so familiar with the wealthy and independent woman. These people, he had always supposed, were under the care and guidance of lawyers, bankers, and investment counselors, as Mrs. Blood and Mrs. Henry Harcourt had been. Although he could see that Mrs. Jacoby was different, he still could not define the difference. He could only listen carefully, but the difficulty was that she talked partly like a woman and partly like a man.

"Now you know as well as I do," Mrs. Jacoby said, "that Manley here hasn't got much business sense."

Willis found himself laughing nervously.

"Oh, I wouldn't go so far as to say that," he said.

"I didn't say you would," Mrs. Jacoby told him, "but you know it and Manley knows it too. You have ideas in your report that I've known all along. Manley has surrounded himself with second-rate people. He has vision but no business sense."

Willis glanced at Mr. Jacoby and was surprised to discover that he was smiling.

"Now, Mrs. Jacoby," Willis began, "I'm not in any position . . ." but Mr. Jacoby interrupted him.

"Now, you see, Edie," he said. "I told you he was good."

"You don't need to tell me anything," Mrs. Jacoby said. "I want to get right down to facts. I'm worried about Manley, Mr. Wayde—I mean Willis. He's always liked that factory. He owned it when I married him. I want him to keep it if he likes it, but he's got to have someone to help him. I think it's time for you to make him our proposition, Manley."

Mr. Jacoby coughed loudly.

"Edie's right," he said, "and we've got to have her on our side. She's got the money, and it looks as though we're going to need some."

"Never mind that," Mrs. Jacoby said. "Make him the proposition, Manley."

"All right," Mr. Jacoby said. "Edie and I want you to be executive vice president of Rahway Belt. We want you to take over so that we can have time to go to Arizona and places like that. We're not getting any younger, and there aren't any young men in the family except our sons-in-law, both of whom are doctors. This may sound sudden to you but Edie and

I have been all over it. We want to sort of take you into the family. Are you sure you don't want a drink?"

"Well, yes," Willis said, "perhaps I wouldn't mind a small one."

He had been right not to have refused that final proffer of a drink. His acceptance finally set the tone for everything.

"Thank you, Manley," he said, as Mr. Jacoby handed him the glass. He had been right in calling Mr. Jacoby by his first name, as Mr. Jacoby had suggested, but he also had been right in speaking slowly and shyly.

"Would you mind telling us," Mr. Jacoby asked, "what your salary is at present?"

"Why, no," Willis said. "It's ten thousand dollars," and he smiled at them. "Just at present."

"That is the figure I guessed," Mr. Jacoby said.

He paused. Somehow people always paused before they made an offer.

"You and I get on all right. You'll be executive vice president down there and I'll back you all the way. You'll get twelve thousand dollars a year and thirty-three per cent of the common stock."

Although it was the percentage that Willis had planned to ask for, he had never thought that Mr. Jacoby would go so far immediately.

"That's quite a lot," Willis said slowly—"the stock, I mean."

"The idea," Mr. Jacoby said, "is to fix it so you won't refuse."

Willis waited a moment. It was no time to be too eager. In fact the size of the offer made him suspicious.

"I'm very much flattered of course," he said. "I didn't know you thought so highly of me, Manley."

He noticed that Mrs. Jacoby had taken off her glasses.

"It's my stock you're getting, not Manley's," Mrs. Jacoby said, "it's never earned me one red cent, and I want Manley to be happy."

It was no time to hurry, and Willis took a deliberate sip of his Scotch and water.

"I think it's very generous of you," Willis said. "There's only one thing that makes me hesitate." He smiled a little sadly. It was like saying he never took a drink in the middle of a business day, and he could see how closely they both were watching him. "Another firm sent me here, you know. I'm not sure it would be loyal, under the circumstances—"

He allowed his voice to trail into silence, and he had a momentary thought of Sylvia.

"Now just a minute," Mr. Jacoby began, "just a minute."

Willis raised his voice slightly, and as he did so he felt a glow of self-righteousness and a warm spot in his heart for Beakney-Graham.

"It may sound a little old-fashioned," he said, "but I'd like to finish my thought, if you don't mind. There's a girl I want to marry. I wish she were here with us now, because I know you'd like her, Mrs. Jacoby. She's the daughter of a Harvard professor. I met her in Cambridge when I was at the Harvard School of Business Administration. She and I were talking about loyalty only the other night. I don't know whether Sylvia would think it was loyal of me if I were to leave Beakney-Graham."

Willis had that quick feeling of triumph that comes of having said exactly the right things. Mrs. Jacoby was smiling at him.

"Manley always told me you were high-minded," she said, "but he never told me you were thinking of getting married."

"That's because he never told me either, Edie," Mr. Jacoby said.

Willis laughed diffidently.

"It's been a secret up to now," he answered. "You're the first people I've told, in fact. You're older than I am and I'd value your advice. I wouldn't want either of you to think I'm disloyal."

He was glad that he had thought to ask their advice, because Mr. and Mrs. Jacoby began advising him simultaneously.

"You're not under any contract with them, are you?" Mrs. Jacoby asked.

"Oh no," Willis said, "no contract, but just the same it bothers me."

"And since when," Mr. Jacoby asked, "can't anyone leave a job and take another?"

"I know," Willis said. "But Mr. Beakney's been especially kind to me. You know what a fine straightshooter he is yourself, and I have some very close fine friends in the office. We're a pretty hand-picked crowd in Beakney-Graham."

"Now listen, Willis," Mr. Jacoby said. "It's time you thought about yourself and this girl you're going to marry. What is her name?"

"Sylvia," Willis said.

"Sylvia," Mrs. Jacoby repeated. "I want you to promise to bring her here, and I think fifteen thousand would be better than twelve, Manley."

"It isn't the money," Willis said. "I only wish I felt right, Mrs. Jacoby."

"Now, Willis," Mrs. Jacoby said, "this is common sense. It's time you thought of Sylvia and any little ones who may be coming along."

Willis was always glad that he had threshed out the matter of loyalty with Mr. and Mrs. Jacoby, because it had started them off on the right foot, and he had Sylvia to thank for it, although she had only seen the picture in a rather schoolgirlish way; and what he had done was for her future as much as his. Nevertheless, sometimes when he had a sleepless night, he would recall his final conversation with Mr. Beakney. He was still sorry that things had ended there with a certain amount of ill-feeling. His interview the next morning was frankly tough, among the worst he had ever encountered up to that date, but, if you had to go through with something, you had to go right through.

Willis had done his morning setting-up exercises as usual, the "Daily Dozen" designed by the late Walter Camp which he had found long ago in a popular magazine, and he had always liked the title—"Take a Tip from the Tiger and Stay Young." Willis had recently been through an optional annual physical examination, which he had passed with an A rating. His eyesight was 20/20, his weight was right, his arches had not fallen, and his heart, blood pressure, and muscle tone were excellent. After a cold shower he had put on his new gray flannel suit, because he wanted to look as smart as possible. He had even taken fifteen minutes before he had gone out for his breakfast of orange juice, a three-minute boiled egg, and raisin bran, to read from William Penn in the Harvard Classics. It had been difficult to concentrate, with half his mind on what he was going to say to Mr. Beakney, but there was no reason to break routine.

He had exchanged pleasant greetings with everyone at Beakney-Graham just as though it were only another September day, and had all his thoughts well organized when Mr. Beakney was ready to see him.

"I thought you were out at Rahway," Mr. Beakney said. "Is anything wrong out there?"

Everything was fine at Rahway, Willis had told him. Then he had given Mr. Beakney the whole picture concisely, without pulling any punches, and he had ended on a note of how grateful he would always feel to Mr. Beakney and everyone in the office. He would never forget what they had done for him but he hoped that Mr. Beakney would put himself in his position and understand his situation. He was always very sorry that Mr. Beakney had not understood.

"Well," Mr. Beakney said, "so that's it. You've been sucking up to a silly old man and his silly old wife while you were on our payroll."

"I'm sorry you look at it that way, sir," Willis had told him. "They've made me an offer and I've accepted it."

Then Mr. Beakney had talked about loyalty, but he could not get away from the basic single fact that Willis was under no contract to stay with Beakney-Graham.

"Let me ask you just one question, sir," Willis said. "Haven't you ever done what I'm doing yourself, in your own career, Mr. Beakney?"

He did not like the look that Mr. Beakney gave him, but it was better than any answer.

"I never thought you'd do this to me," Mr. Beakney said. "I had other ideas about you."

"I'm sorry, sir," Willis said. "I've given it a lot of thought, but I guess this is something that everyone has to do sometime."

"Maybe," Mr. Beakney said. "I fear it would be a waste of time for you and me to argue over ethics, Willis."

"I'm sorry you don't approve, sir," Willis said.

"That's neither here nor there," Mr. Beakney said. "I fear you've grown up to be too much for us to handle. Well, that's the way things go."

"I wish you wouldn't put it that way, sir," Willis said, "because I've always enjoyed working for you."

"All right," Mr. Beakney said, "let's not have any more last words. I'll only say you're graduating, and I'll make just one more remark which maybe is a compliment. I'd hate to run up against you in a controversy ten years from now."

This meant a lot coming from someone like Mr. Beakney. There was no wonder Willis always had a warm spot in his heart for Beakney-Graham.

The next few months of his life were among the busiest and happiest that Willis had ever known, since there was nothing as exhilarating as one's first taste of tangible success and achievement. He only realized later that success had its dangerous aspects, especially early success. Class presidents and football heroes, he had finally come to learn, required careful and suspicious watching. They were like the potted hyacinths and daffodils that he sometimes bought for Sylvia in midwinter—spectacular, but they often yellowed around the edges once you brought them home. The same was true with bright young men who had come along too fast. They were tired because of premature effort, or else over-confidence had made them arrogant. At best the cards were stacked against someone who made good too young. Willis could see now that he had once been in this same dubious category. He could no longer wonder, as he once had, that Mr. Beakney had made no effort to keep him. In fact Mr. Beakney must have been relieved to have let him go —gray suit, trimmed hair, polished Oxfords, sharp mind and everything —because he had come along too fast for the age of twenty-nine.

What really saved him was marrying Sylvia Hodges. It was the most fortunate thing that had ever happened to him, meeting and marrying a girl like Sylvia. Sylvia had better taste than he, better manners and a more cultivated mind. She knew so many things he did not know that he could not help but be very proud of her. Though he was aware of his inadequacies when he was with her, somehow she never made him jealous.

[214]

They were married in Cambridge in October, 1936. There was always a first time for everything. Willis had no idea of the immediate complications. He had not thought of his father and mother as traveling all the way from the West Coast to the wedding until Mrs. Hodges wrote him that she had asked them and that they were coming, and then he had to get them rooms and a room for himself at the Hotel Commander in Cambridge. Then Mrs. Hodges had posed another problem. He had envisioned a small house wedding with no one but the family, but Mrs. Hodges wanted them married in the Unitarian Church off Harvard Square. Laura would be the maid of honor, and Sylvia was selecting bridesmaids. Consequently Mrs. Hodges wanted to know at once whom Willis would invite to be best man and whom he would want for ushers.

Willis never realized until he read Mrs. Hodges's letter at Rahway Belt that in all his years in New York there had not been much time for friendship. Under other circumstances, he could have asked Joe McKitterick and one or two others from Beakney-Graham, but his having left rendered this impossible. This lack of friendship, which had never troubled him before, he felt was something he could not confess to Mrs. Hodges and least of all to Sylvia. He finally felt obliged to resort to bald misstatement when he answered Mrs. Hodges's letter. He simply had to say that the few people he most wanted were unable to leave New York in the middle of the business week, that his father could be best man but that he would have to dispense with ushers.

He had thought that getting married would involve only a day in Cambridge, but instead Mrs. Hodges wrote that he must be there several days ahead to see about the license and to attend a few small parties which her friends and Sylvia's were giving; and then there was the wedding trip, to which he had given no thought at all, but Sylvia had said that they must go somewhere. This was all very difficult, coming on top of everything he had to do at Rahway Belt, and yet as Mr. Jacoby pointed out, after all it might only happen once.

If Willis had no friends of his own, at least he wanted to appear in a proper light. His Ford runabout, which had seemed so desirable only that spring, was not what he wanted any longer and he turned it in for a new green Buick sedan before he motored up to Cambridge. He never forgot Sylvia's expression when she saw the car in front of the house on Craigie Street. Sylvia always did find it hard to understand that you were rated in a business way by the car you drove and by your golf score. People you met in a business way always had to measure you by something.

Sylvia ran down the path to meet him in the late afternoon when he arrived at Craigie Street. He remembered her brown skirt and her white shirtwaist and the rustling noise of her feet among the autumn leaves. Now that she was back in the family she did not look like the girl he had known in New York, and when she kissed him in a shy way, because everyone was watching them, he felt like a distant relative.

"Why, Willis," she said, "where's the Ford?"

Where was the Ford indeed? He was very glad that he could surprise Sylvia at a time like that.

"Why, I turned in the Ford, dear," he said. "This is an improvement, isn't it?"

After all, he did not want to say in so many words that a fifteen-thousand-dollar-a-year man did not drive a Ford.

"Oh, dear," Sylvia said, "I loved the Ford."

"You'll love this a lot better," he told her, "once you get behind the wheel. I've been babying it along, but after two hundred miles more we can run it as fast as we like. I can't wait to knock off those two hundred miles."

"Oh, darling," she said, "I hope people won't think we're throwing our weight around when they see us driving it."

"Why, sweetness," he said, and he slammed the car door casually, "it's only a Buick. You wait till we get a Cadillac before you start to worry."

"Oh, darling," she said, and she linked her arm through his, "we've all been waiting for you all afternoon, and your father and mother are here, and you've got to go down right away to see about the marriage license. Tom will take you. And you've got to see the presents. What do you think Mr. and Mrs. Jacoby sent us?"

"What?" he asked, and it was a lot more important than the Buick. Sylvia laughed in an embarrassed way.

"An enormous silver soup tureen, like a pyramid, and I don't know what we'll ever do with it."

It did not matter what they did with it. It was very kind of Mr. and Mrs. Jacoby.

Getting married, Willis often thought, was like moving without any preparation into a foreign country about whose customs one knew nothing. From the moment he had stepped out of the Buick to the time Sylvia and he finally drove away in it from the wedding reception, he was a stranger in a strange land. Everything was on an entirely different basis from what it had been before, because the Hodgeses were trying to make him a member of the family, and even his father and mother were like strangers. They were all waiting for him in the house at Craigie Street, and he was surprised to have Mrs. Hodges kiss him. Then his mother kissed him, then Laura, and then Tom's wife, Mary, who told him they might as well get it over with now that he was going to be an in-law just like her. Sylvia wanted to see him alone for a minute and so did his mother, because he was her boy and she hadn't laid eyes on him for four years, and he hadn't seen his father yet. No one seemed to know what had happened to Alfred Wayde and Mr. Hodges. They had simply disappeared.

Mrs. Hodges wanted Willis to see the presents right away, but Tom said Willis had to go to the city hall to see about the license before the whole place closed.

"If he doesn't get to City Hall today, he won't get married on Wednesday," Tom said.

This was plain fact, but Willis found that Sylvia was pulling him into Mr. Hodges's study.

"Willis," Sylvia said, "what are you going to get married in?"

"In a church, aren't we?" Willis said. "At least that was the last idea."

"I mean clothes," Sylvia said, and Sylvia looked strained and nervous.

"Well, won't a dark suit do?" he asked.

"No," Sylvia said. "Mother wants you and your father to wear cutaways."

"That's the first I've heard of it," Willis said. "Nobody wore them at Lake Sunapee."

"It's just Mother, darling," Sylvia said. "She's all worn out. You and your father will have to go and rent them, with silk hats."

"Silk hats?" Willis repeated. "I don't know whether I can get my father to do it."

"He's got to," Sylvia said. "And, Willis, have you got the ring?"

"Gosh," Willis said, "I forgot about the ring."

"You forgot it?" Sylvia said, and her voice broke tragically. "I suppose getting married is more serious for a girl than it is for a man. Do you want to marry me or don't you?"

"Now, sweetness," Willis said. "Of course I want to marry you, or I certainly wouldn't have bought the Buick."

"Willis," Sylvia said, "if you mention that Buick again, I'll scream—I really will. That Buick hasn't got anything to do with anything."

"It's only sort of a symbol, dear," he said, "sort of like the ring."

"You come here to get married," Sylvia said, "and all you think about is a motor car."

He knew it was a time to be patient and understanding and that girls were apt to be upset at such a time, but the trouble was he did not know what he ought to understand.

"You haven't even asked to see the presents," Sylvia said.

It certainly was a time to be gentle and understanding, and he supposed all girls were nervous, and he could not blame Sylvia, because he was growing nervous too.

"Now listen, honey," he said. "What's all the trouble anyway?"

At any rate the question changed her mood.

"Oh, Willis, darling," she said, "I know I'm impossible. I'm sorry, dear."

"There, there," Willis said, and he put his arm around her. "It'll be all right when this is over. What sort of a ring would you like, honey? I saw sort of a cute platinum one the other day with little orange blossoms carved on it."

"Oh, God!" Sylvia said. "Why didn't you think of chromium?"

"Why, sweet," Willis said, "why chromium?"

"Because it's all over that Buick," Sylvia said, and she hid her head against his shoulder. He could not tell whether she was laughing or crying, but at any rate he began to laugh himself.

"I was just thinking of something striking, sweetness, that would go with the diamond," he told her.

"Oh, Willis," Sylvia said. "Just put your mind on a plain gold band. I'll go to Boston with you tomorrow."

He was relieved to see that she was growing calmer.

"Willis," she said, "have you done anything about the bouquet?"

"What bouquet, sweetness?" Willis asked.

"Oh, God!" Sylvia said. "The bunch of flowers the girl carries to the altar. The man is supposed to buy it."

"Is he?" Willis said. "I didn't know that, honey, but just you leave it all to me."

"Just don't tell anyone I had to tell you," Sylvia said.

"Now, sweetness," Willis said. "I'm sorry I'm so dumb, but I haven't been married very often." It was a pretty good joke and he had to laugh at it. "Just you wait till you see the bouquet I'll get you. It will be solid orchids."

"Oh, God!" Sylvia said. "Oh no, not orchids."

He was glad that Tom interrupted them. If they didn't go for that marriage license they would never get it.

"And we'll take your car," Tom said. "It's like a motor hearse. I'm dying to ride in it."

It might not have been a very good joke but it did put things on a lighter level.

"Come on," Tom said, "and you're coming too, Sylvia. Where did you get that suit, Willis?"

"Brooks Brothers," Willis said. "What's the matter with it, Tom?"

"I'm only admiring it," Tom said.

Sylvia turned on Tom sharply. There was no doubt she was very nervous.

"You'd better admire it," Sylvia said, "and maybe if you stop being a friend of the Little People, you can afford one like it some day."

There was so much happening that Willis could never get events into chronological succession. He was constantly smiling and chatting with friends and relatives of the Hodgeses' whom he did not know. Sylvia was always saying in amazed tones that she surely must have told him who they were. Although he took pride in sorting out names and faces, it actually took years and several christenings before he got the Hodgeses' connections straight.

So this was Willis Wayde, they were saying. They had heard so much about him that they were very glad finally to see him. Sylvia had always been a wonderful girl. In case he did not know it, he was very very lucky to have found a girl like that. He knew he was very lucky, he answered. They were going to live in Rahway, New Jersey. They had not found a house yet, but they would stay in his apartment in New York until they got settled. Yes, he kept saying, it would be great fun to go house-hunting and buy furniture and things. Yes, he and Sylvia would motor around New England for two weeks, but they had no definite idea just where they were going.

Even his parents treated him sometimes like a stranger. His mother was shy with him at first. She had been worried, she said, as any mother would be, when Willis had written her that he was engaged to a girl she did not know. It was wonderful to discover that Sylvia was just the daughter-in-law she had dreamed of having—a good, sweet, sensible, intelligent girl, whom she seemed to have known always. Her family were all lovely people, too, particularly Professor Hodges. She had never thought that a professor in a great university like Harvard would have such democratic manners or that she would understand nearly everything he said. She told Willis all this when they were finally alone in the hotel.

"You've grown up so, Willis, that I hardly know you," she said. "Doesn't Willis look handsome, Alfred?"

"Yes," Alfred Wayde said. "He's been polished off, all right. How about a touch of rye, Willis?"

"Now, Alfred," Mrs. Wayde said, "I wish you'd ever been polished."

"Anyway you're getting me into a monkey suit," Alfred Wayde said, "just because Willis is getting married."

He was referring of course to the cutaway he was going to rent. Ever since he had heard of it he had not been able to get it off his mind.

"Now don't keep complaining about it," Mrs. Wayde said. "You know you're proud of Willis."

"Why, yes," Alfred Wayde said, "I'd like to see this Jacoby who's giving him fifteen grand a year."

"Mr. Jacoby wouldn't have given it to Willis if he wasn't worth it," Mrs. Wayde said, "and you know it, Alfred."

"Sure I know it," Alfred Wayde said, "and I'm proud to have a boy who can shake money out of anyone." He stopped and looked at Willis in a way that made Willis move uneasily.

"I'm proud of you all right, son. Here you are, not thirty, with motor cars, golf sticks, everything. There's only one thing bothers me about you, son."

"Well, tell me what it is," Willis said. "A lot of things bother me about myself, as a matter of fact."

Alfred Wayde filled a pipe and lighted it. He looked older and heavier than he had at the Harcourt Mill, and all his motions were more deliberate.

"Now, son," he said, and his voice was warm and gentle, "I know you've got to get along like all the rest of us. Boys like you have to try to be something they're not in order to get ahead, and if you try hard enough, no doubt you'll be what you want to be. You're marrying a real nice girl. She's a little thin for my taste, but no doubt she'll flesh out. There's only one thing bothers me."

He stopped and lighted his pipe again.

"Just don't get too smooth," he said, "or you'll turn into a son of a bitch. A lot of people do before they know it, son."

"Alfred," Mrs. Wayde said, "you ought to be ashamed."

"I'm sorry," Alfred Wayde said, "I apologize if I offended you, son."

"You didn't," Willis said, "and I know what you mean, and you said it before to me once. Do you remember?"

"That's right," Alfred Wayde said, "up at Harcourt. I didn't mean to be repeating myself. And the Harcourts sent you presents, didn't they? Old Mrs. Henry and the Brysons, and Bill and Bess. It was nice of them, considering."

"Yes, sir," Willis said, "it was very nice of them."

"Well," Alfred Wayde said, "I'm going to bed now. My feet hurt in these new shoes." He pushed himself out of his chair, walked slowly across the hotel sitting room, and slapped Willis on the shoulder.

XVII

WILLIS ALWAYS liked to think that Sylvia's and his honeymoon had been a very happy one, and certainly before it was completed they had learned a lot about each other in little ways. He had learned, for instance, that Sylvia liked to smoke a cigarette in bed before she went to sleep, a habit which always alarmed him, and that she left shoes and slippers on odd parts of the floor, which one had to be careful not to step on. In fact Willis had almost dislocated his toe on a sharp heel of one of Sylvia's mules the third night of their marriage, and Sylvia had told him that it was his fault because he had insisted on walking around barefoot. Sylvia on her side had learned that he did setting-up exercises for ten minutes every morning and never left the top off his toothpaste tube or his shaving cream. Things like this meant more than you thought, and a honeymoon was surely a period of learning both to give and forgive. He had never known, for instance, that Sylvia wore pajamas instead of nightgowns.

He had heard that the most important recipe for a happy honeymoon was complete physical comfort, and he was glad he had taken this point seriously in spite of what Sylvia had said about economy. He had the good sense not to worry about costs, since, as he told Sylvia, you only had a honeymoon once. He had not told Sylvia where they were going because he had wanted it to be a surprise, and as a matter of fact it had been, very definitely. All he would tell Sylvia was that he had reservations at a place in the Adirondack Mountains and that they would have to hurry through New Hampshire and Vermont in order to reach there on time.

The name of the place was Chieftain Manor, which Willis had once heard Mr. Beakney say was one of the finest rest and recreation hotels that he had ever seen, and Mr. Beakney certainly had been right. Willis had never been to a hotel like Chieftain Manor, and he often said sadly to Sylvia in later years that he wished they might go there now—which was unhappily impossible, because Chieftain Manor closed its doors shortly after Pearl Harbor, never to open them again. It lay back in the past now, as something unique to remember, something never to be spoiled by revisiting later when one's tastes were better formed by wider travel.

Chieftain Manor was gone, and heaven only knew what had finally happened to the immense shingled building or the eighteen-hole golf course, the indoor and outdoor swimming pools, the bungalows and service quarters, the mountain trails and boathouses. Had the hotel burned down, or was it the property now of some real-estate development with ranch-type houses and imitation log cabins, or had the forest that surrounded it rolled back over it again? Willis did not know, nor did he want to know. He preferred to think of it as it had been—as beautiful as a dream of wish fulfillment.

He could seem to see it in his memory just as he had when he drove up over its half mile of driveway with Sylvia beside him. He could remember the autumn sunlight, the gold of turning poplars against the deep green of fir trees. Perhaps the past had given his memories a romantic tinge, but his initial impression persisted that Chieftain Manor contained everything that anyone could need in order to achieve happiness. It certainly had tried to contain everything. Once you passed through its front portals that overlooked the putting green and croquet lawn, there were passages branching off in all directions to shops selling linen and lingerie and jewelry, sport shops, book shops, barber shops, and hairdressers, cigar stands, newsstands, conservatories, and a broker's office. As Willis once said facetiously to Sylvia after they had the ground plan of the main building more or less committed to memory, it must have been that no one coming to Chieftain Manor had decided what to wear until he got there. He was surprised that Sylvia had not appeared amused. Occasionally there were times when Sylvia had not been quite herself at the Chieftain. October was like July, what with the club bar, the golf professional, the card room, the billiard room, the ballroom and the Club Evangeline with its New York atmosphere, and the Turkish baths, and the indoor swimming pool so cozily heated.

The sun was setting and the red glow from the sky was reflected in the still waters of the lake. There was a suspicion of autumn chill that was only enough to make one glad that a day's motoring had ended at just the proper moment. The Manor was really larger than Willis had believed was possible, considering how far they were from anywhere.

"Oh, Willis," he heard Sylvia say, "is this it?"

"Yes, honey," he told her. "It's quite a layout, isn't it?"

"This isn't a hotel," she said, "it's a fantasy."

"A what?" he asked her.

"Oh, never mind, dear," she said. "Isn't it going to be terribly expensive?"

It was strange how apt Sylvia was to miss the point of certain things. For instance she never could understand when it was worthwhile to spend money. Of course the main purpose of Chieftain Manor—or The Old Chief, as Willis came to call it affectionately—was to be expensive. It was a symbolic prize for industry and endeavor, a happy resting place only for those who had made good. Somehow Sylvia never seemed to see that if you worked hard for what you got, it was a pleasure to show that you had money. It never hurt you at all, for example, to be able to say that you enjoyed April at Hot Springs or that you had found that the service at The Breakers at Palm Beach had improved from what you had known of it last. Of course everyone had his own intimate attitude toward money, and he always realized that Sylvia's was different from his, but he did wish she could understand that he had earned his right to be at The Old Chief.

"What's the matter, honey?" he asked her.

"Oh, Willis," she said. "It's just so—Oh, never mind. I only mean that it isn't very cozy."

"But it isn't meant to be," he said. "People who come here don't want anything cozy." And then he could not help but laugh. "I'll make you love it, honey," he said. "We'll do something new every minute we're here. This is going to be a real honeymoon right from now on in."

There was no time to say anything more because a bell-boy in a horizon-blue monkey jacket and white trousers was already beside the car.

"Hello, son," Willis said. "Take out everything, will you? And put the car in the garage."

It was new to him, but then Willis had traveled enough at Beakney-Graham to know his way around hotels. Thus The Old Chief only awed Willis when he and Sylvia first crossed the lobby, with its artistically grouped clusters of chairs occupied by the guests in from golf or riding who were whiling away an aimless hour before it should be time to dress for dinner. By the time he was facing the room clerk he was completely sure of himself.

"Mr. and Mrs. Willis Wayde," he said, "Rahway, New Jersey. Here's a confirmation of my reservation."

The only wrong thing that he had done, of course, was to tell the clerk that he had a confirmation for his reservation, since this indicated an insecurity that he always avoided afterwards. Actually this made very little difference, because, as Willis found out later, the whole staff had been given careful lectures by Mr. Murcheson, the manager, on the arts of hospitality. A guest, as Mr. Murcheson said—and he always made it a point to contact all guests personally—was a member of The Old Chief Club once he had signed the register.

Upon leaving the desk Willis was already able to glance in a calm and friendly way about the lobby. The cashmere sweaters of the younger women reminded him that given the proper things Sylvia could look as well as any of them, and Sylvia was beginning to wear clothes beautifully, as well or better even than Bess Harcourt.

They had the elevator all to themselves, with the two boys and the baggage.

"You have suite C-16, sir," the head boy said.

Willis saw Sylvia glance at him with alarm, and he smiled at her proudly.

"That's right, son," he said, and it was right. The beautifully carpeted hall was almost perfect and so were the sitting room and bedroom, tastefully furnished with chintz and antique maple reproductions.

"Thank you, boys," Willis said, and he handed each of them a dollar, and smiled again at Sylvia.

"Look," he said to her. "Flowers for you with a card from the manager. Well, how do you like it, Mrs. Wayde?"

If he had meant the suite to be a surprise, it had been, but Sylvia's uneasy manner told him that her mind was again on money.

"Willis," she said, "we don't need a sitting room, do we? Really, you're spending money like a drunken sailor."

Somehow the phrase seemed inappropriate and he resented being put in this category.

"Listen, honey," he said. "Let's just sit down and get this straight," and he put his arm around her.

"Darling," Sylvia said, "I don't mean I'm trying to quarrel. I know this is lovely and I love you for thinking of it, but then there's all the money we have to spend for the house and everything in New Jersey."

"Sylvia," he said, "do you remember that green dress?"

It was lovely to see the color rise in her cheeks.

"Of course I do," she answered, "but now we're so much more responsible."

"That's right, honey," Willis said, "but I still feel just the same way I did about that dress. I guess I always will."

"You're awfully sweet, darling," she said.

She said it as though she had made a new discovery, and the warmth of her voice made him happy.

"It is what makes the game worthwhile, honey," he said. "I mean giving you things, having a home." All at once he began to laugh, because finally he had the whole idea straight. "Maybe people like me are like sailors, and do you know why drunken sailors spend their money?"

"No," she answered, "unless because they're drunk."

"No, honey," he said, "they do it because they know that money's meant to spend when they get ashore."

"And you mean you're ashore now?" she asked.

"That's right," he said, "but there's more to it than that. This place means more to me than it does to you, because I've been at sea."

Then her arms were around his neck and her head was on his shoulder.

"I'm awfully glad you told me, dear," she said. "I won't worry any more. We'll have a lovely time."

Sylvia always was a grand girl, once you made her understand, and of course they had a wonderful time. Sylvia's evening dress was not bad-looking at all, and he was wearing his new tuxedo. It was pleasant to see people glancing at them as they walked across the lobby, with looks more wistful than envious; and Willis could understand their attitudes better now that he was old enough himself to look at a nice young couple and remember when he and Sylvia were like that—in love and with years ahead of them. Sylvia was dark and tall and there was character in her face and intelligence that meant a lot more than insipid beauty. Then he was not so bad-looking himself either in those days, as he knew from old photographs.

"Shall we have a cocktail before dinner?" he asked.

"Yes, of course," Sylvia said. "Darling, I keep forgetting how handsome you look, and then I start wondering how I ever found you."

A waiter pulled back a chair for her at a table in the bar, and the happy released chatter of drinkers around them splashed over them like a wave on a coral beach.

"Will you have a dry Martini, dear?" he asked. "Make it two dry Martinis, son, and ask the barman just to squeeze a lemon peel over the surface, not drop it in."

It occurred to Willis after he made the speech that the waiter was somewhat older than he and that it had been inappropriate to call him son, and he made a mental note to use the word less frequently.

"I don't care what it costs now. This is fun," Sylvia said.

"And when we finish these drinks it will be more fun," Willis told her. "Honey, I want to tell you something."

"What?" she asked.

"You said an awfully sweet thing about me as we came in here." He had to raise his voice to make her hear him across the table. "I mean about your forgetting how I look and then remembering. Let's keep on forgetting. Let's never get used to each other."

[225]

"Anyway, let's not get *too* used to each other," Sylvia said.

"All right," he said, "and, honey, you're more than wonderful, you're more than beautiful."

"We ought to stay here permanently," Sylvia said, "if you keep on saying things like that."

Sometimes he echoed that wish in his memory, that they could have stayed on in that bar forever with no more than two Martinis apiece.

"You see," he said, and he wished he did not have to speak so loudly, "you're more than beautiful because you have—you have—I wish I could say it in French."

"Don't," Sylvia told him. "You'll spoil it if you do."

"I know, honey," he told her, "and some day you're going to take me to Paris and teach me how to speak it right. You're more than beautiful. You're distinguée."

"Why, Willis," she said, "you pronounced that rather nicely."

"Excuse my French," Willis said, and he laughed. "I won't say it again, honey, but I will say you're more distinguished than any other girl in this hotel. Waiter, two more of the same, please."

"Do you think we ought to have two?" Sylvia asked.

Willis laughed again. "A bird can't fly on one wing," he said.

They looked at each other and then Sylvia smiled.

"Darling," she said, "do you think I'm as distinguée as Bess Harcourt?"

He was startled when Sylvia brought up Bess Harcourt, because it was neither the time nor the place for it, and also her name evoked a picture and a comparison. He could not help but wonder what Bess Harcourt would be like if she were suddenly to enter that spacious barroom. Would she be handsomer than Sylvia?

"Willis," Sylvia said, "did you hear my question?"

He had forgotten momentarily where he was, and now he was back holding the stem of the glass of his second Martini.

"Oh, yes," he said, "beg pardon, honey. There isn't any comparison. You're both different in your ways, but then no two people can be identical, can they?"

"You know, I saw her once," Sylvia said. "I don't believe I ever told you. I may have been shy about it."

"I don't see that it's anything to be shy about," Willis said. "Where did you happen to see her?"

"Oh, at a Boston dance," Sylvia answered. "She was pointed out to me."

"Well, frankly," Willis said, and as he was speaking he could imagine Bess Harcourt at that vanished dance, with her tawny hair, greenish-blue eyes, and quick smile, "you've got a better figure than Bess. You're

better-looking than Bess. You've got more brains and a better disposition."
And then he laughed. "Of course I may be prejudiced."

Sylvia laughed too. "Just you keep on being prejudiced," she said.

The fine thing was that Willis had meant everything he said. He was
having a very good time. He pulled out his cigarette case and snapped
it open.

"This silver case is going to turn to gold," he said, "when things get
a little better. Have a cigarette, honey?"

"Yes," she said, "but don't you think we ought to go in to dinner?"

Willis lighted a match for her and he made a note as he did so that
he must save some of the Chieftain Manor matches to take back to Rahway.

"Nobody else seems to be in a hurry," he said. "Let's get up an appetite.
Remember, it's all American Plan."

He looked critically around the barroom. Already he felt like a habitué
of Chieftain Manor.

"Wait a minute, honey," he said, "don't interrupt me. I think there's
someone over there I know. Yes, it is. I'm sure of it."

"Who?" Sylvia asked.

"That's Mr. Percival L. Nagel," Willis said, "sitting over there with
that rather heavy blond lady. Yes, I'm sure it's Mr. Nagel."

"Who's Mr. Nagel?" Sylvia asked.

"Why, honey," Willis said—she might know how to speak French but
she did not know everything—"P. L. Nagel is the president of the Simcoe
Rubber Hose and Belting Company."

It was always something to remember, the time he saw P. L. Nagel
sitting across the room at Chieftain Manor. It all went to show that you
never lost money in the end by staying at a fashionable hotel, and it also
went to show that it paid to cultivate a knack for names and faces. The
only time that Willis had seen P. L. Nagel previously was during an
unforgettable episode back in Mr. Harcourt's library, but that had been a
long time ago, in terms of both years and personal development.

Mr. Nagel did not look quite so trim or quite so ruddy, but then seven
years had passed since Mr. Nagel had called on Mr. Henry Harcourt
in June, 1929. The hardness of his face had partially melted into his
jowls. In fact he had put on weight all over, although his double-breasted
dinner coat concealed a good deal of his portliness. His hair, which had
been receding from his florid forehead, had thinned until his shiny
scalp showed through what was left of it, and what was left was benignly
white. It was undoubtedly P. L. Nagel.

"Well," Willis heard Sylvia saying, "and suppose he is the president of the Simcoe Rubber Hose and Belting Company?"

Sylvia's voice was a needless interruption.

"They make conveyor belts in the Middle West, honey, together with a long line of industrial rubber products," Willis told her, and he told her very kindly. "They're the biggest belting company in America, honey. He tried to buy the Harcourt Mill once. That's how I remember him."

"Is that his wife with him?"

It pained Willis that Sylvia sounded disdainful. Of course the lady with him was Mr. Nagel's wife, because, obviously, she could not possibly have been anything else.

It was not difficult for Willis to see that Mrs. Nagel's blond hair was not entirely natural. In spite of facials and beauty creams, her eyes were old, and so were her hands. She was doing very well, but she was hardly the person that one would invite for a surreptitious week end at Chieftain Manor.

"Well, she looks very common," Sylvia said.

It was hard to see how Sylvia had reached that conclusion. It seemed to Willis that Mrs. Nagel looked very well, considering—handsome, blond, in a fine evening dress, with some excellent pieces of jewelry.

"I don't suppose he remembers me at all," Willis said, "but I was right there when he offered to buy the Harcourt Mill. He offered five million dollars."

This sum made no impression on Sylvia.

"I don't see why it is," she said, "that people like that always seem to be the only ones who ever offer to buy something for five million dollars."

Willis only half heard her because the sight of the Nagels had absorbed all of his attention. It was simply one of those times when he could not think of two things at once.

"Nice-looking people," Sylvia said, "never seem to want to buy things for five million dollars."

Willis felt a slight spasm of annoyance.

"Now, honey," he said, "in business it doesn't matter how anybody looks, if he has the money to put on the table."

"But, Willis," Sylvia said, "you're always careful about how you're going to look."

Willis laughed.

"Honey," he said, "maybe I won't care so much if I ever make a million. I think I ought to speak to Mr. Nagel. Don't you think so?"

"Why?" Sylvia asked.

"It would be a wasted opportunity if I didn't, dear," Willis said. It was strange how often he had to spell out things for Sylvia in those days.

He pushed back his chair tentatively, and just then Sylvia spoke with a startling sort of urgency.

"Oh, Willis," she said, "please don't."

He could still remember that Sylvia's voice had sounded half frightened.

"Don't what, honey?" he asked.

"Don't contact him, or whatever you call it," Sylvia said. "We're having such a good time by ourselves." Her words moved more rapidly, more eagerly. "Willis, he'll spoil everything."

Willis patted her hand, gently, reassuringly.

"Don't worry, honey," he said, and suddenly he felt curious. "What is it that upsets you so about my just speaking to him?"

"Oh, I don't know," Sylvia said. "I just don't feel he's good for you."

"Who?" Willis said. "Old P. L. Nagel not good for me?"

"Darling"—there was a sudden catch in her voice—"I don't want you to get to be like him. That's all I mean."

"Who?" Willis said. "Me? Like P. L. Nagel?"

There really had been a moment when he hesitated, since after all it was their honeymoon. There was even a moment when he knew what she meant about getting to be like P. L. Nagel, and then he stood up.

"I wouldn't do this, honey," he said, "if it wasn't important in a business way. I'll be back in just a minute, honey."

As he walked carefully around the tables toward Mr. P. L. Nagel, he had some vague idea of what Sylvia meant. For a second Willis seemed to be leaving something that he and Sylvia were building together which had all sorts of half-realized possibilities. It was, of course, ridiculous. In the end it was more of a twinge of conscience than an idea. At any rate the whole thing was over in an instant. Willis squared his shoulders slightly. He was near the table now. Mr. Nagel was staring at an empty old-fashioned cocktail glass, but he looked up quickly as one does, finally, when someone silently tries to attract one's attention.

"Good evening, Mr. Nagel," Willis said. "I don't imagine you remember me but I couldn't resist the impulse."

Mr. Nagel's timing was slower than it had been years ago. Willis could see him bringing his mind and eyes into focus and for a moment Willis was afraid that Mr. Nagel resented the intrusion. Willis had not learned then that everybody, no matter what superficial annoyance they might show, liked to be recognized and noticed.

"Now just a minute, son," Mr. Nagel said. "Don't tell me who you are. I want to guess. I never forget a name and a face, do I, Myrtle?" He looked archly at Mrs. Nagel.

"It depends on how many old-fashioneds you've had, P.L.," Mrs. Nagel said.

Mr. Nagel shrugged his shoulders.

"Now, Myrt," he said, "I bet you two hundred dollars I guess him."

"How many guesses?" Mrs. Nagel asked.

"Just two," Mr. Nagel said, and sat up straight. "All right. First question. Were you ever in the belting business, son?"

"Yes, sir," Willis said. "I was and in fact . . ."

"Just answer," Mrs. Nagel said. "Don't tell him any more."

"All right, Myrtle," Mr. Nagel said. "I don't need any more questions. This is Jim Budd who used to be in the Chicago office. I remember you perfectly now, Jim. Sit down and have a quick one with us, and bring your best girl over."

"Oh, P.L.," Mrs. Nagel said, and she gave a loud whinnying laugh that made people turn around and look at her. "Two hundred dollars. Look at him. He isn't Jim Budd."

"Now, wait a minute," Mr. Nagel said. "Of course he's Jim Budd," but then Willis's own expression must have told him he was wrong. It was hard to keep from laughing. Mr. Nagel took out his handkerchief and mopped his forehead.

"I'm afraid you've got me wrong, sir," Willis said. "I used to be with the Harcourts—not that there is any reason why you should remember. You had other things to think about at the time."

Mr. Nagel always was very quick on the uptake.

"That's it," he said. "You were the kid who sat with me in that den. Myrtle, sweetie, this is the son of my very close personal friend Alf Wayde. His first name is Harris."

"The name is Willis, sir," Willis said.

Mrs. Nagel gave another laugh. "That's another one on you," she said. "Right on the button, Pops."

Mr. Nagel shook his finger at her.

"Harris is pretty close," he said, "but I admit the drinks are on me, sweetie. Who's the girl you're with, Willis? She's a snappy little babe, if I may say so."

"She's my wife," Willis said. "We happen to be here on our honeymoon."

Mrs. Nagel gave another of her laughs.

"There you go again, Pops," she said. "I told you they were married."

Mr. Nagel raised his eyebrows and cleared his throat.

"You see," he said, "when Mrs. Nagel and I come to a place like this we always have a little game, guessing who's married and who isn't.

Mrs. Nagel's usually right. In fact, personally, she thought we were married a whole year before we were."

When P. L. Nagel laughed you could not help but laugh with him. Mrs. Nagel gave her husband a cold glance and straightened her gold-mesh bag on the table.

"I am sure Mr. Wayde doesn't understand what you're talking about, P.L.," she said.

"Now, sweetie," P.L. answered. "It's just a private joke of Mrs. Nagel's and mine. You understand that, don't you, Harris?"

"Oh, naturally, Mr. Nagel," Willis said. "I just came over to say hello. It's been a pleasure meeting you again, and Mrs. Nagel too, and now if you'll pardon me, I must rejoin Mrs. Wayde."

Mr. Nagel shook his finger at Mrs. Nagel.

"Now you see you've embarrassed him, don't you, Myrtle?" he said. "We're not going to pardon you, Harris, until you bring Mrs. Wayde over here and make this whole thing legitimate."

"Stop calling him Harris," Mrs. Nagel said. "It would be lovely if you joined us for a cocktail, Mr. Wayde."

"Say, Myrt," Mr. Nagel said, "let's get off this formal basis. We're all first names here."

Willis could not help but feel a pleasant glow and a warm spot in his heart that was almost like loyalty.

"I know Sylvia would love to meet you, P.L.," he said. One always had to be careful in the early handling of a first name, but on this occasion he could see that it was exactly what P.L. wanted. "I'll bring Sylvia right over."

"Oh, Willis," Sylvia said, "do we really have to go over there and sit with them?"

It was not fair of Sylvia, because even if it was their honeymoon the Nagels were a very important contact.

"Now, honey," he said firmly but very cheerfully, "it won't hurt. It will be over in a minute."

He could see that there had never been an opportunity for Sylvia in her whole life to meet people like the Nagels, but after all it did not hurt her a bit. In fact after a few minutes he was really proud of Sylvia, and what was more she seemed to know instinctively how to handle types like old P.L. When Mr. Nagel kept holding her hand long after it was necessary, it was a little difficult to know what to do, but Sylvia handled it all herself.

"I'd like it back when you're through with it, Mr. Nagel," Sylvia said. "I need it so I can have a cocktail."

It was pretty good for Sylvia and it started everything on exactly the right note. Mr. Nagel said it was a very funny line and Mrs. Nagel asked right away if Sylvia and Willis would not join them at dinner—that is if they didn't mind sitting awhile with some stuffy old people.

"Don't forget, Myrt," Mr. Nagel said, "it's their honeymoon. But you do have to eat sometime, don't you, kids?"

Willis had a momentary worry that Sylvia might not take the remark in the spirit in which it was intended, but he was entirely wrong.

"There's nothing like a honeymoon," Mrs. Nagel said to Sylvia, "and the first one is always the best one. That's what I always tell P.L., but let's you and I have a little talk and don't mind the men."

"Well," P.L. said, "now the girls have got together, how's Harcourt's?"

It was very easy to tell Mr. Nagel the few lines of personal history. Old P.L. knew all about Harcourt's and Beakney-Graham and Rahway Belt, and he was honestly interested.

"Anyway," P.L. said, "you've got the Planeroid patents." It was a relief to be talking business again.

"That's right," Willis said, "but we're doing some more things to the process."

"Will you boys stop talking business," Mrs. Nagel said, "and let us please go in to dinner."

You could say what you wanted about old P.L. but he did have an intellectual enthusiasm when it came to production and merchandising, and they must have both been a little starved for shop talk. Willis could not remember what they had for dinner or much of what Sylvia or Mrs. Nagel had to say but he could recall all the details of his talk with P.L. Willis could never blame himself for being very proud of that evening. While they drank coffee in the large lounge outside the ballroom, Willis in his thoughts could stand away from himself and enjoy that scene, with its background of ballroom music, as an artist might admire a canvas that was turning out better than he had ever hoped. Furthermore the feeling of well-being that suffused him seemed to Willis to have spread to Sylvia and Mrs. Nagel.

Then everyone talked very happily about antique furniture. It seemed that Mr. and Mrs. Nagel had recently built a new home in the Chicago suburb of Lake Forest, designed on Georgian colonial lines. For ordinary parties you could have a steak fry or some catch-as-catch-can thing like that out by the swimming pool, but there were times when you wanted to do it in a small sophisticated way for some banker or some highly educated corporation lawyer. What P.L. really wanted was atmosphere, and that was why they were getting rid of reproductions and buying genuine antiques. They had a patina all their own.

It was pleasant to hear Sylvia agree with Mrs. Nagel. Old furniture did give atmosphere, and she wished that she could afford to buy some, but of course starting out as she and Willis were made this nearly impossible.

"Say," P. L. Nagel said, "don't let Myrtle give you any fancy ideas now, Sylvia, honey. Speaking of antiques, do you remember old Harcourt's office building? Those were real antiques."

Willis was glad that the subject had got back to the Harcourt Mill, since he could give a few interesting facts about the commercial value of antiques. Finally Mr. Nagel raised his hand and yawned delicately behind it.

"You know, this pine-scented air seems to hit me over the head," he said, "and I have got to hit the hay. How about some golf tomorrow, Willis?"

"Gosh, P.L.," Willis said, "I'm intending to do a little serious work on my golf while I'm here, but I'm afraid I'm not in your league, P.L."

"Oh, just duffer golf," Mr. Nagel said. "I'm not what I used to be. I'll call you at eleven, son. Come on, Myrtle. Good night, Sylvia, precious."

Willis was instantly on his feet, and he stood for a moment gazing after the Nagels before he sat down again beside Sylvia.

"Now, honey," he said, "do you see what I mean about its paying to stop at some place like Chieftain Manor?"

Instead of answering directly, Sylvia put her hand on his arm.

"Now that they've gone, let's go in and dance," she said. It was nice to see how quickly Sylvia was getting into the spirit of the place.

It was agreeable to observe that they were one of the few young couples in the ballroom, for most of the other guests, who sat watching the dancers like village elders, were in stages of late middle age. There were not many people in Willis's age group who could afford the time off for play or the tariff of Chieftain Manor. It was sad to think of this, since The Old Chief had so many facilities that youth appreciated more than age, but at the same time it was stimulating to realize that he was able to make the grade while he was still young.

When they finally reached their sitting room, neither of them, unlike P. L. Nagel, felt like sleep.

"I think I'll read for a while," Sylvia said. "Would you mind getting me *The Oxford Book of Verse* out of my suitcase, dear?"

It was like a preview of an abundance of happy years, to be reading quietly there in The Old Chief with Sylvia. Yet after a space of silence he became aware of a common fallacy in this conventional picture. No husband and wife ever seemed able to sit in the same room and read.

"Willis?" Sylvia said.

"Yes, dear," he answered.

"How is it that someone as stupid and vulgar as Mr. Nagel can be so successful in business? I don't see that he has any brains at all, only a few slow reflexes."

"You don't mean," Willis said, "that old P.L. pinched you or anything?"

He was relieved when Sylvia laughed.

"Why, the thought never crossed my mind," she said, "but I wish he had. It might have made things easier."

Sometimes Sylvia said the most extraordinary things, considering she came from Craigie Street.

"Now, honey," Willis told her, "you've got to—er—kind of expect that sort of thing when you get around with old men over sixty, especially if they're topflight executives."

Sylvia laughed again and something in her mirth began to make him nervous.

"Suppose he starts," she said. "How much should I let him pinch me?"

"Well, now, honey," Willis said, "that's kind of a curious question. I don't see any use in crossing a bridge until you come to it, and maybe you never will."

"You mean I'm not attractive enough?" Sylvia asked.

"Now, honey," Willis said, "I didn't mean that. I was only sort of thinking out loud on general terms."

"Darling," Sylvia said, "what will I do if Mr. Nagel *does* do anything?"

"Well, honey," Willis told her, and he tried to put his thoughts into order, "I've always thought that girls knew how to handle such situations. I don't say it's pleasant the way certain men behave, but then it's sort of an accepted human fact. You know, honey, executives around sixty are all under a heavy strain of responsibility. You ought to feel a little kindly toward them. We can't always be young, honey."

Of course he really did not believe that last thought, because time, in those days, was entirely in his favor.

There was nothing like the Adirondacks to make one sleep when one finally did get to sleep, and there were never more comfortable beds than the twin beds in their suite at The Old Chief. In later years when Willis read the advertisements of the friendly service of certain large hotels which supplied each guest with a mattress equipped with countless thousands of tiny springs, each spring contributing to perfect posture and slumber, and on the occasions when Willis sometimes tossed restlessly upon these mattresses far away from home and worrying about some business interview, he often thought of The Old Chief. No air-conditioned room could ever duplicate the gentle breeze off the lake.

Sometime in the middle of the night, however, he was awakened by a sound from Sylvia's bed and at first he had a startled idea that she was crying, and then he was almost sure that she was laughing. Yet it seemed to him that the hour was inappropriate for joy or sorrow. He could discern the shape of the twin bed across from him, but he could not see Sylvia at all.

"Sylvia," he said, "are you all right?"

"I'm all right," she answered through the dark. "I just don't seem to be able to go to sleep, that's all."

"Sylvia," he asked her, "are you laughing or are you crying?"

There was a silence in the room that lasted a considerable time before she answered.

"I don't know what I'm doing—and don't ask questions, Willis."

"Sylvia," he said, "you've got to tell me what's the matter."

"Oh, please stop it, Willis," she said.

"If it's anything I've said, if I've been too—er—demanding or anything, honey, just tell me," he told her.

At last he was sure that she was laughing more than she was crying.

"It isn't anything like that," she said. "You're awfully sweet, darling, but everything's so different."

"So different from what?" And he waited for quite a while before he asked the question.

"Oh, darling," she said, "just so different from anything I thought anything was going to be. It's on another plane, but I'll get used to it—only please don't talk about it any more tonight."

Often Willis said facetiously that his mind was like an alarm clock and that he never needed to put in a call at any hotel switchboard. At any rate he was always awake by seven, and Sylvia was still asleep that next morning, which was another preview of years to come.

He was delighted to see that it was a beautiful clear morning. The prospectus of Chieftain Manor had made mention of the winelike quality of the pine-bough-laden mountain air, a description that really made sense. He slid out of bed noiselessly, wrapping himself in the silk robe which he had purchased especially for the trip, and, carrying Volume II of the Five-Foot Shelf with him, tiptoed to the sitting room. He customarily did twenty push-ups, but he did twenty-five that morning, because of the elixir in the air. It was still only twenty minutes past seven when he had finished, ample time for his reading. When his fifteen minutes were up he experienced as he always did a fine sense of accomplishment that came of such a combined mental and physical workout, and the indoor swimming pool downstairs was yet to come.

He picked up the room telephone, asking for the pool and speaking softly so as not to arouse Sylvia.

"Am I speaking to the instructor?" he asked. "This is Mr. Willis Wayde. If I came down right now could you give me a half-hour lesson with the Australian crawl?"

He was back by ten minutes past eight prepared to awaken Sylvia, only to find her awake already, with a rather ugly blue-flannel wrapper over her pajamas, which reminded him that he must take Sylvia shopping as soon as they were dressed.

"Willis," Sylvia said, "where under the sun have you been, wandering around in your wrapper?"

"Oh," he told her, "the usual thing—first the old setting-up exercises, and then the Five-Foot Shelf."

"Willis," she said, "you didn't."

"And then," he said, "it just occurred to me that I could have a swimming lesson in the indoor pool, you know. They've got a good instructor there. It was a nice workout, honey."

"What under the sun were you doing that for?" she asked.

"Well," he said, "I've always wanted to learn the Australian crawl."

"The Australian crawl?" she repeated.

He wondered sometimes later whether he would ever have spoken of that incident at another time or place, but the air was like wine that morning.

"You know, in Clyde," he said, "there was a young fellow who could do the crawl beautifully. I saw him do it once in the Harcourt swimming pool after he had whipped me playing tennis. His name was Ed Ewing, the one who married Bess Harcourt—not that any of it makes any difference, honey."

And this was true. None of it did make any difference. Bess Harcourt was a memory almost as distant as his days at the mine in Colorado. He simply remembered that Edward Ewing had been very good at the Australian crawl.

"But, Willis," Sylvia said, "I still don't see why you want to learn it."

It was a rather difficult question to answer now that he was back with Sylvia and calling up room service for breakfast.

"Sylvia," he said, "if we have any—er—children, we've got to get a tennis court—one of those that dries off right after the rain, en-tous-cas I think the name is. They must be taught to play tennis, and how to handle themselves—er—gracefully in a swimming pool."

"You mean," Sylvia said, "it's going to help them in a business way?"

He saw that she was laughing at him, but he did not mind.

"Well, seriously, honey," he said, "both in a business and a social way."

He was feeling wonderful. The coffee and the buckwheat cakes and the small order of breakfast steak and the toast and strawberry jam were all wonderful.

"And, honey," he said, "we'd better lay out our program for the day. First I'll take you shopping. I want to get you some tweeds and a house-coat, and then you and I have both got to have a golf lesson and then I'm going to play a few holes with old P.L. and then it will be time for lunch. Gosh, I'm glad we're here, honey."

He had expected a quick, sympathetic smile from Sylvia, which was the least that he deserved. Instead he was surprised that she looked dubious.

"Don't you think, Willis," she said, "that if you play golf with Mr. Nagel, we'll have to keep seeing the Nagels all the time?"

It amazed him that Sylvia could not see the advantages of their seeing as much as possible of the Nagels.

"Now, honey," he said, and he spoke slowly and carefully, because he knew that he was facing an important moment, "there is one thing we ought to get straight, with all kindness and without emotion. Please don't look so startled, honey."

"Then don't look so stern, Willis," she said. "We were only talking about the Nagels."

"I wish you wouldn't say 'Only the Nagels,' honey," he told her. "They're pretty important, potentially, in my business future, but more than that they represent—well, a sort of principle, a kind of way of life for both of us."

When you came to think of it, that phrase "way of life" pretty well dated the conversation. They were back there in the days before World War II. They were only just beginning to define democracy without knowing what the phrase meant. Still it had a solemn ring.

"For heaven's sake, Willis," Sylvia said, "I didn't mean to upset you, but just what have the Nagels got to do with our way of life?"

"You're not upsetting me, honey," Willis told her. "Just please let me encapsulate my thought, because it is a thought."

"What's that again?" Sylvia asked. "What were you going to do to the thought?"

"Oh," Willis said, and he laughed. "Maybe it's an inappropriate word. We always used to use it back at Beakney-Graham, but never mind it now, honey. You let me worry about business. I'll pay the bills, but you let me run the business end of the combination, honey, and I'll let you run the home. But the Nagels are business, honey, and you let me run business."

Marriage in the final analysis consisted of a series of adjustments.

There was, as that humorist, artist and writer Mr. James Thurber put it, always a war between the sexes, always a kind of competition, no matter how much you loved someone. Somehow he and Sylvia must have worked out those problems more easily than most of their contemporaries. The reason was, he liked to think, that they each had a real respect for the abilities of the other. Right from the beginning he had respected Sylvia's mind and cultivation, and he rather liked it when she laughed at him about words like encapsulate, but they both finally understood that cultivation didn't get you everywhere.

XVIII

PERHAPS THE best way of judging whether or not certain years in your life were happy might be to determine how much you remembered about them; for the happiest years were those in which events blended with each other so naturally that all that remained was a recollection of growth and achievement. Judging the early years of Willis Wayde's and Sylvia's marriage by such a standard, they were very happy ones.

Sylvia and Willis had both been very busy in different ways. The reorganizing of Rahway Belt was combined with all the routine adjustments that most young couples must make. The babies and the obstetrical bills, the buying of furniture, papering the front hall, shoveling out paths to the sidewalk in winter, New Year's Eves at the country club, formed a disconnected chain of recollection. All their friends—the Parkinsons, the Meltons, the Newhopes—friends you played bridge with and friends you just had a good time with on general principles, were also interwoven with these events into a general background. You could recall many incidents, but sometimes it was hard, even with Sylvia's help and with the photograph album, to tell exactly where those incidents belonged, chronologically.

This uncertainty about dates and facts was, perhaps, not as peculiar as it seemed, since life in Orange, when they began it, was on the unstable foundations known to all young couples who have to earn a living. None of their friends, for instance—like the Parkinsons or the Meltons— had the remotest idea that they would live where they were for long. The moment they had higher salaries they would be moving. After all, this climbing up the ladder was all part of the American way. Curiously enough, however, one was not especially conscious at the time of living on shifting sands. To put the thing in purely industrial terms, Willis and Sylvia were in the pilot-plant stage when they lived in Orange, but you learned a lot of things in a pilot plant—you spotted the bugs; you smoothed the edges off generally. When they really went into production Willis realized that they had learned a great deal in Orange.

The home which they had rented was a brown-shingled affair stand-ing on an adequate piece of lawn and shut off from the sidewalk by a privet hedge. Willis never forgot the hedge or the lawn, because he had tended them both himself out of a natural liking for puttering around. They had selected the house with the help of Mr. and Mrs. Jacoby, who felt it was important for Rahway Belt that the Waydes should live in a suitable neighborhood. It had taken them quite a while to furnish the house, or at least it had Sylvia, since Willis had delegated the whole problem to her, Rahway Belt in those days being at least a twelve-hour-per-diem proposition. His idea had been to budget the whole business and get some store like Bamberger's in Newark to furnish and decorate for a flat sum, and they could get a loan, if necessary, from the bank. But when Sylvia objected Willis let her do the furnishing herself. This had kept Sylvia fully occupied during the first months of their marriage, not to mention bossing Minnie, their Irish maid-of-all-work, and the re-sult was not too bad. Sometimes he had to urge Sylvia to spend more money on the right things, like a good Oriental for the living room and a real antique dining-room table, but on the whole he admired her taste. It used to be a lot of fun coming home and examining the new things Sylvia had bought, and he could sympathize, frankly, with Sylvia's great-est preoccupation. She did not want their house to look like a newlyweds' home, even if it was. She wanted it to have both a used and cared-for look.

Willis had always thought of marriage as a process of settling down, whereas he soon discovered it was a series of disturbances. He did not intend this as a complaint, because many of these experiences had been highly enjoyable, such as meeting neighbors, and the first time that Sylvia and he had entertained in their own home. There were invitations to dinner from the Jacobys and various stockholders of Rahway Belt. Then the minister came to call and they promised to attend the Con-gregational Church. Then the Newhopes, who lived across the street, came to call, and Dan Newhope was the one who began talking about the country club. On the whole if you were friendly with people they were friendly in return, and there was a real community spirit in that neighborhood. Willis learned, in the years he and Sylvia were starting out in Orange, the importance of being identified with the place where you lived and of being a useful individual in it. One was bound to derive real personal satisfaction from being on church committees or col-lecting for the Republican campaign or helping with festivities at the country club, and eventually such activities paid off in a very practical way. Local bankers and businessmen whom you had never met began recognizing you as a good sound citizen who was willing to give time and energy to a cause, and this recognition in turn helped the standing of the company you represented.

After a year or two all sorts of people began knowing Willis pleasantly and the labor at Rahway Belt was kind to him. In fact when the CIO struck the plant Willis never had any trouble with the picket line. This was due in part to his practice of knowing as much as he could about everyone who worked at Rahway Belt, but also, he was sure, because he was well-known around town.

It hardly seemed any time at all after they had moved to Orange—in fact before all the drapes were up—that Sylvia announced that she was going to have a baby, except she didn't put it in quite that way. Willis had been making a final check of the Christmas-card list at the office on the afternoon that he found Sylvia waiting for him in the living room. The tea things were ready. Tea had been Sylvia's idea and one he liked, perhaps because tea always made him think of the Harcourt house; and their blue china tea set invariably reminded Willis that some day they must get a silver tea service.

"Willis," Sylvia said, "the doctor says I'm pregnant."

He was startled, not so much by the news as by the way that Sylvia had delivered it, so loudly that he knew that Minnie must have heard it in the kitchen.

"Well, what makes you so surprised, Willis?" Sylvia said. "What did you think was going to happen? Nothing?"

Willis wished, instead of saying that she was pregnant, Sylvia had said that she was going to have a baby or something of the sort, which would have meant the same thing, but then Sylvia was Sylvia.

"Well, well," he said, "so it looks as though we made it, does it?"

Curiously that simple remark of his seemed to startle Sylvia.

"Oh, Willis," she said, "is that all you're going to say?"

Then a wave of emotion swept over him. The news made everything worthwhile, and also it made Willis feel old because he was beginning to march in the procession of generations.

"Honey," he said, "I really think it's swell. In fact it couldn't be sweller."

When he sat down beside her he forgot all the problems of Rahway Belt.

"Willis," she said, "what do you hope it's going to be? Let's make it a boy!" And she spoke as though they could make it anything, and then Willis had another thought.

"Gosh, honey," he said, "I've really got to peel off my coat and go to work now. I want to do something for this kid, no matter what its sex. I want it to have a lot of things you and I didn't have, honey."

Admitted there was something in the maxim that a man with wife and children has given hostages to fortune, Willis never agreed with this entirely. A wife and one or two kids formed a steadying influence for any young fellow who could afford them. When you got beyond the two-children zone, perhaps things did get a little more complicated, but a wife and one or two kids made you feel your responsibility. In picking young executives, Willis was always partial to family men, as long as their families were within limits. Nothing pleased him so much as time went on as the news that a baby was born to someone on the office force. It was a fact that drew everyone closer together, and it always paid to make the news the subject of some sort of small festivity, like the presentation of a pair of knitted booties, or something like that, not as a gag exactly but at the same time in the spirit of fun.

The appearance of that child was a real event which marked the end of a long period of waiting punctuated by moments of being frightened for, and sometimes even of, Sylvia. The progressive change that came over her gave Willis an inordinate sense of guilt. Yet often when he showed solicitude, instead of being grateful, Sylvia seemed cross. As the months went on she snapped at him more than she ever had before and became critical of details in his habits of eating and speech. Even when he made a practice of bringing her a little gift home every day, Sylvia was very seldom grateful.

"I'd just as soon you wouldn't bring any more flowers," she said, "or if you do, won't you give them to me naturally and not make an occasion of it?"

"Why, how do you mean, honey?" Willis asked.

"Oh, I don't know," she said, "except you make me feel like someone in a shrine."

"Now, honey," Willis told her, "of course I don't know what you're going through but I can kind of imagine."

"No you can't," Sylvia said. "You don't even know what you're going through yourself."

Her remark only went to show that Sylvia had lost her balance.

"All right," he said, "all right, but you know I want to help you in any way I can, honey."

"Oh, God," Sylvia said, and her voice choked, and she began to cry in a very hysterical manner, and then she said for no apparent reason that she was afraid he did not love her any more, and then for no obvious reason either she told him she was sorry.

"Darling," she said, "I just don't know what I'm saying. I really do love and I do respect you, even if you are obvious sometimes."

Sylvia was difficult when she was pregnant, but when Willis compared notes with other men, he found that Sylvia was not exceptional. It was just as well to recognize that millions of other human beings, past and present, had shared every experience that one went through.

There had been a lot of talk about the best obstetrician. It seemed that there were a good many of them in the Oranges, which was as it should be with so many young couples making their first homes there. Mrs. Jacoby recommended one, and the Newhopes, who had more recent experience than Mrs. Jacoby, mentioned another whom Mrs. Newhope called a lamb. His name was Dr. Castlebar, and he had played tackle on a Midwestern football team. He was what the *New Yorker* magazine —a periodical which Willis was beginning to read thoughtfully—might have termed affable, florid, and tweedy. He smoked a straight-stemmed pipe and always referred to Willis as "fella." Obviously the main part of Dr. Castlebar's business was to bring babies into the world in rapid succession. Also, since in many ways he acted as a liaison officer between the sexes, his function was highly confidential. Dr. Castlebar's main idea was seemingly that childbirth and the parental manifestations connected with it were really a lot of fun, at least that was what Dr. Castlebar told them on his first visit.

"Now, my dears," he said, "just remember this whole thing is in my hands, and we're going to have a lot of fun out of this before we get through."

Sylvia started to laugh in an alarming way.

"That's all right," Dr. Castlebar said. "Don't worry about her, fella. Let her have her little laugh out, and go fetch her a drink of cold water, will you, fella?"

Willis never knew what was done in his absence, but when he returned from the kitchen with the water, Sylvia had stopped laughing. She was even talking to Dr. Castlebar in confidential tones.

"Now, fella," Dr. Castlebar said, "if the little lady is ever high-strung, just remember that high-strung women make the best mothers, in my book. But as I was saying, we can all get a lot of fun out of this. We will have our ups and downs as month moves into month—and remind me, will you, fella, we've got to be clear on the approximate time of arrival —but there's always one thing to remember."

Dr. Castlebar paused, drew out his briar pipe and tobacco pouch.

"There's going to be a baby at the end of it, and once you see your baby, well, everything you've gone through begins to seem like fun."

Willis could not help but be fascinated by Dr. Castlebar's philosophy. It was like a sales approach, and in fact it was one. Dr. Castlebar, in his simple, direct way made both of them want that baby. When he pointed his finger at Willis and looked hard at him, and said, "Now, fella, you wanted this baby, didn't you?" Willis was able to answer as he should have.

"You bet I did," he said.

The doctor leaned forward and slapped him affectionately on the knee.

"Well, that's fine, fella," Dr. Castlebar said. "Let's hope this will be the first of many and consider this a trial run, shall we? The more you have the easier it gets, and now one thing more."

The doctor looked at the bowl of his pipe and then pointed its stem at Sylvia aggressively.

"I want a breast-fed, not a bottle baby."

All right," Sylvia answered, "anything you say." And then she began to laugh again.

"Stop it," Dr. Castlebar said. "This isn't any joke."

It was remarkable how expertly he could keep Sylvia from laughing.

"Now let's see," Dr. Castlebar said. "The date ought to be August fourteenth, and it cuts right into my proposed vacation."

"I'm sorry about that," Sylvia said, "but I don't see how I can help it now."

Dr. Castlebar shook his finger at her.

"You can't," he said. "That's why I'm against autumn marriages. Next time I want a January baby."

This remark seemed to strike him as highly amusing.

"Go ahead," he said, "laugh. It's a joke. I told you we were going to have a lot of fun out of this."

Willis believed that no man could possibly forget any detail of the experience of becoming a father for the first time, but even so his acutest recollections of parenthood eventually became confused. This may have been only the trick that old Mother Nature plays on men, in a mild way, as well as on women. Willis could remember a lot of things that happened around hospitals while he waited during nervous hours for news, but he could no longer decide whether these events had heralded the appearance of Alfred, who was born in August, 1937, or Paul, in 1940, or Louise, right in the middle of the war.

It often amused Willis to hear Republicans refer scathingly to the Roosevelt administration as "a government by crisis," not that he was not a good Republican himself, or that he approved for a minute of the creeping socialism of the New Deal. Life for any married man was one crisis after another, business or domestic. If a nation was merely a conglomeration of homes, as politicians liked to say, how could government possibly avoid crises?

That summer was very hot in Rahway, and a simplification of the Planeroid process was just going into production. When everything at the plant had demanded his constant personal attention Willis had to remember that Sylvia also might go into production at any moment. Dr. Castlebar had given them a good idea of how the thing would start. First the little fella would have to drop down lower than he was. The fun, as Dr. Castlebar put it, might start unexpectedly after that. It was perfectly simple to tell when the fun was going to start and there was no reason to get into a panic. There would be a series of pains. Never mind one pain, because everybody living could have one pain, even— ha, ha—a prospective father. Hadn't Dr. Castlebar told them they were going to get a little fun out of this?

It was advisable, though not obligatory, to pack a small suitcase with a bed jacket and comb and brush and things like that, and keep it ready. All Sylvia needed to do was pick up the telephone and tell Miss Crump at Dr. Castlebar's office what was going on. There was only one other thing to remember. Never forget it's no disgrace to be having a baby, since it was about the swellest and most natural and useful thing that a woman could do in the world. Everyone always loved a gal who was having a baby and always wanted to help.

Little Al was always a good boy, and it was not his fault that he caused any undue trouble coming into the world. That was something you could blame on Dr. Castlebar, although Dr. Castlebar said it was all a part of the fun that he could not be located and arrived at the hospital only two minutes ahead of Al. After all, he got there, didn't he?

Dr. Castlebar actually was correct in most of his predictions. Even if the whole episode, perhaps, had not been as much fun as the doctor said it would be, there were lighter moments. It surely was amazing how time glossed over grimmer ones. Once you looked through the plate-glass window of the hospital's antiseptic crèche at little Al, you were convinced that all was for the best in this best of all possible worlds. Finally there was nothing so triumphant as the ride home from the hospital and the sight of Al in his own bassinet in the hall bedroom. The world was never the same once you had a baby and once you joined the ranks of parenthood. You were immediately a wiser and a more useful citizen and you had a real stake in the community. It was almost like being gifted with a new language, once you had a baby.

There were plenty of things, businesswise, to take up Willis's attention in those last years of the thirties. There was no doubt—with the assistance of a new sales manager and a general shakeup in the office force, plus the new funds loaned the company by Mrs. Jacoby—that he was getting Rahway Belt into a real competitive position. Willis had made it his personal task to visit every one of Rahway Belt's customers, sitting down with them and talking over their production problems. Also he devoted countless hours to the sales force. He respected the accumulated sales wisdom of several of the older salesmen—in fact he always had an idea that a wise older man equaled an overenergetic and impulsive younger one, but he also injected new blood. Jack Nelson, for instance, now vice president of Briggs, Bryant, had started with him at Rahway Belt, and Buzz Page, whom he first saw as an office boy out in Toledo, was with him still, and there would be no trouble making the list longer.

Yet you always had to remember that a sales force, no matter how effective it might be, was hopeless without a product in which it could believe. It was odd how many people, even in large organizations, were prone to neglect this simple fact. Willis lived, ate, and slept with Planeroid belting. He was only too glad to share his ultimate successes in this regard with Jerry Bascomb, whom he was lucky enough to hire in June '37, just after Jerry graduated from Tech. From the very start Willis insisted on naming Jerry's inventions that improved the Planeroid process the Bascomb patents. This was a good means of insuring loyalty, and to prove it Jerry was with him still, and Willis was the godfather of one of Jerry's lovely children. By the beginning of 1940, the Planeroid line was better than it had ever been, and sales figures and earnings showed that it was going places in a modest way.

XIX

THE YEAR 1940, when you came to think of it, was a headache year for nearly everyone in America, and Willis's personal and private affairs offered no exception. They moved, like nearly everyone else's, against a background of shock and crisis. To begin with, young Paul arrived that February. Rahway Belt was picking up and they could afford with difficulty a nurse for the children. Willis's whole budget was thrown out of balance but this was only the domestic side of the picture. Besides an uncertain business situation and restlessness among plant workers, Mr. Jacoby's health suddenly became so bad that he was obliged to cancel his usual winter trip to Arizona. Willis felt a premonition when he went to call on Mr. Jacoby. Without knowing anything about illness, Willis could tell that Mr. Jacoby, in spite of his high spirits, was far from well, and Willis's gloomiest conclusions were confirmed when he met Mrs. Jacoby downstairs in the living room.

He must have made this call several days after Paul was born, because he remembered apologizing to Mrs. Jacoby for not having come sooner. Willis often thought that everyone's life consisted of a series of repetitions. He had once been the young confidant of Mr. and Mrs. Henry Harcourt, and now his relationship with the Jacobys was on a larger scale, but there was the same atmosphere of trust and friendship. If Rahway Belt meant little to Mrs. Jacoby, except as something that made her husband happy, Willis knew that she appreciated what he had done by way of putting the investment on a paying basis.

Only a few days before his call, Mr. Henry Peters, who was a stockholder in Rahway Belt, had offered Willis some shares of Rahway Belt common. If Willis were to buy this stock, his holdings would be nearer 40 than 30 per cent. This was something which in all honesty he should tell Mrs. Jacoby, but he did not do so immediately when he met her downstairs, because he was still shocked by Mr. Jacoby's appearance.

There was never any use mincing matters with Mrs. Jacoby. She looked worried and unhappy, but like the late Seth Wilfred she knew how to cut her losses.

"There's a heart complication," she said. "Manley won't go to the hospital. He has superstitious ideas about hospitals."

"I'm awfully sorry," Willis told her. "I didn't know things were as serious as this."

"Well, they are," Mrs. Jacoby said, "but something serious happens to everyone some time. Sit down, and I'll ring for Henry to get you something."

"Oh, no thank you, Mrs. Jacoby," Willis said. "I mustn't keep you from anything you're doing."

"Sit down," Mrs. Jacoby said. "You're only keeping me from worrying. How are things at Rahway?"

"Everything's going pretty well," Willis told her.

"I know it is," Mrs. Jacoby said, "and it's a great comfort to Manley. He was reminding me only this morning how I had advised him to sell that plant."

Willis smiled, but at the same time he had a qualm of apprehension. If Mr. Jacoby should die, there might be every reason for Mrs. Jacoby to sell out her interest in Rahway Belt.

It was time to mention the common stock he had been offered. He did not want for a moment to have Mrs. Jacoby gain the idea that he was trying to get control of Rahway Belt. He wanted to explain his motives very clearly, but Mrs. Jacoby spoke again before he could start.

"Henry Peters says you want to buy his stock," she said.

Although Willis was beginning to pride himself on his ability to handle situations, he found himself pausing clumsily.

"Peters offered it to me first, of course," Mrs. Jacoby said, before Willis had a chance to speak. "But I didn't want any more. Why should I, with Manley the way he is?"

Willis often thought it was a pity that Mrs. Jacoby had not been a man.

"I am very glad that Mr. Peters consulted you first about this matter," Willis said, and he hoped he was not speaking too quickly or eagerly. "I was just going to take up the question with you myself, but seeing Mr. Jacoby so ill made it completely leave my mind."

There was a pause, a very brief one, but it was long enough to make Willis highly uncomfortable.

"I'm sure you were," Mrs. Jacoby said.

"I really was, Mrs. Jacoby," Willis answered.

It was a very silly remark to make, and besides, he had answered much too quickly.

"Of course you would really," Mrs. Jacoby said. "You're too shrewd to play around behind my back."

"I'm awfully glad you realize that, Mrs. Jacoby," Willis told her.

"Of course I realize it," Mrs. Jacoby said. "There is no need to worry about me, Willis. I don't want to have control of Rahway Belt"—she lowered her voice slightly—"if Manley should pass on."

The lowering of her voice gave Willis an uncomfortable sensation. It was the duty of anyone in business to discount any unpleasant possibility, but somehow Mrs. Jacoby made the passing on of Mr. Jacoby an accomplished fact.

"Now, Mrs. Jacoby," Willis said, "it's probably the winter climate. I'm sure Mr. Jacoby has many happy years ahead of him."

He was not surprised that Mrs. Jacoby should discount the remark, but he did think that she might have acknowledged it slightly.

"All I care about is the earnings," Mrs. Jacoby said. "Rahway Belt won't mean a thing to me except as another holding in the portfolio" —she lowered her voice again—"if Manley passes on."

Willis cleared his throat. He wished there were not always someone upon whom his future depended.

"Would you mind telling me, Mrs. Jacoby," he said, "if Mr. Jacoby should—er—pass on, are you planning to sell your stock?"

"I won't sink any more money in it," Mrs. Jacoby said. "I've bailed the company out once but I won't again. It's Manley's company, you know."

Willis laughed, but he was afraid his laughter was not very convincing.

"You won't have to bail it out again, Mrs. Jacoby," he said.

He was pleased that Mrs. Jacoby did not pause before she answered.

"No," she said, "you're doing very well, but let's stop beating about the bush. I won't have any sentimental feeling about Rahway Belt—if Manley passes on."

He was always grateful to Mrs. Jacoby for having stated her thoughts so frankly. He could understand that Mrs. Jacoby was actually saying that the end of an era was approaching, and that he must begin looking out for his own interests—if Manley Jacoby should pass on. He was certain that he never would have thought of writing Mr. Bryson Harcourt—that he would only have thought in the vaguest way about combining the Klaus patents with the Planeroid patents—if Mrs. Jacoby had not said that she would no longer have a sentimental interest in Rahway Belt in the event of Mr. Jacoby's demise.

It was a relief to meet someone like Mrs. Jacoby, who did not have the Harcourts' sentiments, because anyone with common sense knew that sentiment had no place in industrial transactions.

As soon as he left the Jacoby house on the ridge, Willis went at once to see Sylvia at the hospital. She was sitting up in her new bed jacket, and there were several new vases of flowers in the room, besides new offerings of booties and knitted blankets, all with a blue motif for a boy. He made a careful note of all the cards so that he might acknowledge them without bothering Sylvia.

"How is Mr. Jacoby, dear?" Sylvia asked.

"I'm afraid he's not very well, honey," Willis said. "There's the usual arthritis, but it is also complicated by a heart condition, but don't worry about it, honey."

"Oh, dear," Sylvia said. "I'm just beginning to get to like Mr. Jacoby."

He did not want Sylvia to be worried, especially now that she was giving little Paul several ounces more milk than she had managed for little Al.

"What is going to happen if he dies?" Sylvia asked.

It was obviously not the time to tell Sylvia about his conversation with Mrs. Jacoby.

"Honey," he said, "you let me worry about that one."

It was fortunate that Willis started that same evening to give serious thought to the possible merger of Rahway Belt and Harcourt Mill, because Mr. Jacoby died two weeks later, just when he was rallying and when preparations were going head for the Jacobys' annual trip to Arizona. Of course the whole picture changed immediately.

The truth was that the time was ripe for a change and everything fitted together in a more perfect manner than any other proposed merger that Willis had ever explored. Usually there were many unexpected obstacles, but not with Harcourt and Rahway Belt. There was no duplication in their products, because Planeroid filled a need completely different from the more ambitious Hartex line. In fact the two plants complemented each other, and the only possible objections to a merger was distance.

Two days after Mr. Jacoby's funeral, Willis decided to get in touch with Mr. Bryson Harcourt, without consulting Mrs. Jacoby, because obviously no one would be committed by an exploratory conversation. In order to avoid office gossip he wrote the letter himself, using his portable typewriter, on a card table in his living room in Orange. Little Paul and Sylvia had only recently arrived from the hospital with Miss Farquahr, a trained nurse who was giving Sylvia a sort of refresher course in baby-tending. Margaret, the new general maid, who had come after Minnie left, had already started quarreling with Miss Farquahr, for no good reason except to prove the axiom that trained nurses and other household employees never could get on together. Sylvia was still not allowed downstairs, and little Al was quite a problem, since he had reached the stage of pulling breakable objects off tables and then of pulling the tables and chairs on top of himself. Just when Willis was preparing to sit down quietly before supper, Sylvia had called to him from upstairs that he would simply have to look after little Al until his bedtime. Miss Farquahr was busy changing little Paul, and Margaret was busy with supper.

Dear Mr. Harcourt,
I am Willis Wayde, whom I hope you will remember from the old days at the Harcourt Mill. Although it has been a long time since we have met, I have a warm spot in my heart for Harcourt, and any news I hear from the mill is still to me like news from home in a very real sense. . . .

There was a crash and a scream from little Al. It was pure coincidence, of course, that Al had contrived to pull over the silver cigarette box which the Bryson Harcourts had sent as a wedding present. The corner of the box hit Al on the forehead, and now the floor was strewn with cigarettes.

"All right, Al," Willis said. "Daddy doesn't want Al to touch. No, no."

It was necessary in those days to speak to Al in simple monosyllables, and even so Al usually went right on with what he was doing. It took quite a while to gather up the cigarettes, and Al roared when the silver box was taken away from his clutches. He did not want the small horse which Willis gave him in place of it, and so thoughtlessly Willis let Al have his fountain pen. In the quiet that ensued Willis returned to his typewriter.

Knowing how busy you must be, I shall state my reason for this letter briefly. I find myself here in general charge of the Rahway Belting Company, and I believe I have an idea regarding its future . . .

Willis observed that Al had completely dismantled the fountain pen and that ink had cascaded over his knitted suit and down to the rug. He immediately took the pen away from little Al, who began to weep again, and then he called first for Miss Farquahr and then for Margaret, but no one answered. Then as long as the damage had been done he turned back to the typewriter.

. . . which I think may interest you as much as it does me. I would prefer to tell you the details verbally and so I ask whether I may call on you at your convenience and by appointment. . . .

There was another crash by the fireplace. Little Al had pulled over

[251]

the fire tongs and shovel, and this time he appeared to be severely injured, but Willis decided to finish the letter because fortunately little Al's screams of pain were changing to a shriller and more familiar note of indignant fury. As Willis endeavored to concentrate, it occurred to him that life was one long journey past milestones of hurt feelings, and though you might learn to suppress the reaction, it was better, perhaps, to scream openly and shamelessly like little Al.

It so happens that I must make a few calls in Boston next week. You may not have heard, by the way, that the Walton people up there are ordering our new Planeroid conveyors, and this is keeping us pretty busy in Rahway.

Willis looked up again from his typewriter. Miss Farquhar had arrived. She stood impersonally in front of the card table in her starched white uniform.

"What have you done to little Alfred, Mr. Wayde?" she asked.

"I didn't do anything," Willis said. "He does things to himself. Would you please mind taking him upstairs?"

"His crying upset Mrs. Wayde," Miss Farquhar said.

"Miss Farquhar," Willis said, and he smiled in an engaging way that usually worked with secretaries and office employees, "I don't seem to be very good at child rearing and I am trying to write a rather important confidential letter. Couldn't you keep an eye on Alfred for a minute, Miss Farquhar?"

After all, he was paying Miss Farquhar a substantial weekly wage, and it seemed to him that whenever she was wanted Miss Farquhar was indulging in necessary rest periods.

"I haven't a minute now, Mr. Wayde," Miss Farquhar told him. "I think Alfred would be quiet if you were to read to him. He's interested in *Peter Rabbit*. Mrs. Wayde read it through to him five times yesterday and he sat on the bed as quiet as a little mousey."

"All right," Willis said. "If you get it, I'll read it to him."

If he had a minute or two longer he might be able to conclude his letter to Mr. Bryson Harcourt.

"*Peter Rabbit* is right on the easy chair by the fireplace," Miss Farquhar said. "Alfred sees it now. Alfred, give *Peter Rabbit* to Daddy, and Daddy read to Alfred."

Then Miss Farquhar was gone and Willis and Alfred were alone again in the living room.

"Alfred," Willis said, "sit down and look at the pretty pictures. Sit down and be quiet, Alfred."

Alfred seemingly respected the change in his father's voice. He sat down quietly on the living-room rug. Of course, it was not a quiet that would last, but it gave Willis an opportunity to collect his thoughts. It was not literally true that he had to go up to Boston to make a few calls, but the statement sounded well.

If you will write me—or better, send me a wire—I can arrange my schedule to fit yours.

It will be a genuine pleasure to see you again and to talk over old times. I hope that Mrs. Harcourt and Bill and Bess are all well and that you are enjoying a good winter.

Sincerely, as always,

Little Al was becoming restive again.

"Here, Al," Willis told him, "sit down on Daddy's knee. 'Once upon a time there were four little rabbits, and their names were—Flopsy, Mopsy, Cotton-tail, and Peter. They lived . . .' "

Although Willis tried to put suspense and conviction into his reading, Alfred would not stay still.

He dropped Alfred hastily to the floor and looked down at his carefully pressed trousers.

"Miss Farquahr!" he shouted. "Would you mind coming down here? Quickly, please, Miss Farquahr."

Thinking it over later, Willis could see that there were a number of things wrong about his letter. If he had done it in the office after hours he could have given his whole mind to the composition. The unevenness and the strike-overs must have shown Mr. Harcourt that it was a home-written effort, and of course it was hastily phrased, but it never occurred to Willis for a moment that Mr. Bryson Harcourt would have thought the letter was merely an application for a job. He was shocked when he found a letter on his desk at Rahway three days later.

"Roger and I delighted if you can return to us again," the telegram read. "Meet me at my house, Beacon Street, five-thirty Tuesday, and please stay to dinner."

There was an overcordiality in the telegram that indicated Bryson Harcourt's transparency. Old H.H. would never have sent such a telegram, but it was clear that Willis was still favorably remembered back at the Harcourt Mill. There was also an indication that things were not going well, since they were overanxious to have him back.

"Delighted to meet you five-thirty Tuesday," he wired. "Sorry gave impression seeking position because am happy here."

He wanted to make it plain from the start that he expected no favors. In the last analysis he was presenting a simple business proposition which even Bryson Harcourt would readily understand.

Boston had been off the track for Willis Wayde for many years, except for fleeting visits with Sylvia to Craigie Street in Cambridge. He had only been back to the city once, businesswise, since he had left the Harcourt Mill, and that was for Beakney-Graham. He had gone on this occasion with Mr. Beakney as a part of what Mr. Beakney called a "presentation team." The presentation team had occupied cramped quarters in the Hotel Statler, while Mr. Beakney had resided in a comfortable suite at the Ritz-Carlton overlooking the Public Garden.

If you were out after a big account, Mr. Beakney would say, a little extra expense money was very often a mighty fine investment. By this he did not mean ostentation, Mr. Beakney used to say, but quiet dignity without a trace of brashness. A well-tailored, unobtrusive suit of clothes, Mr. Beakney used to say, plus the right tie and a well-shined pair of shoes, plus an expensive but worn suitcase, and a fountain pen that wrote at the right time—all these minor factors were better than an hour of sales presentation. Appearance and confidence meant as much as words, Mr. Beakney used to say, and a sound hotel address would back up all those other details.

It was advisable never to forget that someone from your client's office might drop into your room with a message or something. It was always advisable to keep things shipshape, and he wanted everyone who traveled for Beakney-Graham to have a photograph on his bureau of his mother, or of his wife and children. The thought that a man cared about his home had a fine effect on anyone who might drop in. Seriously, as Mr. Beakney used to say, you might as well face it—America was a woman's world. For instance, wasn't 80 per cent of the national income controlled by women? You had better love your mother if you worked for Beakney-Graham.

XX

WILLIS HAD spent many hours planning his approach to Mr. Bryson Harcourt. He knew it was better to show indifference than eagerness. Without undue familiarity he wished to show that he had a warm and loyal spot in his heart for the Harcourt Mill and the memory of Mr. Henry Harcourt. He wished to show that he was calling on Mr. Bryson Harcourt as one who still appreciated the many kindnesses the family had shown him, but he also wanted to have Mr. Bryson Harcourt realize that he was a successful individual in his own right.

Willis had reserved a room at the Ritz-Carlton in Boston. He took the ten-o'clock-in-the-morning train so that he would arrive at the hotel in time to spruce up before he went to see Mr. Harcourt at Beacon Street. He had applied saddle soap himself to the smaller of the two suitcases that he had purchased for his honeymoon. The unobtrusive briefcase he carried was more of a leather envelope for a few documents than a sales-man's bag, but even so Willis decided to leave it at the hotel. He wore a dark overcoat, which he had purchased two weeks before, and a darkish herringbone suit—double-breasted—made for him by the same tailor pa-tronized by Mr. Beakney. Little Paul had been five months on the way when Willis had decided to buy tailor-made clothes rather than ready-made suits. It seemed extravagant at such a time, what with all the doc-tor's bills and hospital bills, but still, as Willis pointed out to Sylvia, a good tailor-made suit would outlast a ready-made one two to one. There was no need for him to worry about his appearance when he registered at the Ritz. Instead he thought of the time when he had reserved a table for Bess Harcourt and himself—it was amazing to think how many years ago. He also recollected he had promised Sylvia to call up Mr. and Mrs. Hodges in Cambridge, but he decided not to do so until he was finished with the Harcourt matter. Sylvia and everything in Orange seemed very far away.

"Front," the hotel clerk called, and he handed Willis's room key to the bellboy. "The room overlooks the Public Garden, as you suggested, Mr. Wayde. Can you tell us how long you will be with us?"

"Tonight," Willis said, and he smiled. "And tomorrow night, I hope. I always enjoy it here in Boston."

When he was alone in his double room, Willis opened his suitcase immediately and hung up his extra suit and put his traveling photographs on the writing table. The photograph of his mother had been with him ever since the Harvard Business School. Beside it was a snapshot of Sylvia which he had taken himself at Chieftain Manor, and a baby picture of little Al. It was still only half past four o'clock by the time Willis had shaved and changed his shirt, and so he had time to sit for a while looking out at the Public Garden. There was no doubt that the days were getting longer. The waning light on the Public Garden reminded him of the light on the snow at the Harcourt place, and somehow the afternoon shadows and the sky itself had a quality that was different from New Jersey—a harsher, plainer quality.

Willis discovered that Beacon Street and the Bryson Harcourts' house only aroused distinct memories without awakening the keen emotion that they had once evoked. He remembered the night he had first walked up the steps with Bess, and he remembered the time when he had asked Bess to dinner and the theater—when Bess had stood him up for Edward Ewing. Thinking of the whole episode made Willis feel like a modern traveler regarding a classical ruin.

The maid who answered the door was a dimly familiar figure from the past. He was surprised that she remembered him much more clearly than he did her.

"I'll take your coat, Mr. Willis," the maid said.

"Oh, thank you," Willis said. "I hope Mr. Harcourt is expecting me."

He glanced unobtrusively at his wrist watch as he spoke. It was two minutes after five-thirty.

"Oh yes," the maid said, "Mr. and Mrs. Harcourt are expecting you upstairs, Mr. Willis."

Although it had been nearly ten years since Willis had seen them, Mr. Bryson and Mrs. Harcourt still had the durable outdoor quality that he remembered. There were gray streaks in Mr. Bryson's dark hair, but he still had a young look. There had always been a warmth and kindness about Mr. Bryson and this quality had not gone. There was a moment, as Willis stood in the doorway of the upstairs parlor, when he realized that the balance between them all had changed. He knew before either of the Harcourts spoke that they were anxious to see him in the way people were when you had something that they wanted.

"Why, Willis," Mrs. Harcourt said, "how well you look!"

"And you too, Mrs. Harcourt," Willis said. She had the florid complexion he remembered, but her hair was growing becomingly white. "It is a genuine pleasure to see you again."

"I told Bryson that I wanted to have a glimpse of you and then I'd go," Mrs. Harcourt said. "How are your father and mother—well, I hope?"

"Oh, yes thanks," Willis said. "They're on the West Coast, you know."

"You're staying to dinner, aren't you?" Mrs. Harcourt asked.

"If it would not be an inconvenience, it would be a great pleasure, Mrs. Harcourt," Willis said.

"That's splendid," Mrs. Harcourt said. "I've asked Bess and Edward over. She's terribly anxious to see you."

"Let's see," Mr. Bryson Harcourt said, "maybe you don't know that Bess married Edward Ewing. I don't remember whether you were with us or not when they got engaged."

"Oh yes, I was, as a matter of fact," Willis said. "It will be a great pleasure to see them both again."

"Why don't you take Willis across the hall, dear," Mrs. Harcourt said, "for your little talk, but don't be too long because we all want to hear about him."

"It is just like old times having you here, Willis," Mr. Harcourt said, and he took Willis by the arm and led him past the stairs into the smaller sitting room that looked out on Beacon Street, and closed the sliding door. "Will you have a cigar, Willis?"

"No thank you, sir," Willis said, and he laughed. "Mr. Harcourt taught me a lot of things, but he never could get me to like cigars."

"Well, I'll have one if you don't mind," Mr. Bryson said. "Father taught me the cigar habit earlier than he expected. I used to steal cigars out of the humidor in the big house when I was thirteen, and I don't think he ever knew. You're looking very fit, Willis."

"I always make it a point," Willis said, "to do a little bending and stretching and a few push-ups every day, but sometimes I think I thrive on hard work."

"Let's see," Mr. Bryson said. "What is the name of that place where you are working?"

A feeling of frustration, which Willis had forgotten, returned to him when Mr. Bryson asked that question.

"It is the Rahway Belting Company, sir," Willis said, and he tried not to speak too slowly. "You may have heard of the Planeroid conveyors that we manufacture. They fill a different need from Hartex. Incidentally, the Walton people are using them here in Boston."

"Oh, of course," Mr. Harcourt said, "Rahway Belt."

Willis settled himself more comfortably in his chair.

"Of course, it is a small company," Willis said. "I happen to be the head of it at the moment." He tried to speak as casually as possible, and he smiled. "That's why I came up to see you, sir."

Willis's instinct was telling him that the amenities of the interview were over. Mr. Bryson nodded as he always did when he was trying to put facts together.

"Dear me," he said, "I had no idea that you were so responsible there. I'm sorry, selfishly, because you see, we are looking for a new plant manager at Harcourt. I thought of you in that connection just as soon as I got your letter."

Mr. Harcourt paused and Willis smiled sympathetically.

"Of course," Mr. Harcourt said, "Father was under the impression that you would move ahead quickly, but I hadn't thought of you as being at the head of your own organization."

Willis laughed in a deprecating way.

"It really isn't my own organization, sir," Willis said. "I'm acting as president only for the moment. I'm sorry you have to look for a new plant manager, because I know they are rather hard to find."

Mr. Bryson shook his head.

"It isn't finding them—it is keeping them," he said. "You may remember my cousin Roger, don't you?"

"Oh yes," Willis said, "I remember Mr. Roger Harcourt very well."

Mr. Bryson puffed for a moment on his cigar.

"Of course," he said, "I keep forgetting. Of course you know Roger Harcourt as well as I do. He had a disagreeable streak, but I frankly don't know what I'd do without him."

Willis nodded understandingly but he did not answer. It was far better to let Mr. Bryson go on talking.

"Roger was delighted," Mr. Bryson said, "when I told him I had heard from you."

"I am very pleased that Mr. Roger reacted that way," Willis said. "Of course I will always have a warm spot in my heart for the Harcourt Mill."

"There is such a thing as sentiment even in business, isn't there?" Mr. Bryson said. "It is like old times talking to you, Willis. I had half forgotten what good friends we used to be, and how you used to come over to see Bill and Bess."

"It will be a great pleasure to see Bess this evening," Willis said, "and I hope that Bill is well."

"Bill." Mr. Bryson laughed exactly as he had long ago when Bill's name was mentioned. "He's down in Bermuda now. Ever since he married Anne Gresham they stay at her family's place there for most of the winter. I keep trying to talk mill to him but he'd rather work for his father-in-law. Let's see, Willis, how old are you?"

"I'll be thirty-four in November, sir," Willis said.

"Just Bill's age. I should have remembered." Mr. Bryson laughed again. "It must be great to mention your age at your next birthday so happily."

Willis felt uneasy for the first time since they had been talking. He did not realize that he had been so transparent.

"Well, it is surprising how time marches on," Mr. Bryson said, "and you're married too. I remember now—to a girl Bill used to know in Cambridge, the daughter of a professor at Harvard."

"Yes, sir," Willis answered, "Sylvia Hodges."

"Well," Mr. Bryson said again, "time certainly marches on, but there is one thing that puzzles me."

"What's that, sir?" Willis asked.

"You know," Mr. Bryson said, "Father always used to tell me not to exhibit undue curiosity when I was talking business. He used to say to let the situation develop without forcing it, but I can't help being curious. If you don't want a job, why have you come up here to see me, Willis?"

Willis waited for a moment, deliberately, because he wanted to be sure of Mr. Bryson's full attention, and the time had come to put things into very simple terms.

"Well," Willis said, and he tried to speak slowly, "I don't want to startle you, sir, and maybe this whole thing should have something more of an introduction." He checked himself and sat up straighter. "I was wondering if you would be interested in buying the Rahway Belting Company, Mr. Harcourt."

It was the most decisive thing that he had ever said. The words were out in the room and all his imaginary talks with Mr. Bryson were swept away.

"Good God!" Mr. Bryson said.

"Just a minute," Willis said. "Please do not turn it down without thinking of it, Mr. Harcourt. You see, there would be no cash involved, only a negotiated exchange of stock. You could call the whole thing Harcourt Associates, if you wanted, and if you want, you can get me with the deal. I don't see why I couldn't manage both the Rahway plant and the Harcourt Mill."

Mr. Bryson sighed.

"I wish Roger were here," he said, "but as long as he isn't, you had better begin at the beginning, Willis."

[259]

Past associations were so strong, as Willis gave his explanations, that it was hard to remember that he was no longer Mr. Henry Harcourt's assistant engaged in explaining, at Mr. Harcourt's request, another business detail to Mr. Bryson.

"Frankly, Willis," Mr. Bryson said, "I'm looking for fewer and not more complications and I don't exactly see how any sort of combination could possibly simplify any of our problems."

"I think I can show you," Willis said—and it was not hard for him to present his ideas, because he had rehearsed them so often—"that things will be much simpler and that you will have much less personal responsibility. Do you remember what Benjamin Franklin said—at least I think it was Franklin, check me if I'm wrong—when the Declaration of Independence was being signed?"

Mr. Bryson frowned and shook his head.

"Let's see," he said—"the Declaration of Independence? No, I don't seem to remember at the moment."

"Well, I don't know if I've got it straight myself," Willis said. It was not a time to appear too bright, and his age was a handicap in talking with Mr. Bryson. "I think Benjamin Franklin said that if we don't hang together we will hang separately."

"That's right," Mr. Bryson said, "but I don't see what it has to do with the subject."

It was a childish sort of maneuvering but at the same time it was effective, and there was a grim menace in that statement about hanging separately.

"Please don't think," Willis said, and he laughed heartily, "that I am offering any threat to the Harcourt Mill. It is larger and stronger, of course, than the little show I'm running. I am only stating a business axiom, Mr. Harcourt, in rather theatric terms—only saying that if two businesses combine they are much stronger in the face of competition. Small businesses don't have the chance they had a few years ago."

"I know," Mr. Bryson said. "That's what Roger is always saying—we're losing money and we ought to sell out. He hasn't any sense of responsibility."

Willis nodded and watched Mr. Bryson gravely.

"Mr. Harcourt," he said, "what I'm about to say comes from the bottom of my heart. I think I know the belting business. I ought to because my father and your father taught it to me."

He stopped, and when he went on the conviction of his own voice impressed him.

"I'll guarantee that none of us will lose money if we can get together, and if Mr. Henry Harcourt were here he would be the first to agree with me."

Willis had been a good salesman even before his final training at Beakney-Graham. There was no trouble, he always said, in selling anything to anyone, whether it was an article or an idea, provided you believed in the thing you wished to sell—but belief should be harnessed with knowledge. Willis had never believed in anything as fully as he had in joining the Harcourt Mill with Rahway Belt. He had his facts so clearly that eloquence was not necessary. All he needed was patience. One always had to be patient with Mr. Bryson. Willis went over the facts very slowly and he asked for a pencil and paper so that he could set down figures.

If you thought of selling as a form of sport, it could be the most fascinating game in the world. Willis could turn his mind, if he wanted to reminisce, to some of his outstanding achievements in salesmanship which were as tangible to him as a big-game hunter's trophies, but nothing had ever been as perfect as the Harcourt-Rahway Belt promotion. It had not been difficult in detail, because Mr. Bryson had been with him all the way.

The beauty of the whole thing lay in what you might call the *rapport*, to use a French word. Right from the beginning, he and Mr. Harcourt were in tune and in step. Mr. Bryson was confused and weary of the details of the Harcourt Mills. He had never wanted to be the head of it, and he had assumed the leadership only as a family duty. The beauty of the Rahway-Harcourt promotion was that Willis and Mr. Bryson desired two different things which fitted together like a jigsaw puzzle. Willis wanted a chance to move forward, while Mr. Bryson wanted to move back. It was a very pretty problem of balance. It was beautiful to see Mr. Bryson react to every stimulus.

"I really think you have something, Willis," Mr. Bryson said. "Of course I'm not much of a judge of these things, but the further we go into this the better it seems to look."

The time had come to draw back slightly. Willis paused for a moment seemingly lost in thought. His hesitation was a little like Tom Sawyer's reluctance to allow the other boys to paint the fence, and it also resembled Antony's feigned alarm when he had aroused the Roman mob.

"I agree with you, Mr. Harcourt," he said, "but I think we both ought to remember that there may be some sort of catch in this thing that neither of us sees, and fortunately we both have plenty of time to think it over."

"I'm glad we have time," Mr. Bryson said, "because I can see that this is pretty complicated. It does take thinking over."

"It certainly does," Willis said, "and I can't tell you how glad I'll be to get someone else's reaction. I may as well tell you frankly that I haven't discussed this with any of our people at Rahway—in fact, not even with my wife." Willis laughed. He had thought of everything and now as the time for a lighter, friendlier touch. "Of course Sylvia isn't in a position to be interested right now. She's just back from the hospital with our second child."

It always paid to bring family into such discussions. If any proof of stability was needed, there it was, with Sylvia just back from the hospital.

"Really?" Mr. Bryson said. "Is it a boy or a girl?"

"A boy," Willis said. "He's actually our second boy. The first one's Al, named after my father. "Al's quite a little rascal—always pulling things off tables and things like that. But, honestly, I didn't mean to bring the little fellows in to interrupt this talk."

Willis laughed but he immediately became serious. "I'm sorry I digressed, because the beauty of our situation lies in the fact that we are both thinking out loud and that neither of us is committed to anything whatsoever. In fact, it may very well be that our majority stockholder, Mrs. Jacoby, may be entirely against the whole transaction."

"Let's see," Mr. Bryson said, "who is Mrs. Jacoby?"

"The widow of the late president of Rahway Belt," Willis told him. "Mrs. Jacoby has an excellent head for business. She is the daughter of the financier Seth Wilfred. I don't know whether you have ever heard of him."

"Oh," Mr. Bryson said, "was he the Wilfred that was mixed up with the Erie Railroad?"

Willis nodded. The mention of Mr. Seth Wilfred, he could see, gave Rahway Belt a new stability and a brighter background, but a disturbed look had come over Mr. Bryson.

"I can't understand why you haven't talked this over with Mrs.—er—Jacoby," Mr. Bryson said. "It would seem to me that she is a key figure in your picture."

Willis nodded in grave agreement and at the same time like a younger man acknowledging an older man's rebuke.

"I suppose I should have," Willis said, "before I came up here to bother you about something which is so theoretical, but the truth is I was hoping I might get a little something more concrete to give Mrs. Jacoby when I finally did see her." Willis shook his head slowly. "Frankly there has been no opportunity to take up any matter with her because of Mr. Jacoby's illness and death. His funeral was only a very short time ago."

For a few seconds they both were gravely silent. The mention of death was often useful in pulling together the loose ends of a business conversation.

"I wish I had some way of predicting," Willis said. "I hope Mrs. Jacoby will see things my way."

He felt a sharp sense of elation as he glanced at Mr. Bryson Harcourt. There was no doubt of Mr. Bryson's concern now that he saw bright prospects moving away from him.

"I certainly hope she will," Mr. Bryson said, "and I don't see why she shouldn't. Suppose we go on the assumption she agrees."

"I think that is a very good idea, Mr. Harcourt," Willis answered, "as long as we are just thinking out loud."

"Good heavens!" Mr. Bryson said. "I haven't been so absorbed for a long while. It is quarter of seven o'clock and I hear voices. It must be Bess and Edward. You'll stay over tomorrow, won't you? I'd like to have you talk to Roger."

"It would be a great pleasure, Mr. Harcourt," Willis said, "as long as it is definitely understood that we are just thinking out loud."

Willis was beginning to be interested in how the years had treated people. When Mr. Harcourt pulled open the sliding door, Willis could see that Mrs. Harcourt and Bess and Edward Ewing had already gathered around a tray of cocktails in the sitting room across the hall. Mrs. Harcourt had changed into a black velvet evening gown, and Bess was dressed in green. A green dress, as Willis had told her once, went particularly well with her greenish-blue eyes. Her hair, Willis could see in those seconds while he walked across the hall to the parlor, was still yellow but, like his own, darker. She looked taller than he remembered; and he could tell—because a man could always tell such things—that Bess Ewing had made a special effort for him. The gloss of her hair and its somewhat aggressive curly quality told very plainly that Bess had been to the beauty parlor that morning. It was pleasant of course, particularly under present circumstances, to realize that Bess wanted to look well on his account, but Willis was sure that his interest was now based on nothing but pure expediency.

When he had last seen Bess, his knowledge of young women had been confined only to her, to the few girls he had known at the Clyde High School, or had met in classes at Boston University, and to one or two of Bess's friends, who had seldom bothered to converse with him. It was very different now. Mrs. Harcourt and Bess, in her green satin and pearls, had a slightly provincial look. Sylvia, even in an old dress, would have attracted more attention than Bess Ewing. The truth was that Sylvia had lived in a real world, while Bess—and Edward Ewing too—had only existed under a permanent umbrella of financial protection.

Bess's voice had a high note which Willis had always associated with her when she was pleased and elated.

"Why, Willis," she said, and she held out both her hands. "You don't look a bit different."

He thought that her hands held his a moment longer than was necessary before they dropped away.

"I hope I've changed a little for the better," Willis said. "This is a very great pleasure, Bess."

"Well, you sound just the same," Bess said. "You always did sound like Emily Post."

Willis felt his cheeks reddening.

"And Uriah Heep," Willis said, and he laughed louder than was necessary. "Don't forget Uriah Heep."

Suddenly Bess's lips lost their malicious smile.

"That isn't accurate now," she said. "You don't look humble any more."

"Uriah Heep stopped being humble too," Willis said, and he laughed again—"that is, if I remember Dickens."

"Oh, Willis," Bess said, "let's stop. I'm really dreadfully glad to see you." Then she must have remembered that Willis had not yet said a word to Edward Ewing. Edward was standing waiting, wearing a dinner coat, which made Willis wish that he had brought his own tuxedo.

"Willis," Bess said, "you remember Edward, don't you?"

It seemed to Willis that they shook hands in very much the same way they had across the tennis net at the Harcourt place, but Willis was also aware of certain shades of difference. He felt no wishful envy of Edward Ewing now. He felt not only a mental but a physical superiority, because Edward had accumulated a corpulence about his face and waistline, clearly indicating that he did not put saccharine in his coffee, sprinkle wheat germ in his orange juice, or do bending-and-stretching exercises and push-ups in the morning. His brownish eyes had a dull, contented look, giving an impression, which Willis was beginning to recognize, of someone who had never moved forward, in a career or business sense.

"I certainly do remember," Willis said.

"I'm awfully glad to see you again, Willis," Edward said. "How's everything going?"

"Fine," Willis said. "Fine. I'm living in Orange—married and have two children—and you, Edward?"

"We have four," Edward said. "That is, the last time I counted up. Four's right, isn't it, Bess?"

"Right," Bess said. "And no more in sight on the immediate horizon. But then, Edward and I had a head start over you and—oh, dear, I have forgotten your wife's name, Willis."

Willis laughed heartily and hoped that he did not sound nervous.

"Her name is Sylvia," he said. "You can remember it by the quotation 'Who is Sylvia? What is she?'—from Shakespeare, if I'm not mistaken."

"My God!" Bess said. "Since when did you take up Shakespeare?"

"I wouldn't say I have taken him up," Willis said, "but I like to relax with a book now and then when little Al isn't pulling potted plants off the window sill on top of himself."

"Little Al sounds very active." It was Mr. Bryson Harcourt interrupting.

"Indeed he is," Willis said, "considering his age."

"Well, boys will be boys," Mr. Bryson said. "See here, hasn't anyone given you a drink?"

"Edward," Bess said, and Willis remembered her executive tone of voice, "you're keeping bar for Father, aren't you?"

"Sorry, dear," Edward said. "My mind was on little Al and the flower pots. Dabney used to do it. You remember, in the conservatory."

"Never mind Dabney, Edward," Bess said. "Go and please get Willis his cocktail. What else do you relax with besides Shakespeare, Willis?"

"I always try to relax with something worthwhile," Willis answered.

"What do you consider better?" Bess asked. "A blonde or a brunette?"

Willis laughed heartily.

"Gentlemen prefer blondes," he said.

Of course Willis meant it only in a kidding way, but still it was not such a bad remark as a comeback after the one Bess had handed him, and it seemed to please Bess very much.

"Do you still like blondes?" she asked.

"Oh yes," he said, but he did not like Bess Ewing in that way any longer, and he was sure that pique or resentment did not enter into his feeling.

"What was it we were talking about before Father interrupted us?" Bess asked. "Oh, I remember. About good books. What do you read besides Shakespeare?"

"Well, I don't get a chance to tackle anything much except business reading," Willis said, "but I am making my way through Dr. Eliot's—I mean President Eliot's—Five-Foot Shelf. I'm almost through volume ten right now."

"Oh, dear," Bess said, "not the Five-Foot Shelf of Books." And then she began to laugh.

Willis was not annoyed because he was already training himself to rise above annoyance, but before he could answer, Bess had stopped laughing.

"I was only laughing at one side of you," she said. "You used to be so

[265]

persistent that you frightened me sometimes, and you still do, Willis."

"Oh, come, Bess, I am a very mediocre person, and you know it," he answered, and then Mr. Bryson interrupted them again.

"I don't know what you two are talking about," he said, "but it's time to go down to dinner, and before we go—" and he spoke in a louder tone—"as long as we are all in the family here, I have a word to say that may interest us all. Willis and I have been having a very interesting and worthwhile talk. It may very well be that we will have Willis with us again, at least for part of his time, at the mill." Mr. Harcourt raised his glass. "Here's hoping so, Willis, and you'd better have another before we go downstairs."

"Oh, no thank you, sir," Willis said. It was not what he would have called a two-drink night, and he needed to watch everything. He was surprised that Bess looked as though she had just received an answer to an outlandish wish.

"Oh, Willis," she said, "I'm so glad."

Willis had been in the Bryson Harcourts' Boston dining room on several occasions years ago, but he saw it with a new eye while he told Mrs. Harcourt about Sylvia and the children. It looked more worn than he remembered, but he had to admit that the added dinginess only indicated that the Harcourts were not obliged to care how things looked. He and Sylvia, he was thinking, would have been criticized, but not the Harcourts, and, besides, the room was durably handsome. The pedestal table, without an extra leaf since it was only set for five, was late-eighteenth or early-nineteenth century. The sideboard was of the same period as the table, but rather heavy for Willis's taste. The plates were simple blue Canton—traditional New England, of course—but they really made quite a show since, what with the Japanese invasion of China and then the European war, no Canton china had been available for years. The heavy pretentious flat silver dated from the middle eighties but the candlesticks and a very handsome *épergne,* he believed, were Georgian. There was a long gilt-framed mirror behind the sideboard, and on the wall opposite Willis was a portrait which he recognized at once, from the neck-constricting costume of the eighteen-twenties, as that of Mr. William Harcourt. It must have been a copy, like the one in the president's office at the mill, because they surely would not have removed the original from the big house.

"What a very beautiful *épergne,* Mrs. Harcourt," Willis said.

Sylvia had said that he was never good with French words, but he was sure that he had pronounced it correctly.

"Why, Willis," Mrs. Harcourt said, "I didn't know you were interested in old silver."

There was wine, which must have been a claret—red wine with red meat. Willis took a sip of it before he answered and made a mental note that he must read up on wines.

"Well, frankly," Willis said, "it was Mr. Henry Harcourt who obliged me to take an interest in antiques. You see, one summer he had me make an inventory of all the antique furniture in the office at the mill." Willis smiled and shook his head as though he faced a rather hopeless situation. "Now antiques have become a hobby with me, and a recreation which Sylvia and I can share. It's sort of fun to hop in the car on Saturdays and go around to antique shops. And I've found that antiquing is a hobby that pays in other ways."

He paused and glanced around the table, and finally he encountered the stern gaze of the portrait on the opposite wall, and felt pleased, as he had often felt previously, that he had never been obliged to work for Mr. William Harcourt. Bess, who was sitting on his right, had stopped conversing with her father.

"How do you mean, antiquing pays in other ways?" she asked.

Willis had not meant to deliver a public dissertation, and as usual Bess had caught him off guard.

"Why," Willis said, "I only meant it never hurts to have an interest that you can talk about intelligently. Frankly, it interests me that the heads of a great many large businesses seem to collect antiques. They're apt to appreciate someone who knows about them."

"Is that why you mentioned the *épergne?*" Bess asked.

Willis felt his face redden. He wished that he could outgrow this telltale habit.

"No," he said, "it was only that I happened to like it. Isn't it here to be admired?"

"Oh," Bess said, "well, come around and see some of my *épergnes* sometime."

It was a little hard to interpret this remark, but everyone began to laugh.

"I certainly will," Willis said, laughing with the rest, "now you ask me."

Then Willis had an unexpected shock. Bess's knee was touching his beneath the table. The dessert was floating island, not a favorite of his. He could not very well draw his knee away, considering the status of the Harcourt-Rahway deal.

"Don't you like your floating island?" Bess said.

"Why, yes," Willis said, "very much, Bess."

"It always makes me feel young and childish," Bess said.

"It always makes me think of home and the children," Willis answered.

It might have been difficult to have made Sylvia understand that he could not very well withdraw his knee, considering the Harcourt-Rahway situation.

"Willis," Mr. Bryson said, "what do you think of this 'phony war' in Europe? Do you think they are waiting until spring?"

Frankly Willis was not able to react to war news in the emotional way that Sylvia did. He did not know much about Hitler or Nazism, and he was bored by arguments on the subject.

"Well," he said, "of course I don't know anything except what I read in the papers and hear over the air, but I don't see how they can all sit around doing nothing indefinitely. Someone must be getting ready to do something."

"That same thought has been running through my own mind," Mr. Harcourt said. "I can't help wondering what that something's going to be."

It was difficult to consider the world situation with Bess's knee pressed against his. Government interference in business was enough, without having to think about war.

"Hitler hasn't got the resources," Edward said. "His whole machine is stopped and the French will put on an offensive this spring. It will all be over before we get a chance to get into it."

At first Willis thought that Edward Ewing was joking, when he hinted at a chance of getting into it, but Willis was learning that war and politics got people unnecessarily stirred up, and so he tried to speak as lightly as possible.

"As far as I can see," Willis said—"and I base my knowledge on market letters, especially the Kiplinger Letter from Washington—"

"What on earth is the Kiplinger Letter?" Bess asked.

Willis felt somewhat constrained explaining Kiplinger, because he suspected that she knew all about it, although she was looking at him brightly.

"Well, the Kiplinger Letter," Willis said, "is edited in Washington by a man named Mr. Kiplinger."

"You said all that the first time," Bess said. "When you mentioned the Kiplinger Washington Letter, of course I knew that it was written by a man in Washington by the name of Mr. Kiplinger."

"Well, I suppose you're right," Willis said, and he joined in the laugh at his expense. "But this Mr. Kiplinger does get around a good deal, and he has important contacts that he naturally can't quote."

"I should like to see one of those letters," Bess said. "Make a note of it, will you, Willis?"

"Indeed I will, Bess," Willis said, and he took out his pocket notebook and his pencil.

"Oh, Willis," Bess said. "I only meant a mental note."

Willis wanted to answer Bess sharply, but he couldn't, what with the Harcourt and Rahway deal. He was relieved when Mrs. Harcourt pushed back her chair.

"Come on, Bess," Mrs. Harcourt said. "You and I can talk about Dabney's school while the men talk about war and business."

"If it is war, Edward will like it," Bess said. "He won't rest until we can get into the war."

There was a moment's comfortable silence in the dining room when Mrs. Harcourt and Bess left them. Willis's mind had moved momentarily into the future. He was thinking of a dining room that he and Sylvia might have some day, with a table and a dozen very good Chippendale chairs from Mallet's of Bath—and then his thoughts were interrupted by Mr. Bryson Harcourt's voice.

"Are you sure you don't want a cigar, Willis?"

"No thank you, sir," Willis said, "but if I might I would like a cigarette."

"By the way," Mr. Harcourt said, "I should have asked you if you wanted to wash up before dinner. There is a lavatory in the closet below the front stairs, in case you need it, Willis."

"Thank you, sir," Willis said, "but I really have no need of it."

"Well, then," Mr. Bryson said, "your constitution's stronger than mine. If you will excuse me, I shall visit it myself, and then I think I'll call up Roger Harcourt so we can be sure to meet with him in the morning."

"Brandy, Willis?" Edward asked.

"Just a little, thank you," Willis said. "Just a very small touch."

When he tasted it, he knew it was some of Mr. Henry Harcourt's brandy, and he thought of Mr. Percy Nagel in Mr. Harcourt's private study long ago.

"I don't know what it was that you were talking to my father-in-law about," Edward said, "but if it involves your coming back to the mill, I hope it works. I gather things are rather confused up there. I don't know anything because I am in a law office, but Bess is always fussing about the mill—not that we depend on it much."

Willis discovered that he suddenly had a warm spot in his heart for Edward Ewing.

"Of course the plant is small in a modern sense," he said slowly, "but still it has real possibilities. I remember that Bess used to be sentimental about it."

"Sentimental is right," Edward said. "Her family is always quarreling about the mill."

It was just as well to assume that Edward Ewing might not be as dull as he looked. It was not a time to show undue eagerness or a time to be fishing for information. It was better to drop the subject of the Harcourt Mill.

"How's the tennis?" Willis asked.

"Tennis?" Edward repeated, and it was clear that he had entirely forgotten.

"I don't suppose you remember," Willis said. "No reason that you should. We played a set at the Harcourts' one summer when I was working in the mill office." He laughed easily. "I was lousy, perfectly lousy."

"Oh," Edward said, "yes, I remember, and we had a swim in the pool. I've given up tennis and taken up golf."

"Is that so?" Willis said. "Well, I'll take you on at that sometime. I'm not so lousy at golf."

It would be a compensation, a squaring of the circle, if he could play golf and beat Edward Ewing.

"Not that I'm any good," Willis said, because it was never correct to say that one was good at golf. "But I get a whale of a lot of fun out of it."

Edward Ewing nodded and Willis had the pleasant feeling one always has when a difficult conversation ends on a common ground of interest.

"How much do you go around in?" Edward asked.

"Oh, just a beginner's score," Willis said. "In the middle nineties or perhaps a stroke or two below."

"Oh," Edward said. "Well, we must have a game."

Since Edward had not mentioned what he could go around in, he was, of course, a better player. It was ridiculous that Willis should have had a faint feeling of frustration. It was a relief when Mr. Bryson returned to the dining room. He was like the map of a familiar country, although the map had been stored away for many years.

"Don't get up," Mr. Bryson said, "please. I'm sorry to have taken so long, but Roger wouldn't let me go. He hopes we can both be down at State Street at half past nine tomorrow morning. I hope that isn't too early."

"Oh, no," Willis said. "It will be a real pleasure to see Mr. Roger again."

"I can drop by and pick you up," Mr. Bryson said. "I forgot to ask where you were stopping, Willis."

"Thank you very much, sir," Willis said. "I'm at the Ritz."

"Well, that will be no trouble at all, if you're at the Ritz," Mr. Bryson said.

It seemed to Willis that there had been a shade of surprise when the Ritz had been mentioned.

"I usually stop at the Ritz when I'm in Boston," Willis said. It was a little crude, he thought the moment after he said it, and not quite accurate, perhaps, because he had never stopped at the Ritz before.

"I suppose if we don't go upstairs we will be criticized," Mr. Bryson said.

"That's right," Edward said. "Bess gave me the word for us to come up as soon as possible, and you know Bess."

"Oh, yes," Mr. Bryson said, "we all know Bess."

"Come here and sit beside me, Willis," Mrs. Harcourt said, "and please tell me some more about the children."

"Well," Willis said, "there isn't much to tell about Paul except that he's a pretty hefty youngster, Mrs. Harcourt, but Al's quite a boy—just in what I think is called the toddling stage. I wish I had a snapshot of him here. You know I really have a pretty warm spot in my heart for Al."

"Of course you have," Mrs. Harcourt said. "I'm sure you're a very good father. Doesn't—er—Sylvia think so?"

"Why did you name the second one Paul?" Bess asked. Her voice came to him from across the room, showing that she had been listening all the while.

"Sylvia named him after her grandfather," Willis said.

"Well," Bess said, "as long as no one robbed Peter."

Willis smiled carefully and looked at Mrs. Harcourt.

"I just meant robbing Peter to pay Paul," Bess said.

There was an undercurrent in her voice that puzzled him. "Paul is going to get along all right," Willis said, "without anybody doing any robbing for him."

The edginess in his own voice made Willis uneasy. It was not the way one should sound, considering the Rahway-Harcourt merger, and Willis turned quickly back to Mrs. Harcourt and to little Al and Paul and Sylvia's ideas of decoration and nurses and hospitals, all subjects which Mrs. Harcourt understood and commented on intelligently.

And yet, he was thinking, could anyone in Mrs. Harcourt's position really know about himself or Sylvia? There was luck in everything, but people like the Harcourts scarcely needed it. The money their family had accumulated had been increased by the clever management of other people, until the Harcourts were free from the Harcourt Mill itself. Mrs. Harcourt could give her dinners, Mr. Harcourt could sail his yacht races, and Bess could send her boys to Groton School, or some such place, no matter what happened to the Harcourt Mill.

Of course, Willis was thinking, he had been lucky, but he had worked to earn his luck. What did the Harcourts know about scrimping to pay insurance policies and saving for new clothing, let alone a new car?—absolutely nothing. What would happen to the Harcourts if they were thrown into the world? Bill Harcourt could not have held a clerical job and Bess could not be a secretary or a switchboard operator.

"You're quite right, Mrs. Harcourt," Willis said, "Orange is hot for Sylvia and the children in the summer, but she and the children do get off to Lake Sunapee for a month. The Hodgeses have a little camp there by the lake. . . ."

It was lucky for the Harcourts that they did not have to earn their living. Willis stood up when he had finished talking about Lake Sunapee.

"It's been delightful renewing old associations, Mrs. Harcourt," he said, "and thank you for asking me to dinner. I've enjoyed every minute of it, but I must go now so that I can be ready for Mr. Harcourt in the morning. I think—at least I hope—that we are going to have a busy and worthwhile session."

He shook hands with Mrs. Harcourt. Then he squared his shoulders, assuming the alert posture that he had learned at Beakney-Graham.

"Good night, Bess," he said. "It's been a real pleasure seeing you again. It's been just like old times."

Bess had assumed her most tantalizing expression—at least it had been tantalizing once.

"Well, not quite like old times," she said.

"Well, no," Willis said, "not quite, Bess."

She dropped his hand but she was still smiling.

"If you finish all this business," she said, "that you have to be so fresh for in the morning, would you like to come and have tea with me or something stronger? You'll need it after a day with Cousin Roger."

"Well, I wouldn't quite say that, Bess," Willis said, "but it would be a great pleasure to have tea and to talk over old times with you and Edward."

"Edward won't be there," Bess said. "He has to have his squash at teatime. It will be just you and me. The children never come to tea."

"Well, that will be all the better, Bess," Willis said, and he laughed. "Tea for two is a wonderful idea. As soon after four-thirty as possible. By the way, I don't think I remember where you're living."

Willis whipped out his notebook and his Eversharp pencil. Dinner at the Harcourts' was over and he was feeling more tired than he had expected.

XXI

In those hectic years before and during the war Willis did not have much time for non-business reading except for his fifteen minutes a day with the Harvard Classics. There was no time for reading during the day, and frankly he was pretty tired by the time he got home before supper for his play hour with the children. Usually, in the evenings he and Sylvia dined out with some of their new friends at the country club or had a couple in at home to play a rubber or so of bridge. Briefly, like most men he knew, Willis did not have much time to read. Yet some of the best people Willis knew gave serious thought to reading. Joe McKitterick, for whom Willis had a deep respect and a warm spot in his heart, always knew about the best plays and latest best sellers if only because he read the book-review section in the Sunday *New York Times*. In fact nearly all the other topflight people whom Willis met could cope intelligently with talk about the international situation, the columnists, Broadway hits, and best sellers.

These things helped form the interests of a well-rounded man, and some of the best-rounded that Willis contacted frankly gave every appearance of enjoying this sort of talk. Almost in self-defense Willis began doing a little reading when he was laid up with a cold or on Sunday mornings when Sylvia was servicing the children. Even when he was rushed he skimmed through the *New York Times Book Review,* and finally at the suggestion of Ted Perlman, one of the new salesmen he had hired at Rahway, Willis bought a useful periodical called *The Book Review Digest.* It was a relief to Willis that he already had acquired a certain literary background. The Dickens and Thackeray, the Scott, the single Austen, and the Brontë which his mother had read to him in his childhood began to pay real dividends by the time he reached forty. Also he discovered that there were ways of knowing about a book without having read it. For example, book reviewers, especially in the Sunday supplements, usually told you what it was all about.

Besides reviews and condensations, Willis also read several full-length novels, simply because Sylvia had talked so much about them. He read *Babbitt* by Sinclair Lewis only because Sylvia had once said, playfully, that he would get to be like Mr. Lewis's Babbitt if he did not keep in touch with a few intellectual things. He also read *The Prodigal Parents,* and he got through half of Steinbeck's *Grapes of Wrath,* but could not finish it because of its manifest unfairness. Somehow or other these other novels, which, he thought, might have had a few cheerful thoughts in them, always left a bad taste in his mouth. Frankly, Willis preferred a plain down-to-earth writer like Dale Carnegie. It was shocking to Willis, but he had to face it, that the men who wrote these books really did not seem to like America. They did not like their country in spite of all the fine things America had done for them, such as the education it had given them and the chance to sell their books and motion-picture rights for enormous prices. They did not like America in spite of the opportunity American gave them to acquire lovely homes and have their pictures in *Life* and *Time*. These people were constantly sneering at solid institutions, snapping at the very hand that fed them. When they wrote about business, they looked upon people who earned an honest dollar by selling products, running banks or production lines as crass materialists, devoid of ideals and social conscience. Businessmen in all these novels were ruthless and very dumb. Willis often wished that he might have a talk with some of these writers. He wished that he could show them that men who ran factories and sold the products and dickered with bankers, tax examiners, and labor-union organizers were not as dumb as a lot of novelists who always seemed to be at Palm Beach with some blonde.

It was the American businessman and not the novelist who had created Palm Beach, and Willis was willing to bet that any top-flight businessman, like old P. L. Nagel for instance, could take any blonde away from any novelist. The truth was that businessmen had a lot of good ideas outside their fields. They understood, for one thing, a lot about human relations. Anyone who ran a big office force was naturally a better judge of character than a novelist. Businessmen could also put their thoughts succinctly into a few sentences, without writing pages and chapters.

In this regard Willis never forgot the advice of old P. T. Green, president of the Green Gauge and Roller Company, who once did him the real honor of asking him to come over to Green Gauge. When you are out on a business trip, old P.T. used to say, whether or not you had been playing with other gals on the road, be sure to come with a present for the wife and kids. Willis recollected that homely advice when he took the midnight home from Boston—not that he had anything whatsoever for which to reproach himself. He had gone to Boston for an important piece of negotiation, and he had succeeded far better than he had hoped. By four o'clock the next afternoon it had been obvious that he and Mr. Bryson and Mr. Roger Harcourt had talked the whole deal into being and that all the dangerous corners had been rounded. It was a great relief to go and have tea with Bess.

He and Bess had had tea entirely by themselves, sitting side by side on a sofa. Bess had asked him in a rather pointed manner to close the door to the hall. The Ewings were living in one of those old houses on Chestnut Street, and Bess had said that the house was very draughty, particularly in March. The only way you could keep warm was to close every door possible. It seemed to Willis that Bess, in spite of all her joking, was impressed by him, and in all modesty, he could see why, considering Edward Ewing—not that Bess had not spoken of Edward Ewing with warmth and affection. You always knew where Edward stood, she had said, and that was something. Edward was just as easy as an old shoe, Bess had said, that never pinched you, and strangely enough, she could occasionally do with a pinch.

By the time Bess had made this remark she had opened a small cupboard and had produced some of Edward's Scotch. Then they sat in a relaxed way on the sofa while Willis gave her a few highlights about Rahway Belt and the Harcourt Mill. It had been a friendly worthwhile visit and a useful one, because Bess had been right on his side from the very beginning.

"Well, it will be like old times if you're to be at the mill," Bess said.

It was an improvement over old times, but Willis had not forgotten Sylvia for a single minute. When Bess had suggested that he stay for dinner, he had refused at once, because he had promised to go to the Hodgeses' for supper. He had to bring Sylvia the news about her family.

After an early breakfast in the Grand Central Station Willis began to look for something to bring home, and it was a real pleasure to be thinking of Sylvia. It was so early that the gift would have to come from the Liggett's, and fortunately this store contained a large selection of articles which had nothing to do with drugs. When one of the salesladies asked if she might help him, Willis smiled at her disarmingly.

"Frankly," Willis said, "I can't go home without some little gift for my wife and the two babies." It always paid to take someone into your confidence. In half a minute he had bought a Teddy bear for Al and a rattle for little Paul.

"We've got some cut-price electric hair dryers," the saleslady said.

"Oh, no," Willis said, "not a hair dryer."

"Bath salts?" the saleslady said. "We have some very nice geranium bubble-bath salts."

It was close to half past nine o'clock, and he could only stay at home for a few minutes, but there was nothing like that sense of homecoming. Little Al was in his play pen and he was very glad to get the Teddy bear.

"Yoo hoo," Willis called at the foot of the stairs. "Are you up there, honey?" He felt an indescribable sense of relief when he heard Sylvia call back. Of course he knew that she would be up there but, at the same time, there was a shade of doubt, which perhaps other husbands shared.

"Come on up," Sylvia called. "I'm giving Paul his breakfast."

Willis knew enough about child rearing to understand perfectly that a breast-fed baby had a far better chance in later life than a bottle-fed baby. Breast-fed babies were less subject to adenoids; their teeth came in straighter because their jaws were better developed. There was no real substitute for mothers' milk.

"Maybe I'd better wait until Paul is finished, honey," Willis said.

It did not help the situation any to have both Sylvia and the trained nurse laugh.

"Now, Willis," Sylvia said, "it's time you learned the facts of life. Sit down and tell me everything."

It was not the time or place to tell Sylvia everything and besides he had to get to the office.

"I brought you a little present, honey," Willis said.

"Oh, Willis," Sylvia said, "how sweet. What is it?"

"Bath salts. Geranium effervescent tablets."

"Oh, God," Sylvia said, "not geranium!"

Sylvia was putting Paul through a process technically known to young mothers as bubbling. The resultant digestive sounds from Paul interrupted Willis's train of thought.

"How's Mother?" Sylvia asked.

"She's wonderful," Willis said. "And so is your father. It is always a real pleasure to have a talk with him. Laura was away, of course." Willis glanced nervously at Paul. "You're not going to keep on feeding him, are you?"

"Why, he's only started," Sylvia said. "What else?"

"Well," Willis said, "everything is going even better than I hoped."

"Oh, I don't mean that," Sylvia said. "I mean about Father and Mother and Laura and Tom and everybody."

"Oh, Willis said. "Well, frankly I wasn't there long enough to learn everything—but I did gather from your mother that Laura has an admirer."

"Did Mother call him an admirer?" Sylvia asked. "What's he like? Who is he? Please try to remember."

It went to show how far women were removed from reality, that Sylvia should have expected him to remember details about a young man whom he'd never seen.

"His name just came up for a minute in the conversation, honey," Willis said. "The only thing I can remember is that he goes to the Harvard Business School."

"Oh, no," Sylvia said, "not the Harvard Business School!" She began to laugh; and until she did the connection had never occurred to Willis.

"Honey," he said, "I'm sorry if you look down on the Harvard Business School."

"I don't, dear," Sylvia answered, "but you must admit it's a coincidence."

"Honey," he said, "I know this house is sort of tacky and it is a little small for two babies. I don't honestly blame you if it makes you restless, and certainly a Harvard Business School graduate ought to do better. I promise to do something better as soon as I can."

"Why, Willis, I don't know what put that into your head," Sylvia told him. "I love this house and I keep asking you not to do extravagant things. Just tell me everything that happened up in Boston."

It was obviously neither the time nor place for giving any account of what had happened, and besides he had to get down to the plant. And he also wanted to call on Mrs. Jacoby at the earliest possible moment. Yet in spite of all his preoccupation, that talk with Sylvia had given him a new idea. It was time they moved into a home of their own, and if you kept your eyes open there were some pretty good real-estate buys around the Oranges.

Sylvia had asked him to tell her everything—a familiar but vague expression. Willis was only thirty-three, but his business experience was beginning to approximate, in many respects, that of someone close to forty, and he knew already that you never could tell anyone everything about anything, even yourself. For instance, there was one story which had to be prepared for the Rahway stockholders and another story for Mrs. Jacoby and still another one for the negotiating lawyers. These stories all differed in detail, not because concealment was advisable but because certain people were more interested in certain facts than in others.

When everything was over and the final agreements for the merger of Rahway Belt with the Harcourt Mill were signed, Willis had attended a small dinner that the new company—now called Harcourt Associates—tendered to the new officers, directors and to some of the key personnel; and the various negotiating lawyers were also present. Among the latter was Mr. F. Augustus Tremaine, who had always handled Mrs. Jacoby's affairs and who had negotiated in behalf of the Rahway interests. Then there had been Mr. Tom Bolsen, Sr., and his son T. Bolsen, Jr., of the Boston firm that represented the Harcourts. Mr. Earl Decker had also been present in his capacity as general counsel for the Harcourt Mill. It had been a happy and friendly dinner. Even Mr. Tremaine, who had never missed a trick that Willis could remember, had been in a pleasant glow and had referred to Mr. Decker handsomely in his after-dinner speech as his learned friend and advisor.

Willis, as first vice president of Harcourt Associates, had made one of the main speeches of the evening, speaking not only as an officer but as a stockholder, since he owned personally 15 per cent of the common shares of the new company. Willis had given much time and thought to its preparation, and had been assisted now and then by a bright young Harvard Law School graduate who had recently entered Mr. Tremaine's office. This assistance, however, was of a very minor nature, consisting of a little brushing up of paragraph and sentence structure—more of a clerical service than otherwise, and one which any executive expected from his organization when he had to make a speech. But all of the ideas the speech contained were original with Willis. It was highly gratifying that the speech made an even better impression than he had hoped. He had started slowly but he had built up to a real climax.

"What is an idea?" he asked in the beginning, adding facetiously, "I ought to know, after the last three months, when Mr. Tremaine and Mr. Bolsen and Mr. Decker have tossed around so many good ones." It was a relief to feel that his dinner audience knew what he meant by tossing ideas around.

Willis was never quite sure whether he or the Harvard Law School graduate had set up these sentences, but it made no difference, because Willis was positive that the general conception was basically his own.

"I may as well face the fact," he continued, "that I may have been responsible in the beginning for the idea of merging Rahway Belt with Harcourt into our new strong company. But seriously, gentlemen, let us never forget that no idea can stand by itself. It must be activated to have value. A team must be behind it, and I think tonight we all know we have a real team.

"Yes, gentlemen, an idea must be activated, and to achieve this end patience is necessary and an ability to understand what the other fellow has on his mind, but above all else, good fellowship and team play are the true ingredients of success."

He had to stop at this point until the applause died down.

"Now I don't want to talk too lengthily," Willis said, "but I would like to leave just one more thought before I close. As a good sailor steers by a star let us, too, keep our eyes on the main objective. And what is that objective? It is basically the joining of the Planeroid with the Hartex line—two complementary lines which will make a perfect unity of production. There is new competition in the belting industry tonight and new vigor. Let us all who have been responsible for this latest achievement rededicate ourselves anew to pushing forward a new sort of belting gospel. May I raise my glass in conclusion—and I wish it were a loving cup—to the unlimited future of Harcourt Associates."

The setting and the mood were exactly right for everything that Willis had said. They were obviously on the threshold of new and unpredictable demands for conveyor belting, and a new aggressive company like Harcourt Associates could compete for those demands.

"Willis," Mr. Bryson Harcourt said, "that was a magnificent speech."

"Why, thank you very much, sir," Willis said. "I'm very glad indeed if you think it went all right."

He could be deferential to Mr. Bryson Harcourt still, but they were both perfectly aware of a new relationship. Even if Mr. Bryson or Mr. Roger wanted, neither of them could push him out of Harcourt Associates. Some such thoughts had been in back of Willis's mind when he returned from Boston after that dinner. The Harcourts could not put him out of the new company, but still he would like to have a larger control of it. There was a chance of buying Mrs. Jacoby's stock, if he only had the money. It would not hurt, he thought, to stop for a few hours in New York on his way home from Boston and talk things over with a bank —and on this trip Willis never thought of bringing Sylvia a present.

During the Harcourt negotiations Willis had begun to learn the banking facts of life. Among other things, he learned that bankers could be more generous than otherwise with money, given the proper stimulus. Never be afraid to ask, and when you did, make it a substantial sum— the more the better, provided you came with a program of what you were going to accomplish in a business way. You had, of course, to develop a warm relationship with a banker first, so that he had a real belief in you and a keen personal interest.

One of the best contacts along these lines that Willis had made was with a Yale graduate some ten years his senior named Gilbert Bakeliss. Gil, as Willis learned to call him, had sat in as one of the underwriters' representatives on a lot of the Harcourt conferences. Willis admired the way Gil could keep facts in order, and he also admired Gil's prematurely graying hair. He found that Gil, who was married and lived at Cos Cob, had a lot of good ideas about physical exercise and diet. When Willis had told Gil about sprinkling wheat germ over tomato juice Gil had been really interested, and several times Gil had asked Willis to lunch at the

Yale Club. It had been a pleasure to be in a position that enabled him to return the compliment. At Mr. Jacoby's suggestion, Willis had joined the New York Harvard Club, a move which he had never regretted, either in a social or in a business way. Willis had explained to Gil, without unduly underlining the fact, that he was not really a Harvard man but a graduate of Boston University. He had, however, attended the Harvard School of Business Administration, which rendered him eligible for the New York Harvard Club.

Much as Willis would have enjoyed hurrying back to Orange to Sylvia and the children when he reached New York after the Harcourt dinner, he had determined to see Gilbert Bakeliss first. He had never felt so much like a Harvard man as when he arrived from dinner in Boston and had breakfast at the Harvard Club. He seemed to be more a part of the handsome dining room than he had ever been before. He knew better than to show undue eagerness by calling Gil Bakeliss at the stroke of ten, and ten-fifteen would look like a self-conscious delay. Willis actually did not call Gil until ten-twenty-three. It was pleasant to note that Gil sounded more than conventionally cordial.

"Well, well," Gil Bakeliss said, "so the Pilgrim has returned."

Willis laughed with real appreciation.

"That's right," Willis said, "I missed you at that dinner, Gil."

"You know I'd have come," Gil said, "if Geraldine and I hadn't been in one of those duplicate bridge tournaments. It must have been quite a love feast."

"Well, it frankly wasn't so bad, Gil," Willis said. "I mustn't take up all your time, but if you've nothing to do for lunch I'll be right here at the Harvard Club."

"Let's see. You mean lunch today?"

Willis laughed again.

"I know there's not much chance with anyone as popular as you, Gil. I just thought something might have broken in your schedule, and it isn't often that I can get to town from Rahway."

"There isn't anything I can't put off," Gil said. "Will twelve-thirty be all right?"

If Willis had not known many bankers, it had been his privilege to meet and chat on friendly terms with many top executives in other lines of business. A proven knowledge of his own ability and worth gave him an ease more genuine than that possessed by the usual bright young man. He was beginning at last to achieve naturalness, because there were not so many things about himself which now demanded his attention.

When Gilbert Bakeliss entered the Harvard Club at twelve-thirty precisely, Willis was able to meet him with this new naturalness. Gil

Bakeliss was in his middle forties, and his business suit—a dark gray flannel—though correct in every detail, hung in a studied careless manner. The wear and tear of competition had only sharpened Gil's aquiline features, making them more alert and intelligent. He could afford, like Willis, to be natural and the bridge of years between them was not disturbing.

This is a nice thought of yours to ask me here," Gil Bakeliss said. "Frequently when I enter this place I wish I had been a Harvard man."

"I always have the same wish myself, Gil," Willis said. "Would you care to visit the bar before we go to the dining room?"

Willis asked this last question in a most tentative manner, because he never dreamed that Gil would touch a drop of anything in the middle of the day.

"Let's see," Gil said. "The meeting I was to attend this afternoon was called off. Under the circumstances I should like a Martini, just in the nature of a celebration after what you and I have been through together."

This was a compliment and Willis knew it. A man like Gil Bakeliss would never have taken a Martini on a business day without a very good reason.

"I'm awfully glad to hear you say that, Gil," Willis said. "And it will be great fun to join you."

Willis smiled at the barkeeper.

"Two Martinis, please, very dry," he said. "That is, if that's all right with you, Gil? I'm somewhat of a fanatic on the subject of dry Martinis."

Neither of them spoke as they watched the barman fill the glasses.

"Well, here's to Harcourt Associates," Gil said.

"Thank you, Gil," Willis answered. "That is something I can drink to with genuine enthusiasm."

"How was Mr. Roger Harcourt last evening?" Gil Bakeliss asked.

Willis was listening carefully for any change of tone.

"He was very mellow last night, for Mr. Roger," Willis said.

Gil Bakeliss took a small sip of his Martini.

"I suppose it's *lèse-majesté* to speak disparagingly of one of your substantial stockholders," Gil said, "but I have very seldom seen anyone whose personality was so annoying."

They were obviously on a very pleasant and friendly basis, and they said a few words about everyone else—Mr. Tremaine, Mr. Bolsen, Mr. Decker, Mr. Bryson Harcourt—before they reached the dining room.

"It isn't every day I entertain a banker," Willis said, and he laughed. "I need hardly say we'll sit at a table and have the food passed to us, shall we? Instead of getting it ourselves?"

At the beginning of lunch talk turned to the war in Europe. It was surprising to Willis that people like Gil Bakeliss should worry about the war, not for business but for purely personal reasons. One explanation of this, Willis supposed, was that many men in the Bakeliss age group had participated in the last war, and memories and old reactions clouded their perspective.

"The trouble seems to be," Willis said, "that the Allies don't seem to have many tanks."

He was sure he was on firm ground when he advanced this idea because he had read it that very morning in the *New York Times*.

"I don't know whether that's so or not," Gil Bakeliss said, "but you can't tell me that the French haven't made as good a study of this so-called mechanized warfare as the Boche. But don't discount the French."

"That's what my wife keeps saying," Willis said. "Sylvia's crazy about France. She spent a winter in Paris once."

"You never forget it if you've lived there," Gil said. "Well, let's talk about something more cheerful." He glanced at Willis and his expression changed. "It seems to me you ought to be pretty well pleased about this Harcourt Associates thing, Willis."

It was a time to display restraint, because anyone who was too pleased about anything aroused opposition.

"Well, it was my baby in the beginning," Willis said, "so maybe I'm prejudiced. I hope this is just a start, that's all."

When Gil Bakeliss glanced at him again, Willis was sure he had said the right thing.

"Well," Gil said, "maybe they don't know it yet, but you're running the whole show."

"Oh, come now, Gil," Willis said, "I wouldn't say that exactly."

"Perhaps not exactly," Gil Bakeliss said. "And you made a nice deal in the common stock."

"Well," Willis said, "neither Harcourt nor Rahway common has paid a dividend for years. It's just a gamble, Gil."

Gil Bakeliss smiled.

"If there's any more lying around loose, I should think you'd want to buy it," he said. "I wouldn't mind owning a bit myself."

It was clever of Gil to put his finger on the stock, because it was the heart of the situation. Gil Bakeliss must have been wondering why Willis had asked him to lunch.

"I'm glad you brought that point up," Willis said.

Gil Bakeliss did not laugh, but his expression was amused.

"I had an idea you might be," he said, and he put the tips of his fingers together and looked at Willis. "Do you know if there is any common stock floating around for sale?"

"Well, frankly," Willis said, "I think I know where there is quite a little. You remember Mrs. Jacoby's interest, don't you, Gil? Of course she relinquished some of her shares, as others did, to induce me to remain with the management. Everybody was most kind that way, but I think she has some more."

It was beautiful to see how accurately Gil Bakeliss did business. "If you think she'll sell I'd buy," Gil said. "I don't know what she'd want for them, but you ought to be able to figure some sort of price."

A time for frankness always arrived in any sort of interview, and there was no doubt any longer that the time was there; and yet one could be frank without being flat-footed.

"Mrs. Jacoby's not interested in things at Rahway any longer," Willis said, "not since the death of her husband. I wish you could have known Mr. Jacoby, Gil. He was quite a character. I think she would rather like me to have those shares. There's only one great difficulty."

He paused, and Gil Bakeliss smiled again.

"How much money do you think it would take, Willis?" he asked.

The way that bankers spoke of money was always interesting. They made it seem like any available commodity, and after all it was.

"I don't exactly know, Gil," Willis said, "and the question's merely academic for anyone in my position. I only wish . . ."

He paused and shook his head in a defeated way.

"It's funny how people begin wishing as soon as they get near a bank," Gil said. "How much do you wish?"

Willis's instinct told him it was not the time to set a figure. He smiled and shook his head again.

"That isn't the point, Gil," he said. "I was wishing that Harcourt Associates' common stock would be decent collateral for a bank loan, but of course it isn't."

The cards were on the table now, and there was one of those indecisive moments when everything was in balance, but in a second it was over.

"Now, Willis," Gil Bakeliss said. "It happens that we're interested—in a small academic way, of course—in Harcourt Associates. Why else do you think I came over here for lunch?"

XXII

SYLVIA, AS she sometimes told Willis, had graduated with honors from Radcliffe, and therefore she could add, subtract, and multiply without his having to tell her how to do it. Willis was the first to admit the agility of Sylvia's mind, and yet sometimes he was not sure whether Sylvia had ever understood fully what had happened to them both when Harcourt Associates was formed. Once he had spent a whole evening explaining to her the complementary qualities of Planeroid and Hartex belting. Willis knew that he was eloquent and accurate whenever he preached the union of Planeroid and Hartex, but when he had presented his thoughts to Sylvia, his words fell like twigs upon a passive pool, leaving scarcely a sympathetic ripple. Sylvia must have known, because he had told her again and again, that the 15 per cent of the common stock which had been allotted to him when the Harcourt Mill absorbed the Rahway Belt had only a nominal value at present. If, however, the stock eventually increased in value, they might finally have quite a lot of money. She must have understood this, but even when she saw Harcourt Associates Common grow in years to come until it paid dividends and split itself into parts like the amoeba, she showed no marked elation. The truth was that Sylvia, like everybody else, had certain intellectual blind spots. In this regard Willis had to admit that he felt a twinge of disappointment in Sylvia's reaction when he returned late in the afternoon to Orange after his luncheon with Gil Bakeliss at the New York Harvard Club.

It was half past five before Willis reached the house in Orange. Holding his suitcase, he paused on the front path and looked at the brown shingles and at the Indian pipe that was beginning to leaf on the porch. It was May, and the season in Orange was considerably more advanced than that in Boston. There was that note of promise, that note of hope, that always comes with spring. The house had never looked better and yet it had never seemed so impermanent. It was high time that they moved into a more spacious neighborhood, especially after his talk with Gil Bakeliss.

Still he was fond of the old house because of the many pleasant memories that clustered around it, but everyone grew out of everything, particularly houses. When the front door closed behind him, Willis understood that the house was typically young-married, filled with little pretensions and hopes but not with real solidity. It was far too small. They needed a couple and a nurse. They were out of the one-maid bracket now.

"Yoo hoo," Willis called. "Yoo hoo, honey."

As it was half past five he shouted his greeting up the stairs, where Sylvia would be bathing Paul, and where Al would be playing in what was called the nursery. He was surprised when Sylvia answered him from the kitchen.

"Oh," she called, "is that you, Willis?"

Willis had to laugh at her question.

"No, honey," he called, "it's the president of the Aluminum Company of America."

He even made his voice sound like the imaginary voice of the president of the Aluminum Company of America, but Sylvia did not catch the spirit of it.

"Well, now you're home," she called, "come here and help me, or we won't get any supper."

Sylvia was in the kitchen looking hot and tired. Her sleeves were rolled up and she was wearing one of Margaret's aprons, which did not give her the appealing look of the little housewife in the movies. The table was covered with mixing bowls and pans and there was a heap of dishes in the sink.

"Why, honey," he said, and he kissed her, "where under the sun is Margaret?"

It was a natural question to ask and he was sorry that it made Sylvia impatient.

"She left at three o'clock for good. She was cross about cutting up Al's chop. She said it was Miss Farquahr's work or my work, but not her work."

"But we haven't got Miss Farquahr now, honey," Willis said.

"I called her, and we've got her for a day or two," Sylvia answered. "Thank heavens she just left a case. She's going to stay until we get someone new in the kitchen."

It was perfectly all right to have Miss Farquahr, but it did not seem fair to have all this happen on top of the good news he was bringing.

"I'll tell you what we'll do, honey," Willis said. "We'll just leave everything, and you and I will hop in the car and go somewhere for a bite to eat. Frankly, I'm just bursting with a lot of things I want to tell you."

"Oh, Willis," Sylvia said, "you know we can't possibly go anywhere. I have to get supper for Miss Farquahr and Al."

"Now, wait a minute," Willis said. "Why can't Miss Farquahr throw something together for herself and Al?"

"Of course she can't, Willis," Sylvia said. "She's a trained, not a practical, nurse, and besides she has to bathe Paul and Al and besides . . ."

"Besides what?" Willis asked.

"Besides, you know very well I have to give Paul his supper at seven o'clock."

"Well, anyway," Willis said, and he laughed at the idea, "you and I won't have to cook Paul's supper."

"I wish you wouldn't try to be so funny about Paul," Sylvia said. "Really, a little goes a long way, Willis."

"Now, honey," Willis said, "I won't say anything more about Paul, and I'm going to help you with the dishes and everything. It was silly of me to think that we should go anywhere in the car, but I do have one suggestion."

"All right," Sylvia said, "I don't mind suggestions, if they're sensible, darling."

After all, it was nice to be home, even if everything was in disorder.

"You'll be crazy about this one, honey," Willis said, "and it's very simple too. Before we do anything more about supper you take off that apron, go and get the cocktail things and I'll get some ice and we'll have a quiet Martini just to celebrate."

"To celebrate what?" Sylvia asked.

"Why, my being vice president of Harcourt Associates, darling," Willis said, "and several other things. Just take off that apron."

"I don't know whether it would be very good for Paul," Sylvia said.

"Just exactly what has Paul got to do with it?" Willis asked.

"I wish I didn't have to underline everything," Sylvia said. "I told you I was giving Paul his supper at seven o'clock, and I don't know whether a Martini would be good for him."

Willis had to laugh in spite of himself.

"Listen, honey," he said, "have you asked Castlebar whether Paul will get soused because you take a Martini? I'd really like to know, honey."

"I wouldn't dream of asking Dr. Castlebar," Sylvia said.

Willis could not help laughing again.

"But, honey," he told her, "we've asked Dr. Castlebar a whole lot more embarrassing questions."

"Oh, Willis," Sylvia said, "I suppose I'm silly, but it doesn't seem decent to take a Martini and then go up to little Paul with liquor on my breath."

It was funny, but it was advisable to be serious.

"Now, honey," Willis said, and he took her firmly by the shoulders and pushed her playfully out of the kitchen. "Let's compromise on half a Martini. I certainly don't want to get Paul into trouble any more than you, only let's see if we can't forget him for about ten minutes. I've really got something to tell you. You get the shaker and the glasses, and powder your nose while I do the rest."

"What's the matter with my nose?" Sylvia asked.

"Your nose is very cute, honey," Willis told her. "I just said that as a joke."

It was always sad when one person was in a happy mood and another could not get the contagion. Sylvia had simply not realized, as he had, that a maid-of-all-work was not important any longer, or that they could keep Miss Farquhar permanently, if they wanted her.

If Willis did say so himself, he had been learning lately to mix a rather good Martini. He had learned long ago from old Mr. Harcourt that it was not how much one drank but how a beverage was prepared that gave lasting satisfaction, and now he further realized that if you were fussy about a Martini cocktail, you were apt to be remembered—and with respect if you turned out a good product.

Making a Martini that afternoon was a capstone to his day. It was a pleasure to get everything in order, the shaker and the glass stirrer, the bowl of ice—they could easily, now that he came to think of it, afford an ice thermos now—the lemon peel and the sharp little vegetable knife, because he was not of the school of thought that believed in having a lemon peeled out in the kitchen. He was of the school of thought that did not believe in measuring either, except by eye and ear. The results were excellent this afternoon—two glugs from the gin bottle and only enough dry vermouth to make a faint discoloration.

"You act exactly like an old maid making tea," Sylvia said. "You didn't use to fuss about a cocktail."

He had not intended to be conspicuous. He had simply arranged everything thoughtfully beforehand, and not fussily like an old maid either. Actually he had made the Martini very quickly, and it was excellently blended.

"I don't care how long it takes you to make Martinis usually, dear,"

Sylvia said, "but right now we've got to get supper—and then there's Paul."

"Now just relax a minute please, Sylvia," Willis said. "I haven't told you anything about what happened up in Boston, or anything else."

"I know you haven't," Sylvia said, "and I'm dying to hear."

"Well, in the first place, honey," Willis said, "let's you and I be frank, shall we? I wouldn't talk this way to anybody else, because it might sound boastful. The first thing is that it's all sewed up. As of yesterday noon, you became the wife of Mr. Willis Wayde, executive vice president of a very streamlined and aggressive concern known as Harcourt Associates, who now has a salary of twenty-five thousand a year, and any time Mrs. Willis Wayde wants she can get new drapes for the living room."

The moment he used it, he remembered that Sylvia disliked the word drapes.

"Darling," Sylvia said—her voice rose, but he felt that there was something restrained about her enthusiasm—"I'm glad, but then you've been talking about twenty-five thousand a year for weeks."

"Well, it's in the bag now, honey," Willis said. "And that isn't all, honey. As a special inducement to retain my services they loosened up and let me have fifteen per cent of the stock. They were really rather fine about it. I was willing to settle for ten, but there it is, fifteen."

"Why, Willis," Sylvia said, "I think that's perfectly wonderful."

He did not know why he should have been annoyed, because it was exactly what Sylvia should have said.

"It's going to be a lot more wonderful," Willis said, "when that common stock begins paying dividends. You wait. It won't be long, honey."

Now that Willis had finished his Martini he knew it was not going to be long at all before they began retiring some loans and paring down on the preferred.

"You remember that speech I was working on, honey?" Willis said.

"Oh, yes," Sylvia said. "I'm sure it went wonderfully."

There was no reason, under the circumstances, why he should not have another Martini. Willis smiled at her and lifted up the gin bottle, listening for the requisite two glugs.

"I wish you'd been there," Willis said. "That speech really got them, honey. I never knew that I could be so good."

"I knew you'd be," Sylvia said, "because you're good at everything, dear, but now perhaps if you'll take your cocktail into the kitchen, we might start getting things organized. I don't want Miss Farquahr to be cross and hungry."

"Now, just a minute, Sylvia," Willis said. "Let me make my point.

They were all behind me when I made that speech. It had just the right amount of sentiment, now I come to think of it, and just the right amount of humor, not that I mean I'm a funny boy, exactly."

"You're pretty funny sometimes," Sylvia said. "Please finish your Martini, Willis."

"I don't know whether you remember that part where I defined an idea, honey," Willis said. "It went this way, just in case you've forgotten. 'There is one thing of which I am sure, and that is that no idea is original *per se*. It is nothing but a minted coin with an imprint similar to that of a million other coins, but it is never a counterfeit. . . .'"

It sounded exactly as well as it had up in Boston, and he was sure now that he had written that part himself.

"Willis," Sylvia said, "don't you think you could tell me the rest of it in the kitchen while I start supper? Would you like an omelet?"

"Why, certainly," Willis said, "I should enjoy an omelet very much, and pardon me for inflicting my speech on you. I only had the idea you'd be interested. Shouldn't married people share each other's interests?"

"Oh, Willis," Sylvia said, "please don't be huffy."

"I'm not huffy, honey," Willis said. "I merely said I should be very interested in having an omelet for supper."

"Oh, Willis," Sylvia said, "I'm awfully sorry, but I just can't seem to keep my mind on your speech, what with one thing and another."

Of course he realized that she had been working hard all day and was tired. He could see it clearly—the drudgery of the little house, the babies, and then that scene with Margaret. He felt a deep tenderness and sympathy for Sylvia.

"Now, honey," he said, "forget the old speech. In just a second flat we'll go out in the kitchen, where you can watch *me* make that omelet —but there's something else I haven't told you, honey, that's just so wonderful that I think maybe I'll have one more tiny bit of Martini, and won't you join me so we can drink together to it, honey?"

"But, Willis," Sylvia said, "so many wonderful things have happened already that I don't see how any more can."

It was something to laugh about, the way Sylvia put it. He lifted up the gin bottle and listened. One glug was enough, because it was a good idea never to carry anything too far.

"I guess you're right," he said. "It certainly looks as though we've hit the jackpot today. Now give me your attention, honey. Are you listening, sweetness? I think we've got a real chance to accumulate some property, and somebody else can make your omelets in the future, Mrs. Wayde, and it isn't going to be Mr. Wayde either."

[289]

It should have been a moment that made life worth living. The only real purpose in working and striving was to be able to say at home that you were really getting somewhere. This was like the redemption of a vow, and also it was a rededication. It was more blessed to give than receive, as the Bible said. It was a wonderful thing to be able to tell Sylvia that all sorts of little hardships were about to become matters of the past. It was no wonder that he could hardly blame himself for being depressed by her vagueness.

"Well, it certainly will be nice to be rich," she said, "and I'm dying to hear all about it, dear, but right now it's a quarter past six."

Willis felt a touch of honest indignation.

"And suppose it is six-fifteen?" he asked. "What of it, honey?"

"Willis, dear," Sylvia said. "There *is* supper for Miss Farquahr, and then there's Paul. Can't the rest of it wait till later, when we have more time?"

Willis paused before he answered, because he wanted to be absolutely fair.

"All right, honey," he said, "let's skip the whole thing, and we'll go into the kitchen and make that omelet. I guess you're right—the rest of it can wait."

"Oh, Willis," Sylvia said, "you're not angry? I didn't mean to hurt your feelings."

The last thing he wanted was to have Sylvia think that she had hurt his feelings, and consequently he laughed in what he hoped was a light, friendly manner.

"Of course I'm not mad," he said.

"Then don't try to look like Ronald Colman," Sylvia said.

"Honey," he said, and he tried to measure his thoughts and words, "I can't help feeling offended when you think an omelet is more important than our acquiring a new block of common stock in Harcourt Associates."

"I said the omelet was more immediate—not more important," Sylvia answered.

There was a sharper note in Sylvia's voice. Willis stood up straighter by the empty fireplace and looked at his half-empty Martini glass. The high spirits and elation with which he had faced the future were diminishing, like the Martini.

"Skip it," he said. "I just came to tell you what I thought you would think was good news, but let's skip it."

"No," Sylvia said, "of course I won't skip it, Willis. I didn't know we were going to have such an important conference, but now you can sit right down and tell me about this common stock, as long as it makes so much difference."

Sylvia rose from the sofa as she spoke, and neither of them had the slightest inclination to sit down again.

"There's no use talking to you about plans, when you take this attitude," Willis said, and he spoke very carefully. "I'd prefer to delay our conversation until you are in a happier mood."

"There isn't anything wrong with my mood," Sylvia said, "except I don't care to have you address me as if you were speaking to the Rotary Club."

Willis drew a deep breath. Strangely, a number of small things had become large. It was Sylvia's remark about the Rotary Club, of course, which had achieved this unhappy result. It was a fine organization, in spite of the jokes that people like Sylvia made about it. He finished his Martini and placed the glass on the mantelpiece beside him, where it balanced for a moment before it fell to the hearth.

"Oh, Willis," Sylvia said.

"Don't say it," Willis said. "I know I'm clumsy, because I did not come from a professor's family in Cambridge. I'm a crude fellow who tries to get a little culture by reading Dr. Eliot's—excuse me, Sylvia, President Eliot's—Five-Foot Shelf of Books. Wait, don't interrupt me, honey."

"Then don't call me honey," Sylvia said, in a strained voice. "I can't stand it."

"All right," Willis said, "I won't, Sylvia. Please let me make my point. I've called you honey because I've loved you. I didn't know you couldn't stand it. Maybe it hasn't occurred to you that there are some things I can't stand either. I can't stand—" he had to raise his voice to drown out Sylvia's—"I can't stand being laughed at because I can't quote Keats and Shelley. Maybe you didn't marry me for that. I know why you married me—and don't interrupt me, please."

"I married you because I thought you had a little common sense," Sylvia said.

"Oh no," Willis said, "that wasn't why you married me. You're not as dumb as that, Sylvia."

"Won't you please keep your voice down?" Sylvia said. "Miss Farquahr can hear every word you're saying."

"Miss Farquahr is at perfect liberty to hear every word," Willis said. "You married me because you wanted dresses and a comfortable home and because you like new cars and the country club and Chanel 5 and Paris underclothes, and don't you tell me any different. I've been aware of that from the beginning, Sylvia, and I haven't demanded very much personally, except for a little peace and quiet in the home, which

I have never got. There is, however, just one thing that I think I have a right to ask."

He paused. He was amazed and appalled that he should have said so much, because he had never before dreamed of having such a scene with Sylvia.

"Don't interrupt me, Sylvia," he said, "please. I want to make my point. I think I have a right to ask, when I come home tired, after working my fingers to the bone for you and your two children, that you might at least listen to me politely when I am trying to explain to you how I am trying to make the money that you married me for. Does that or does it not seem reasonable?"

"Willis," Sylvia said, "you're being ill-bred and insulting. All you ever think about is money, but that doesn't mean I do, too."

"You have not answered my question," Willis said. "Does the point I am trying to make, or does it not, sound reasonable?"

"Willis," Sylvia said, "please don't shout at me. I'm not used to it."

Willis found himself answering with elaborate gentleness.

"My dear Sylvia," he said, "I had not the slightest intention of raising my voice, but now that I have made my point I will not bother you any longer. I will go to the country club and have a quiet dinner, and when I return I should like to spend the night in the spare room."

"Miss Farquahr's in the spare room," Sylvia said.

Willis ignored the fact, and it was not a time to take up Miss Farquahr.

"I presume you have no use for the car this evening, Sylvia," Willis said.

"Willis," Sylvia said, "do you think you're in any condition to drive a car?"

It was a question which did not require an answer. Willis turned on his heel and walked into the front hall.

"Willis," he heard Sylvia call.

Willis picked up his hat and topcoat and slammed the front door behind him. He had never said so much before to anyone in anger. That question of Sylvia's about his being able to drive a car was ridiculous. After his apprenticeship at entertaining Beakney-Graham customers, he could drink six Martinis, if necessary, without showing it.

Yet there was always a reaction to everything, and reaction came as soon as he reached the country club. There was no one in the bar. He was entirely alone except for Joseph, the steward, who sat behind the cigar counter.

"Everyone's off tonight, Mr. Wayde, sir," Joseph said, "but I can fix you a lamb chop and some French fries."

"I'm sorry I came so suddenly, Joseph," Willis told him. "A lamb chop and some French fries would be excellent, and I wonder if I might have a dry Martini? If you're too busy, I should be glad to mix it personally."

He was certain he had been right in everything he had said to Sylvia, and on the whole he was glad that he had stated his position, but, in spite of his conviction of having been absolutely right, Willis had a sense of remorse as he absently stirred his third cocktail.

Perhaps he had been too hard on Sylvia, although he had been absolutely right. While he had been away making his speech at the Boston dinner and negotiating with Gil Bakeliss what had Sylvia been doing? She had been performing what to him were horrors of household drudgery, wiping purée of beets and spinach from the chin of little Al, ordering the meals, answering the telephone. He should have had a more sympathetic understanding.

"Your chop is ready, sir," Joseph said. "I can serve it right here, if you'd prefer it, sir."

"Thank you, Joseph," Willis said. "If it is not too much trouble, I should appreciate it very much."

The truth was that he must do something for Sylvia. She and the children needed a home that would afford a truly permanent background, and in that home they could gradually make a good collection of antiques. There would be a note of happiness and order, a nurse for Al and Paul, and a good couple—a cook and a houseman—and a two-car garage with a chauffeur's quarters over it.

Willis did not want to stay at the club too long, because that might have given Sylvia the impression that he was seriously angry, but he was sure that Sylvia would be in bed and asleep by the time he did return. Instead, to his surprise, she was sitting in the living room knitting on a sweater for little Paul.

"Did you have a good dinner at the club, dear?" Sylvia asked.

"Oh, a fine dinner, honey," Willis said—"er—sweetness."

"Call me honey, if you like," she said. "I'm used to it by now."

She looked at him shyly, and all at once he felt absolutely happy.

"Listen, honey," he said, "I know I'm crude in spots, but I want to do the best I can for you and the babies."

"Oh, Willis," Sylvia said, "please don't think I'm ever laughing at you seriously. I believe in you all the time."

"It makes me feel good to hear you say that, honey," Willis said. "It gives me a chance to dedicate myself."

"I wish you'd kiss me, dear," Sylvia said.

"Why, certainly," Willis said. "It will be a pleasure, honey."

All that scene seemed relatively unimportant, but something had changed between him and Sylvia. It seemed to him that she had put a different value on him. Once when he had pronounced Botticelli wrong and Sylvia had given the artist's name the right pronunciation, she actually had blushed.

"I'm sorry, dear," she said, "I didn't mean to do that."

"Honey," he told her, "I know I can't play every instrument in the band."

As a matter of fact, the sooner you learned this homely truth, the better. Back there in Orange, before Pearl Harbor, before Louise was born, back there when he had started Harcourt Associates, he and Sylvia had struck a balance, and you had to strike one somewhere in a marriage. On the whole it had been a very good balance.

XXIII

THE WAR YEARS, conferences with government bureaus, interminable trips to Washington, labor disputes and the renegotiation of contracts, were already approaching rapidly. Compared with the constant shift of scene and nervous tension which had already begun mounting, the days that marked the fall of France and the Battle of Britain always seemed peaceful to Willis. It had not occurred to him yet that his country might be in danger, but he had realized that business was on the threshold of great industrial expansion.

The stockholders' meeting of Harcourt Associates was called in late June that year, and Mrs. Henry Harcourt, in keeping with the old tradition, had invited the stockholders to luncheon at the big house on the Harcourt place. The stockholders' meeting turned into a bright and significant event for Willis Wayde because the whole occasion tied the present to the past in a very welcome way. It touched Willis especially that Mrs. Henry Harcourt wrote asking him and Sylvia to stop at the big house during the meeting.

"Honey," he said to Sylvia the evening he had received the note, "I have a very gracious letter from Mrs. Henry Harcourt, asking us to be her guests at the big house. I hadn't thought of bringing you up there, honey, but I do think it would be a very nice idea, both personally and businesswise."

"I think it would be lovely," Sylvia said. "I'd love to see the place. Let's see, Mrs. Henry Harcourt is the old Mrs. Harcourt, isn't she?"

"Good for you, honey," Willis said. "Yes, Mrs. Henry Harcourt lives in the big house. She used to be mighty kind to me when I was a kid."

"The more I think of it, the better I like the idea of going," Sylvia said. "Oh, by the way, a man called you up just before you got home. He said his name was Mr. Lever."

"He did, did he?" Willis said. "Well, that's another story we'll have to go into later, sweetness."

"He wanted to talk to you about a house, I think," Sylvia said.

The whole thing was meant to be a surprise, and it was annoying of Ted Lever almost to have spoiled it.

"Oh, I've only had a vague idea," Willis said, "but let's schedule our visit to the Harcourt place. I hope we can manage to get Miss Farquahr."

As a matter of fact, Sylvia called up Miss Farquahr right away, and luckily Miss Farquahr was both able and glad to come.

"Now, honey," Willis said, "I'm going to be pretty proud of you up there, and I want everybody to see how beautiful you are. So I'm going to write you out a check and send you into town tomorrow to Bergdorf Goodman's."

"But I've plenty of clothes, Willis," Sylvia said.

Willis smiled at her. He did not mean to be critical of Sylvia's clothes, but without being too personal, dressing was difficult for Sylvia, having babies and moving from one dress to another.

"I always think you look lovely, honey," he said, "in whatever old thing you wear, but this is a sort of special occasion, and besides, you've just weaned Paul." He did not want to hurt Sylvia's feelings. He was very glad that he was beginning to make his point. "If you were in overalls, sweetness, you'd look beautiful. Just the same, you do like clothes, don't you?" It was a rhetorical question which he did not mean her to answer. "How about getting a lot of new things—a suit, an afternoon-and-evening frock, and a light coat, and shoes and accessories?"

"But, darling," Sylvia said, "I don't believe you have any idea what all those things will cost."

"Listen, honey," Willis said, "you go get them. Here's a blank check and you fill it in."

It was naturally important that Sylvia should make a good impression on the Harcourts and on other stockholders and officers at the luncheon, and it also was high time that she had a little pleasure. He felt deeply tender toward Sylvia when he pulled out his pocket checkbook and signed a check and handed it to her.

"Don't you think you ought to put on a limit, Willis?" she asked him. Basically Sylvia was always a wonderful girl.

"Only a lower limit," he told her. "I'll feel hurt, sweetness, if that check is filled in for anything less than six hundred dollars."

There were a great many things he could not say, but he liked to think that he had implied most of them when he mentioned the minimum figure.

"You're awfully sweet, dear," she said, "and you don't have to explain. I'm not so dumb."

"Okay, honey," Willis answered, "as long as you know I love you."

"I love you too," she told him. "I used to think it was bad being a woman, but perhaps being a man is worse."

"Let's put it this way," Willis said. "Everyone has a rough time occasionally, regardless of sex."

It was not a tough time then; it was a rare moment when two people understood each other so well that they could talk without worrying what the other might be thinking.

"Men have so many more loyalties," she said. "It's simpler for me, because I have only you and the children."

It had paid, he was thinking, to have had that quarrel with Sylvia. Each of them knew much better where the other was, and they could touch each other mentally, without either of them drawing away.

"There's something I've been meaning to tell you," Willis said. "You were mighty sweet about Paul—I mean, weaning him, honey. I hope you didn't do it because of the stockholders' meeting or anything."

"Oh, no," she said. "I did it because I was getting selfish. Maybe nursing mothers always are."

"Nursing mothers aren't as good pals," he told her, "as nonnursing mothers."

Both of them laughed, and it was the finest thing in the world when he said something that made Sylvia laugh with him and not at him.

"Honey," he said when they finished laughing, "there's something else I maybe ought to tell you but I won't right now except to say I think it's something that you're going to like."

He could see now that he should have discarded his romantic idea of giving her a big surprise. He should have realized that a home, even though located in a topflight development like Northfield Park in West Orange, was not like a diamond-and-sapphire clip. No one, he knew now, should ever flash a new home as a surprise on any wife, but Willis was still only thirty-three. After all he could not know everything.

As long as they were going to make the trip, Sylvia had suggested very sensibly that they might add a day or two more to it, so that she could have a chance to see her family in Cambridge, and Willis had concurred most cheerfully. There was only one thing upon which he insisted, and he hoped that Sylvia understood his point. He had insisted that before going up to Clyde they should occupy a small suite at the Ritz instead of staying with the Hodgeses at Craigie Street.

They took the Merchants Limited to Boston, and Willis was pleased that the clerk and the assistant manager of the Ritz both knew who he was. As Willis said facetiously to the assistant manager, the Ritz was getting to be a home away from home. It was gratifying to have the assistant manager say that he hoped this would always be the case and that he wished to extend an especial welcome to Mrs. Wayde. Sylvia looked perfectly at home at the Ritz. He was very proud of Sylvia.

The stockholders' meeting had been called for a Friday, and they had arrived in Boston on a Monday evening. Consequently Willis wrote to Mrs. Harcourt that they would motor from Boston, arriving at the Harcourt place in time for dinner on Thursday, staying through the stockholders' lunch Friday and returning to Boston directly afterwards. This would be quite enough, Willis thought, for both himself and Sylvia, because any stockholders' meeting, with its inevitable encounters and minor crises, was always more of a strain than one expected.

Willis had not anticipated how busy he would be in Boston. The telephone began ringing almost the moment they got to the suite, and by breakfast time next morning his schedule was almost entirely filled for the two ensuing days, and would have been for the nights, too, if he had not insisted on some leisure. Yet in the midst of those crowded hours, each packed with its own problems, Willis frequently found himself worrying about the trip to Clyde. Instead of its being something that he could look forward to with pleasure, it began to loom up like an ordeal. If they were motoring to Clyde, they should leave Boston at four o'clock, to avoid commuter traffic, but if they left then, they would reach the Harcourt place too early. He compromised on four-thirty.

"Willis," Sylvia said, "isn't everything going all right?"

He was startled by the question, because everything up in Boston had been going very well indeed. The sales organization was in fine shape and already beginning to deliver. Production was being stepped up as much as possible, both at the Harcourt Mill and at Rahway, because, with existing world conditions, he could see no danger in piling up an inventory. The quicker you got the rubber into the carcasses of conveyor belts, where the Government couldn't get it out, the better; and he explained this carefully to Sylvia.

"So you're asking a very silly question, honey," he told her. "What made you ask if everything wasn't going all right?"

"You just seem tense," Sylvia said, "but then I suppose you're worried about the meeting."

"Oh, no," Willis said. "The meeting's going to be a real love feast to which I'm frankly looking forward, honey, and I have a sort of selfish feeling that I want to show you off to all those people. I sort of hate to wait."

"Then why don't we leave at four instead of four-thirty?" Sylvia asked.

"Because it's a sort of waste of time sitting talking," Willis told her.

"I hoped we could see the place before dark," Sylvia said. "You've always told me so much about it—the walk by the brook, and the greenhouse with the hothouse grapes. Do you suppose the grapevine is still there?"

Willis was mildy shocked by the question, because he passionately wanted to believe that everything was still exactly as it had been when he had first seen the Harcourt place years ago late on an August afternoon. In spite of the depression, he was sure that Mrs. Harcourt had the money to keep it up. He wanted everything to be the way it had been.

"It won't be dark when we get there, sweetness," Willis said. "We're right around the longest day of the year, and that reminds me, I've completely forgotten to call up a Cadillac renting service. I must make a memo to do it in the morning."

"What kind of a renting service?" Sylvia asked.

It was high time that he took Sylvia on a few business trips. She had been cooped up in Orange too long with the children, even if she did look at home in the Ritz; but once they got moved into a new home they would have to get adequate help so that Sylvia would be able to move around.

"It's one of those services that supplies a Cadillac and a liveried chauffeur," Willis told her. "Now, I know what you're going to say, sweetness. Sure we could go up on the train, but this is going to give me a chance to relax."

"But what are people going to say," Sylvia said, "when we drive up that way? It's going to look awfully queer."

"Just exactly why is it going to look queer?" Willis asked her.

"Oh, well," Sylvia said, "it looks so ostentatious, Willis."

He understood what Sylvia meant by ostentation, but he could not see why Sylvia should always be afraid of it.

"There's a whale of a lot of difference between ostentation and intelligence," Willis told her. "It's just being plain intelligent to go up there with a car and a driver. "Also, sweetness, I'd rather have people up there think I can afford it than have them think I can't."

He was sure this was what old P. L. Nagel would have said. He could remember old P.L. driving up there in a Cadillac, but of course this had no influence on his judgment.

Willis had been absolutely right about the Cadillac, and he was very glad to be motoring through a green June country, instead of catching the train for Clyde. His mind went back to that first day he had gone to Clyde with his mother on that blistering-hot August afternoon. He could see his father at the station, and Patrick, and the old Locomobile. The country had seemed strange to him, and in spite of all the time he had lived in New England he still could not feel a part of it as Sylvia did, although Sylvia was seeing Clyde for the first time. It was strange that Sylvia saw a great many things that he had never noticed—gardens, and peculiarities of architecture.

"I don't see why you never told me it was so beautiful," she said.

It would have put him in a highly embarrassing position if he had confessed to Sylvia that he had never thought of the town as beautiful. Willis was still convinced that a lot of it was unnecessarily old and that more of it was run-down. The mellow brick of the Federalist buildings, and the fresh green sweep of the elm trees, superficially, he supposed, were beautiful, but none of it fitted his taste.

"If you like this," he said, "just wait until you see the Harcourt place."

He could not exclaim, as Sylvia did, at the farmhouses along the river or at the views of the river, because he had seen too much of them when he was younger. He was waiting for his first glimpse of the Harcourt Mill, with an odd feeling of suspense. He first saw the new chimney on Building 4 and then the bell tower on the old warehouse and then the newer construction. The sight of the buildings gave him a rather good idea for a piece of Harcourt Associates promotion—a pair of balanced pictures of the two plants: "Harcourt Mill, Home of Hartex; Rahway Belt, Home of Planeroid." Then Sylvia's voice interrupted his thoughts.

"What's that place?" she asked.

Very few groups of industrial buildings made an aesthetically attractive picture, and the Harcourt Mill had grown in a purely functional manner.

"Don't be too hard on it," Willis said, and he laughed. "That's the Harcourt Mill. There wouldn't be any Harcourts or you and me here if it weren't right here with us."

He did not speak in a reproving manner, because he did not care what Sylvia's opinion of it might be. Now that he had seen the mill, he felt better about everything. It relieved him to realize that there was no sentiment in his allegiance to the Harcourt Mill, and that environment had nothing to do with the problems which the mill presented, many of which, for example, were interchangeable with those of the Rahway Belting Company.

Willis could not develop these thoughts because he had to direct the driver through the mill village.

"You'll see the stone walls and the gatehouse," he said, "and when you see a pond on the right-hand side of the drive, bear to the right. It's a large granite house."

The rhododendrons and the laurel were out, making, as always, a fine show, and the rose gardens were at their best.

"You never told me it would look so English," Sylvia said.

The grounds looked as trim as they ever had. They were passing the pond, and Willis saw that there were still swans.

"Didn't I?" he said. "Well, it's a real family place, but the Harcourts can explain it better than I can, sweetness."

There was no reason why he should have told Sylvia much about the Harcourt place. He had been in New York when they were engaged, and they had a lot of problems of their own without dragging in the Harcourt place.

"What are you laughing at, honey?" he asked.

"It's so English, Willis, that it makes you English, too," she said.

"Frankly, I don't quite get you," Willis told her.

"You take it for granted," Sylvia said. "You act like a county family."

"I've been around here quite a lot," Willis said, "but I still don't get you about taking things for granted."

The car had stopped at the flagstone veranda with its Gothic columns, and there was no time to say anything more, but he was thinking that Sylvia might have been correct about the taking-it-for-granted aspect. As someone who controlled the destiny of the Harcourt Mill, he did have rights on the place which he could not entirely express. The driver had opened the door of the Cadillac, and Willis saw that Selwyn, who looked old and frail was stepping down from the veranda, followed by a younger man, who must have been a gardener.

"Hello, Selwyn," Willis called, and he turned quickly to the driver. "Please be sure to come back here at three-thirty tomorrow afternoon. I hope you can come personally."

"Yes, indeed, sir," the driver said, in a confidential undertone. "It would be better if I did, because I know the way."

He was relieved that there was no need to press a furtive bill into the driver's hand in front of the Harcourt house and Selwyn, but this was only a transient worry. Now he was able to give his full attention to Sylvia, holding her elbow solicitously for a moment after she had stepped from the car. Her gabardine suit looked just as attractive as it had at the Ritz.

"You have your purse and everything, have you, sweetness?" he asked.

"Yes," Sylvia said, "everything, thanks."

He stood for a moment, as a good traveler should, checking the pieces of baggage.

"Five pieces, weren't there, sir?" the driver asked.

Five pieces sounded like a good deal for overnight but one was his attaché case, and the three small matched pieces belonged to Sylvia.

"That's right—five," Willis said, and he nodded smilingly to the driver.

He was sure that Selwyn was glad to see him. Willis had always had a warm spot in his heart for Selwyn.

"Well, Selwyn," he said. "It's wonderful to lay eyes on you, and it's been much too long a time," and Willis shook hands at once with Selwyn, "and this is my wife," he went on. "Selwyn, dear, was my guide, philosopher and friend for many years."

"I'm ever so glad to meet you," Sylvia said. "I think you did very well with him on the whole."

Willis could not help being proud of Sylvia.

"It's a great pleasure to meet you, Mrs. Wayde," Selwyn said. "We tried to do our best with Mr. Willis, and I'm glad if you approve."

It was time to laugh and to move toward the veranda.

"Things all look very well, Selwyn," Willis said, and then he remembered Sylvia's remark about county gentry, but what else could one say?

"Yes, the place looks well," Selwyn said, "but of course there have been changes."

Willis nodded. Selwyn was obviously referring to the deaths of Mr. Beane and Patrick and the retirement of Mr. MacDonald.

"Yes," he said, "we can't set the clock back, can we? No matter how much we wish we might."

He was thinking that he did not wish the clock set back a single instant and that he was quite happy with things as they were. As he reached the front door he had a queer thought that Mr. Henry Harcourt would be inside waiting to receive him, and the thought made him square his shoulders.

Mrs. Harcourt stood, as they entered the hall, in the exact spot where she and Mr. Harcourt had greeted the guests at that stockholders' luncheon years ago. She looked almost as Willis had remembered her. After all, there came a time in the lives of women when decline was much less marked than in the lives of men. She stood there, white-haired, plump-faced, and durable in a handsome purple-brocade dress.

"My dear, I'm so glad to see you," she said to Sylvia, and she kissed her. "And I'm going to kiss Willis too."

She laughed and turned her cheek to him.

"Now let me have a good look at you," she said, and she still held his hands. "I do wish Henry were here. He would be so pleased."

"It makes me very proud to have you say that," Willis answered. "I was just hoping this moment that I hadn't altogether let him down."

His glance traveled beyond the staircase to the shadowy corridor that ran under the upper landing; he was already sure that nothing in the house had been changed since he had seen it last.

"You must be exhausted, dear," Mrs. Harcourt said to Sylvia. "The tea things are in the library, but perhaps you'd rather go right upstairs and have a bath and get ready for dinner."

Sylvia looked at Willis questioningly, and at that very moment the hall clock struck six, and it was followed by the chiming of the clocks in the corridor and in the library.

"I'm afraid time rather speaks for itself," Willis said, "if you still have dinner at a quarter before seven."

The whole house was cool and smelled of flowers, as it always had.

"Yes, dinner's still at a quarter of seven," Mrs. Harcourt said, "and only the family are coming—Bryson and Mildred—and Bryson wants to have an hour with you in the library afterwards to go over all the final meeting details."

"I suppose we should have a talk," Willis said, "but I'd much rather have a talk with you, Mrs. Harcourt."

"Have you noticed," Mrs. Harcourt said to Sylvia, "that Willis is always sweet to old ladies? They'll all be going home early, and then I do hope we can have a quiet visit and that I can see the photographs of your babies, Sylvia. I do wish you could stay tomorrow night."

"I wish we could," Sylvia said, "but I've never left the children so long before."

"You must bring them with you the next time," Mrs. Harcourt said. "You could stay in the garden house, where Willis's father and mother used to live. Bill and Anne come there sometimes with their children."

"That sounds wonderful," Willis said, "but I'm afraid you'll get tired of me before that. I'll have to be making a lot of flying visits to the mill this summer."

"Bill and Anne will be here," Mrs. Harcourt said. "Bill always comes for the stockholders' meetings—and then of course Bess and Edward. I thought of asking Roger for dinner and the night. Since Catherine has the shingles and couldn't have come anyway, it would have evened the table but I couldn't bear to do it."

Willis laughed, remembering things that Mr. Henry Harcourt had said about Roger.

"We'll be seeing plenty of him tomorrow," he said, "and now perhaps . . ." he looked at Sylvia and smiled at Mrs. Harcourt, "we'd better start to get ready, if dinner's a quarter before seven."

"You'll be in the east room," Mrs. Harcourt said. "It has a sitting room so that you can have your breakfast quietly. Selwyn will take you up, and you know Selwyn well enough to ask him for anything you want."

"I certainly do," Willis said. "Lead the way and we'll follow, Selwyn."

Their footsteps were deadened by the thick stair carpet.

"The upstairs maid's name is Elsie," Selwyn said, "if Mrs. Wayde should ring. There won't be any need to dress, unless you care to, Mr. Willis."

Willis wanted to ask Selwyn whether he thought Mr. Bryson or Bill or Edward would be dressing, but then he remembered Mr. Henry Harcourt had liked as a rule to be the only one who dressed. It was curious, Willis thought, that he had never spent a night in the big house, in spite of his having been in it so often. Thus the east guest room was only vaguely familiar to him—cool, with its green glazed chintz, heavy mahogany furniture and a massive four-post bed. Selwyn coughed discreetly and opened a door, explaining that there was also a bed in Mr. Wayde's dressing room.

Willis and Sylvia were both silent for a while after Selwyn left them. Willis kept thinking that Sylvia would speak first, as she usually did, but instead she stood looking at the four-post bed and at her luggage. Then she looked at her own bathroom, at Willis's dressing room and bath, and then at the sitting room with its open fireplace.

"Well?" Willis said.

Sylvia sighed.

"I don't know why you've never told me anything about all this," she said. "It's beautiful, but there's one queer thing about it. I keep thinking there are lots of invisible people around."

Willis was startled, because from the very beginning he had always thought this same thing about the Harcourt house.

"It's what happens if one family lives in one place," he said, "but don't let it get you down."

"It doesn't," Sylvia told him. "I'm dreadfully glad I'm here."

The windows were open and the birds were still singing. It was the end of a cool June day. Willis turned on his bath and hung his coat on a hanger. He never knew what had prompted him to put on a dinner coat and a soft shirt, except that he had a feeling that Mr. Henry Harcourt would have approved. He was glad to see that there was a desk in the sitting room on which he could sort over some papers after dinner, but when he thought of work he became conscious of a reluctance that was almost lassitude. It was exactly the same sense of peace that used to come over him when school was over. Then his mood changed abruptly. Mrs. Harcourt's words of welcome, he was thinking, implied that he was still a dependent of the Harcourt world and that he owed a debt to the Harcourts which could not be repaid. He wished there might be some way of making it clear that this was contrary to fact. He was deeply obliged to Mr. Harcourt, but he had paid everything back and the slate was clear. He was responsible to the stockholders of Harcourt Associates and not to Mr. Henry Harcourt's family.

"Willis," Sylvia called, "would you mind coming in and doing me up my back?"

Sylvia wore the flowered silk that she had bought at Bergdorf's, and he approved of the flare of the skirt. The back, he was glad to see, was secured by a series of hooks and snaps and not by a zipper.

"It's rather tight, isn't it?" Willis asked.

"I'm planning to lose five pounds," Sylvia said, "and then it will be all right, but don't pull so hard. Willis?"

"Yes, honey?" Willis said.

"I want to see all the place before I leave."

"You certainly must," Willis said. "Someone will take you around while we're having the meeting at the mill. I wish I had time but Mr. Bryson wants to see me after dinner."

"I wish you could," Sylvia said. "The grounds are so beautiful. I keep thinking of England."

"I know, honey," Willis said. "I've told you, haven't I, that the house and grounds were planned by a British architect?"

"Why, no," Sylvia said. "You never told me that. Of course that explains everything."

"That's funny," Willis said. "I must have told you."

"You never did, Willis," Sylvia said. "It's so queer that you've always spoken of the Harcourts so casually, because it must have meant an enormous lot to you to have lived here. It would have to anyone."

"I suppose it did at one time," Willis said. He had finished the back of her dress. "But you get accustomed to anything you see a lot of—I lived with Ma and Pa in the garden house way across the lawn. I must have told you that."

Sylvia frowned in a puzzled way.

"You've never told me much of anything," she said. "I don't see why you have been so secretive."

The word secretive annoyed him, but he laughed.

"Now listen to me, honey," he said. "I never thought you'd be so interested in any of this, and besides, I'm not good at painting word pictures, and you couldn't understand a layout like this unless you saw it."

"It makes me wonder what you're really like," Sylvia said, "to have kept this locked inside you all this time, when it couldn't help but have an influence on you."

"Listen, Sylvia," Willis said, "Lake Sunapee had an influence on you, didn't it, and you don't—thank God—always talk to me about Lake Suna-pee."

"But you hardly even told me about Mrs. Henry Harcourt," Sylvia said.

"Oh, hell, honey," Willis said, "please don't keep saying I haven't told you."

"But she loves you," Sylvia said. "She's devoted to you and you never told me."

"Now, Sylvia," Willis said, "I've always had a warm spot in my heart for Mrs. Harcourt, but she isn't devoted to me."

"I don't see how you can be so oblivious," Sylvia said. "She adores you, and so does that old butler, Wilson."

"Selwyn," Willis said, and lowered his voice soothingly. "Just calm down, honey. This isn't Buckingham Palace or anything, really. It just happened that old man Harcourt employed my father as an engineer at the mill, and I may also tell you confidentially if my father hadn't induced Mr. Harcourt to buy the Klaus belting patents, maybe this estate might have turned into an insane asylum or something. I don't see why I should have talked about it all the time. I like it out in Orange."

He stopped, surprised by his own vehemence, but Sylvia went right on.

"I wish I could have seen Mr. Harcourt," she said. "He must have been a remarkable man."

"I wouldn't say he was remarkable," Willis said, "but he was a nice old gentleman. I've certainly told you I have a warm spot in my heart for him. And now come on. You've fixed your face already, honey."

"I should think you would have a warm spot in your heart for him, as you put it," Sylvia said, "seeing that he put you through the Harvard Business School."

It was upsetting, because Sylvia was simply not being factually correct.

"Now listen, honey, let's get this straight once and for all," Willis said. "I don't owe the Harcourts anything even if they try to give that impression. Mr. Harcourt did pay my way through the Harvard Business School, but it was also in his interest, and every cent he gave me was paid back at six per cent. I definitely don't owe the Harcourts anything."

He had never said so much before, even to himself. It was the place, of course, that had compelled him, and the birds and the smell of the syringa bushes, and the voices downstairs of the surviving Harcourts. His mother had given him the money to pay Mr. Harcourt, but he had paid her back as soon as possible. Although he was talking to Sylvia, he seemed to be entirely alone.

"Why, Willis," Sylvia said, "I don't know why you should get excited."

"I'm not excited, sweetness," Willis said. "I only want you to get things in their proper perspective. Now I'll tell you who's going to be there, so you won't get mixed up. First there's Mr. and Mrs. Bryson Harcourt— he is Mr. Henry Harcourt's only son and president of Harcourt Associates—and then there's his son, Bill Harcourt, and Bill's wife, Anne. You can't help liking Bill . . ."

Willis was still describing the Harcourts to Sylvia when he heard the dinner chimes in the hall. He had forgotten the dinner chimes. They rang now strongly and musically through the house with the good-natured authority of the ship's bells struck by the watch at sea. Willis took a hasty glance at himself in the mirror. His dinner coat hung with a studied negligence that only a good tailor could accomplish. He had passed the stage where self-analysis and checking-up were necessary, until he was at last rather close to those people he most envied, who did not need to bother about appearance or behavior.

"Do I look all right?" Sylvia asked.

"Honey," Willis said, "I'm mighty proud of you and you look just wonderful."

When they reached the door of the drawing room, Willis knew the Harcourts thought so too. The Harcourts could not help but have been wondering what Sylvia would be like, and now at the sight of her all of them looked relieved. As Willis had thought, none of the men had dressed, but he passed off the situation by simply saying that he had to change anyway, and he had smiled at Mrs. Henry Harcourt, implying, of course, that he had put on his dinner coat out of respect.

"I'm not sure whether you have met all the family or not, my dear," Mrs. Harcourt said to Sylvia.

"Well, well, my boy," Bryson Harcourt said to Willis. "It's a sight for sore eyes seeing you here again."

There was no doubt that his contact with Mr. Bryson Harcourt had sweetened itself enormously. Even a few weeks ago Mr. Bryson would not have thought of calling Willis "my boy," but now he exhibited a touching trust and dependence, and he lowered his voice to a confidential murmur.

"The report is splendid, my boy," he said. "I've been practicing reading it all afternoon."

Bill Harcourt was even gladder to see Willis. Some people would have forgotten old associations but Bill had never been that sort. He slapped Willis on the back and shook him playfully by the shoulders.

"It's good to see you, boy," he said. "I was just telling Anne this evening that I won't have the mill on my conscience ever any more. And look at Sylvia. Don't you forget who introduced you to her."

Momentarily Willis had forgotten, and now it seemed inappropriate to remember.

"And here's Anne," Bill said. "I don't think you've ever met Anne, have you, Willis?"

"Why, no," Willis said, "I've never had the pleasure. Good evening, Mrs. Harcourt."

"Call her Anne," Bill said. "We're all of us family here."

Bill's wife was a dark, acidulous-looking girl with beady black eyes and too much lipstick.

"It would be a great pleasure to call you Anne," Willis said to her. "Bill may have told you that we used to see a good deal of each other at the Harvard School of Business Administration, and in fact Bill only just reminded me that he was the one who introduced Mrs. Wayde and me—or rather Sylvia."

"Bill's told me all about it," Anne said. "Bill's very fond of you."

"I've always had a warm spot in my heart for Bill," Willis said, "and I hope that you and I will be good friends always, Anne. I greatly admire your father. I had the pleasure of greeting him for just a moment at the last meeting of the National Association of Manufacturers, but of course he wouldn't remember." He laughed lightly. "Why should he?"

Then he shook hands with Bess and Edward Ewing.

"It's always like pulling teeth to get Edward down to the meeting," Bess said, "and it was particularly God-awful this year, because all Edward wants to do is sit and try to hear the war news. He can't sleep, worrying about the war. Do you worry about it, Willis?"

Willis laughed.

"I've got more pressing worries right now," he said—"the ordeal tomorrow, for example. The war's only a sort of general worry like the weather."

"But you think we're going to get into it, don't you?" Edward asked. "You see it's historically impossible to let England be defeated, don't you?"

"Please for God's sake," Bess said, "let's not talk about a cross-Channel invasion—at least not until we get to bed—and ask Selwyn to come over here with the cocktails, Edward. Willis won't get one for himself because he's always so abstemious."

"The place is more beautiful than ever, Bess," Willis said. "I mean it, with no exaggeration."

Then he saw her greenish-blue eyes watching him.

"You look more handsome than ever yourself," she said, "with no exaggeration."

"It's nice of you to say so, Bess," Willis said.

"I only mean it in a purely friendly way," she told him. "This room hasn't changed at all, has it? Do you feel queer being back?"

"No thank you, Selwyn," Willis said when Selwyn came with the cocktails, because he was counting on champagne for dinner. "Why, no, it all seems natural, Bess."

"Well, I feel queer seeing you here," Bess said. "But I'm awfully glad you're here, because I can't begin to tell you how much we all need you, and we're all going to be good friends, aren't we, all of us, always?"

You could never tell when Bess would do something unexpected. She held out her hand to him impulsively.

"Why, Bess," he said, "of course we always will be."

"Sometimes I don't know where I am with you," Bess said, "and I'm not sure what you're going to do. I don't blame you, altogether, but it makes me nervous."

"Why, Bess," he said, "you mustn't feel that way."

"Why didn't you tell me," Bess said, "that Sylvia was so perfectly lovely?"

Willis laughed, and he was very glad indeed that they were finally on another subject.

"And you were surprised, were you?" Willis asked.

"Now, don't be disagreeable, Willis," Bess said. "I didn't mean it that way. I only meant I didn't know she'd be so outstanding, and I hope we're going to like each other. I'm going to try my best with her right after dinner when the boys are listening to the war news and you're talking to Father."

"Come on, you two," Bill called. "We're going in." And then Bill turned to Sylvia and laughed. "Willis and Bess were always the darnedest people for arguing when Willis used to be living in the garden house."

According to Willis's recollection, there was only one change in the dining room. One of the mirrors had been removed, and Mr. Henry Harcourt's portrait hung in its place. The mouth looked as though it were about to smile, and the slightly protuberant lower lip almost trembled. The moment Willis saw the portrait, its eyes met his and seemed to follow him through all the dinner, and once when Willis looked up from his plate he had the idea that Mr. Harcourt actually was smiling at him, mockingly or approvingly. There was no way of telling which.

Most of the evening Willis was giving thought to the personalities of the various stockholders he would meet the next day. In his desire to know as much as he could about everyone, he went over the list first with Mr. Bryson and later on with Bess. He also asked Mr. Bryson if they could not meet at the mill at half past eight next morning—an early hour, but he and Mr. Bryson should certainly make a tour of the plant together and meet the production heads. The keynote of the meeting was to be one of triumph, and at all times good will. For this reason Willis asked Bill and Bess to be near him when the guests came to the luncheon after the meeting in order to remind him of names he might have forgotten. This was a practical step. It would be a help to have branches of the Harcourt family see that he and Bill and Bess, not to mention Mr. Bryson, all formed a solid front.

In the library after dinner, Willis took up another, more difficult, subject with Mr. Bryson personally. It was advisable to tell Mr. Bryson frankly about the common stock he had acquired from Mrs. Jacoby before Mr. Bryson found out from some other source, and the library seemed a better place for the disclosure than the mill office the next morning.

"By Jove, Willis," Mr. Bryson said, "I can't tell you how I admire the way you can take hold of everything and smooth it out. I feel that I can let everything go, just the way I could when Father was alive."

"It naturally makes me happy to hear you say so, sir," Willis told him, "but I'm going to be on your doorstep, I'm afraid, asking advice about all sorts of things. You know, I haven't been very close to the Harcourt picture for quite a while."

Mr. Bryson laughed in a very friendly way.

"From the way you take hold," he said, "no one would think you'd been out of it for a minute, Willis, and I wish you hadn't. As I said to you on that morning you were leaving . . ."

Willis had not forgotten what Mr. Bryson had said to him, but it was entirely beside the point.

"I know," he said. "I've always treasured in my memory the kind things you said, but in another way it may have been better for all of us that I left here when I did. I may have gained a wider perspective."

"Perhaps you're right, Willis," Mr. Harcourt said. "You have had a great deal new to offer all of us—and now perhaps we'd better go and see what the ladies are doing without us."

"That's a very sound idea, sir," Willis said, "but there's just one more detail that I've been meaning to take up with you privately. I hope this won't offend you."

An opaque look came over Mr. Bryson, which always indicated that he was completely confused.

"I can't imagine what you're talking about," he said.

Another moment had arrived for directness, and Willis had learned never to shirk on such occasions, because when the time came to advance, the slightest hesitation often spoiled everything.

"You may remember that Mrs. Jacoby was allotted a block of common stock in the reorganization, Mr. Harcourt," Willis said. "She was kind enough to offer this to me for sale, and the transaction was completed the day before yesterday. This may make me a larger stockholder than you had planned, but I hope you'll accept me as such." He raised his voice when he saw that Mr. Bryson was about to interrupt. "And remember that my desire to make a success of everything will be proportionately greater."

Mr. Bryson looked blankly at the end of his cigar while his mind worked with painful slowness.

"You say you bought it?" he said. "I don't exactly see . . ."

"I was able to raise a loan," Willis said. "You see, I have great faith in Harcourt Associates."

"Well," Mr. Bryson said, "I think that's splendid, and thank heaven Roger didn't know there was any loose stock for sale. I don't know anyone I'd rather have own it. Congratulations, Willis."

"Thank you very much, sir," Willis said. "And now there's one final matter. We were talking the other day about enlarging the base of the board of directors of Harcourt Associates, and you were kind enough to ask me for a name. I think I have a very good one. It's Mr. Gilbert Bakeliss, the bank representative, you remember, who did so much toward adjusting shares and refinancing. It occurred to me that we might offer his name at the meeting tomorrow, if you have no objections. I can prepare a proper motion for you the first thing in the morning and have it fitted in very nicely on the agenda."

He did not add that the motion nominating Mr. Gilbert Bakeliss was typed already and in his confidential briefcase, because such information did not seem necessary at the time.

The whole evening was over at half past ten, and the last half hour of it had been consumed in chatting alone with Mrs. Henry Harcourt. Everything was finished early and sensibly, so that everyone might have a good night's sleep in preparation for the rigors of the meeting. Nevertheless something about the evening disturbed Willis, without his being able to tell what, because logically he had every reason to be satisfied and not disturbed. He had looked forward, for instance, to considerable trouble in inducing Mr. Bryson to advance the name of Gilbert Bakeliss for the board of directors, knowing Mr. Bryson's slow approach to strangers, and there had been no trouble whatsoever. Mr. Bryson had remembered Gil Bakeliss favorably and he had readily agreed with all Willis's arguments on the advantages of having an investment banker on the board. Superficially it had been a very pleasant evening among old friends.

The moment Sylvia and he reached the east guest room, Willis was surprised to have her throw her arms around his neck.

"Oh, darling," Sylvia said, "I'm so glad I came."

"I'm glad you did too, sweetness," he said.

He thought at the moment that Sylvia's burst of affection was the result of dull weeks and months in Orange, and he was happy that he had been able to give her a pleasant change.

"They're such fine people, all of them," she said. "It makes me very proud of you, darling."

The uneasiness in back of his mind grew more acute because of her enthusiasm.

"I don't quite get you, Sylvia," he said. "What is it that makes you proud of me?"

"Why, that they should all be so deeply fond of you," Sylvia said, "and that they should all have such trust in you, Willis."

"Oh, come now, honey," Willis said. "You're exaggerating quite a lot. They don't trust me as much as all that."

"Oh, yes, they do," Sylvia said. "I wish you could have heard the things they said about you."

It was hard to explain why instead of being warmed by Sylvia's remark, it aroused a hostile and resentful feeling. The Harcourts, of course, had to depend on someone because of their utter incapacity, and he was surprised that Sylvia did not appear to recognize this fact.

"Well," he said, "it's nice to know they feel that way."

"And why didn't you tell me that Bess was so sweet?" Sylvia said.

"Why, Sylvia," he said, "I think she's got a lot of personality, but I wouldn't call her sweet."

"Well, congenial then," Sylvia said. "She's awfully congenial. We got along right from the very start, and we've made a date for tomorrow morning. She's going to show me the place and the town and everything."

"You mean Bess isn't going to attend the meeting?" Willis asked.

"She says she's been to enough of them," Sylvia said, "and she'd much rather show me around. You don't mind, do you, Willis?"

"Why, no, honey, I don't mind at all," he told her. "But just see you both get back in time to help with lunch."

"She has a lot of character, hasn't she?" Sylvia said. "All Bill's charm plus character."

"Yes," Willis said, "I guess that's so. It's funny, I never pictured you getting on well with Bess."

"I don't see why not," Sylvia said. "She has such a wonderful sense of humor and she's so outgiving."

"Outgiving?" Willis repeated.

"Why, yes," Sylvia said. "She's so well adjusted that she has time to be kind. That's what I mean by outgiving."

"Well, well," Willis said, "she must have made a real effort over you, honey."

"Oh, no, she didn't," Sylvia said. "We just happened to get along. Aren't you pleased about it, Willis?"

"Why, yes, honey," Willis said, "I think it's swell."

"Well, you don't look pleased."

"Never mind how I look, honey," Willis told her. "I've got a lot on my mind. This meeting's pretty serious tomorrow and I'd better get some sleep."

Bess had obviously made an effort over Sylvia, which might have been kind and generous of her, but then there might have been another reason. He recalled her remark about their all being friends always. It was almost as though she doubted his sincerity, as he was doubting hers. He wished the Harcourts were not all so dependent and trustful. You could like people, but business was always business, and the Harcourts should have remembered that.

While he was hanging up his coat in the dressing room he heard Sylvia laughing.

"What's the joke, honey?" he called to her.

"It's just a technical question," Sylvia said. "Are we going to sleep together in the four-poster or have you other plans?"

"They've got the bed turned down here, honey," he told her.

"Well, come in here for a while anyway," Sylvia said. "Do you realize we've never had a chance to be in a double bed?"

It took Willis an unusually long time to fall asleep when he returned to the single bed in the dressing room. Usually at the end of a hard day he could drop off very quickly, lulled by the noises of distant traffic. He was no longer accustomed to the quiet of the Harcourt place, not that the place was really quiet. The tree toads in the oak woods made the night full of sound. Their melancholy vibrant song mingled with the scent of the syringa bushes. The passage of summer at the Harcourt place was marked by a succession of choruses. Next would come the katydids and then the crickets. He wished that his thoughts would not move uneasily. It was logical and eminently fitting in every way that a man of the outstanding caliber of Gilbert Bakeliss should be a Harcourt Associates director, and yet he wished that Mr. Bryson Harcourt had not accepted the suggestion so readily, because there was something defenseless about Mr. Bryson's guilelessness. When Willis had mentioned Mrs. Jacoby's common stock, anyone except Mr. Bryson would have recognized that the placing of Gil Bakeliss on the board represented a return for a favor. There was nothing wrong about this fact, and Willis would have gladly admitted and defended it, but Mr. Bryson had seen nothing. Willis could not understand why Mr. Bryson's blindness should bother him when there had been nothing wrong about the whole transaction. . . . The song of the tree toads was continuing and the chorus would go on till dawn, but Willis remembered the crickets best, because the season of the crickets was beginning when he had first seen the Harcourt place.

XXIV

THERE WERE days when everything went wrong, in spite of the most careful planning. There were others when everything ran smoothly, and thank goodness the stockholders' meeting was one of those. From first to last, it had been a very lovely occasion, without a dislocation or a trace of overemphasis. Mr. Bryson had read the report very well indeed, and what was more, it had held the attention of the audience, especially the five-point program for the coming year. Willis was especially pleased with the reception of the final paragraph, over which he had spent considerable thought and the sentences of which he had personally polished.

"The management of Harcourt Associates," it went, "is not a group of crystal gazers. We cannot foresee the future or predict war and peace. There will surely be unexpected problems to be faced. We can only promise to do our best to face them. However, in spite of uncertainty, our attitude is one of quiet confidence. Come what may in the turbulent future, the production of our nation is expanding and with this expansion will grow the demand for our product. We are confident that we can deliver and produce. We are confident that the earnings of your company are on an ascendant curve. Optimism is the thought which your management wishes to leave with you today."

The thing that made Willis proudest to remember in the whole general picture was that he had behaved tactfully, which was an achievement, considering his age. However, he had already learned some of the basic facts and dangers in human behavior. No one living could wholly suppress a feeling of ill will and suspicion toward anyone who had moved too quickly into a prominent position, but it was possible to take defensive measures. Without being anonymous, Willis had not obtruded himself at the meeting. In fact rather than prompt Mr. Bryson too often, Willis had allowed him to fumble and to make several minor mistakes. He applauded the report and congratulated him on it, and stood respectfully beside Mr. Harcourt while others did the same.

It did not matter much where you were, as long as you had the power and control, and Willis had seldom felt the pull of power more strongly than he had at the Harcourt Mill that June.

After the meeting, Willis was able to have a few moments alone with Mr. Bryson in the family office while guides were showing stockholders through the plant. Willis observed that he felt more at ease than he ever had previously. The portraits of the Harcourts seemed to know, like the office force, whose brains and ability were running Harcourt Associates. Nevertheless Willis stood up until Mr. Bryson asked him to sit down.

"That was a very successful meeting," Mr. Bryson said, "but thank God it's over."

"I want to congratulate you on the way you conducted the whole thing, sir," Willis said, "and I think the report has got us squared away to a fine start."

Sometimes Willis was reminded of old Mr. Henry Harcourt when Mr. Bryson smiled.

"I agree with you about the report, Willis," Mr. Bryson said. "Although it was your composition, I do hope you think I read it well."

Willis smiled and then he shook his head reprovingly to Mr. Harcourt.

"I hate to seem to contradict you, sir," he said, "so early in our association, but there's one thing I think we ought to get absolutely straight before we adjourn to the house for lunch. That report was really much more yours than mine, and I can't emphasize this point enough, Mr. Harcourt. I really can't."

Willis paused and looked at Mr. Bryson earnestly. Though he could admit to himself that what he was saying was sophistry, there was still a grain of truth behind it, and Willis believed in that grain. In fact he was beginning to be moved by it.

"I know what you're thinking, Mr. Harcourt," he said. "I admit that I wrote that report, or at least a good part of it." Willis paused and laughed. "Between you and me, young Sol Bradley—that new promotion man of ours, you know—helped to polish up quite a lot of it. I don't mind that either, because I can't impress on you too strongly, sir, that the physical writing of a thing is not important. As Mr. Beakney used to tell us back in Beakney-Graham, you can buy a writer a lot easier than you can get a sales manager. And as I mull it over in my mind, there's a whale of a lot of truth in that remark. It isn't the written words in that report that count, or in any other report, Mr. Harcourt."

Yet words did have their value. Willis realized that he was being carried away by words, even as he belittled them.

"Basically," Willis said, "it's the spirit and the inspiration behind words that count, and you have given me the spirit and inspiration. In fact,

Mr. Harcourt—and I may as well face it—I drew every basic idea embodied in that report from our conversations. I only put your own thoughts into words."

Willis smiled again at Mr. Bryson when he had finished, and he was glad to see that Mr. Bryson had followed him.

"That's awfully nice of you to say that, Willis," he said, "and I understand what you mean. An older man can't help but have a few ideas, and it's very pleasant to have a bright fellow like you respect them."

A generous kindliness suffused Willis. He had never felt so warmly disposed toward Mr. Bryson Harcourt.

"Of course I respect them," Willis said, "and if you ever find I don't please put me in my place. I'm only here to help you, sir, and take routine details off your hands and I'm not forgetting for one minute, Mr. Harcourt, that you're boss of the works. When we get up to the house to lunch, I want everyone to know that I'm right behind you and not in front of you."

Mr. Harcourt was obviously moved, and Willis was moved himself. They were friends standing shoulder to shoulder, and that was the way that Willis wanted it to be, up there at the stockholders' luncheon.

"Willis," Mr. Harcourt said—and he had to stop to steady his voice— "you've always been true blue and a yard wide, but you mustn't be too modest, Willis."

Willis laughed. It was nice to know that he could laugh affectionately with and at Mr. Bryson Harcourt.

"Don't worry about that," Willis said. "I'll handle the modesty department, Mr. Harcourt."

"I suppose I'll have to say a few words at lunch," Mr. Harcourt said. "I've been up half the night trying to piece together some ideas. I wish I could speak like Father. He could always handle everything at those luncheons."

"I know before I hear them that you're going to say some very gracious things," Willis said, "and I know you'll agree with me that, after the report, you won't have to say too many, because you've really told them everything already."

"By Jove," Mr. Bryson said, "that's an idea, Willis. I suppose I could say just that to them at lunch."

"I think you've hit on exactly the right note, sir," Willis said, "and then you might say a little something about loyalty, or dedication, or something along those lines, but not too much."

"That's right," Mr. Bryson said. "By Jove, Willis, if you wouldn't mind I'd like to repeat what you just said about being here to help me and backing me up in every way. You see, I'll have to introduce you, Willis."

"Do you really think that's necessary, sir?" Willis asked. "I admit I had thought of the possibility but I hadn't entirely envisaged it."

This statement was only partially correct, for Willis, like Mr. Harcourt, had been thinking of a few words.

"Of course you'll have to say something, Willis," Mr. Harcourt said. "After all, who had the idea of combining the Planeroid and Hartex lines? It was entirely yours, Willis."

Willis sighed and squared his shoulders.

"If you think it's necessary, sir, of course I'll do it," he said. "But do you mind if I ask you a little favor? Don't tell them that the Harcourt Associates was my idea. If you have to say anything, say what I told you about backing you up in every way, and let it go at that."

There was a discreet knock on the door and Mr. Bryson looked questioningly at Willis.

"I guess that's about all there is, isn't it?" Mr. Bryson asked.

"Yes, sir," Willis said quickly, "I think we're all quite clear."

"Come in," Mr. Bryson called. "What is it?"

The door to the secretary's room had opened and for a moment Willis expected to see Miss Jackman, but Miss Jackman had been retired for several years, and it was her understudy, Miss Nellie Bailey, who had been a year ahead of Willis at high school.

"The car's waiting, Mr. Harcourt," Nellie Bailey said.

"Oh, thank you, Nellie," Mr. Bryson answered. "You remember Mr. Wayde, don't you?"

At the age of thirty-three Willis was so young that faces lost from the ranks and new faces filling old formations did not move him as they did later. Still, at the Harcourt house it was hard to place some of the people he had previously known. Heads were grayer, bodies were more corpulent. Time had altered the features of the more-distant Harcourt relatives so that they looked like prints from an overexposed film, and Mr. Eldridge Harcourt was deaf as a post. In fact it was a tribute to Willis's memory that he hardly mistook anyone.

Mrs. Henry Harcourt and Mrs. Bryson Harcourt were both already in the hall receiving guests when he and Mr. Bryson arrived from the mill.

"Thank heaven you've got here finally, Bryson," Mrs. Henry Harcourt said. "Don't you think Willis and Sylvia should stand here with us?"

Unexpected as the question was, Willis was able to answer very promptly.

"That's a most generous and lovely suggestion, Mrs. Harcourt," he said, "but I honestly think this is the president's luncheon, and the emphasis should be entirely on the president." He laughed because he wished his refusal to be as friendly as it was honest. "I'll go into the living room and help Bill and Bess pass appetizers."

Then just before he reached the living room, Selwyn stopped him.

"There's a telegram for you, sir," Selwyn said. "I took the liberty of taking it myself over the telephone. I hope you don't object."

"Why, Selwyn," Willis said, "I'm proud to have you take any telegram."

Still smiling, he opened the paper that Selwyn handed him.

"Browning place yours at your price," he read. "Congratulations, boy. Lever."

It was one of those days when everything broke all at once. Willis never had dreamed that anyone would take his low offer. It would be a surprise for Sylvia, and now there was no immediate opportunity to tell her, right in the middle of everything.

The moment Willis entered the living room he saw that Sylvia was safely back. She looked very well indeed in the second suit, of natural linen, that she had bought at Bergdorf's, and she looked very happy as she stood talking to Bill and Mr. Roger Harcourt.

"Oh, there you are, Willis," she called. "We were wondering what under the sun had become of you."

Willis wished very much she had not called across the room when he saw faces turning toward him, but all he could do was hurry toward her, smiling like a devoted husband.

"So you got back all right, did you, honey?" he asked. "Did Bess show you all the sights?"

"I wish you'd been with us, darling," Sylvia said. "We were looking at some perfectly wonderful old houses by the river. We've been having a lovely time."

"I'm delighted to hear it, sweetness," Willis said, and immediately included Mr. Roger Harcourt in the conversation. "I gather you didn't visit the plant, Mr. Harcourt?"

"I'm too fat to be wandering around," Mr. Roger said, "and in that connection, do you remember what the Chinese Ambassador once said at a Washington party when he was asked if he did not want to dance?"

"Why, no," Willis answered, and he assumed an air of happy anticipation. "What did he say, Mr. Harcourt?"

"He said," Mr. Roger answered, "why should he dance himself if he could pay someone to do it for him?"

Willis laughed with genuine amusement. It was a very good story, and one that he could write down in his notebook of anecdotes.

"That's a lovely story," Willis said. "I never heard that one before."

"I'm glad to have contributed to your education, Willis," Mr. Harcourt said. "You get my point, don't you? Why should I walk through the fumes and noise of the mill when I'm paying you to do it for me?"

"I certainly do get your point, Mr. Ambassador," Willis said, and he laughed again, on a diminishing key. "Seriously, that's an anecdote I'm going to treasure, Mr. Harcourt."

"Listen, Willis," Mr. Roger said, "I wish you'd get off this Mister business and call me Roger, now that it looks as though we're going to see a lot of each other."

Willis had never seen Mr. Roger in such a completely genial mood, and as soon as Mr. Roger looked at Sylvia, Willis knew the reason for it. Anyone who said a wife wasn't a help in business was wrong, dead wrong.

"Why, I'd be greatly honored, Roger," Willis said.

"Now get along and mingle with everyone," Mr. Roger said, "and allow me to entertain your wife. Why should I mingle with everyone when I can pay you to do it for me?"

Nearly all the luncheon guests were standing in watchful groups drinking cocktails or sampling the claret punch in the green Canton bowl that stood on a long table near the terrace windows. They sipped their drinks like connoisseurs, seemingly comparing their quality with the memory of other drinks they had consumed previously in the Harcourt house.

Willis was glad that Bill stuck by him when he greeted the Haywards and some of the others, and he was gladder still when Bess joined them.

"You've got to talk to Aunt Ruth," she said. "She's over near the fireplace."

"You mean Mrs. Blood?" Willis said.

"Yes, she came at the last minute," Bess said. "No one ever knows exactly what she's going to say."

Willis had been careful to make inquiries regarding Mrs. Blood, and he had been sorry to hear that she was not in good health, though this was to be expected, considering her age. She was really quite a wonderful sight, sitting near the fireplace like a living portrait, the last of the old line. She sat, disdaining the back of the stiff chair she had selected. Her face, always reminiscent of Mr. Henry Harcourt's, was no more sallow or lined than Willis had remembered it, and her white plume of hair was done in its old pompadour. Willis had been told that Mrs. Blood's memory was not what it used to be, but obviously she was still aware of her own importance, as she received the compliments of the guests.

"You remember Willis Wayde, don't you, Aunt Ruth?" Bess asked.

When Mrs. Blood's tired old eyes gazed at him, Willis remembered the evening he had first met her, his own first evening on the Harcourt place.

"Of course I remember Willis Wayde," she said. "How you've grown, Willis."

He could only make the best of the startled looks around him, and answer before anyone could interrupt.

"I suppose I have," he said, "at least I hope I have, in some ways, Mrs. Blood."

"I know you've been away," Mrs. Blood said, "at school or somewhere," and then without a pause her mind was back in the present. "I'm very glad you're back to take care of the mill," she said. "Bryson is incapable and Bill has no ability. Bess should have been the boy of course. It's the only wise thing that Bryson has done in years, getting you back."

If only from embarrassment none of the group around Mrs. Blood's chair could help laughing.

"You certainly ticked us all off, Auntie," Bill said.

"In any event, Mrs. Blood," Willis said hastily, "it is a great pleasure and an honor to be back and a greater pleasure to see that you are ticking us all off, as Bill puts it."

A minute later Willis crossed the room to say a word to Mr. Decker. Willis's high opinion of him had increased during the negotiations. In spite of being in his late seventies, Mr. Decker was very alert indeed.

"Well, Willis," Mr. Decker said, "so you and I have joined forces again to look out for the family." He paused and coughed. "You remember Steve, don't you? I've been divesting myself of a little property, and Steve is a stockholder now."

Willis had not observed Steve Decker, because Steve had been standing a step or two behind his father. Now Steve moved forward in a cynical way. If there was one thing Willis hated, it was cynicism.

"Hello, Steve," Willis said. "What have you been doing all these years?"

"Nothing to write home about," Steve said, "but then I've been home so I don't have to write—just in my father's law office."

"Not married or anything?" Willis asked. Neither he nor Steve Decker had the slightest interest in each other, but still they had to talk.

"The girls seem to shy away from me," Steve said.

"Sylvia's up here with me," Willis said. "I hope you've had a chance to say a few words to her."

"Oh yes," Steve Decker said. "She's looking very well. Congratulations on that and on setting the world on fire and everything, Willis."

It was a relief when Mr. Bryson interrupted them. Luncheon was ready, and Willis was to sit between Mrs. Bryson and Mrs. Henry Harcourt, which meant that no great conversational effort was required. It was only necessary to say that the dining room had never looked more beautiful, which was true. There were few dining rooms in existence with a green Canton dinner service, and there were not many sets of heavy-cut champagne glasses left in the world either. Except for his approaching speech, the worst of the day was over. He was able to enjoy the clear soup and the fresh asparagus and the dry champagne. When Mr. Bryson rose to speak, Willis finished his glass carefully, and he was pleased when Selwyn refilled it, because he would be glad to have a little more when the speaking was over.

Willis listened with great attention to Mr. Bryson and honestly admired his measured manner.

"It has been the custom," Mr. Bryson said, "for the president of this company, after welcoming our guests, as I do now, to say a few words. On this occasion they need be very few, because I have said what there was to say in my report to you this morning.

"I only have one additional remark before I offer you a toast. After the meeting I had the occasion to talk for a few moments to one of your employees. All he wants, he told me, is to have our enterprise succeed, and then he added that he would always stand loyally behind me. Knowing him, I have learned to accept his loyalty and integrity as axiomatic. It is with more reluctance that I accept his modesty. I ask you for a rising toast to our new vice president, Mr. Willis Wayde."

It was difficult to sit alone when everyone at the long table had risen, and equally hard to rise gracefully when everyone around the table settled back into their seats. As Willis stood for a moment waiting, he was conscious of his comparative immaturity, and although he had rehearsed his words, they all completely left him. The table blurred in front of him but a second later everything returned in sharp focus. He looked up at the portraits in the dining room, a gesture which he had not intended, but one which was a happy accident.

"Mr. Harcourt," he said, "old friends and new ones, I am deeply moved by your courtesy, but believe me, please, I realize better than any of you that the toast you have just been so kind as to drink is not intended for me alone, but for all representatives of your new company, Harcourt Associates. I am, as Mr. Harcourt said, your employee, and I hope you will consider me always as someone you have hired to listen to your suggestions, and whom you can discharge at will if he does not bring you the results you have every right to expect. I have no other purpose for being here than to be heart and soul an integrated part of your new company. The gracious and lovely past of the Harcourt family is with us, and with us too are the lessons of Harcourt ability and integrity. The future still lies ahead of us. All I want is to help in some small, modest way with that future. May I raise my glass and drink to the man who will lead us there, to Mr. Bryson Harcourt?"

A speech was only a vehicle of one's character and personality. As Willis heard his voice, he was pleased by its earnestness and the almost passionate desire to convince that underlined every word. The truth was, of course, that he had been in deadly earnest. When he had finished, he took care not to sit down too rapidly, because he had seen too many dinner talks lose their effect when speakers slumped too hastily into their seats. For a second or two everything hung in dull suspense, lost in the silence of the table. Then even before the applause started he knew that he had accomplished what he desired. The applause was loud and cordial, and before it was over Mr. Bryson rose and clasped his hand. Then, just before he smilingly acknowledged Mrs. Henry Harcourt's congratulations, his eyes met Bess Ewing's across the table. She smiled back, but her eyes were inscrutable. Of course he knew better than to feel that he could impress Bess Harcourt, but he wished for a moment that he had not been quite so humble, because she might have known that this was an exaggeration.

Luncheon was over. The chairs were being pushed back. Mr. Bryson said, as Mr. Henry Harcourt always had, that there would be coffee and cigars for the men in the library, when a thing happened which Willis did not wish but half expected. He could never say that he was surprised to find Bess standing beside him.

"Let's go outside and smoke a cigarette," Bess said. "I don't believe you've seen the garden or anything."

She should have known that it was no time for them to be walking in the garden or anywhere else, and he wanted to refuse but at the same time he did not want to be curt.

"That's correct, Bess," he said. "I've had little or no time to do any of the things I should have liked to do most, but I hope, when I'm here next, as I must be before long, that I'll have more time on my hands."

"You don't have to talk as though you were addressing a meeting any longer, Willis," Bess said. "It's only me."

"Only 'I,' Bess," Willis said, "only 'I.' "

"Oh, my God," Bess said, "I bet you clipped a coupon and bought one of those courses in proper speech. Come on outside. We'll stand on the lawn if you like, within sight of everybody. I won't compromise you, Willis."

"Why, with pleasure, Bess," he said, because the only polite thing he could do was go out on the lawn with her.

"Willis," she said, "that was quite a little speech."

"I'm glad if you liked it," he said. "Anyway, I meant every word of it."

"Did you?" she asked.

"Yes," he answered, and he looked at her steadily. "I did, and what's more, I'm in the habit of meaning what I say."

His answer was unmeasured enough to give him genuine satisfaction. After all, he was thinking, now that the Harcourt-Rahway deal was finished it was not as necessary as it had been to be on good terms with Bess.

"Don't get angry," Bess said. "I loved what you said, Willis, I really did. But I got you out here to tell you something else. Sylvia and I have been talking things over, and we don't see why you don't move up here from New Jersey."

"What's that again, Bess?" Willis asked her.

"That plant of yours in New Jersey is just a subsidiary, isn't it?" Bess said. "This is the main plant and the main office is in Boston. Well then, why isn't it only sensible for you to move up here?"

Willis put his thoughts carefully together before he answered. He wanted to give a balanced reply, which could, if necessary, be quoted.

"You know, I've already given that idea careful thought, Bess," he said, "but Rahway Belt happens to be an important subsidiary, and I am more familiar with the processes there than anyone else and I also hope we'll need more and more to cover the New York field. Besides, your father will be in the Boston office."

"Sylvia would love it here," Bess said. "She says it's terribly hot for the children in New Jersey in the summer. We were looking at some of the old houses by the river this morning, and you could live in the garden house until you got settled."

"You say you were looking at some houses this morning?" Willis said. "That's awfully kind of you to take such an interest, Bess, but I really don't think the step would be sensible."

They looked at each other for a moment, and Willis later wondered whether Bess Harcourt had an idea of what he was thinking. The old loyalties were all around him; the Harcourts were trying to draw him back because they needed him, and he was never coming back. Willis tossed his cigarette on the lawn and stepped on it carefully. They were standing outside the living room, and the voices of the stockholders of Harcourt Associates came to them through the open windows. It was time to make a speech that was even more sincere than the one he had delivered in the dining room.

"I'm afraid I must speak a little as though I were addressing a meeting, even if you don't like it, Bess," Willis said. "If there is any problem or confusion here, I shall always come up immediately, and I shall also be making regular visits, but I don't think it would be advisable, not for any of us, for me to be here permanently."

He spoke as genially as he had learned to do whenever he made a decision; he was glad to see that Bess Harcourt was impressed by what he said.

"But, Willis," she began, "I don't see why you're being so illogical."

Willis paused and he was always glad that he looked straight into her eyes.

"I'm being very logical, Bess," he said.

He had always thought of that conversation as a clear-cut victory, and he always liked the final thing he said to Bess as they walked across the lawn.

"Not that we won't always be friends, Bess," he said. "We're bound to be, because there are a great many things that neither of us can forget."

Willis was glad to know that Sylvia and Bess had been looking at houses, because his knowing enabled him to handle intelligently what might have been a very difficult scene if he had faced it unprepared. As it was, the scene began five minutes after he and Sylvia were in the Cadillac on their return to Boston.

"Willis," Sylvia said, "Bess and I saw the dearest old house down by the river this morning. Its date is some time around the Revolution and it has all its old woodwork in very good condition. Of course it needs repairs, but it will be fun fixing it."

"That sounds very interesting, sweetness," Willis said. "I'm glad you had an opportunity to see some of the old colonial houses here. I know many are considered as unique. By the way, did you see Steve Decker?"

"Yes," Sylvia said. "He was frightfully unattractive. I don't know what I ever saw in him. If we have to come here to live, you don't have to worry about Steve Decker."

"And now we're on this subject," Willis said, and he took her hand and kissed it, "you needn't worry about Bess either. I had a few words with Bess after lunch."

"I've never been worried about Bess," Sylvia said. "What did you say to her after lunch?"

Willis spoke gravely but firmly.

"Bess seemed to think it would be more efficient if we all came up here to live," he said. "I told her it was impossible."

"But, Willis," Sylvia asked, "why is it impossible?"

Again and again Willis was to meet individuals with executive drive and brilliance who failed because they could not handle women. These people were not able to say no at the right time, or to make the negative stick. Thank heaven he had learned to say no.

"It's impossible for several reasons, sweetness," he said, "one of which is because I like New Jersey. Another is that I don't want you or me or our children to be bossed around by the Harcourts, and I really mean this, sweetness."

"Willis," Sylvia said. "They're not bossing you. You're bossing them around."

"Very well, sweetness," Willis said, "if that is so, I would rather boss them from New Jersey. I want you and me to be completely independent, honey."

"Willis," Sylvia said, "no one is ever independent."

"And besides, I have another reason, sweetness," Willis said, "something which I hope will be a happy surprise for you. What do you think, Mrs. Wayde? As of today you and I are the owners of an estate near Orange. The view is like the Jacobys'. You can look right across over to New York, only this home is Georgian and brick, sweetness, with a swimming pool and a three-car garage, and five acres. It's a sweet little investment, because we can always subdivide the acreage eventually. The grounds are beautifully landscaped and there's a rose garden. I can't wait to see the kids playing around the lawn—slate roof, copper gutters, oil heat, an electric kitchen. They were in a hurry to settle the estate, and you'll laugh when I tell you what I offered. You may want to pick out a few wallpapers, but we can move in any time. Don't say I haven't been thinking about you, Mrs. Wayde. Are you surprised? I thought you would be, sweetness."

Willis could never have acquired the Browning place in Northfield Park at the figure he offered except for a chain of favorable circumstances each of which was linked with the other in a way that only happens once or twice in a lifetime. The affairs of Mr. Hubert H. Browning, the owner, were found to be in a highly tangled condition after his decease. Also, large pieces of real estate were growing hard to move. You could not blame anyone in June, 1940, or the next year either, for waiting to see which way the cat was going to jump. Later, when the cat had jumped, a number of good friends told Willis Wayde confidentially that he had certainly had a hell of a nerve to buy the Browning place.

They said this in a laughing way, of course, at lunch at the outdoor grill or around the swimming pool, which was not a bad pool considering its rather small size. They would never have elected Willis treasurer of the country club if they had known he was up to his ears in debt when he bought the Browning place. He had a hell of a nerve to do what he did, the kind of nerve you only had when you were just a kid and knew everything was going your way.

Nerve was a mighty useful asset if you could back it up by faith. They were getting into a seller's market and Willis had faith that it was going to last for years. He knew as sure as fate no matter what the international situation might be, and no matter what punitive taxes the Roosevelt administration might slap on business, Harcourt Associates was going to amortize its obligations and would pay dividends on its common stock in a year or two.

There was seldom anything dramatic in building up industrial units, since progress was only made by sticking everlastingly at what you were doing. Years, when Willis came to think of it, blended all together into a larger unit when you looked at the Associates picture. When he thought along these lines, he always liked what he had once written about Harcourt Associates:

> I was one of those instrumental in combining Rahway Belt with Harcourt Mill in the spring of 1940. The Planeroid of Rahway and the Hartex line of Harcourt met shoulder to shoulder the shock of Pearl Harbor with a staunchness that would have been impossible for either individually. They went to war shoulder to shoulder, doing yeoman service in production lines everywhere in America. They are still doing yeoman service in this uncertain period of reconstruction.

This was one way of putting it, and a somewhat conservative way, considering the Harcourt profits. Right from the start it had been an essential industry, and as one who headed its management, Willis often felt that he had been in the war himself. In fact he had seen much more of wartime Washington than many army officers who were stationed in that city. Harcourt won the Army-Navy "E" award three times, beginning with the autumn of 1942, and if Willis had joined the armed services, he would not have made the contribution to his country that he had. He was told this personally by Rear Admiral Charles G. Spoonholm over cocktails in the men's bar of the Hotel Mayflower. Admiral Spoonholm, on this occasion, had told Willis that he was more valuable than a destroyer screen—an exaggeration but a pleasant one to remember. Also at a cocktail party in the same hotel Brigadier General Hugo A. Brass had said affectionately that he wouldn't swap Willis Wayde for a couple of North African combat teams.

It was a pleasure sometimes to read the many kind things that had been said about Harcourt Associates from the first days of its inception. There were some fine clippings from the financial pages of New York and Boston dailies and from Chicago, including a nice picture taken after Willis assumed the presidency of Harcourt, when Mr. Bryson Harcourt was elected chairman of the board in 1943. The items that interested Willis most were the pieces about Harcourt Associates that began to appear in market letters and in Washington gossip sheets. He particularly liked the piece which appeared in *Crown Capital News* in 1944 under the title "Thought of the Week."

Harcourt Associates

Although common shares were split five for one recently, these are still closely held and not yet available on the big board, where we predict they will be eventually. Though called today a war baby, Harcourt Associates has placed itself in a fine position to reap rewards in the field of consumer production. A small company, compared to its larger competitors, such as Simcoe Rubber, its compact size has added to its mobility under the efficient and aggressive leadership of its president, Willis Wayde, whose face is well known here in Washington at the WPB and Army and Navy Departments. The dividend on Harcourt common, initially declared a year ago, was raised for the last quarter to two dollars, which is said to be a fraction of the current earnings. Several investment trusts and the trust department of a large New York bank are now taking a lively interest in the Harcourt picture.

On the whole this piece was factually correct. As Willis always said when he was asked how things were going, Harcourt could speak for itself. Once things were shaken down, there was a fine team at Harcourt, and he had contacted some very nice young bright army and navy boys who augmented that team splendidly when the war was over. As Willis often said facetiously to Sylvia, what would they have done if they had moved up to Clyde, Massachusetts? Sylvia would have been a real war widow then, whereas living in Orange, Willis simply had to drive to Newark and get a train to Washington in no time flat. With earnings rising as they were, and with all the red tape and renegotiation of contracts, a small suite at the Mayflower Hotel in Washington became a legitimate company expense. There wasn't much home life in wartime but there was more in Orange than there would have been if they had moved to the vicinity of Boston.

When Harcourt began paying dividends on the common, Willis was even able to talk to Sylvia facetiously about the Browning place and to remind her how shocked she was when she had first seen it. In fact at one point she had begun to weep.

Willis would have thought that anyone would have fallen in love, as he had, at first sight with the bronze of the casement windows and the forced hot-air heating and the laundry with its electric clothes dryer, but he was soon to learn that women as a whole never cared for basic beauties of construction. It took Sylvia a long while before she realized that they had really got in on the ground floor when they bought the Browning place and that it could not possibly have been duplicated for many times the original investment. The truth was that the Browning place may have been a little too large for them in the beginning and a little tough to swing, but they grew up to it pretty quickly, and Sylvia did wonders with it, once she got the spirit of the thing.

Willis had arranged that Sylvia and he should see it just by themselves and he had looked forward with keen pleasure to Sylvia's reaction. It disconcerted Willis to have her laugh, when he stopped the car in front of the Georgian doorway, with ivy swarming up the warm brick façade and with those completely satisfying copper conductors and a fine original bronze ship's lantern to light the steps at night.

"What's so funny, honey?" Willis asked.

"Now, Willis," Sylvia said, and she still laughed, "let's get out of here and go where we're going before someone sees us and asks us what we want."

"What's that again?" Willis said. "I don't quite follow you, honey."

"Oh, Willis," Sylvia said, "a joke is a joke. Let's get on and look at the new house. I've got to get back and see about the children."

That first reaction of Sylvia's was really something to remember and to tell about in later years.

"But, sweetness," Willis said, "believe it or not, as Mr. Ripley says, this really is the house, and all of it is yours, Mrs. Wayde."

"Oh, come now, Willis," Sylvia said, "it's awfully tiresome to go too far with a practical joke."

"But, honey," Willis said, and he opened the door of the car and got out and took the front-door key out of his pocket, "it isn't a practical joke. It all belongs to you and the children, honey, and don't you ever say I didn't get you something. Look at those casement windows—all bronze framed—and wait till you see the plumbing. You and I are each going to have a bathroom—in fact everybody's going to have a bathroom."

Sylvia said, "Oh no, Willis."

It was a little hard to follow her mood but he tried to do his best.

"I frankly felt a little the same way when I saw it first myself," Willis told her. "It doesn't seem possible, does it? Now you get out of the car and I'll tell you what I'll do—I'll carry you over the threshold."

"Oh, Willis," Sylvia said. "Have you really bought it?"

"It's hard to believe, isn't it?" Willis said. "But it's really and truly ours, sweetness. Now step into the front hall and wait till you see the wood-work."

Every guest who ever came to "Waydeholm"—a name which they finally adopted at Willis's suggestion in order to have something to put on the social note paper—always commented favorably on the beauty of the hall, which ran spaciously through the house, and on the fine broad staircase. It was disappointing that Sylvia had different ideas when they first entered Waydeholm.

"If you have really bought this," Sylvia said, "can't you sell it over again?"

"Well, for goodness gracious sakes alive," Willis said. "That's the queerest question I've heard in a dog's age, sweetness."

"Oh, my God," Sylvia said, "I think I'm going mad."

"What's that one again?" Willis said. "I don't get you, honey."

"Either I'm going mad or you are," Sylvia said, "and I don't think it's me," and then she began to cry.

It was hard to follow Sylvia, but the fact that she had made a grammatical error showed how upset she was.

"Now, honey," Willis said, "tell me what's the matter and let's see if I can't fix it."

"I always thought you had common sense," Sylvia said. "Now look what you've done."

"You mean," Willis told her, "that you don't consider this a practical home, Sylvia? If that's what you mean, I really just don't get it."

"Oh, please," Sylvia said, "don't say any more about it, Willis."

"But I got it for you and the boys, sweetness," Willis said. "Can't you visualize the children in a year or two sliding down the banisters?"

Somehow or other the mention of Al and Paul seemed to calm Sylvia. At least she opened her purse and took out a handkerchief and blew her nose. At least she listened to him and gave him a chance to convince her that they really had a home.

"You've got to get the whole picture, dearest, before you jump to conclusions," Willis said, "and then you'll have the same vision I have. I know you will."

"Willis," Sylvia asked, "for heaven's sake, what sort of vision?"

"A vision of the future, honey," Willis told her. "I don't even have to shut my eyes to picture you and me eventually entertaining all sorts of people here. For instance when we are once established we will be able to ask Mr. and Mrs. P. L. Nagel out for a week end when they come to New York. This is going to be a real center for you and me and the children, and it's also going to offer a type of business entertainment which I am very confident can be written off on the income tax."

At least Sylvia was listening to him and thank goodness she had stopped crying. "I never thought you could be so fantastic, Willis," she said. "Have you ever thought that it will take three servants to run this place, let alone a nurse, and those lawns, Willis—you'll need a man all the time."

Willis was glad at last that they were getting down to brass tacks. In the last analysis, taking over a house like Waydeholm was a simple question of faith and courage. It had never occurred to him until he had observed Sylvia's reaction that women, as a rule, were more timid and conservative than men.

"Actually I've given the service angle some real serious thought," Willis told her, "and I've noticed, sweetness, that it is an occasional habit of yours to exaggerate difficulties. If we temporarily close off some of the rooms in the third story, I believe that two maids will be able to look out for things, considering the kitchen's all electric. That only means one more maid than we have already."

"But what about the children?" Sylvia asked, and her voice rose in a plaintive way.

"Now that's a very reasonable question, honey," Willis told her. "It will be just as easy to take care of the children here as it would be anywhere else, and we can start budgeting right away for a nurse."

"But you don't get a nurse by budgeting," Sylvia said.

"Oh yes you do," Willis said. "You wait and see, sweetness. You're going to be surprised. If I was able to get Rahway Belt on its feet, I guess I can manage this house all right, just so long as I have your cooperation. Wait till you see the washing machines in the basement and the electric dryer. As far as the lawn goes, there's a honey of a motor lawn mower out in the garage. Just for a starter I can do the lawns personally."

When Sylvia listened, she was always reasonable.

"But, Willis," she said, "what about furniture?"

That was what convinced Sylvia eventually. He had entirely forgotten to tell her about the furniture.

"Sweetness," he said, and he put his arm around her, "you wait and see. All the essential furniture comes with the house. There are rugs and drapes and beds and sofas. We will now visit the living room." He stopped and kissed her gently on the cheek. "Honey, I will have your cooperation, won't I?"

"I'll do the best I can," Sylvia said, and she sighed, "but it's all so ostentatious, Willis."

Right from the very beginning Sylvia always worried about ostentation, and yet in certain ways Willis knew she loved it, as soon as she became accustomed to an ostentatious phase.

"Sylvia, dear," he said, and he did not realize until he had started that he was going to state a clause or two of his personal philosophy, "if there's any ostentation, we'll outgrow it mighty quickly. Some day, maybe before too long, this house is going to look small to you and me."

"I don't see how you can say that, Willis," Sylvia told him.

It showed she did not have his vision, but it was rather a cute remark, and he kissed her cheek again.

"Let's consider this home as a symbol, dear," Willis said.

"What sort of a symbol?" she asked him.

What he answered might have been unduly sentimental, but he meant every word he said then and he meant it still.

"A symbol of faith, dear," he told her, and when he saw that she looked startled, he enlarged upon his thought. "Maybe you think I'm going overboard, sweetness, but I mean our faith in each other, and our faith in the future and the children and everything. Maybe it's fantastic, as you say, sweetness, but let's look upon this whole home venture as a dream we want to make come true."

Maybe he had said it in a corny way, but he was expressing in his own personal terms the thoughts and wishes of any man who tries to build a home, and Sylvia understood him.

"Darling," she said, "I wish I didn't keep forgetting how generous and sweet you are. I see what you mean, dear. Of course I'll help you make it all come true."

Essentially Waydeholm did turn into a dream come true. Willis was not there much during the war and he was pretty busy afterwards, but it was always a place of happy memories. As P. L. Nagel said when they walked around the grounds once, it was a sound, efficient home and a good place for showing off antiques, but it was a whole lot more than that. It was where the children learned to walk and talk and play. It was where Sylvia and he cemented many friendships and it was where he bought Sylvia her first mink coat—if you wanted to think of anniversaries. All sorts of birthdays and Christmases and happy sentimental times transpired at Waydeholm, and furthermore servants always liked it. Willis had a real lump in his throat when he parted with Waydeholm finally, dividing up its five acres into lots and selling the main house as a convalescent home, all for double the original investment. It was sad to pack up and go away, but as he told Sylvia at the time, that was America. Life and progress always meant moving into something new— and better. In life and in business you couldn't stand still in America.

XXV

WILLIS FOUND himself telling that story about the Chinese Ambassador again in—of all places—the spacious glassed-in terrace of the Hotel Carolina in Pinehurst in May of 1948. He had just come in from a very happy afternoon of golf, and he was enjoying some good talk before going up to the suite to change before the cocktail hour and the banquet.

They were serving tea, as was the custom at the Carolina, but not many were having any. Willis had been sitting with Jerry Bascomb, who had been his foursome partner and whom Willis had asked down with him for the Pinehurst convention because he thought that Jerry needed a little fun away from Helen and the children, and also because it was a great help to have Jerry at his elbow in case something came up of a technical or engineering nature. If anybody in the Associates deserved a good time at company expense, it was Jerry, and Willis made a mental note to send Jerry to some convention every year in the future. He was just telling Jerry that Pinehurst was an ideal place for business meetings —what with the mild dry air and the four golf courses—when Alec Bingkrampf came up and spoke to him. He was of course the Bingkrampf who was president of Swanee Power, and this year he was chairman in general charge of all arrangements for the Production Liners Convocation at Pinehurst. It was one of Alec Bingkrampf's duties to mingle with everyone, and Willis had meant to help by coming up himself and shaking hands at an early opportunity and asking Bing if he remembered the good times they had had in Washington together during the war. There was no necessity for this, however, because Alec Bingkrampf came right over himself.

"Well, well, Willis," Bing said. "I've been looking for you ever since I saw your name down on the list."

"Well, well, Bing," Willis said. "It's been a long time no see, hasn't it? By the way, I don't know whether you remember my associate, Jerry

Bascomb. He was down at Swanee on a little problem a year or two ago."

Evidently Bing did not remember Jerry Bascomb, but then, as Willis was beginning to learn himself, no one could ever remember everything.

"So you were down at Swanee, were you, Mr. Bascomb?" Bing said. "I certainly hope the bunch treated you all right. Well, well, Willis. It's quite a while since we fought the war down in Washington, isn't it? Say, Bascomb, did the chief ever tell you what went on in Washington?"

Jerry was not such a bad mixer, considering he was a graduate of Tech.

"Not much," Jerry said. "I gathered most of it was top secret down in Washington."

It was not a bad line and both Willis and Alec Bingkrampf indulged in a moment of reminiscent laughter.

"That's one way of putting it," Bing said. "We really did have some high old top-secret times down there—and don't you give me that vague look, Willis."

There was nothing like a little good-natured kidding at the end of a long day.

"Well, now, Bing," Willis said, "I wasn't like you. I was generally pretty tired at night."

"You old rascal," Bing said, and he slapped Willis's back affectionately. "Say, I wonder what's happened to the old crowd. Do you remember— who was it—the fellow who kept playing the guitar? I've got it—Red Flyrood."

"Oh, yes," Willis said. "He's still down there on the National Labor Relations Board."

"And what about General Pottle?" Alec Bingkrampf asked. "Do you remember the bourbon he used to keep in his desk? I wonder where old Gus is now."

"We exchange Christmas cards each year," Willis said. "And I'll tell you whom I do correspond with sometimes, and that's old Charlie Spoonholm."

"By God, the admiral," Alec Bingkrampf said. "I'm glad you brought him up. Now there was someone who could really put away the bourbon. I wonder what ever happened to old Charlie when he retired."

"I can answer that one for you, Bing," Willis said. "He's down in Florida and he owns a small alligator farm."

"Well, well," Bing said. He was showing signs of restlessness, and it was kind of him to have stayed chatting so long. "Think of old Charlie wrestling with an alligator. Well, I've got to be thinking up some remarks for my speech tonight. Well, so long fellows, and bellyache to me if there's anything wrong with your room or anything." Then just as he was leaving he stopped, and his voice became mellow and vibrant. "Well, well, look who's here. If it isn't the old horse thief himself! If it isn't old P.L.!"

Alec Bingkrampf was referring, of course, to P. L. Nagel, and Willis had just been wondering what had happened to P.L. and whether P.L. remembered that they had made a cocktail date.

"Is everything all right, P.L.?" Alec Bingkrampf asked. "Did you get the suite you wanted?"

"Yes, thanks, young fellow," P.L. said. "I hope to welcome you to the suite and return your hospitality some time with a small libation."

"That will be swell, P.L.," Alec Bingkrampf said, "and you got your locker at the club and everything?"

"Never mind my locker," P.L. said. "I don't think I'll enter in the Tombstone tomorrow. I'm just going to sit and bend my elbow and let the young fellows do the work."

That was the moment when Willis was reminded of the story of the Chinese Ambassador in Washington.

"You know that reminds me of a story," Willis said. "Stop me if you've heard it. It's the one about the Chinese Ambassador in Washington."

It was always hard to tell whether someone was being polite or whether he really had not heard the story.

"Well, it's just a quickie," Willis said, "but it might help Bing here at the banquet. It seems that this Chinese Ambassador was at a party in Washington, and when his hostess asked him if he would not like to dance, he said, Why should I when I can pay someone else to do it for me? That's like P.L., isn't it? Letting young fellows win the Tombstone for him."

It was gratifying that the story made a real hit, because P.L. and Alec Bingkrampf were by way of being connoisseurs of stories. Their laughter, Willis was sure, was genuine, and as he listened to it Willis thought that telling a story was an art in itself. Once he had been too quick and nervous with the Chinese Ambassador story, but now he had the timing right. Then he remembered the first time he had heard it. Roger Harcourt had told it to him eight years ago, before the stockholders' luncheon at the Harcourt place. It did not seem possible that it was eight years ago, but it was.

"Well," Willis said, "I suppose we've all got to prepare to foregather for cocktails."

"As long as we foregather," P.L. said, "let's go easy on the preparing. Will you come to the suite, Willis?"

"Come on over to my place, P.L.," Willis said, "and try some of my stuff. It's all pure, because it comes from the Alcoholic Beverage Control store."

Eight years ago, when Willis had first heard the ambassador story, he might have been hesitant about asking someone of P. L. Nagel's stature around to the room to have a drink, but things were different now. Willis knew that people like P. L. Nagel liked to be treated by younger men in a spirit of equality. After all, Willis was forty-one, although he didn't look it. At least Sylvia, and some of the boys at the office too, said he didn't look it. Even though there was a touch of gray in his hair, Sylvia had pointed out that people who started out blond were apt to turn gray earlier. This indication of age, at any rate, did not look badly on the president of Harcourt Associates. Frankly, Willis was getting a little tired of youth.

"All right," P.L. said, "but don't ask in a crowd."

It was a little sad to hear him, Willis thought, because once there was nothing P.L. had liked as much as a crowd. It never occurred to Willis for a moment, that afternoon at the Carolina, that P.L. could want a quiet conversation with him. He never realized until later that P.L. might very well have come to the Production Liners Convocation at Pinehurst exclusively for that purpose.

They weren't building monumental hotels like the old Carolina any more, and Willis was sorry. The enormous hallway stretching the length of the building afforded perpetual interest in leisure moments. Walking over the springy carpet of that corridor was like drifting down a Venetian canal—a fanciful simile, because Willis had not had time to get abroad as yet. On either side of the corridor was a shifting series of attractions. Shops full of sporting clothes for men and varicolored gowns for women were blossoming out like the late Carolina spring, and there were all sorts of unexpected consumer gadgets, now that the war was over. Then there were gift shops with novel souvenirs suitable for carrying home to wives, children, and sweethearts, and besides these attractions there were lounging alcoves and card and cocktail rooms, not to mention the ballroom. This vast caravansary, beautifully run despite the constant turnover of guests, reminded him of Chieftain Manor because, though somewhat smaller, The Old Chief had been a part of American hotel tradition, as practiced at the turn of the century—and what a tradition it had been, exemplifying the spaciousness and breadth of American belief, in the first flush of America's industrial youth. It spoke of plenty and of a boundless opportunity inconceivable today, when one was hemmed in by socialistic restrictions. There would never again be a time similar to the era when the Carolina was brand new, but the Carolina was still far from being a mausoleum. Thousands of people who loved it were making it right now the background of a new America.

There was no hotel, in Willis's opinion, as suitable for housing a large-scale and active business convention. There was room to turn around at the Carolina and space to get away from the crowd if you wanted to discuss facts and figures. Then of course there was the country club and those great Pinehurst golf courses that siphoned off junior executives and their wives and left lots of opportunity for quiet, orderly discussion, if you wanted round-table or committee talks. The Carolina could handle a big crowd comfortably, and the Production Liners Convocation needed a lot of space.

It had started as a casual group of Midwest industrialists with a common interest in promoting industrial efficiency. Once it had been an informal discussion group with a humorous angle which it had never quite lost, as was illustrated by the somewhat irreligious name "Convocation," but then this was a word that distinguished the Production Liners from the ordinary convention. Now few people on the list could afford to miss the annual meeting, which the press itself rated as important as that of the National Association of Manufacturers. Now on the afternoon of the opening day tardy Production Liners were still streaming in with gigantic leather golf bags and other suitable pieces of luggage. Tables were still set up near the desk with a large banner emblazoned, "Welcome, Production Liners," and smaller signs saying, "Get Your Badges Here." As Willis saw the sign, he reached guiltily into the pocket of his windbreaker, pulled out his gold-framed badge and pinned it on his chest. "Willis Wayde," it read, "Harcourt Associates, Pres."

"It's funny," he said to Jerry Bascomb, "how I keep forgetting to put on this thing."

"Oh hell," Jerry said, "why don't you forget it? Everybody here knows you anyway."

All Jerry's reactions made Willis very glad that he had brought him along to the Convocation. It showed that you failed to notice people sometimes in the daily routine of a plant or office. Jerry had a fine appearance and a very easy, congenial manner, not to mention brains and ability. Given the proper driving force, he might very well be high-executive material.

"I hope you enjoy being here as much as I enjoy having you, Jerry," Willis said.

"Why, thanks a lot, Chief," Jerry answered. "I'm having a swell time. The impact of all this is terrific."

Although Willis knew the assistant manager of the Carolina personally, having been careful to keep up the contact he had made during his first stop there in 1945, the bedroom and sitting room that he and Jerry shared were smaller than he preferred, but then you couldn't expect everything at a Production Liners Convocation, and it was all a whale of a lot better than what he had been able to secure for Will Freeman, Harcourt's assistant sales manager, and his cute little wife, and for Mr. and Mrs. Fred Seagurt from the Rahway plant. Still, the Freemans and the Seagurts, though promising, were only kids who deserved the outing.

"Personally, I showered at the country club, Jerry," Willis said, "so the bathroom is yours."

It only took a short time to change into a fresh linen suit and white buckskin shoes, but still time was limited, because Willis wanted to have things right when P. L. Nagel got there, and suddenly Willis was worried about how Jerry would fit in. Willis was still considering the matter when he picked up the telephone.

"Head bellman, please," he said. "Jerry, when you get out of that tub, would you mind getting the liquor and setting it out here on the writing table?—all the bottles. P.L. likes to see lots of bottles."

"Hello, Mr. Wayde, sir," the bell captain said.

It was an amazing achievement, when you stopped to think of it, that the switchboard operator should have known his name and passed it on to the bell captain. It was something new in service.

"Hello there, Archie," Willis said. He always made a point of knowing bell captains. "Could you rush up some ice to my room and about four Martini and four old-fashioned and four highball glasses, and about six bottles of soda?"

"Would you like some crackers and cheese and a few appetizers with it, Mr. Wayde?" Archie asked.

"As long as you can get it all up in ten minutes," Willis said, "and I won't forget your cooperation, Archie."

It was impossible not to have a sense of well-being on that waning sunny day of a Southern spring. Outside the windows of the sitting room were the fine glistening leaves of a large magnolia and from its branches came the liquid notes of a mockingbird. The room looked homelike, with the bottles and ice and glasses and a few random copies of periodicals including his company house organ, *Harcourters Only*. The Wayde family photographs stood upon a long console table. The bottles and ice and glasses probably should have been put there, but the photographs in their leather frames would have looked crowded elsewhere. One was of Willis's mother, and then of equal size was a fine study of Sylvia seated in the library reading. Sylvia had said facetiously that it represented the first chance offered her to read in weeks. Then, in smaller frames, appeared the children. Al was in his Scout outfit, indicating that Willis believed strongly that the family should be an integrated part of the community. Paul, in the ridiculous long trousers that little boys now wore, was playing with their new retriever, whom Paul had named Hugo. Louise was simply standing out on the lawn with Miss Farquahr, and Willis was glad to have Miss Farquahr included, because she was getting to be quite an old retainer now. Finally there was an enlarged snapshot of Waydeholm as seen from the garden and the swimming pool. Combined, those pictures made a good sound gallery.

"Say, Jerry," Willis said, "I particularly want you to observe P. L. Nagel. Although a competitor, Jerry, I really have a warm spot in my heart for him and a deep admiration. He's a fine type executive, who keeps a youthful outlook. He gives the air of being a playboy, but don't let that deceive you."

"I hear Simcoe is going into foam rubber in a pretty big way," Jerry said.

"Yes," Willis said, but he did not want to be talking about foam rubber when P.L. came in, so he changed the subject.

"Jerry," he said, "I was watching you this afternoon, particularly on the twelfth and fourteenth. You're developing the makings of a good sound game."

"I work at it," Jerry said. "I admit golf's a fascinating game, just from the point of view of precision."

Willis smiled. There was no doubt that Jerry Bascomb was executive material.

"Golf is something you've got to cultivate pretty prayerfully," Willis said. "I used to be a duffer, and I'm not proud at all of my ninety-one today, but that trap on the tenth set me back three strokes. I've got to remember to look around the golf shop tomorrow for another wedge."

He looked at his wrist watch. P.L. was a little overdue.

"Basically," Willis said, "a golf game is like a man's character, or like integrity or loyalty. It mellows with experience. Come to think of it, the first time I saw that golf was a significant game was during my honeymoon. Sylvia and I spent it at a place called Chieftain Manor in the Adirondacks. It happened—it's quite a coincidence—that I played several times there with old P. L. Nagel, who was vacationing there with Mrs. Nagel when we were honeymooning. P.L. studies every shot. He never lets anything get by, and that's just the way he is at Simcoe."

He had gone on about golf deliberately, as a sort of test, and Jerry had listened without allowing his attention to waver for a moment.

"It's interesting," Jerry said, "that you speak of golf in terms of philosophy, while I think in terms of ballistics. It's fascinating that the power of a swing, properly exerted, can send a ball so far and so straight."

Those remarks of Jerry's showed that he could talk interestingly on a general subject, and Willis hated to break up the conversation, but he was thinking about the two young couples, the Freemans and the Seagurts.

"The whole secret of golf," Willis said, because he did not want to change the subject too abruptly, "is hitting from the inside out. Get a nice pivot, and if you make a good clean finish you don't have to worry. By the way, Jerry, after you've had a little visit with P.L., maybe you'd better get in touch with the kids down the hall. I've just remembered that P. T. Green is throwing a little shindig in the Pine Room—you know, president of the Green Gauge and Roller Company."

"It sounds like a kind of plum, doesn't it? I mean Green Gauge," Jerry said, and Willis laughed perfunctorily.

"It sounds good to us right now, Jerry," he said, "because they've just put in an inquiry for Planeroid. I don't know whether I can induce P.L. to go down or not, but I'd like you and the Freemans and the Seagurts to show up in the Pine Room, and you might indicate indirectly to P.T. that you're our Planeroid specialist. You don't mind, do you, Jerry?"

"Mind?" Jerry said. "Why should I mind?" And then there was a banging on the door, and Willis heard P. L. Nagel's voice.

"Open up there," P.L. was calling. "It's the house detective."

When he was playing, P.L. always was a lot of fun, although Willis sometimes suspected that those playful moods were a sort of iron curtain that concealed many of P. L. Nagel's thoughts and motives. The truth was P.L. was not really an entertainer like the regular pranksters and jokesters who would appear at the banquet. No matter how he tried, he was not a natural-born comedian, because comedians did not have steel-trap minds. And yet out of courtesy to an older man, Willis had to act up to the horseplay.

"Don't put the bracelets on us yet, Chief," Willis said. "And how about a drink?"

If it was a flat answer, it had the advantage of stopping P.L. from being a house detective. In spite of his corpulence, which had been catching up with him in the last few years, P.L. looked sharp in a beautifully pressed Palm Beach suit and a canary-yellow necktie, and his growing bald spot gave the illusion of an island surrounded by white breakers.

"Just a tetch of bourbon," P.L. said. "Say, I've just been down at Alec Bingkrampf's with a crowd of wild men. It's my considered prognostication after *several* drinks, that they're going to tear this caravansary apart tonight."

Willis laughed in the way one should when playboys and fun were mentioned.

"I don't think it's such a bad idea, seriously speaking," Willis said, "to have some informality at an opening banquet. Jerry, as long as you're being barkeep, I'll have a little bourbon too."

But P. L. Nagel's mind had not yet left the Bingkrampf get-together.

"Have you seen the song sheet those boys have got printed?" P.L. asked. "They've got a real theme song for this convocation. Just hold onto your chairs and listen.

> Nothing could be finer
> For an old Production Liner
> Than the Hotel Carolina
> In the morning."

It seemed to Willis that this was a very obvious effort, but P.L. was watching him critically, so Willis had to be careful of his reaction.

"Well," he said, "I guess it has the makings of a theme song, but I'm not much of a judge of music."

"Say, Bascomb," P.L. said, "how about sweetening up this drink a little? Say, Willis, someday I'm going to snake Jerry away from you. He's too smart to be in a one-horse show like Harcourt Associates."

Willis rose, laughing heartily, and slapped Jerry affectionately on the shoulder.

"Oh no you don't, P.L.," he said, "because Jerry's smart enough to know he's all fixed right where he is."

"I wish you young fellows wouldn't get steamed up at a little clean fun," P.L. said. "When did I ever hire a man from out of a friend's office? Just when did I?"

Willis burst into another hearty shout of laughter.

"You mean just when *didn't* you, don't you, P.L.?" he said.

After all, part of the game was being able to joke with competitors in a friendly way. Wllis had P.L. there, and P.L. beamed at Willis and Jerry Bascomb.

"You ought not to tempt me by having Jerry here," P.L. said.

"I guess the boss would feel better if I pulled out of here then," Jerry said, "and seriously, some of our crowd has got to show up at Mr. Green's. It's been a real pleasure seeing you, Mr. Nagel. Table Fifty-two, isn't it, Chief?"

It was Table 52, and everything about Jerry confirmed Willis's opinion that Jerry was topflight material. He had handled P.L. very nicely, but even so Willis had a twinge of uneasiness, because you could not always tell what anyone, even as loyal as Jerry Bascomb, might do when brought into contact with someone like P.L. This was one of the dangers in conventions that sometimes offset advantages, and it seemed to Willis that P.L. looked at him in a questioning way when Jerry closed the door.

"Seriously and all kidding aside," P.L. said, and he rattled the ice in his glass, "it's nice to snatch a moment of peace and quiet up here. Listen to that God-damn bird singing in that God-damn tree out there. He sounds like a professional bird-caller, doesn't he? Seriously, I'm mighty glad to have a little get-together alone with you, because you've kind of been on my mind lately, Willis."

Willis looked carefully at his old-fashioned glass. He was old enough by now to conceal surprise and old enough also not to indulge in a series of guesses as to what was coming.

"I hope I've been on your mind in a nice way, P.L.," Willis said.

When you were dealing with someone of P.L.'s caliber, you were playing in the big league. You needed to be careful if you wanted to keep your shirt. Willis saw P.L. watching him, and he gazed back innocently, but then before P.L. could make a further move the telephone on the console table rang.

"Sit right where you are, P.L.," he said, "and sweeten up your drink. I was so absorbed in what we were saying that I completely forgot I put a call in for home for six-thirty—just to say hello to Sylvia and the kids."

The telephone rang impatiently before Willis could reach it. Then he sat down with the instrument propped expertly against his ear and smiled at P.L. hospitably.

"Speaking," he said. ". . . Hello, sweetness . . . How's everything going in the park? . . . Oh, I couldn't be better, honey. The weather's wonderful and this is going to be a real party. I do wish you were here to enjoy it with me, but Jerry Bascomb's mighty good company. . . . Yes, I've been out already, but I only shot a ninety-one today. I took three strokes getting out of a trap on the tenth on Course Two. . . . Oh, no no, I'm not at a cocktail party or anything. I'm just lazing around up here in the suite, and who do you think is up here with me? Old P. L. Nagel."

"Oh, my God," Sylvia said, "not that terrible old bore."

Willis had been careful to hold the receiver tight to his ear because you never could be sure what Sylvia might say, but still he was glad to remember that someone had said that old P.L.'s hearing was not what it used to be.

"Now, sweetness," Willis said, "I certainly will give him your love. I wouldn't forget it for the world."

"Give him my love but don't have him or that wife of his here if you can help it, darling," Sylvia said.

"Right," Willis said, "right, sweetness, and now if the kiddies are there, how about my saying a few words to them?"

"First about the Packard," Sylvia said. "You never told me you were going to turn it in. Really, Willis, it's just as good as it ever was."

Willis smiled at P. L. Nagel. Conceivably, it might be valuable if P.L. overheard this part of the conversation.

"Now, sweetness, let's get this straight," Willis said. "The Packard is obsolescent, and I've had my name in for a Cadillac for months, sweetness."

"But, Willis," Sylvia said, "we don't really need a Cadillac."

"It isn't a question of needing a Cadillac," Willis said. "The point is we can readily afford a Cadillac. Just to reassure yourself, you might look up Harcourt Associates in the *New York Times.*" Willis laughed and winked mischievously at P.L. "Just see what a share is quoted at now, and remember what I paid for it. In fact I'm willing to get two Cadillacs, sweetness."

"Oh, Willis," Sylvia said. "Let's not have people think we're Miami gamblers."

As Sylvia spoke, Willis released the telephone from his ear so that Sylvia's rather high voice could carry across the room.

"All right, honey," he said, "we'll leave it at one for the present, and you can keep the Packard and turn in the Ford if you want to. Well, if that's all—oh, just a second. I hope you called up Boston in my behalf and that the news is still reassuring."

"He's had a very good day," Sylvia said, "and he sent you a special message not to break things off at Pinehurst, and now Al's waiting for you. He's crazy to speak to you about something."

Willis put his hand over the transmitting end of the telephone.

"That's about Bryson Harcourt, P.L.," he said. "There's been no publicity but we've had some bad news in that direction—a slight stroke in the Boston office ten days ago—very slight, thank goodness, but his left side is still affected. It's upsetting because he's a very splendid person."

"That's very tough," P.L. said. "I didn't know."

He spoke as one who recognizes we must all meet an inevitable ending but also like a soldier who sees his comrade fall in the ranks. They could not go on with the conversation, because Willis could hear Al's voice, still the falsetto of childhood, calling to him from hundreds of miles away.

"Hey, Dad," Al was calling.

"Hello, son," Willis answered. "How's every little thing with you, Al?"

"Dad," Al said, "we're going out for a two-day hike beginning Friday."

"For a two-day hike," Willis repeated after him. "Well, well. Where are you going to sleep, Al?"

"In the woods in pup tents," Al answered. "Troop A and Troop B."

Willis was about to ask what woods, until he remembered that a large area in New Jersey had been left to the Scouts for just such purposes, but he still could not understand this desire for woods and woodcrafts when there were no frontier days any longer.

"That sounds wonderful, Al," he said. "Don't chop your finger off or anything and don't run if you see a bear."

"Say, Dad," Al said. "When are you coming back?"

"Why, Al," Willis answered, "I'll see you Monday night, and I want to hear all about that hike."

"Okay, Dad," Al said, and his voice sounded fainter.

It was something like a spiritual seance, speaking to one's children hundreds of miles away, and now Paul's voice was speaking through the unsubstantial distance.

"Well, well," Willis said. "How's Hugo, Paul?"

"Hugo's okay," Paul answered. "Say, Dad, will you bring me a present when you come back?"

"Yes," Willis said. "I'll see what I can do, Paul."

"Okay," Paul said. "I've got to be going now."

"Daddy." It was Louise speaking, and her voice was fainter still, giving Willis the impression that Sylvia and all the children were drifting away into space. "Daddy, I'm on the second spelling book now."

"The second spelling book," Willis said. "Well, my little honey bunch."

"Well, that's all, Daddy," Louise said.

"Good-by, honey bunch," Willis said. "Give Mommy a big kiss for me. Good-by, honey bunch."

Willis smiled at P.L. as he put down the telephone. The Carolina Hotel suite was more like home and P. L. Nagel like a house guest because of those brief domestic speeches.

"I wish Myrtle and I had ever had kids," P.L. said, "but Myrtle was always against babies. Those kids of yours must be getting to be quite a handful now."

Willis laughed the way a family man should when his children came up for discussion.

"You've got to watch yourself at the Wayde house," Willis said, "so as not to trip over roller skates and doll carriages, but I'm willing to settle for the lot of them, frankly, and besides, we have Miss Farquahr to look after them. Miss Farquahr's a real wonder. She showed up when Paul was born. We couldn't do without Farky now—that's what the kids call her, Farky."

"No," P.L. said, "there's nothing like kids to make a home, and it's sort of tragic that Myrtle thinks so too, now it's too late. There we are in Lake Forest in a house just made for kids and grandchildren and everything, and no kids. Pour me out another tetch, will you? On the rocks. I wish you lived next door, boy, so I could see your kids running around our lawn. Those are their pictures over there, aren't they?"

"That's right," Willis said. "There they all are, to keep Daddy on the straight and narrow."

"It's quite a display, isn't it?" P.L. said. "I'd like to take a look, if it isn't too impertinent, son."

P.L. pushed himself up and put on a pair of massive horn-rimmed spectacles of the type used by Hollywood producers.

"I always feel better about anyone," P.L. said, "when I see him traveling with a picture of his mother, and your mother's a lovely little lady, Willis. Old Alf introduced her to me once while he was working for Harrod Cash. Where are your parents now, Willis?"

"They're pretty much retired now," Willis said. "They're living in a very attractive ranch-type house in a development near San Bernardino— or San Budoo, as they call it in California."

"That's a lovely part of the world," P.L. said. "Do you know old Ralph Schultz in Hocking Aircraft?"

"I surely do know old Ralph," Willis said. "I look upon him as one of my sweetest West Coast contacts. The last time I was out there he was kind enough to lend me a car and a driver to take me out to San Budoo."

"It is, I repeat, a lovely part of the world," P.L. said. "It's too bad you're not living nearer to it, Willis. As I always say to Myrtle, a man can have a lot of wives, and a great many do—" P.L. chuckled but sobered up immediately—"but, boy, you only have one mother."

"That's right, P.L.," Willis said. "I've never heard it said in quite that way." But P.L. had turned to continue his inspection of the photographs.

"That's a sweet shot of Sylvia," he said. "Remember back at The Old Chief? Been fond of Sylvia ever since."

"Sylvia will love to hear that, P.L.," Willis said, "because frankly she feels just that way about you."

"And look at those kids," P.L. said. "Sylvia's looks and your brains, boy—not that Sylvia isn't a pretty brainy gal herself. It does make me wish they were all running around using my pool and facilities at Lake Forest. What is it the poet said—about the phrase 'it might have been' being the saddest in the world? Willis, you don't know it but you're a lucky damn horse thief."

"Yes, P.L.," Willis said, "I guess I am pretty lucky."

"And that's a nice shot of your home, too," P.L. said. "But, say, come

[345]

across clean now. Isn't it a little cramped now that the kids are growing up?"

"Well, now you mention it," Willis said, "I do wish we had another ell or something."

Willis could not avoid a feeling of suspense, knowing there was something behind every one of old P.L.'s verbal maneuvers, but at the same time it was a pleasure to watch P.L. at work. P.L. was looking in a surprised way at his empty old-fashioned tumbler.

"Hell," he said, "my tongue's hanging out. Say, rush me over some more bourbon, and what about you, son? You've been nursing that drink ever since I've come in here. You act as though you're suspicious."

"Why, I was just thinking we might be going down to Green Gauge or somewhere, P.L.," Willis said, "and I was merely saving a little space."

"Well, you just start in filling it, son," P.L. said, "because I like it here. I like to hear that God-damn bird outside. Take a real shot of bourbon, son, and here's to our not being too smart with each other. Get me?"

"Why, no, P.L.," Willis said. "I don't exactly get you at the moment."

P.L. took out a handkerchief and patted the bald spot on his head.

"Well, I rather think," he said, and shook his finger slowly at Willis —"I rather think before we're through here you'll get my meaning, eventually, and now let's you and me stop horsing around."

Willis had to laugh, although it was a time when he should watch himself.

"Why, P.L.," he said, "I didn't know we had been."

"Now stop," P.L. said. "You know damned well you and I have both been horsing. Finish that drink and take another and sit down."

"If we're stopping horsing," Willis answered, "and if you have something you want to tell me, maybe I'd better not have another drink until I get the news."

Willis laughed as he said it. Even though he felt annoyed at P.L.'s tactics with the bourbon, Willis was relieved that the horsing around was over. The whole texture of P.L.'s expression changed. He was like an actor off-stage in his dressing room at the end of a performance.

"Son," P.L. said, "when you get to be my age, maybe you'll find yourself dreaming dreams like I do. Right now I would like for you to dream back with me to the time when you and I first met. At that period I was suffering from a head cold, and my sinuses haven't improved any since. I made, you may recall—in fact I know you do—an offer to Mr. Henry Harcourt of five million dollars for that mill of his. I was not interested in the physical plant, since I am a believer in concentration, and Simcoe is situated in the Middle West. I wanted the Klaus patents and other parts of the Harcourt process, and Mr. Henry Harcourt knew it. Well, he turned me down for sentimental reasons, which surprised me, because I know, and you know too, that nothing runs long on sentiment —businesswise."

P. L. Nagel seemed to be in no hurry, and Willis began to wish that he would make his point. It was growing increasingly difficult to stop himself from leaping ahead to conclusions.

"I hope you're dreaming right along with me," P. L. Nagel said. "When old H.H. turned down that offer, I wasn't worried any. Time solves most things, and I could foresee what would happen under Bryson Harcourt's management. It was my idea they'd be glad to sell me that property, and they would have—if it hadn't been for you, son. You're the nigger in the woodpile—you fooled me."

Willis could not help but feel flattered, not so much by what P.L. said as by his utter seriousness.

"Oh, now, P.L.," he said, "you know I couldn't fool you."

Willis watched P.L. carefully, but P.L.'s features did not relax.

"Maybe you wouldn't have fooled me," P.L. said, "if I had got my facts straight. I didn't know at the time you had some of the best organizing ability I've ever met—and guts."

It was dangerous to be moved by flattery, but no one familiar with P. L. Nagel could have helped feeling a secret sort of pleasure.

"Oh, come now, P.L.," Willis said. "Seriously, I'm not as good as that."

"I wouldn't be sitting here if I didn't know you were, son," P.L. said, "but just you let me make my point. When you combined Harcourt with Rahway I thought it would be a bust. I didn't envisage how the Planeroid and the Klaus patents were going to fit. I never thought you'd be giving Simcoe competition and that you and I would be talking serious business."

P.L. paused again and Willis waited for him to go on until he saw that P.L. was also waiting. It was one of those tense moments that demanded care.

"Are we really talking serious business, P.L.?" Willis asked.

"You're damned well right we are," P.L. said, "and to prove it I'd like you to kindly get up and turn the night latch on the door."

Willis was glad of the opportunity to move across the room and the click of the latch made a satisfactory decisive sound.

"All right, P.L.," he said, "go ahead and tell me what you want."

Willis was in the better position, of course. One always was when someone else wanted something. He walked across the room and stood in front of P.L. waiting, and he hardly needed to tell himself to be relaxed.

"Sit down," P.L. said. "It hurts my neck looking up at you. All right, I want you in the first place, son, to come in as first vice president and

[347]

in three years to be president of Simcoe. That's one thing I want and I'm not kidding."

Willis crossed his right knee carefully over his left. It was important to show no surprise or excitement, and this was very difficult because he had never given any serious thought to being president of one of the biggest belting and industrial-rubber concerns in the country.

"Of course I'm very flattered, P.L.," he said. "But obviously this is something that requires a lot of considering and I should have to familiarize myself with the whole Simcoe picture."

P. L. Nagel waved his hand carelessly.

"Of course it needs thought," he said. "With this God-damn punitive income tax there's no use saying much about salary, but I'm confident we can do something interesting with stock. I don't want to name a figure now but I want to leave one thought. You're about as far as you can get where you are, son. On the other hand, the sky will be the limit at Simcoe."

Willis smiled courteously. There was no use in giving any indication of anything until there was a definite offer.

"That's right, P.L.," he said, "I'm about as far as I can go in the Associates, I suppose, but I'm happy where I am and I know my way around."

Willis's words fell into a void of silence.

"You won't be happy there eventually," P.L. said. "Anyway, I want you to be running Simcoe in my place. I want the very best, and that means you, son, and that isn't all I want."

Apparently P.L. wanted to be asked what else he wanted, but Willis's instinct told him it was a time to wait, and it was amusing to outwait someone like P.L.

"I also want Harcourt Associates," P.L. said. "I regret it's going to cost more than five million. The figure I'm thinking of is in the neighborhood of twenty-five, and now that you know what I want I wish you would sweeten up my glass."

Willis took the old-fashioned glass from P. L. Nagel. It was not a time to be superficial and he spoke very gravely.

"Frankly," he said, "I need a minute to catch my breath, P.L."

Willis had received several offers to leave Harcourt Associates, and the Nagel offer, though more flattering, could be considered as another of the lot, but the idea of the sale of Harcourt Associates was new. He balanced it quickly as he poured the bourbon into P.L.'s glass, and that vague offer of twenty-five million was skillful. It had been dangled out like bait, obviously after P.L. had made a careful study of the Associates, and was conceivably not a top offer. Willis saw that the picture had the unsavory implications of a package deal; but he also knew that he was facing a moment in his life that was fraught with possibilities that might never come again.

"Well, P.L.," he said, "I'm somewhat curious as to why you want to absorb Harcourt Associates, but then I suppose it's more your business than it's mine."

While P.L. took a sip of his bourbon, Willis tried to recollect how many drinks P.L. had taken, but the number made no difference in P.L.'s mental processes or control.

"I think you know the answer, son," he said. "I like your conveyor belting, and there are certain parts of your process that I would like to combine with Simcoe. It's a high price but part of it would be an exchange in stock." P.L. paused and looked thoughtfully at Willis. "I think, son, if this went through you could buy Rolls-Royces instead of Cadillacs."

Willis cleared his throat.

"I suppose," he said, "you wouldn't keep using the Harcourt Mill or Rahway."

He could see already that this was the most disturbing problem in the picture and the one which he least wanted to face, and he was relieved that P. L. Nagel did not wish to face it either.

"We would have to make some experiments regarding integration," P.L. said, "but this seems a small detail."

"I'm not sure whether it is or not," Willis answered. "Very frankly the prospect of closing the Harcourt Mill disturbs me. You remember, don't you, what Mr. Harcourt said about the family feeling for the mill?"

"I'd like it," P.L. said, and his voice had an imperious sound, "if we laid aside this angle for the moment. If you want my guess a lot of the Harcourt family would like to take that offer. Why don't you face it? With those two little factories of yours, one in New Jersey and one in Massachusetts, you're swimming against the tide. I'm throwing you a life raft, son, because I want you up at Simcoe and I want those processes."

Willis glanced at his wrist watch. It was almost seven, and the discussion could not continue much longer, and that glance at his watch at least showed that he was not too impressed by the conversation to forget the time.

"Well, I must admit that this is all most interesting," he said, "but there's one thing about your general approach that leaves a rather bad taste in my mouth. I may as well be frank, P.L."

"Why, yes," P.L. said gently, "what is it, son?"

Willis stood up and squared his shoulders. He deliberately took a few moments to set his thoughts in order. It did no harm to keep P.L. waiting. When he did speak he was carried away by his sentiments, and each of his words gave strength to the others.

"P.L.," he said, "I believe that sincerity and integrity are the cornerstones of any relationship. I am sure you will understand that in my position as the head of my company I am not a free agent because I am the servant of my stockholders. I can recommend but in the end I must follow their wishes. Also I must add that I believe in loyalty, P.L., and my loyalty to the Harcourt family ranks as high as what I owe my own, especially with Mr. Bryson Harcourt incapacitated. I have to think of these things very carefully, P.L. I want to do what's best for everyone, and what is best for myself comes last."

Willis stopped. He was moved by what he had said. He had clarified his own thoughts.

"That's fine, son," P. L. Nagel said. "I like the way you put it. We both of us are servants to our stockholders, and I counted on you being loyal."

Willis paused for a moment before he answered. It was growing late but the mockingbird was still singing.

"I merely wanted to make this clear, P.L.," he said, "because there was one part of your offer to me personally which I do not like. I refer to my future in the Simcoe Company. I hate to say a hard word but I'm afraid I must, P.L. That offer sounds to me somewhat like a bribe, an inducement to facilitate the sale of my company and perhaps to forget certain loyalties and obligations. I'm not saying you meant this, P.L., but it's the way it sounded. I want you to know in a very friendly way that you can't bribe me in that manner."

Willis looked at P.L. steadily, and P.L. set down his glass. For a moment their glances met, but Willis did not allow his to waver for an instant, because it was a time for absolute sincerity.

"Why, son," P.L. said, and his voice was surprised and sad, "I guess I'm getting to be mighty clumsy. I like straight shooting as much as you do. I never intended any ulterior motive in that personal offer to you—none whatsoever. I want you as president of Simcoe because you're the best man your age in belting and because I love you—yes, I love you—for the honest things you've said and for the very lovely and fine way you've presented them." P. L. Nagel pushed himself up from his chair. "And now if I may use your toilet, son, I think we had better prepare to go down to the banquet, and suppose we meet in my room at ten o'clock tomorrow morning and go on with this little talk. And now let's shake hands, and no hard feelings, because I really love you, son."

As Willis often said later, the admiration he felt for P. L. Nagel was always pretty close to hero worship. When they shook hands, everything in their relationship reached a new high and all sorts of doubts were gone from Willis's mind. Although nothing was settled at all, a good deal appeared to have been, and Willis was at peace with himself.

It was strange to think that an hour before he had not imagined he would be in the position he now occupied. When he walked down the broad staircase of the Carolina beside P. L. Nagel into the wave of voices that rose from the Production Liners filing into the banquet room, Willis could almost believe that he was already an integral part of Simcoe Rubber Hose and Belting. Nothing at all was settled, but he was already wondering how much he ought to tell Sylvia and how Sylvia might react to moving to Lake Forest. It was ridiculous to let his imagination run away with him, because the whole thing might evaporate into thin air, but Willis was already thinking of what he should say to Mrs. Bryson Harcourt and to Bess and Bill in order to put the situation into an agreeable light.

The halls of the Carolina Hotel were ringing already with the song which P. L. Nagel, good old P.L., had rendered already in the suite upstairs:

> Nothing could be finer
> For an old Production Liner
> Than the Hotel Carolina
> In the morning.
> Aspirin and coffee
> Coming in the door
> And you only have to holler
> To get some more,
> If you're an old Production Liner
> In the Hotel Carolina
> In the morning.

There was one thing of which Willis was positive. If these things came to pass—and every moment he felt more and more sure that they would—he would do everything to keep the Harcourt Mill in operation, out of loyalty to old memories. He could see its buildings in his memory, ugly individually but combined into a fine progression. He thought of Mr. Henry Harcourt's office and its hard chairs and its portraits and the coal fireplace. Willis had come close to forgetting what a warm spot he had in his heart for the Harcourt Mill. He certainly would do everything he could—within reason—to keep it in operation.

XXVI

WILLIS WAS not a believer in elation, because elation was an emotional state which clouded judgment. He was not elated when he returned home to Orange after the Production Liners Convocation. There had been time to sort facts and to file them in back of his mind so that he could face the immediate problems which he naturally found waiting for him after a few days' absence from the New York office. In fact he went through the whole business day exactly as though there were no prospects of a merger between Harcourt Associates and Simcoe Rubber Hose and Belting. Still, in back of his thoughts, resting like a handsome balance in the bank, lay the final impressions of his conversations with P. L. Nagel. They had passed out of the zone of agreement in principle to tentative agreements on certain basic facts. It was rewarding to remember that they both had seen the central core of every problem almost simultaneously, but then as P. L. Nagel had said, minds in the high brackets were generally congenial.

If Willis was not elated when he returned to Orange, he could hardly blame himself for having a feeling of well-being and of achievement. After all, like everyone else who had to start with nothing—and this was a proper way, the American way, for anyone to start—Willis had been striving for security. No matter how well things had gone in the last few years, there was always the besetting worry as to what might happen if death or accident should suddenly remove him. Could anyone else taking over Harcourt Associates keep up the level of earnings? Willis could see a gloomy picture of decline, of dividends falling off and of Sylvia and the children suffering the pinch. Everything was different now that an offer had been made for Harcourt Associates in tangible figures. Once the deal was consummated there would be no need to worry. If he wished to sell his common stock once it was converted into Simcoe, he would be rich enough to retire, not that he had the slightest wish to do so.

Without being elated or dazzled he had to admit that these prospects made him happy. The best of it was that they were fruits of his own labor. No matter what credit he might give to the fine team at Harcourt, it was due to his leadership that Harcourt was where it was. The haste and rush of years were not wasted and he was about to reap a just reward. He could not blame himself for being very happy when he got out of the taxicab at Waydeholm.

Al and Paul were playing catch out on the lawn. It seemed to Willis that they had grown even during his short absence from home. They were very handsome boys. They had their mother's features but their yellow hair reminded Willis of his own when he was their age. Besides being handsome, they were real sturdy boys and they looked as though they were going to make good athletes. They dropped their mitts and ran to meet him, and a lump rose in Willis's throat. After all, he had not let them down.

"Hello," he said. "How about helping me wrassle with this luggage, fellers? And let's see if we can find Mommy and Louise."

The whole house never had looked better. Dogwood and paper-white narcissus decorated the hall. The really beautiful claw-and-ball-foot table he had bought to stand under the Chippendale mirror was freshly waxed, and the tall clock at the end of the hall, which he had bought at the Parke-Bernet Gallery after very brisk bidding, gave balance to everything around it. After all, acquiring good pieces of antique furniture really was the same as putting money in the bank, provided you could keep the children from doing damage. Right at that moment Paul was leaning on the arm of the end chair that flanked the claw-and-ball-foot table.

"Remember what I said, son," Willis told him. "You mustn't do that with good furniture. You've got to learn to respect good furniture."

"Okay," Paul said. "Sorry." There was no doubt they were both fine boys with very good manners.

"Besides, boys," Willis said, "you've always got the rumpus room downstairs."

Then Sylvia came out of the dining room and kissed him, and Carl, the colored houseman, came to get his bags, and Louise and Miss Farquahr appeared on the stair landing.

"Daddy," Louise called, "Daddy!" She had dark hair like her mother, and her eyes were shining. It was ridiculous, of course, to say that Louise was like a little princess, but still that was how she looked.

The whole scene in the hallway added up to something that was greater than any good news, because without a happy home, everything else was pretty hollow.

"Hello," he called to Louise, "my darling little pussykins." Then he added in a very cordial way, "And it's nice to see you, Miss Farquahr."

"Did you have a good time at Pinehurst, dear?" Sylvia asked him.

Somehow wives always thought that conventions were only intended to supply a good time.

"There was a fine crowd, honey, and fine papers and discussions," Willis said, "but frankly I'm a little tired, and now if you'll all forgive me I think I'll go up and shower and get into a pair of slacks."

"The boys want to show you their garden," Sylvia said, "and Louise has a garden too, with radishes."

"Well, well," Willis said, "yum, yum, radishes."

"Maybe you'd like to have Carl bring us cocktails on the terrace, dear," Sylvia said. "It's such a nice warm day."

Willis was aware of a slight headache, although nothing that a cold shower would not cure.

"Let's make it a little tonic water, dear," he said. "I'm pretty well cocktailed out for the moment."

He laughed and kissed Sylvia again and started up the stairs. It was amusing to remember that Sylvia had once been appalled by the size of the house, while now she was finding it difficult to discover a suitable place to hang the Winslow Homer he had given her for her birthday. The clothes closet in his dressing room was too small, and the two guest rooms might easily have been more gracious. He was thinking of a house made to his own order and of the fun he and Sylvia might have poring over the blueprints. It was a daydream, perhaps, but if they moved out to Chicago, as they undoubtedly would if he accepted P. L. Nagel's offer, that daydream became a real possibility.

Dinner was wonderful—green-turtle soup and guinea hen—and Sylvia had brought up a bottle of Veuve Cliquot from the cellar, to celebrate, she said, his safe return. If you had lived in a place long enough, there could not help but be memories, and memories crowded around Willis in the dining room. The chairs, the pedestal table, and the sideboard all brought memories of how he and Sylvia had searched for these objects. After all, good silver and furniture were money in the bank.

"I suppose I should have asked you," Sylvia said, "whether you wanted a rough-and-tumble family supper, but I guessed you'd rather have the children with Miss Farquhar in the nursery. I thought you might be tired after—what was the name of the convention that you went to, dear?"

"The Production Liners, sweetness," Willis said, and he smiled at her through the candlelight.

"Darling," she said, "I have a confession to make—a reluctant sort of confession."

"A confession, honey?" Willis asked, and he was aware of a slight discomfort, because you could never tell about confessions.

[354]

"Yes," Sylvia said, "I thought you'd like to know that I'm getting so used to this house that I wouldn't want to live anywhere else. I'm even getting used to calling it Waydeholm. My spirit must be broken or something, darling."

Willis raised his champagne glass to her. Her speech upset him but it still called for some sort of gesture.

"Well, well," he said, "congratulations, sweetness, and how about having coffee in the library after we've kissed the kids good night?"

"We can kiss Louise and Paul," Sylvia said, "but you keep forgetting that Al goes to bed an hour later."

"Gosh," Willis said, and he shook his head, "I do have a lot of things to remember, honey."

"But then I forgot," Sylvia said. "The Crosby boy asked Al over to his house for the night. I wouldn't have accepted if I had been sure you were coming back today."

"Why, that's all right, honey," Willis said. "In fact it's just as well, because I have a real budget of news for you—news that I hope is going to give you the same sort of thrill that it's giving me."

The library was a room of which he and Sylvia were justly proud. It was well-proportioned, with a beautiful open fireplace and mantel, and it was furnished with English armchairs still in their original leather. There was a Kermanshah rug for floor covering, one of the most beautiful Willis had ever seen, unobtrusive in design and with soft colors matching the window curtains and the waxed pine paneling. There was also the flat desk of the General Grant period, which had been with them ever since his New York apartment. It served to give the room the informal, unstudied appearance that reminded him of the rooms in the big house on the Harcourt place, and the Persian rug itself was worn, and this too reminded him of the Harcourt rugs. It was what you might call a cultivated, lived-in library.

Usually when they were alone Willis was content with nothing but a small cup of Sanka, but since he had some really important news to impart to Sylvia, he had Carl bring in liqueurs.

"Brandy, sweetness?" he asked Sylvia.

"Oh, I don't think so, dear," Sylvia said. "I don't want anything, really, but if you want me to keep you company I'll have a little *crème de menthe*."

"Well, as I've said before, but I'll repeat, sweetness," Willis said, "it's great to get home. I hope everything's been going all right."

"Oh yes," Sylvia said. "I don't think I told you over the telephone that Al was almost selected as Toby Tyler in the parish-hall play."

[355]

"Well, that's fine," Willis said. "It makes me feel good, dear, that the kids are beginning to take their place in the community."

"I know it, darling," Sylvia said, "but you don't have to keep on saying it. We are a real integrated part of the community, but what with Open House Week for the church and everything, do you think I still have to be on the program committee for the League of Women Voters?"

"Well, now, sweetness," Willis said, "I know these activities, from my personal experience, are time-consuming and often dull, but you know how I feel about everyone in Harcourt Associates pulling his weight in the community boat, but well—" Suddenly he thought of the future, and he had to admit that this changed the present picture. "Well, sweetness, if you're awfully busy, never mind the League of Women Voters."

"Why, darling," Sylvia said, "this doesn't sound like you at all, but thanks for letting me off," and she put down her liqueur glass and kissed him.

"Why, sweetness," Willis said, and he had to laugh, "you sound like a kid excused from school."

"If you want to know, I feel like one," Sylvia said. "Willis, dear, isn't this a lovely room? I feel at last that it represents us, even your old Five-Foot Shelf of Books. I feel that we've finally fitted into it in a sort of permanent way."

Willis sniffed his brandy conventionally for a moment before he answered.

"It *is* a lovely room," he said, "and I congratulate you on the thought and taste you've put into it—not that there aren't some things about the fenestration and the paneling that we could improve if we were building it ourselves."

"But we didn't," Sylvia said, "and we aren't going to, so let's enjoy it the way it is."

Willis nodded gravely.

"Honey," he said, "just supposing—I'm only thinking out loud—but just supposing we did have a chance to build a home of our own, wouldn't you sort of enjoy it, honey?"

Sylvia sighed.

"Oh, I don't know, dear," she said. "There would be all the details and arguing with an architect, and a new house always looks so new. No, frankly, I'm awfully glad that we don't have to build a house."

"But, honey," Willis said, "wouldn't you look forward to the adventure in it? The reaching out for something new? What was it Oliver Wendell Holmes said?"

"Please," Sylvia said, and the line between her eyebrows deepened, "if you mean 'Build thee more stately mansions, O my soul,' this one is perfectly good enough, Willis."

Willis laughed apologetically.

"I suppose the quotation does sound a little shopworn," he said, "but you can't deny progress, sweetness. It isn't wholesome to keep standing still."

Sylvia looked at him in a way that made him slightly uneasy, and lighted a cigarette. It was not fair, he was thinking, that she should smoke a cigarette and look doubtful just when he was about to tell her one of the most important things that had ever happened to them.

"Willis," she said, "you aren't thinking of building a new house or anything like that, are you?"

"Well, only indirectly, dear," Willis said, "but still that might be part of the fun if everything I've been mulling over in the last few days comes true."

"Oh, Willis," Sylvia said, "what under the sun are you talking about?" And instead of looking at him with pleased anticipation, she seemed almost apprehensive.

"Sweetness," he said, "it's been a real strain on me to have waited so long before telling you what has happened, but I had to wait until we were alone because it's still very confidential. Frankly, here it is in a nutshell, and I want you to hold tight to your chair, because it's really 'sumpin'—as they say. If things work out right, I honestly think we can start relaxing a little and take that trip abroad, honey, and all sorts of things, and build a whole new house, if we want to, and landscape it just the way we want. You're following me, aren't you?"

He had asked the question because she still looked apprehensive.

"Yes," Sylvia said, "I follow you, but I wish you'd tell me what it's all about, Willis."

"All right, sweetness," Willis said. "I think that's just the fair sort of request that one partner ought to make of another, and we always have been partners, sweetness."

"Yes, although I seem to be a pretty silent partner right now," Sylvia said. "For goodness' sake, go on and tell me. Don't make me sit here being frightened."

That last remark really broke the tension, and without intending to, Willis shook with convulsive laughter.

"You know, that's one of the funniest things you've ever said, honey," he told her. "Frightened? Now hold onto your chair and listen to this. In a nutshell, sweetness, I've been offered the first vice presidency of the biggest belting company in existence, the Simcoe Company, with the assurance that I will be president inside of three years. Aside from the salary, there's a very intelligent common-stock setup going with it." Willis had to laugh again. "And you were making uncomplimentary noises over the phone when I told you at the Carolina that old P. L. Nagel was in my sitting room. Well, that's what he was there for—and what do you think of that one, Mrs. Wayde?"

Willis stood up and paced across the Kermanshah rug, smiling at her. Sylvia had put out her cigarette. The whole thing was what the moving-picture people called a "double take."

"But, Willis," Sylvia began and then stopped, and she still did not seem to get it.

"Now, honey," Willis said, "there are no ifs and buts about this. I'm not thinking out loud. This is a firm and clear-cut offer—not that I can blame you for being the least bit incredulous, considering where Simcoe stands tradewise."

As Willis watched her, Sylvia shifted her position, and her worried look, instead of evaporating into relief, grew more pronounced.

"But, Willis," she said, "I know your mind is very quick about these things and that mine isn't, and so I hope you won't be impatient with me. I don't see how you can leave Harcourt Associates, especially when so many people depend on you as much as they do. It doesn't seem to me exactly fair."

It irritated Willis that Sylvia should think for an instant that he would have done something that was not fair—but then he remembered that he had not yet presented the whole picture.

"I'd rather you'd let me make my point," he said, "before you jump to conclusions, Sylvia. You haven't heard the whole of the offer, and the best part is coming, honey." He laughed lightly, because in a way the situation did have an element of humor, what with Sylvia's doubts and hesitations. "It just so happens," he went on, "that Simcoe is offering to merge with Harcourt Associates, and the figure, honey—now hold onto your seat again—is in the neighborhood of twenty-five million dollars. Now how do you like that one, Mrs. Wayde? And before you answer just remember that you and I own *several* shares in Harcourt Associates."

Perhaps it was the sum of money that he mentioned—because large sums of money always startled Sylvia—that seemed to help Sylvia to grasp the general situation. She sat with parted lips, gazing at him.

"I've had to hold onto my chair several times before," she said. "I do wish these things didn't come so suddenly."

Sylvia was adopting a proper attitude. She might be a little slow on the uptake but in the final analysis he could always count on Sylvia.

"Frankly I was pretty surprised myself, sweetness," Willis said, "so I don't blame you for one moment, honey, if it makes you kind of woozy.

If you will just excuse me, honey, I think I'll take another little tetch of brandy."

He realized the instant he said it that "tetch," like "severial," was P.L.'s word, not his.

"You're beginning to see, aren't you," Willis asked her gently, "why I feel so happy about this whole picture? Not so much for myself as for you and the children, sweetness. It's mighty hard to accumulate property today with things the way they are taxwise."

It did seem to him it was about time for Sylvia to share at least a little in his own spirit of euphoria, but then Sylvia was always slow on the uptake.

"But, Willis," she said, "you can't sell Harcourt Associates yourself. The Harcourts and other people will have to agree to it, won't they?"

No wife, no matter how loyal and lovely she might be, ever seemed to be able to grasp the principles of corporation management—but then after all why should she?

"Right, sweetness," Willis said. "The offer must be accepted by a majority of voting stock, and I think that's the way it will happen when the offer is presented, because in its essence it's a very generous offer."

"I suppose it is," Sylvia said, and she sighed and the line was deep again between her eyebrows, "but there's one thing I don't like about it, Willis, one thing that I think sounds tricky."

Willis sat down in one of the leather armchairs and held the brandy inhaler between his hands.

"I just don't get what you mean," he said, "by the word 'tricky.' I don't find anything 'tricky' in this offer—not a single nigger in the wood-pile, honey."

He realized again that he was using one of P.L.'s phrases, and the thought added to the disturbance that Sylvia's question had created.

"I know I don't understand these things," Sylvia said, "but it does seem to me that what they want most is Harcourt Associates, and that they are offering you a position in their company so that you can help them get what they want. It seems something like a bribe, Willis."

He wished that Sylvia had not hit upon that final word, because it sounded like an echo of his own conscience, but he knew Sylvia would be right with him as soon as she got the whole picture.

"I'm glad you brought up that point, honey," he said, "because it was one that disturbed me very deeply first off, and in fact I went right to the mat with P.L. about it. The two offers aren't tied together in any sort of a package deal, sweetness. P.L. really wants me at Simcoe. He's reaching retirement age, you know, and he said I was the best man there is for the job. There it is in a nutshell, and I hope it makes you as proud as it makes me, Mrs. Wayde."

He had told Sylvia everything frankly and sincerely, but the furrow between her eyebrows was still as deep as ever.

"Willis," Sylvia said, and her lack of enthusiasm made him feel very uneasy, "did you ask Mr. Nagel whether he wants you in his company, if he can't get Harcourt Associates?"

He must have looked startled because she repeated the question almost sharply.

"Did you ask him that, Willis?"

For a moment it seemed to Willis that he was balancing on the edge of nothing. It was a question that he should have asked and he was trying to cast back into his memory for some explanation of why he had not asked it.

"No, honey," he said, "I didn't. Very frankly the thought did not occur to me."

"But why didn't it, Willis?" she began, but he stopped her before she could finish.

"Please," he said, "please, sweetness. Let me go on with what I'm saying. If I had thought of the question, I wouldn't have dreamed of asking it—for a single very good reason. It would have been very insulting to P. L. Nagel, sweetness. I know he wants me, no matter what —but of course I can't go with him and leave the Harcourts in the lurch. You see my point, don't you, dear?"

He felt relaxed and happy now that Sylvia had the true picture. Anyone could see that he could not leave the Harcourts in the lurch.

"But, Willis," Sylvia said, "I shouldn't think the Harcourts would like it, I mean the Bryson Harcourts and Bill and Bess. I mean about selling their business that's been in the family so long. You know they have a sense of obligation to everyone who works there. Of course it's old-fashioned but that's the way they feel."

Willis examined the intricate pattern of the Kermanshah rug before he answered Sylvia. He wished she could understand that anyone in his position could not indulge in personal whims when making a decision, that he was not a free agent. Sentiment had nothing to do with business. In the last refinancing Harcourt stock had been listed on the New York Stock Exchange, so that he was responsible to hundreds of unknown investors.

"You've made a very valid point there, sweetness," he said. "You don't have to tell me how the Harcourts feel about the Harcourt Mill. It's like a sort of an old home to me, too, honey."

He had not expected that there would be a tremor in his voice but there was, and he paused and cleared his throat. He was thinking of faces gone forever and of the years he had spent at the Harcourt Mill. No other plant could ever be quite like it.

"But here's the point, sweetness," he said. "We are living in a world of change, and I am as sure as I can be morally that nothing physical is going to happen to the Harcourt Mill. In the final integration with Simcoe, if I have anything to do with it, it won't even lose its name. Of course there'll be different control, but such things are inevitable, honey."

He had given everything he had to his exposition, and at last Sylvia followed his logic.

"I see what you mean, dear," she said, "but I do feel sorry, just in a sentimental way."

Willis nodded slowly and he sighed.

"It might clarify both our thinking if we looked at the picture from another angle," he said. "I always will be loyal to the Harcourt interests. They're the same as my own family, honey. But look at the present offer —twenty-five million dollars. Very frankly and without fanfare, they wouldn't be getting one fifth of that if it hadn't been for me."

"I know you've worked day and night, dear," Sylvia said, and she nodded her head slowly.

"And nobody knows better than you that it's been quite a strain, sweetness." Willis spoke quickly, because he did not want Sylvia to interrupt him. "When a chance like this comes for you and me and the children, we've both of us got to take it, if it doesn't involve integrity, which this doesn't. You've got to keep on moving and growing. That's the American way, sweetness."

Willis wondered where he had picked up that thought about the American way. Then he remembered that he had said much the same thing to Sylvia years before when they had moved into Waydeholm.

"But, Willis, dear," Sylvia said, "we're always changing. First there was that time when you resigned from Beakney-Graham because Mr. Jacoby wanted you at Rahway."

"Yes, dear," Willis said, "and shall we admit, in the light of the present, that I was quite correct in doing so?"

"Then after we were all getting on comfortably at Rahway Belt," Sylvia said, "you started Harcourt Associates, and now just when we're all happy, this new thing comes along. Willis, can't we forget about it and let things stay the way they are?"

This was the last question Willis would have expected. Just when he thought that things were settled the argument had shifted ground.

"How do you mean, sweetness," he asked, "leave things the way they are?" His voice betrayed an undercurrent of irritation which he had not intended, but then he was pretty tired after the Production Liners Convocation.

"I mean why do it?" Sylvia said. "Let's just let things go on the way they are, as though this offer never happened."

While Willis was trying to pull his thoughts together, he was conscious of the silence that surrounded them, as though an unseen audience were waiting for his reply.

"I can't believe that you're serious about that suggestion," Willis said, "when this is a chance for everything we want—leisure, trips to Europe. We're going to be in the big league, honey."

"Oh dear," Sylvia said, "I suppose men are different from women."

Willis laughed briefly.

"In this case," he said, "thank heaven, they are different."

"Darling," Sylvia said, "don't be angry with me, I really do appreciate you and all the things you do for us."

Willis smiled and shook his head.

"That's the way you always are, sweetness," he said—"objecting when I bring home a new antique, saying that the sapphire-and-diamond clip is ostentatious, but I know you. You like them in the end. And how about admitting it and giving me a kiss?"

He crossed the room and kissed her and held her hand for a moment.

"Oh, darling," Sylvia said. "I suppose you're right. I do like money, and maybe I'm even beginning to like ostentation, but I'm getting tired of change. For instance, if you do become the president of this new company, we won't be able to live here, will we?"

"No, honey," Willis said, and he laughed again, "we'll have to pack up the old covered wagon and move West, honey, right out to Chicago. That's where their main offices are."

"Willis," Sylvia said, "I suppose it sounds easy to you, but we've got all our roots here, all our friends and the children's friends. I really hate the prospect, darling."

Willis put his hands in his pockets and walked slowly three times back and forth across the rug.

"I don't know why you haven't got any sense of adventure, sweetness," he said. "It's going to be something new. We're going to build a home of our own, and Lake Forest, where we'll look for a building site, is a much more lovely and more gracious suburb than any I can think of around New York. We'll have new friends, honey, but we'll be coming to New York frequently." He bent down again and kissed Sylvia. Then he patted her head gently, just as he patted Louise's. "And besides, I'll make you a little promise. The boys will go to school in New England, some fine school with high ideals, like Middlesex, and then of course they'll go to Harvard."

He gave Sylvia's back a friendly slap.

"And I can promise you we're going to have one whale of a fine time, honey," he said, "from now on in. Europe, Claridge's in London, the Paris Ritz. Believe me, honey, you're going to love every minute of it— and now how about our going upstairs to bed? I'm feeling pretty tired, what with one thing and another."

XXVII

WILLIS WAS rapidly learning that if you had to do a thing, no matter how difficult, delay only made it more difficult, and in the case of the Simcoe proposal time was of the essence. As P.L. himself had said, there was nothing to be gained by horsing around on such a proposition, and consequently the day after Willis arrived in Orange he took the Merchants up to Boston in order to present the situation promptly, and also to have a night's sleep at the Ritz without his mind's being disturbed by any further questioning by Sylvia.

He was relieved when he showed up at the Boston office the next morning to observe no trace of undue curiosity or restlessness. As a matter of fact some new orders had come in and there was a prospect of still more in the near future. Although Willis reminded himself that the whole Harcourt picture was fluid, he already found himself viewing it like an artist who had finished a canvas and was able to put down his brushes with a clear conscience. When he smiled at the people already working at the central desks and shook hands with Sol Bradley of promotion and Dana Britchbury of sales and Hank Knowlton, the general manager, who would have been tops in any organization, Willis felt a warm spot in his heart for everyone.

With the upward business trend continuing, Willis had been quite right in moving everything from an obsolescent building on State Street, where the Harcourt Boston office had always been located, into the Tewkesbury Building near Park Square. Here he was able to start afresh with a preconceived floor plan of a great central room indirectly lighted, carpeted to avoid noise, and divided in an informal but effective way by glass partitions into cubicles. Then around the central room were the executives' offices, furnished by a firm of home, not office, decorators. It had been Willis's thought to keep something of the old simplicity of the original Harcourt Mill office, and to this end he had collected some captain's chairs and pine desks. He had personally bought three industrial oils by Sheeler which made a fine show in the reception room; and to carry out the same thought, he had made a collection of early industrial prints. His own office was small, although he had been president of Harcourt Associates for the past four years.

When Mr. Bryson Harcourt had retired from the presidency to become chairman of the board, he had instantly offered Willis the president's room, but Willis had immediately refused. Willis had even heard Mr. Bryson say that he was less disturbed in his office than he had ever been at home, and finally when Willis presented him with a discreet portable bar for purposes of business entertainment, Mr. Bryson had said the office was better than his club. Willis was glad to see that its door was open and that everything inside looked as though Mr. Bryson might appear at any moment.

"Hank," Willis asked when the first-minute greetings were over, "what's the latest about Mr. Harcourt?"

He spoke in a low solicitous voice, and Hank Knowlton answered in the same manner.

"The picture, as we got it yesterday afternoon," Hank said, "is about the same. His left side and his speech are still affected. We called up Mrs. Ewing personally instead of bothering Mrs. Harcourt."

"You're right, I think," Willis said, "to make inquiries through Mrs. Ewing. I'll call this afternoon. By the way, whose idea was it to have fresh flowers on his desk?"

"Oh, that was Miss Bailey's idea," Hank said. "It takes a gal to think of a thing like that."

"Well, it's a nice idea," Willis said. "It's the sort of thing that highlights the spirit that you and I are trying to create. You might tell Nellie Bailey to get fresh flowers every day. You know, Nellie and I used to go to school together. Did I ever tell you that?"

"It seems to me that perhaps you did at one time or another," Hank said, "but I'm not exactly sure."

Willis set that answer down as a reminder not to reminisce too often.

"Well, Hank," he said, "it might be a good idea if you were to get the department heads together in the conference room for a general briefing, say in half an hour. I'll be making a couple of telephone calls but interrupt me right away when you're ready."

The windows of Willis's office looked over the Charles River toward Cambridge. The surface of his desk was clear, except for his group photograph of Sylvia and the children, and Willis sat down in the special posture chair he had ordered—not a thing of beauty, he had to admit, but effective for the purpose intended. Before starting the day, he had a pleasant word with the switchboard girl, because few things were more important in an office than a good switchboard operator who remembered customers' voices and who took an intelligent but not an intrusive interest in everyone.

"Hello, Nancy," Willis said. "I hope everything's going all right with you, and I hope that asthma prescription I got for your mother was of some help."

"It was a real help, Mr. Wayde," Nancy said.

"I'm very glad to hear that, Nancy," Willis said, "and please don't hesitate to let me know if I can do anything further. And now I wonder if you will get me Mrs. Edward Ewing, please."

Until the telephone rang, he sat looking over the roofs of Commonwealth Avenue and Beacon Street, planning what he would say to Bess.

"Hello, Bess," he said. "I hope I haven't waked you up or anything."

"Oh," she said, "is that you, Willis?" He would have known the slightly husky quality of her voice anywhere, and he was glad she remembered his. "Where are you? I hope you're somewhere where we can see you."

"Why, Bess, dear," Willis said, and he laughed reassuringly, "of course I am. I'm right up here at the Boston office. Can you tell me how everything's going at Beacon Street?"

"I just finished talking to Mother a minute before you called," Bess answered. "He's able to sit up for two hours in the afternoon now. He can get downstairs to the library, and he was asking for you only yesterday."

"Well, that's the best news I've heard in a dog's age," Willis said. "Maybe you wouldn't mind finding out whether I ought to see him or not. It would be good to see him if it wouldn't make him overtired."

"I know he'd love to see you," Bess said. "The doctor said only the family, but we'll let you in on the ground floor."

"I've never felt more like family," Willis said, "than I do right this minute, Bess. I don't suppose I could have a little visit with you sometime later this afternoon myself."

"Why, Willis," Bess said. "Alone?" and she laughed.

He was glad that he was still able to keep on a friendly, bantering basis with Bess.

"Yes," he said, "alone, if you can stand it, Bess, but then we've been without chaperones before, haven't we?"

When she laughed, he could not help joining in with her.

"Why, Willis," she said, "have you got something special and private to say to me?"

Willis waited a moment before he answered. A pause over the telephone had more dramatic value than in a conversation face to face.

"Well, to be serious for just a minute, Bess," he said, "I frankly want to ask your advice about something that's been on my mind recently involving a decision I have to make. Ordinarily, of course, I'd ask your father, but in any case I'd value your reaction, Bess."

"Oh, dear," said Bess, "is it something about business? It isn't bad news, is it?"

"Oh, now, come," Willis said, "I wouldn't be joshing with you over the telephone if I had bad news. Why, frankly I think it's pretty good news, both of a business and a personal nature. After I've seen your father, why don't we meet up here in the office?"

"In the office?" Bess said. "Why the office, Willis?"

"Only because it's a place where we can be quiet and undisturbed," Willis said. "Maybe on second thought you'd better ask Bill to come up with you, Bess."

"But what under the sun is it about, Willis?" she asked.

"Now, Bess," he answered, "I can't explain it over the telephone, but as I say, I think it's pretty good news for all of us. The more I think it over the better I like the idea of Bill being with us. Let's make it half past four in your father's office." Then he ended on a more playful note. "You know, there's a portable bar up there, or perhaps you didn't know."

"Well," Bess said—and she laughed but her laugh was still worried— "as long as there's a bar, that's something, and I know that will interest Bill."

"That's fine then," Willis said. "I'll have seen your father then and everything will have been squared away, and don't worry about anything, Bess, dear."

Willis stood still for nearly half a minute after he had put down the telephone. The conversation had been more difficult than he had expected, because instead of keeping to the straight track, his thoughts kept running off on tangents, as they frequently did when he talked to Bess Ewing. They had known each other too long and sometimes too well, and long familiarity made impersonality impossible, but he had achieved his purpose. He would see Bess at half past four; and her brother Bill would be with her, if he knew Bess.

Yet instead of concentrating on what he must do next, Willis found his thoughts moving backwards. For a second he was with Bess that evening long ago when she had filched a bottle of her father's Scotch and brought it out to the swimming pool. It was a little pathetic how glad Bess had been to hear his voice. She could not be wholly happy with Edward Ewing, but it was too late now.

Willis pulled his wits together. In fifteen minutes he would have to be in the conference room going over sales and production figures, and he had another call to make.

"Oh, Nancy," he said when he picked up the telephone, "will you get me Mr. Roger Harcourt, please."

Roger Harcourt was in his office. Everything that day had run very smoothly.

"Hello, Roger," Willis said, "it's good to hear your voice. . . . Yes, I'm up here for the day, and just parenthetically, Roger, before I forget it, while I was down in Carolina at the Production Liners Convocation, whom should I meet there but P. L. Nagel, but that's a point, Roger, that I wish to take up with you later. What I wanted to say over the telephone is that I told that story of yours about the Chinese Ambassador. I wish you had been there to see how well it was received."

Willis waited a moment for some comment, but there was only silence.

"Are you there, Roger?" Willis asked.

"Yes, I am, unfortunately," Roger Harcourt said. "What else is it you want?"

Willis laughed, and the possibility of moving to Chicago seemed pleasanter than ever.

"I was only hoping that I might have a bite of lunch with you, Roger," Willis said, "over a little matter that Gil Bakeliss and I were talking about yesterday, and Gil concurs with my views. You'd be pleased if you knew how highly Gil thinks of you, Roger."

"And I'd be pleased if I knew what in hell you were talking about," Roger Harcourt said. "What have you and Nagel been cooking up together there at the Hotel Carolina?"

It had never been wise to discount Roger Harcourt's perspicacity. Willis found himself speaking more tersely, because Roger Harcourt always misunderstood if one was polite or ingratiating.

"I'll tell you that at lunch," Willis said. "I suggest we have it here at the office at twelve-thirty sharp. I'll add that it's an important enough appointment to break any others that you may have, Roger. I have a piece of news that I think will please you, and I have one more suggestion."

Willis paused. There was nothing like a slight wait over the telephone.

"Hello," Roger Harcourt called, "are you there?"

"Yes," Willis said, "I'm right here, Roger. I said I had one suggestion. See if you can make an appointment to see Mrs. Henry Harcourt's trustee for later in the afternoon. And now I must bid you good-by because I'm going into a conference."

It was strange when one grew older how age differentials leveled off. Roger Harcourt was nothing now but a peevish, ill-mannered old man who happened to be a director of Harcourt Associates and the owner of a considerable block of stock. There was nothing else to Roger Harcourt any longer.

The idea of office luncheons and of the office as a place for entertaining had always appealed to Willis. Guests were impressed by the office setting and liked to meet the department heads, even if the food was austerely simple—usually cold meat, a salad, a thinning dessert and plenty of coffee. The food came from outside, but as Willis had once said hilariously, saccharine for the coffee was supplied by the management.

Guests or not, Willis had always made it a point to have lunch in the office with the executive staff whenever he came to Boston. He could not help it if Roger was annoyed by having to eat clear consommé, cold tongue, and cole slaw in the conference room with Sol Bradley, Dana Britchbury, Hank Knowlton and two juniors from the sales department. He was sure that he needed only a half an hour with Roger after lunch, and as matters turned out his foreshadowing had been correct almost to the minute.

"Roger," Willis said, "suppose you and I go into Mr. Bryson's office for our coffee. You can have sugar if you like, but I find saccharine keeps my weight down, and saccharine is thoughtfully supplied by the management."

It was one of those office jokes that never grew stale, but Roger Harcourt did not join in the communal laughter.

"I'd like a digestive tablet instead of saccharine," Roger said. "I never could stand raw cabbage, but I would indeed appreciate a minute alone with you, Willis, since you asked me up here for a talk."

Once Willis would have been alarmed by this display of temper, but he knew that basically Roger Harcourt respected him. It was even barely possible that Roger Harcourt was fond of him.

"Oh, Hank," Willis said to Hank Knowlton, "would you just pass the word around that I don't want to be disturbed for half an hour, and no incoming calls?"

Willis closed the door of Mr. Bryson's office and his gaze traveled over the copies of the Harcourt portraits on the walls. None of the former owners of the Harcourt Mill had ever looked at home in the Tewkesbury Building.

"Have a cigar, Roger," Willis said, "and settle down in a comfortable chair. I know you don't approve of the captain's chairs, but there's a soft leather one over by the window."

Willis poured the coffee, and Roger Harcourt grunted painfully as he sat down.

"All right," he said in his high voice, "now that you've got me placed with the light on my face and the office door closed, perhaps you'll pull the God-damned rabbit out of your hat, Willis. I don't underrate your ability for a single minute but I wish you didn't always find it necessary to set the stage."

Willis laughed affectionately.

"I think you'll agree with me in just a minute," he said, "that this moment needs a little setting, Roger. I'm sorry you were bored at lunch. I wanted it to look as though you dropped in casually, because, very frankly, our meeting mustn't be underlined at all. But before we start, could you tell me what the doctors say about Mr. Bryson's condition?"

"I don't think I can bear it, Willis," Roger Harcourt said, "if you tell me again that you have a warm spot in your heart for Bryson. If he had worked harder and hadn't indulged in violent exercise, he wouldn't be in his present unhappy condition. From everything I can gather, he will never recover sufficiently to participate further in Harcourt Associates matters—not that this will be a loss to anyone."

Willis put down his coffee cup carefully on Mr. Bryson's desk and looked sternly at Roger Harcourt.

"I hope you'll forgive me, Roger," he said, "if I say I resent your attitude. Simply because our business has been expanding—this does not mean for a minute that my loyalty to Mr. Bryson and his family has altered in any way. I want to make that quite clear from the outset, Roger."

Willis was moved by the ring of his own voice, but he could not tell whether or not Roger Harcourt was impressed.

"I don't give a damn how loyal you are," Roger Harcourt said, "as long as this firm keeps on making money. Just as soon as the stock gets up to a hundred, I'll sell out, and maybe I'll have a warm spot in my heart for you when that happens. Now let's get down to brass tacks. What is it you've been talking about with Mr. P. L. Nagel?"

Although Willis was not sure that he liked Roger's attitude, he could always take a hint. It had never occurred to him until then that perhaps he had overworked that phrase about having a warm spot in his heart, and he was very glad to know it.

"I often think the best thing about maturing," Willis said, "is being able to collect a fine assortment of pleasant memories. I have a lot of them, including a few about you, Roger. We both remember, don't we, when old P.L.—who, by the way, is a very remarkable person when you get close to him—came down and offered to buy the mill from H.H. Five million dollars was the price, and you wanted to sell, as I remember. It's worth a good deal more now, Roger."

Roger scowled and flicked the ash from the end of his cigar onto the immaculate carpet.

"I was basically right then and I still think the property ought to be sold," he said.

Willis nodded slowly. At last all the facts were maneuvered into a correct position.

"I agree with you, Roger," he said gently, "one hundred per cent."

Roger Harcourt gave a clumsy jerk and half pushed himself from his chair.

"What's that again?" he asked.

It was a pleasure to be able to surprise Roger, and now that he was surprised the news would be more effective.

"It hurts me, very frankly, to say that we are in agreement, Roger," Willis said, "because in a way this contradicts a number of my public statements regarding the future of our company, but privately I've been thinking for a long while that we must expand or sell out."

Willis waited but not too long. There was no need to be over-dramatic.

"P. L. Nagel could naturally put the case more strongly than I," he said. "Briefly, Simcoe wants to absorb us for a figure in the neighborhood of twenty-five million dollars. I think we ought to accept, Roger. Of course I would have taken it up with Mr. Bryson, had he been well, but I think the family should consider this offer very seriously and in the next few hours."

The words had been in his thoughts for so long that it was a little strange to hear them molded by his own voice.

"Good God!" Roger Harcourt said. "Twenty-five million?"

Willis was glad that he had gone so far beyond Roger that he was no longer bemused by high figures.

"In cash and in an exchange of stock, Roger," he said. "I'm pleased to see by your reaction that you agree with me that the offer should be taken very seriously. I don't know how Mr. Bryson will like it, or Bill and Bess, but I'm going to talk to them this afternoon. You see, there's another angle I haven't mentioned—a personal angle."

"Oh?" Roger Harcourt said. "Well, what's the personal angle?"

It seemed as though their conversation had been written beforehand, since it moved smoothly and inevitably.

"I hate to bring it up, Roger," Willis said, "since it involves a question of divided loyalty and one that I have not entirely worked out as yet to my own satisfaction. I like to think I deserve the trust you've all put in me during the last eight years, but I also have another loyalty—my obligation to my family. I want to be absolutely sincere about this, Roger. I've been offered the first vice presidency of Simcoe, which means the presidency when P. L. Nagel retires—but don't think for a minute these two offers are contingent."

Roger's smallish mouth creased into an unpleasant smile.

"Oh, no," he said, "no, not for a single minute, Willis."

It was not a time to be angry, but it was a time for sincerity and for the display of one's innermost convictions.

"It's only fair to tell you," Willis said, "that I don't like your tone of sarcasm, and I resent your implication. If there had not been this offer to buy, I would not dream of going to Simcoe, no matter how alluring the future. I want to impress this very seriously on you, Roger. I would never leave this organization in the lurch. I have my stake in Harcourt too, if you want to think from a mercenary angle. Everything aside, I think we'd better sell, but I won't have you or anyone else casting a reflection on my motives."

Roger Harcourt had stopped smiling, but his lips still puckered in a disagreeable way.

"Don't get excited, Willis," he said. "I don't give a damn about your motives, but I want the facts."

"I'm not excited," Willis said. "I simply want to set the facts straight, Roger."

Roger Harcourt smiled at him again.

"You know," he said, "I sympathize with you. Nothing anyone ever does is clear-cut. Everything has rough edges. Are you going to go over to Simcoe?"

It was a question that had to be answered, but as Roger Harcourt had said, everything had its rough edges. Willis spoke slowly, raising his voice slightly, simply for the sake of emphasis.

"For the sake of my wife and family," Willis said, "I feel very nearly compelled to accept the flattering offer that Mr. Nagel has made me—and the offer that Simcoe is making the stockholders of Harcourt Associates eases my conscience in this regard. If I am repeating myself, I am only doing so to be absolutely clear."

The point had arrived when further talk was unnecessary, and both of them must have seen it.

"You've been very clear," Roger said. "I'm completely with you about selling, and I see what you mean now about my seeing Mrs. Henry Harcourt's trustee."

"I'm glad you get my point," Willis answered. "It seems to me only fair that he should know of my personal intentions."

"I'll see he knows," Roger Harcourt said, and he laughed briefly. "He'll vote her stock with ours. By God, I'm glad I don't have to play poker with you, Willis."

The tension inside of Willis relaxed, but he still spoke carefully.

"I'm afraid I don't quite follow you," he said. "I don't want you to feel that I'm using the personal offer that Mr. Nagel made me as any sort of a threat. It isn't. It's an integral part of the general picture."

"Don't worry," Roger Harcourt said. "He'll vote Mrs. Harcourt's stock with ours. I'll call you up as soon as I've seen him."

Roger pushed himself up from his chair.

"I always enjoy it when you and I think alike," he said. "Thank you for the luncheon, Willis, and as I exit may I add that I feel I've been in the presence of true greatness? It is a pleasure to see an artist working."

"I wouldn't say that I'm an artist, Roger," Willis said, "but I am grateful for our little talk and relieved that we have reached an area of agreement."

In later days Willis often wondered if there were any way in which he could have made a better presentation. On the whole he was reasonably sure that he had done the best he could. At least he had stated the facts candidly, and in a difficult negotiation it was always best to choose candor.

The worst part of the day was his visit to the Bryson Harcourt house on Beacon Street. That visit, more than anything else, indicated a severance, and it was always painful to view the end of old associations. Willis might have been less shaken emotionally if he had been accustomed to serious illness, but his own father and mother had always been in excellent health, and when Sylvia's father, Professor Hodges, had died at the Mt. Auburn Hospital two years before, his death had been so sudden that there had been no atmosphere of the sickroom.

Willis had always hoped that he had not shown his consternation when he saw Mr. Bryson Harcourt seated in a wheel chair with Mrs. Harcourt standing in the background. He managed to smile in spite of the sagging appearance of half of Mr. Bryson's face.

"It's so good to see you, Willis," Mrs. Harcourt said, and she shook hands with him in her old vigorous way. "This is Willis, dear."

But Mr. Bryson recognized him, though he spoke so thickly that Willis could only distinguish half the words.

"He's asking if there's anything new at the office," Mrs. Harcourt said.

"Nothing that isn't first-rate news," Willis answered, and he found himself speaking loudly. "Everything is under control until you get back with us."

Then Mr. Bryson's speech grew clearer, or perhaps Willis had become accustomed to it.

"How was the golf at Pinehurst?"

The question made a lump rise in Willis's throat.

"Pretty good, considering," Willis answered.

He could not get Mr. Bryson's next question, but Mrs. Harcourt did.

"He wants to know what you went around in," Mrs. Harcourt said. Though Mr. Bryson was lingering in the shadows, he still wanted to know about the golf.

"Well," Willis said, "I got a ninety-one on Course Two but I took three strokes getting out of the trap on the tenth. That's a very tricky hole, the tenth."

Half of Mr. Bryson's face was like a mask but the other half followed every word.

"Which trap?"

"The first on the right, sir," Willis answered. "The deep one." He laughed. "It was like being in the crater of a volcano, taking those three strokes."

A minute or so later Mrs. Harcourt nodded meaningfully to Willis.

"It's great to see you, sir," Willis said, "and I'll be looking in again sometime very shortly. Now don't worry about the office. Everything's all right."

Mrs. Harcourt walked down with him to the front door.

"Oh, Willis," she said, "we all thank God that you're here looking after everything." He had never felt so close to Mrs. Harcourt.

"Believe me," Willis told her, "I'll always do the best I can, the very best for everyone."

He was always glad that he had made this promise to Mrs. Harcourt, and he believed that he had kept it. All anyone could do was do one's best.

All that day left an impression of hurry, but there was plenty of time between appointments. It was only his mind that was hurried. There were fifteen minutes to spare, when he reached the office, before Bill and Bess could possibly arrive, plenty of time to compose his thoughts, but there was still that sense of haste.

"Hank," he said to Hank Knowlton, "when Mrs. Ewing and Mr. Bill Harcourt are here, keep me off the telephone. And I wish you'd find out where I can reach Mr. P. L. Nagel in Chicago, because I may want to speak to him after they are gone."

It was almost like letting the cat out of the bag to mention P. L. Nagel, but then Hank Knowlton was reliable.

"If it gets to be after five o'clock," Willis said, "send everybody home except Nancy at the switchboard, and I wish you'd stay too, Hank. There may be something I want to take up with you."

There was no use telling him what it was, because Hank was pretty good at educated guessing.

Actually the meeting with Bill and Bess had not been nearly as difficult as Willis had anticipated. Although of course there had been the emotional strain and the sentiment about the Harcourt Mill, it had been a warm and friendly meeting, with kindness and sympathy on every side, a sympathy which was intensified by his call on Mr. Bryson, because Willis was still distressed when he saw Bill and Bess.

"Well, well, Bess," he said, "how lovely you look this afternoon."

There was always something fresh and out-of-doors about her, although she never had the taste for clothes that Sylvia had, and Bess was not careful of her weight like Sylvia.

"Oh, Willis," Bess said, and she kissed him and clung to him for a moment and he was as touched as he was surprised, "isn't it dreadfully sad?"

"Yes, Bess, dear, it is," Willis said, "but your mother's wonderful."

"She is wonderful," Bill said, "and so is Father. He shows a lot of sportsmanship, I think."

"That's very true, Bill," Willis said. "You know, he asked about my golf score down at Pinehurst."

"Did he?" Bill said. "Well, that's just like him."

Everything they had said was simple, but taken together their words wove themselves into a fabric of genuine affection.

"Your mother," Willis said, and he was aware of a catch in his voice, "said a very sweet thing to me just as I was leaving, something I shall never forget—'We all thank God,' she said, 'that you're looking out for everything.'"

"We do, Willis," Bess said. "We really do."

It was the real Bess speaking, without mockery, that afternoon. In fact they all of them were at their very best.

"Well," Willis said, "I'm glad it's that way, and I'm glad we all know each other well enough to trust each other—but let's all sit down, and, Bill, if anybody wants a drink, there's everything in that portable bar there. Do you remember how tickled your father was with that portable bar?"

There was a proper interlude of small talk, when Bill said that he would like a Martini cocktail and that he would make it, and Bess said she would like a bourbon on the rocks. Who was it he had seen last who drank bourbon on the rocks? Willis remembered that it had been Mr. P. L. Nagel.

"I hope you noticed the flowers on the desk," Willis said. "I want to tell you who thought of that little touch, because I think it's rather moving—Nellie Bailey."

"Why, that's sweet of her," Bess said.

"I think so too," Willis answered. "Fresh flowers every day." He paused and cleared his throat. "You know, I'm glad I called at Beacon Street before I saw you, because now I'm pretty sure that what I have to say will relieve you, Bill, and you too, Bess, of a lot of worry. I may as well be terse about it. One of the largest belting companies in the country wants to buy Harcourt Associates—the Simcoe Company to be exact. It's located in the Midwest, in case you don't remember. The offer's in the neighborhood of twenty-five million dollars. I know what you're thinking, Bess, but don't interrupt me. I think we ought to sell to them and I want to tell you why."

The art of persuasion, Willis believed, was the very keystone of American business and the basis of American industrial prestige, and he was never more convinced of its importance than during his talk with Bill and Bess. Without exaggeration, never in his life had he so keenly wanted two people to understand and sympathize with his point of view and to agree with his conclusions. It would have been unthinkable to have quarreled after so many years. It was a time for a sincere interchange of reaction, a time when every question must be answered.

The strength of his approach, as he talked to Bill and Bess, lay in his sincere sympathy. No one knew better than he how genuinely the Harcourts had regarded the conduct of the Harcourt Mill as a family obligation. In his own small way, he told them, he shared that obligation. He knew that Bess and Bill looked upon the workers of the Harcourt Mill, as he did too, almost as members of the family, and why not? There were dozens he could name—because he never liked to regard labor as a commodity—whose families had worked there for three generations. This was a proud record and Willis shared in the Harcourts' pride—just a little. He shared this fine tradition, having been brought up in it like Bess and Bill, and he was as loyal to it as any Harcourt. And yet—and yet they were all old enough now to see how times were changing, and even traditions had to be reactivated—sometimes.

Without delving into the history of American industry, they were all aware of the almost explosive expansion of business that was going on around them. He hated to say it, but they would have to face a painful fact. The day of family ownership in business was disappearing. Within a radius of fifty miles of where they were sitting, there were hundreds of factories that had been in family hands for over a century now being merged into larger groups. There was nothing to be ashamed of in this situation, for merging, very frankly, set new blood and new ambition coursing through fine old arteries. This was not exactly a happy simile, as he could tell from Bess Ewing's changed expression.

"Sorry, Bess," he said, "I didn't mean to get poetic, but believe me, basically the thought is sound."

And it was—so sound that Willis was carried away on the wings of it. There was no use standing against change. One had to accept it as one accepted old age and death—not that he meant for a single moment that the Harcourt Mill or the Harcourt tradition would dissolve if it merged with Simcoe Rubber Hose and Belting. Eventually the time was bound to come when they would have to sell the Harcourt Mill because, very frankly, it could not stand alone as an isolated unit. Frankly—because they were all talking almost like brothers and sisters now—in his opinion the Harcourt Mill would have closed its doors long ago because of competition if he had not happened to think of integrating the Planeroid patents with Harcourt when he was at Rahway Belt. Fortunately at the moment Harcourt Associates was in a fine position. They had many assets which might never be so valuable again, which explained why P. L. Nagel, whom he hoped Bill and Bess would get to meet and love as much as he did, had made this generous offer. All change was painful, but very conceivably there might never be such a chance again. Willis was reluctant, being humanly proud of Harcourt's achievement, but—to encapsulate all his thought—he must recommend that the stockholders accept this offer, and he knew that Bill and Bess, when they thought it over, would stand right there with him to be counted.

You could always tell from the feel of things around you whether or not a presentation had moved toward success. It gave Willis a fine glow of pride that he had been sincere and had used the straightforward approach without dialectic tricks. He had not lost their attention for an instant, but it might have been dangerous to have gone on further.

"Well," he said, "I'm afraid that was a pretty tough sermon, and I really did feel a couple of times that I was sort of in the pulpit, but I do think that's about the picture as it looks to me, and now I know you'll have a lot of things to ask."

Bill was the first one to speak. He rose from the captain's chair in which he had been sitting, walked to the portable bar, and poured the ice water from the Martini shaker.

"That was quite a speech," he said. "I never knew you could lay it on the line like that. I'm always convinced by the last person who talks to me but that's because I'm said by little sister here to have a weak character. Maybe Bess had better pick up the thread of the discourse while I mix another round of drinks. Will you have one now, Willis?"

"Er—well, no thank you, Bill, not at the moment," Willis said. "Not that I won't have one later."

Bess was the one, of course, whom Willis was watching, because he valued her reaction as much as he valued her opinion. He was too well aware of her devastating observation and her capacities of derision not to feel uneasy. There flashed unexpectedly across his mind the occasion when she had compared him to Uriah Heep, and he dismissed this from his thoughts as abruptly as he could. It had never struck Willis that Bess's lower lip was so nearly a replica of Mr. Henry Harcourt's, or that her eyes, though of a different color, had the same qualities of contemplation he remembered in old H.H. Willis was happy to observe that Bess looked intensely serious. At least she was not in the mood to ask some frivolous or disconcerting question.

"I'm glad you've been so frank, Willis," she said. "I know you have been."

"Why, Bess," Willis answered, "I couldn't possibly be anything else."

"And I'm glad you feel the way Father and all the rest of us do about the mill," Bess said. "I know it's old-fashioned, and I suppose we'll have to face the inevitable, but there is one thing I'm sure we will all want to know. That offer will make us quite rich, but I'd like to know, if we're bought out, what assurance there is that those people won't close the mill. There is still our obligation to the people working there."

Of course he had known that the question was coming, just as he had known previously that Sylvia would ask it.

"Bess, dear," Willis said, "of course I knew you'd bring that matter up, and it is the sixty-four-dollar question, isn't it, as they say? Frankly it's been bothering me from the first moment that P. L. Nagel approached me with this proposition. Believe me, I've been right to the mat with P.L. on this subject, and in that connection I think I can deliver some reassuring news—not, mind you, that anyone can ever promise anything beyond the foreseeable future—you know that, don't you, Bess?"

He never forgot that he had made this proviso and he saw Bess nod her assent to it.

"Bill," he said, "since you are being barkeep maybe I would like just a rather small one after all." He must not be tense, he was telling himself. It looked better to appear relaxed.

"Thanks, Bill," he said, "and as one Martini authority to another, my heartiest congratulations. Well, I hesitate to obtrude my personal problems at this time but here's the news I was speaking of. It seems they've been looking for a new president at Simcoe, and well, to make matters brief, they've offered it to me—first vice president to start with, and president when Mr. Nagel becomes chairman of the board. It's a pretty hard matter to turn down when I remember Sylvia and the kids."

He raised his hand quickly when he saw that Bess was about to speak.

"Please, Bess," he said, "just let me make my point." He leaned slightly forward in his chair to emphasize his point and allowed his voice to drop to a lower scale. "If we should sell out to them and if I should take that position, you know and I know, Bess, that the Harcourt Mill and all your feelings about it will be one of my first cares. In fact, Bess, P. L. Nagel and I have had some discussion about integrating Harcourt Associates and we've pretty well decided to leave it where it is and call it the Harcourt Division, so the name will still be there."

He should have realized long ago that the very fact that he would be the president of that larger company was a favorable argument.

"Why, Willis," Bess said, and she smiled and not at all in a mocking way, "that makes everything sound much better. Why didn't you tell us that before?"

"Oh, it was only a personal matter, Bess," he told her, "and, as I said, you and Bill have problems of your own."

Bess leaned forward and rested her hand on his knee for a moment.

"Well, I'm awfully glad for your sake, Willis," she said. "In fact, if things happen that way I guess I'm pretty glad for all of us."

Then Willis had the most glorious feeling that anyone can have, a conviction that everything was resolved, and this was due to Bess. There was no one in the world quite like Bess Harcourt. She had made him feel happy and at peace with himself for the first time since P. L. Nagel had passed the word. It was all due to Bess, to her generosity and her lovely understanding. It had not been necessary at all to bring up the subject of Roger Harcourt or Mrs. Henry Harcourt's trustee. After all there was nothing like an old friendship.

Yet Willis had learned long ago to conceal blatant feelings of triumph and elation. It was a part of office discipline always to be measured and controlled.

"Good-by, Bill," he said, when he escorted them around the glassy island of cubicles to the reception room. "Aside from everything else, it's been swell seeing you and I hope we can repeat the process soon again."

He meant it, because he had always had a warm spot in his heart for Bill, and then he remembered that this was a hackneyed phrase. In all the years he had known Bill he never could help liking him.

"Good-by, Bess, dear," he said. "May I?"

[379]

"Well," Bess said, and she laughed, just as she had in the old days, "it wouldn't be the first time, Willis."

She turned her cheek to him and he kissed it, in the most formal possible way, since Bill was there.

"And it won't be the first time I've thought you were a very wonderful person, Bess," Willis said, "and I know furthermore that it won't be the last."

It was a quarter before six when Bill and Bess left, and the office was deserted except for Nancy Sullivan at the switchboard and Hank Knowlton.

"Thanks a lot for staying, Nancy," Willis said. "I hope I haven't made you stand your boy friend up."

"Oh no indeed," she said. "It's been a pleasure, Mr. Wayde."

"I won't forget your kindness, Nancy," Willis said, "and now before you go will you see if you can get me Mr. P. L. Nagel, please, in Chicago? And, Hank, will you come back with me to Mr. Bryson Harcourt's office for a moment?"

Willis rested his hand affectionately on Hank's shoulder. There was nothing like loyalty, and when loyalty was obtained it should be nourished by appreciation.

"I wouldn't have kept you around here, Hank," he said, "unless I had had something pretty big to say to you, and maybe if Elly wouldn't mind at this short notice, you might call her up and say I'd like you to dine with me at the Ritz. You see, very confidentially, Simcoe Rubber has made an offer to buy Associates, Hank, and if it comes through I'll want you to be the head of the Harcourt Division—temporarily, at any rate, until we solve the problem of integration. Of course, operationwise the Harcourt Mill may be something of a headache in the future—not that I haven't got my fingers crossed in the hope that it won't. . . ."

It would mean a lot to Hank Knowlton, but that was the way the world was. You either moved down or up. As soon as Willis had invited Hank to dinner he was a little sorry, because he was so tired that it would be hard to make a further effort. His words and gestures already seemed to be spoken from a distance. He was moving away from everything inevitably, as though a tide were moving him faster and faster, now that he had seen Bill and Bess. He wondered for a moment how this thought had come to him of moving faster and faster, and then he remembered that it must have stemmed from his mother's reading him *Through the Looking Glass*—a book which had always made him uncomfortable and which he had asked Sylvia as a great favor not to read to their own children. He was like a passenger on the observation platform of an outgoing train that was gaining in acceleration as it left the station. He was moving away from his years of contriving as head of Harcourt Associates. Memories and figures were growing smaller, losing their validity. He was moving out of one square into a larger one, and he was moving faster and faster.

XXVIII

CLYDE, LIKE any self-sufficient New England town, had a long if inaccurate memory. In fact the better one came to know Clyde the more one grew impressed with the town's inability ever wholly to forget anyone who had ever dwelt within its limits. Instead of forgetting, Clyde inhabitants, through their exaggerated powers of recollection, were able in each generation to elevate two or three of their fellow townsmen to a folk status that approached the myth. After all, memory and mythology go hand in hand, and on any afternoon, a dozen or so members of the Clyde Men's Club could be found there working in the field of legend, and the same was true of the women's clubs and the church alliances and sewing circles. From its earliest days, Clyde had always preferred legend to scientific history.

Willis probably was never aware that Clyde was in the process of making him a Great Figure. Since he had never been obliged seriously to consider local town opinion businesswise, he was not aware of the great number of persons in Clyde who eagerly watched his every move.

As president of Harcourt Associates Willis had made a few public appearances there for the benefit of good plant relations. He had once spoken at a Rotary Club luncheon to the largest attendance there had ever been in Clyde, although he had not been aware of this fact. Willis had been deeply flattered when Mr. Roderick Holhalter, Clyde superintendent of schools, had invited him to address the graduating class of Clyde High in June, 1944. He was delighted to do so because the stockholders' meeting of Harcourt Associates came only two days later. He never knew, when he made some sound inspirational remarks on the subject of success, that the high-school auditorium was unduly crowded and that there was a large crowd in the corridor outside. Willis was also glad to accommodate the Reverend Morton J. Heatherby, who had been minister of the Congregational Church when he and his mother had attended there, by giving a talk during Young People's Week. He had not realized that plans to hold the event in the parish hall had been canceled because of the turnout—not only of youths but of older people —and that the church had finally been opened for the meeting. Willis certainly never suspected that most of the people in Clyde who greeted him with courteous applause when he stood before a lectern were not gathered to hear what he had to say as much as to observe him.

He was not a snappy dresser, according to Clyde standards. His double-breasted business suits disappointed many, and also the words he said were only what could be expected from someone in his position. Nevertheless his presence was impressive. He was tall and he had good features, and his manner conveyed earnestness and self-confidence. His shoes were beautifully shined and his trousers accurately creased, which may have been the basis for the rumor that a personal valet always traveled with him. Willis always came to town in a chauffeur-driven Cadillac, and there was some debate as to whether or not this was a Cadillac hired in Boston or one owned by Willis Wayde in Massachusetts. On the whole better-informed people were sure that the Cadillac was his own. He would have been ashamed to ride in a hired car. There was also some debate as to whether Willis Wayde's chauffeur might not be a valet on the side, since one read about valet-chauffeurs in light fiction, but on the whole this theory was not accepted.

When Willis became first vice president of Simcoe, and when the Harcourt Mill became the Harcourt Division of that corporation, nearly everyone in Clyde reacted with great pleasure to the news; for it meant that the small-town boy had risen higher, to a plateau far beyond Clyde experience. Simcoe, as everyone knew, was a multi-million-dollar corporation, or a billion-dollar corporation, now that a billion dollars had grown to be an ordinary unit of financial measure. There could not be the slightest doubt that Willis Wayde had acquired a great many million dollars through the deal. Even skeptics began to accept the Wayde legend when the Meltonian Publishing Company succeeded in selling to the Clyde Public Library a volume entitled *Industrial Leaders of America*, which contained a photograph and a biography of Willis Wayde. Willis must have been surprised, during his last visit to Clyde while he was still working on the integration of Harcourt Associates with Simcoe, to be approached by a committee of Clyde businessmen, including his friend John Sparks, vice president of the Dock Street Bank, who asked him, because of his well-known love of sport while at Clyde High, if he would not donate a football stadium to the town, suitably lighted for night games. No one could seriously have believed him when he said he could not afford the five hundred thousand dollars necessary for the project. Clyde was already drawing an idealized portrait of Willis Wadye, and everyone had already begun to scorn any homely truth that did not fit in with this ideal.

Mrs. Willis Wayde had seldom appeared in Clyde, but a number of readers in the periodical room of the Clyde Public Library had seen her picture in the Willis Wayde family group on the lawn in front of his house called "Waydeholm" that had appeared in *Fortune* magazine. In fact there had been complaints in the reading room when it was discovered that some reader had abstracted the picture from the pages. At any rate, those who saw the picture said that Mrs. Willis Wayde was very beautiful and quite a lot like Dorothy Lamour, and that she was wearing a diamond bracelet, a diamond clip, and an enormous diamond ring.

When the Wayde family moved to Chicago, and when finally an article appeared in *Town & Country,* handsomely illustrated, describing the new Wayde home at Lake Forest recently built by the Chicago architectural firm of Guthrie, Gompers, and Clutch, the myth of Willis Wayde assumed greater stature. In a sense this was a proof of the old adage that absence made the heart grow fonder, but other reasons also could be ascribed to the rise of Clyde interest. Now that no one saw Willis Wayde, it became necessary to draw his character with broader strokes, making still fuller use of the material at hand. Bowker's newsstand on Dock Street sold out its supply of *Town & Country* three times over, and might have sold even more if Mr. Bowker had not said he was tired of reordering. But there was also eyewitness evidence, because Howard Twining, the president of Willis's high-school class, who ran Twining's Real Estate and Insurance, had the energy and vision to make a business gamble. He had personally boarded a Chicago plane at Boston's Logan Airport, had flown to Chicago, and had personally called on Willis Wayde at the offices of Simcoe Rubber. The Twining version of the whole meeting may have become garbled but it was, at least, based on fact.

It seemed that Willis had a very large private office that looked out over Lake Michigan, and, believe it or not, Mazie Minton, a Clyde girl herself—and who did not remember Mazie?—was his head private secretary, right up there wearing a gold charm bracelet, with lots of other private secretaries under her. Mazie had received Howard Twining herself in the outer waiting room, it being her duty to screen visitors for Mr. Wayde. She had recognized Howard right away and said it was just like Old Home Week to see him. With a start like that it took almost no time before he was led right up to Willis Wayde's private office, and Willis was very glad to see him too. Willis had remembered Howard Twining very well, although he started in by calling him Harold. As

Howard said at the outset, he did not want to take up too much of Willis's time but he had dropped in to have a little talk about life insurance. No matter how much insurance a man had, he could always do with some more, and how about remembering the good times they used to have together at the old Cylde High?

Nothing could have been more gratifying than the reaction of Willis Wayde to these remarks. It showed what everybody knew, that Willis was a man of high caliber who could take time out to be a human being. Willis said of course he remembered the good times they once had at the old Clyde High; and then he began asking about people, calling them all by name. He asked personally for Steve and Winnie Decker. He asked for any news about Miss Minnie Wilson, whom he remembered very well as their room teacher back in Clyde High. He would always have a warm spot—that is to say a lasting and genuine affection—for Miss Minnie Wilson. And he hoped that if she was retired she was comfortable on her pension.

Seriously, those had been great days at school; and he wished he were not so far away from Clyde, because he would have loved to have sweetened some of those old contacts. Unfortunately, the manifold responsibilities of running an organization the size of Simcoe contrived to keep him chained to the Chicago office. For the last few years, frankly, he was only able to keep in touch with the Harcourt Division in New England through correspondence, the telephone, and through memory, but he did know that Hank Knowlton was doing as fine a job as he could under the circumstances. Willis would always have a warm spot—that was to say, a very abiding sentiment, a weakness almost—for the old Harcourt Mill. Well, well, time moved on, didn't it?

When Willis made this remark about time, Howard took him right up on it, saying it was wonderful to have had this visit, but he knew that Willis had every minute occupied, so how about getting back to insurance? At this point, Howard had stated very categorically that he never did think that talking about insurance was an intrusion on friendship. In fact the most friendly thing a man could do was to talk insurance. It was warming to see how heartily Willis responded to that idea. His insurance schedule, he said, was pretty well filled up but he wouldn't mind considering a hundred thousand more in straight life, if only because Howard had come all the way to see him.

At this point Mazie Minton came back. It seemed that they had the display of Simfoam cushions set up now in the conference room, and that Mr. Gregorian from the agency wanted Mr. Wayde's reaction. Willis was dreadfully sorry, but if Howard wouldn't mind waiting they could go on with their talk. Then Willis asked Mazie for his engagement calendar and looked at it. Then, after a moment's thought, Willis had extended a very gracious invitation. He asked Howard if he wouldn't come out to Lake Forest and take potluck at supper, since just the family would be at home. They could talk business going out in the Cadillac. Howard would not have dreamt of accepting this invitation if Willis had not urged him warmly. After all, as Willis had put it in a very graceful way, Howard Twining was a sort of ambassador, a liaison link between him and his many dear friends in Clyde. Frankly, they had just moved into a rambling and rather informal home. It had been built by the Chicago architectural firm of Guthrie, Gompers, and Clutch, and he and Mrs. Wayde had given many happy hours of thought to the plans and to arranging their antique furniture, which was more of an investment than a luxury. The landscaping was well along now, and being in the real-estate business, Willis was sure that Howard understood the intangible plus values which surround a home, and the latch-string was always out for old friends from Clyde High. It was a play day for the kids, and they could both have a dip in the pool, a cold drink and a pick-up supper, after which Howard could be returned to his Chicago hotel in the Caddie. It was a fact that Willis Wayde called it a Caddie.

"Mazie, my dear," Willis said, "would you see if you can get me Mrs. Wayde? And then I'll go right into the conference, and maybe Mr. Twining won't mind waiting here, and you might show him our new booklet, the one called 'Simcoe Magic' I mean."

Until the telephone rang, Willis talked about the thought behind the booklet called "Simcoe Magic." His basic idea had been that Simcoe and its conveyor belting had formed a magic carpet that now was girdling the globe.

"Is that you, sweetness?" he said when the telephone rang. It was a fact that he did call Mrs. Wayde sweetness, and there was something rather nice in the way he said it. "I'll be starting out in about a half an hour. I want to see the end of the tennis and also the Australian-crawl lessons, so please ask Mr. Crock and Mr. Ginsberg to synchronize their schedules, based on a normal run between home and office, beginning in half an hour, sweetness. And by the way, who do you think is sitting here right beside me this minute? Howard Twining. Isn't that something, after all the times I've talked to you about Howard? I've asked him out to have a bite and Howard's gracious enough to say he can come. He understands it's a wife-and-kiddies' day, and Gus can take Howard back right after supper. If the children want to go to the movies Axel can drive them in the other car, or I could, myself, in the convertible. Well, I'll be home in no time now, sweetness."

Howard Twining wished he had the powers of description to paint a real word picture of the Wayde home at Lake Forest. He could only say that even in that suburb of magnificent homes the Wayde home took its place with the best of them. He could only say that the whole place had a welcoming, outgoing quality—and Howard was sure that he was not influenced in his judgment simply because he had made a hundred-thousand-dollar sale. Curiously enough the estate reminded him in a funny, though in a quite different, way of the old Harcourt place. The rhododendrons on the drive were like the Harcourt rhododendrons; and believe it or not, there was an artificial pond with a swan on it. When Howard spoke of this resemblance Willis Wayde was delighted.

"You're the first one who's ever said that, Howard," he said, "and I'm flattered you perceived it, because I did draw quite a lot of inspiration from the Harcourt place while Sylvia and I were pooling our ideas."

The house was made of gray stone like the Harcourt house and it had a gray slate roof; but the whole thing was modern, with picture windows and things like that. To Howard's regret he never did get upstairs. He washed up in a very commodious downstairs lavatory that had a cloakroom as a vestibule, evidently designed for large parties. His main impression was made up of gracious hallways, large rooms with oil pictures, and very lovely furniture. There was not much time to see all this because, being summer, they dined outdoors on a terrace overlooking the pool, on a lovely glass-topped table lit by hurricane candles, and were served by a butler named Axel in a white coat. The whole family were at the table, seeing, as Willis said again, it was a wife-and-kiddies' night. But a whole lot of interesting things happened before they ever sat down to dinner.

Mrs. Wayde, Howard Twining said, was a lovely, gracious hostess. If she had seemed vague as to who he was, then why shouldn't she have? You could see, though, that she was used to making people at home, proving that Willis must have used the place freely for business entertainment.

"Howard," Willis said shortly after they arrived, "why don't you and I take off our coats and relax? Sylvia won't mind, will you, sweetness?"

Howard had to confess that he was wearing suspenders, but Willis said that Mrs. Wayde would not mind in the least, this being in the nature of an old Clyde High reunion, and Mrs. Wayde didn't mind. You could see at once that there was a lovely relationship between her and Willis, that she was a real wife and mother, and very handsome too. She was wearing a lovely tailored linen dress, and everything about her was spic and span. Incidentally she wore no jewelry except for a diamond bracelet and a very handsome solitaire diamond ring.

"And now, Howard," Willis said, "let's all go down and see the kids.

This is one of their sport afternoons. They have tennis and swimming instruction three times a week. I feel these skills are important for them, and Sylvia and I try to see that nothing interferes. Are they down at the court now, honey?"

"Yes, dear," Mrs. Wayde answered. "Mr. Crock is finishing up with Paul. And Mr. Crock is very anxious for you to see how much Al has improved with his forehand."

"Has Louise picked up any on her serve?" Willis asked.

"Mr. Crock said he was very happy with her serving, darling," Mrs. Wayde said. "But you must hurry if you want to see Paul."

You could see that a beautiful relationship existed between Mr. and Mrs. Wayde.

"Crock thinks Paul has the makings of an outstanding player," Willis said. "I always maintain you have to learn the rudiments of tennis when you're young. Is Ginsberg at the pool yet, dear?"

"Yes," Mrs. Wayde said, "I think he's getting ready, Willis."

"I wonder if you'd tell him, sweetness," Willis said, "that he needn't get out the dumbbells or the mat? I won't have my workout as long as Howard's here."

As a matter of fact Willis Wayde looked fit enough to skip the workout. Even at the end of a hard day he was right on his toes showing off the place. The tennis court was very beautiful, and when Howard mentioned it, Willis confessed he had constructed it mostly from his memories of the court at the Bryson Harcourts'.

The children had lovely manners. One of the boys was playing tennis with a muscular young man, and another boy, Al, about thirteen, with a sweater around his shoulders, was sitting beside a very cute little dark-haired girl aged eight.

"It looks to me," Willis Wayde said, "as though you were having a happy time, kids."

You could see that there was a real and deep affection between Willis and his children. They all gave a big shout when they saw him, and the little girl, whose name was Louise, jumped right up into his arms.

"How's Daddy's darling?" Willis said. "And now I want you all to meet Mr. Twining. Believe it or not, Mr. Twining went to school with Daddy."

There was no doubt at all that the Wayde children were good at tennis, and when it came to swimming Howard Twining was frankly a little embarrassed to put on a pair of trunks and get into the pool with the Wayde family and Mr. Ginsberg. He did not mean that the pool was small. It was oversized and beautifully landscaped, with dressing rooms, and showers, and foam-rubber chairs, and everything. Howard Twining only meant that he was embarrassed because he could merely do the side and breast strokes, whereas Willis and all the Wayde children swam the Australian crawl. But Mrs. Wayde put him at his ease.

"I think Willis overdoes the Australian crawl," she said. "It's always been an obsession with him. He even took crawl lessons on our honeymoon."

"Oh, now," Howard said facetiously, "not on your honeymoon, Mrs. Wayde."

She laughed. She had a lovely sense of humor.

"Well, you know Willis, if you went to school with him," she said. "And now I see Axel's bringing down some cooling drinks. If Willis will stop doing the crawl he'll make you a Martini. He's quite an authority on the making of Martinis."

What Howard Twining always tried to emphasize when he told of his visit was its homey informality. You could see that there was lots of money around—swimming pools, old silver, butlers, chauffeurs, Cadillacs, tennis instructors, and things like that; but none of this made you self-conscious. All that mattered was the hospitable friendliness of Mr. and Mrs. Wayde and the beautiful relationship they and the children all shared together. It was a privilege to be taken into the bosom of such a family, every member of which tried to make a guest happy. Howard was very deeply regretful when Gus came with the Cadillac, but he carried the picture back of the Waydes in their lovely Lake Forest setting. Furthermore he could never say too often that success and riches had not changed Willis Wayde. Willis was the same fine modest Willis Wayde who had debated at Clyde High on whether capital punishment should be abolished, and had walked in the grand march with Patricia Ryan at the graduation dance. In conclusion there was one remark of Willis's that Howard always remembered.

"Howard," he said, "although we live here in Lake Forest and try in our small ways to play our part in the community we are essentially New England folks. Sylvia is a Cambridge girl essentially and my heart is right back there at Clyde. Sylvia and I have put our heads together to see what we can do to give our children the benefits of that New England heritage that you and I both value. That's why Al is going to Middlesex School this fall, just outside Concord, Massachusetts, and Paul I hope will follow him later—but Louise will stay with Daddy, won't you, honeybee?" At least these were approximately the words of Willis Wayde, and at least Howard Twining had conveyed the sense and spirit.

Howard Twining had made his trip to visit Willis Wayde in the summer of 1950, just at the bginning of the Korean difficulties. The signs on the Harcourt Mill had been changed almost a year before to read "Simcoe Rubber Hose and Belting," and underneath in smaller but highly legible lettering "Harcourt Division." There were no rumors then or undercurrents of uneasiness in Clyde regarding the future of the Harcourt Mill. Why should there have been, as long as Willis Wayde had a personal interest in the mill and was also first vice president of Simcoe Rubber? Willis was actually not moved up to the presidency of Simcoe until 1953, when P. L. Nagel finally became chairman of the board of directors—later than P.L. had promised, but then, older people always liked to hold on.

Clyde myths seldom died easily, and in a town like Clyde, disillusion could never wholly destroy belief. When Willis Wayde became president of Simcoe Rubber the news was announced in headlines that extended clear across the front page of *The Clyde Herald,* and everybody loved the news, for Willis Wayde was too great now to be the target of envy or malice. It was clear to everyone in Clyde that the town at last had a great protector. If there was any jealousy at all, this uncomfortable sentiment was directed toward the lucky executives and employees of the Harcourt Mill, who, under Willis Wayde's especial care, would always be employed, in good times and in bad, and who would always have prompt support in sickness or in sorrow.

It was, therefore, a shock to Clyde when the disaster finally struck, the more so since there were no rumors to precede it. The news first took the form of a brief notice placed on all the bulletin boards at the Harcourt Mill, almost two months to the day after Willis had been made president of Simcoe. The next morning there was another banner headline across the front page of *The Clyde Herald:*

SIMCOE CLOSES HARCOURT MILL—PROPERTY FOR SALE

There was, of course, an official explanation carefully prepared by the management of Simcoe Rubber Hose and Belting. It said, among other things, that this step was taken only after long deliberation, and with deep regret, due to the necessity for closer integration of the Simcoe processes, thus achieving greater economy and efficiency. Positions, it was added, would be made available as far as possible to employees who might want to work at the Simcoe Ohio or Illinois plants. And out of consideration to all employees, operations at the Harcourt Mill would not be discontinued for two full months. The announcement was signed by Willis Wayde as president of Simcoe.

This last was very hard to believe, because the announcement was completely devoid of his well-known warmth and sympathy. In fact, after a few stunned days when no one could talk of anything else, a group of die-hards, including many Harcourt laborers, who still had faith in Willis Wayde, banded together in his defense. They knew that if the Harcourt Mill had closed it was because Willis Wayde could not help it. He was sick about it, he had fought against it every inch of the way. It was not Willis Wayde who had closed the Harcourt Mill. It was a ring of Wall Street bankers who had secretly gained control of the Simcoe Company, and who had forced this humiliation upon Willis Wayde.

Thus the final dissolution of the Harcourt Mill was perhaps not quite so tragic as it might have been. True, it disrupted the economic life of Clyde and the private lives of many families who lived within its limits. It was an especially heavy blow because it soon was clear that the Harcourt property was unsalable for future industrial purposes. There were many hard words spoken, both in sorrow and in anger, but there was one thing which was a real tribute to the town, and a fact of beauty, when one came to think of it. Treachery and disaster—such was the loyalty of Clyde—could not destroy the myth of Willis Wayde. There were those who believed in him still, and who even believed he would return in his Cadillac some day and repurchase and run the Harcourt Mill again.

XXIX

OCCASIONALLY there were times when Willis wondered whether he should not have hopped a plane or a train in Chicago and gone straight to Boston to tell the Harcourts personally—particularly Bess—the exact and compelling reasons that made the closing of the Harcourt Mill necessary and the genuine grief and concern he felt personally for having to take such a seemingly drastic step. It might very well, on thinking it over, have been more considerate to the Harcourts, if not to himself, if he had made such a personal presentation. Sylvia, he admitted very frankly, had advised him to do so as soon as he had told her about the unpleasant step that he had been obliged to suggest to the Simcoe directors. Willis had been surprised, in fact, at how seriously Sylvia took the news, because Sylvia, what with the children and her many social and community activities of Lake Forest, had not of late taken much interest in business matters. It actually took Willis some time to convince Sylvia that the closing of the Harcourt Mill was a business and not a personal matter. Although no one was a better wife than Sylvia, she never cared to face statistical facts. Instead she worried about the more bothersome, but actually less important, angles.

"But, Willis," she said, "you don't seem to think at all about what this will do to the Harcourts."

Of course Willis had thought of it, as he told Sylvia very distinctly.

"It's just as painful to me, sweetness," he said, "as it is to the Harcourts themselves. But really, honey, I wish you would try to see, for one single, little minute that I'm not my own agent in this. I have to do what is best for Simcoe. You wouldn't want me to be disloyal to my trust, would you?"

"No, Willis, of course not," Sylvia said, "but it seems so—" She stopped, as though she were groping for a word, and her forehead wrinkled.

"So what, honey?" Willis asked, and he asked very gently.

"So cold-blooded—and after all the years you worked there, Willis," Sylvia said.

Willis sighed. Although he knew he was absolutely right, it was an unhappy conversation.

"I've told you I feel as badly as anyone," he said, "but you've got to realize these things sometimes can't help but happen. Frankly, from the very beginning I think both P.L. and I were a little afraid that it would be eventually impossible to integrate the Harcourt Mill into the bigger picture; but, of course, the same is true with the Rahway plant. I wish you would believe me when I tell you, sweetness, that I've tried for several years to do my level best to maintain a *status quo*. The result has been some very discouraging sheets of figures, and the situation simply can't continue. Sometimes, one has to be cruel in order to be kind."

"Willis," Sylvia said, "I know you're kind but I don't see why you don't think about what's going to happen to everyone working in the mill. You know that will bother the Harcourts terribly."

It was difficult for Willis to listen patiently to Sylvia's remarks, which were tangential and had no bearing on reality. Her attitude was only another proof of the old adage that home and business do not mix. In the home, for instance, there was opportunity for a graciousness which did not operate in a corporation, and much more leeway for human kindnesses; and these home kindnesses and home charities were different from those of business. Willis could, for instance, add to the comfort of his own parents and that of Sylvia's mother, and he could also lend a helping hand to other individuals without rendering a cost accounting. One's very responsibilities altered when one stepped into the office elevator. They grew until they ended by becoming responsibilities to groups. He was conditioned to this sort of thinking now, and of course Sylvia had never been exposed to it—but Willis did wish that she would understand.

"I know, honey," he said. "I know. I've given a lot of thought to those workers. I realize as well as the Harcourts that there will be very considerable distress, but I wish you'd try to see the main point, which is that no broad decision can ever be made without someone's getting hurt. Frankly, the Harcourt Mill must eventually be abandoned by somebody because it isn't a modern plant and it's too far away from large centers of production. You must realize that all sorts of small plants are closing every day, and you and I cannot change the trend."

Irritating as it was to be obliged to repeat such obvious facts, it was more irritating to have Sylvia dismiss them and turn to something else.

"But, Willis," she said, "didn't I understand you to say that you knew from the beginning that this was going to happen to the Harcourt Mill if Mr. Nagel bought it?"

Frankly Willis had to admit that he was upset by the question. Irrational and unjust though it was, it contrived to disturb the balance of his facts.

"Now, now," Willis said, "just wait a minute, honey."

But Sylvia did not wait for him to finish.

"Because if you knew it," Sylvia said, "I don't think you were fair to the Harcourts. I don't see how you could have advised them to sell out."

"Now wait a minute," Willis said, and he forgot for a moment that he was talking to Sylvia, because he was aroused at last and anxious, for his own sake, to set the matter right. "Let's get this perfectly straight. I can't let you or anyone—anyone, understand—make such implications. In the first place, I said I was afraid it might be impossible to keep that plant. I only promised the Harcourts to do the best I could, and I have. In the second place, I was perfectly right in advising them to sell when I did, and my own personal interest had nothing whatsoever to do with that advice."

When Willis stopped he realized his voice had risen.

"Willis," Sylvia said, "please don't get excited. Of course you did the right thing. I was only making a comment."

"I'm not excited in the least," Willis said, "really, Sylvia. I'm only dealing with plain fact. They sold for twenty-five million dollars, as you very well remember."

"Yes, dear," Sylvia said. "Yes, I remember."

"And while we're on the remembering side," Willis said, "you might remember, too, that they never would have got any such price for their holdings if it had not been for my management over a period of years. I have nothing to apologize for, sweetness, when I can't stop the inevitable. I can be sorry, but that doesn't stop the inevitable either."

It was a very painful conversation, but Willis could finally see from Sylvia's expression that she had followed his line of logic. After all, she had a good mind, once she faced facts.

"I understand what you mean, dear," she said, "and I can see how hard it must be to try to do what is right for everyone. I do hope you're going to see the Harcourts and explain things to them, just the way you have to me."

Instead of answering directly, Willis bent over Sylvia and kissed her forehead. He always loved it when she finally understood him.

"I'm pretty busy right now, sweetness," he said, "but I'll mull over that suggestion. I'm not sure how this should be presented, yet, but don't you bother your head about it. And by the way, I think I'm going to have a nice surprise for you tomorrow."

Sylvia looked up at him, and the line between her eyebrows deepened.

"What sort of surprise, Willis?" she asked. And he really had to laugh at the worried note in her voice.

"Nothing to bother you a bit, honey," he said, "but something I think will give you a real thrill—something we've often talked about, and dreamed about together, for many years. Now don't try to guess because guessing will spoil it. Just wait until tomorrow."

It might actually have been better if he had taken Sylvia's suggestion and had gone to Boston to see the Harcourts, but at the time this seemed impossible. A very tight schedule of meetings had been arranged in Chicago, the disruption of which would have been embarrassing and difficult. Besides, it was November, 1953, with hints of recession in many lines of business. The problem of inventory was acute, and one which Willis felt demanded his full attention. Also, the monthly directors' meeting was coming up, which required not only his presence but his personal report on the whole Harcourt situation. If he were to see the Harcourts, he would have to drop everything and leave for Boston immediately, since any delay involved the risk of the Harcourts hearing the news from other sources. It simply did not seem possible to drop everything, and besides, though 1953 had been the greatest year that Simcoe had ever known, Willis was quite frankly feeling tired and not in the mood for the emotional upset which he knew would face him if he were to see Mrs. Bryson Harcourt and Bess and Bill. It seemed far more sensible to set aside several hours in which to write a series of warm personal letters to the large stockholders of the old Harcourt Mill.

Willis reached this decision on his way from Lake Forest to the city the very next morning after he had taken the matter up with Sylvia, and he activated this decision immediately after his arrival in the office. Since he was most anxious to approach this delicate problem with a fresh mind, he asked his secretary, Mazie Minton, to clear his desk and make him unavailable to everyone. He even dismissed the idea of dictating the letters. This could be done for the final drafts, but he wished to formulate the first drafts entirely alone and undisturbed.

It was a much harder assignment than he had thought it would be. It had been a long while since Willis had done any writing by hand, so his thoughts necessarily moved slowly. He had started with a letter to Bess Harcourt, in the belief that it might serve as a model for others. On the whole, Willis was satisfied that his letter to Bess said everything completely but concisely, with the spirit of old friendship in every line. He was never surprised that Bess did not acknowledge it, for after all no acknowledgment was necessary, and the effort of answering would have been a strain on Bess.

Dear Bess,

    I can't help wishing as I write these lines—and believe me I'm writing the first draft by hand—that I were physically nearer to you, your mother and Bill, so that I might tell you what I have to say here personally. I wish, too, that such a long time had not elapsed without our seeing each other personally, because I strongly feel that this is an occasion when contact would be conducive to a sympathetic understanding. However, due to distance, and due to business pressures here, this letter must act as a substitute—an adequate one, I hope.

Believe me, Bess dear, I have signed the enclosed notice, which will appear within a few days on the bulletin boards at the Harcourt Mill, with the utmost pain and regret. The business wisdom of this step is, I am afraid, irrefutable, but this does not assuage my personal reluctance. I hope you will remember, Bess, dear, that when I advised the selling of Harcourt Associates—advice which I, and I trust you, have never regretted—I promised you that the old Harcourt Mill would always receive my fullest and sincerest interest because I felt, and still feel, toward it almost what any true descendant of your grandfather must. I am proud to say, in this moment of self-examination, that I believe I have kept this promise to the letter. Not our wishes, but economic forces, have been against us, Bess. Tender as my memories are that cling to the Harcourt Mill, its integration into our broader picture here has never been successful. Its plant is obsolescent and its day, quite frankly, is over.

But, Bess, dear, let us not repine, but instead keep the memory of the Old Mill green in our sentiments. Agonizing though this whole decision is, I know that you and Bill, who now hold substantial blocks of Simcoe stock, will in the end come to my way of thinking. In the final analysis, deeply though our affections may be rooted in the past, you and I and all of us who have homes and families to care for, must look down the road ahead. As a fine, old New England preacher (was it Ralph Waldo Emerson?) once succinctly put it: "Look up, not down. Look forward, not back, and lend a hand."

If I may, Bess, dear, I'd like to close my letter on that final note. As I say, I wish I might be sitting with you now in your welcoming library, or taking a late-autumn walk with you in the country, perhaps up to the pine woods that you and I explored so thoroughly so many years ago, so that I could give you personally some sense of the loyalty and affection I have ever had for you and yours. Let me only conclude that in the midst of the very heavy burden of responsibility that this very active company has placed upon my shoulders, one of the things that makes the work worthwhile is the belief that I am in a position to lend a hand. If there is ever anything I can do for you, please call on me in that spirit.

Sylvia, by the way, who also loves the Harcourt Mill, has asked me particularly to extend her most affectionate greetings to you and Edward; and she adds—and in this I heartily concur—that any time your journeying may lead you to Chicago, don't forget the Waydes are always waiting in Lake Forest.

Sincerely as always and devotedly,
Willis Wayde

Perhaps, instead of relying solely on his own judgment, it might have been the better part of wisdom to have shown his letter to Sylvia before he mailed it; but as it was, it seemed to Willis that it was a good letter. He never had any valid reason to revise his opinion of it, and the other letters he wrote appeared to him equally satisfactory. What with the series of drafts, and then luncheon, and finally some absolutely essential afternoon appointments, the business day was almost over by the time he signed the letters.

"Mazie," Willis asked, when Mazie Minton finally placed them on his desk ready for his signature, and stood prepared to blot and fold them, "do you think those letters were adequate under the circumstances?" It was a great consolation to have someone like Mazie there, who had worked in the Harcourt Mill so long. Willis's doubts were dispelled by Mazie's immediate and enthusiastic comment.

"I think they are all just wonderful, Mr. Wayde," she said, "especially the one to Mrs. Ewing. That one, I think, is especially lovely."

"Thanks, Mazie," Willis said. "At any rate, no one can say I didn't try." And then he changed the subject. As he had said to Bess, it was always better to be looking forward, and he had not forgotten the surprise for Sylvia.

"I wonder if you'd slip the travel folders and our itinerary for May and June into my briefcase so I can take them home with me," Willis said. "I want to show them to Mrs. Wayde. Now that this Harcourt matter is settled, I believe we can keep the schedule. Mazie, would you see if Mrs. Wayde can be reached at home?"

By the time that Sylvia was on the telephone Willis was deep in the travel file. Though it was only November and they would not be leaving until May, he seemed already to be on the threshold of a wonderful experience.

"Sylvia," he said half playfully, but still seriously, "how would it be if you and I took a trip to Europe? Not immediately, but next May and June. . . . No, I'm serious about this one, honey, just you and me, and nothing for you to worry about because I have everything arranged already. We have a suite on the veranda deck of the *Elizabeth,* and a car and chauffeur to meet us at Cherbourg, and reservations at the Ritz in Paris. I'll bring the full details back with me tonight, sweetness. It's sort of like the story of the magic carpet, isn't it? All the things we've talked about for so long being brought to pass. So beginning now, we've got to be making our plans, Mrs. Wayde."

It was strange, he was thinking, that they had delayed that dream so long, and that they had never been to Europe, in spite of all their conversations. The war, of course, had intervened, and after the war one thing had seemed to follow another, but at last life seemed to be on an even keel. Besides, he had been invited to attend the Paris convention of International Industrial Production in June. This was really a must, and old P.L. himself had said that Willis really ought to go. Besides, he and Sylvia had always dreamed of Paris.

XXX

IT WAS not fair to say that Stephen Decker was unfriendly to Willis Wayde, because the word "unfriendly" was too definite, and indefiniteness had come to be one of Steve's outstanding weaknesses, when he had been able to retire after his father's death. It was not fair, either, to say that Steve disliked Willis, because he was too easygoing to dislike anyone aggressively. But then, as he always said when he described the time he and his wife, May, met the Waydes at a sidewalk café on the Champs Elysées, he had never liked Willis very much.

The Deckers ran into the Waydes in Paris late one June afternoon. There was no place like Paris, Steve pointed out, to create cleavages of taste between men and women. Just when you had an opportunity to participate mildly in a Continental way of life, women became seized with a thirst for culture. That very morning May had expressed a wish to motor through the château country—a very girlish desire, and May no longer was in pigtails.

"But, Steve," she said, "we can't ever be sure when we are going to be able to leave the children again."

"That's exactly it," Steve said.

"I don't see any use in coming here," May said, "and then playing dominoes with an old man in a *brasserie*—and don't make a joke and call it a brassière."

There had been a time when May would have been amused by this mild humor, but now she wanted to get something out of their trip to Europe, and the days were going by with absolutely nothing worthwhile to show for them. To prove her point she went on to say that all Steve wanted to do was to look in the shop windows of the rue de Rivoli, and read off-color jokes embroidered on ladies' handkerchiefs—in English, of course, for the American trade:

Oh, please do not kiss me
Oh, please do not kiss
Oh, please do not
Oh, please do
Oh, please
Oh.

He might at least try not to be an adolescent himself. There was no reason for Steve to be so utterly American.

"We haven't even seen Sainte Chapelle," she said, with an impeccable accent, since as a *jeune fille* she had spent a year with a French family in Paris on the rue de l'Université. He had compromised that morning by going with May to Sainte Chapelle. She, in turn, had compromised that afternoon by attending the races at Longchamp, in a car which she knew cost them twice too much, but there was not much room for argument, because he had won ten thousand francs.

It must have been close to six when they returned from Longchamp. The sun was low and made the Champs Elysées, in spots, a golden street.

"Let's pay off the driver," Steve said, "and stop at the café over there and have a bottle of champagne."

"Oh, Steve," May said, "at least we might stop at some interesting place. There used to be a lovely little place near the Luxembourg Gardens that only the French knew about. This one will be full of Americans."

He could see that May was right. It was exactly the sort of café that would attract American tourists. It seemed to Steve that American women in Paris, especially May, enjoyed pretending that they were Continentals.

"How would it be," he asked, "if we pretended we were Americans for an hour?"

May was amused, in a cosmopolitan way.

"You don't have to pretend. You really don't," May said, "and please don't try to ask for the wine card in French."

They sat down in wicker chairs beneath the café awning, and the babble of voices around them was very cosmopolitan.

"*Garçon*," Steve said, "*la carte des vins, s'il vous plaît.*"

"Well," May said, "at least the children aren't here to hear you. . . . I told you that this place would be full of Americans."

May was right as usual. There were several middle-aged American groups around them, all identified beyond any chance of error. The men wore expressions of confused discomfort, and each of the women seemed to be living in her own small world of fantasy.

"I don't see why American men invariably look undistinguished," May said.

Instinctively Steve sat up straighter.

"Maybe they're tired," he said, "at the end of a long hard day."

"They might try not to look tired," May said, "and they don't all have to look as though they were doing mental arithmetic."

"They have to," Steve said. "They're all changing dollars into francs."

"If we were to speak to any of them," May said, "they would all say just the same thing." May looked around her serenely, conscious that at least she was not an ordinary American. "They all might just as well have stayed at home. None of them is getting anything out of being here. . . . Steve, look directly behind you."

"Why?" he asked.

"There's a very nice distinguished-looking couple directly behind you, and I think we've seen them somewhere."

"How do you mean, they're distinguished?" Steve asked.

"Well, she's exquisitely dressed," May said, "and he looks interested in everything, and he has a nice profile, and I like the way he smiles. He's in a gray flannel suit that's really well-cut, and he has grayish-blond hair, and he sits up straight."

"Maybe he's a Britisher," Steve said.

"No," May said, "but I think his clothes were made in London, and he has such a nice smile. He's smiling at her now. I wish you'd turn around. They're four tables directly behind you."

"How do you know he isn't British?" Steve asked. "Does he look cornfed?"

"No," May said, "no. He has very heavy tortoise-shell glasses, and those aren't British. He's reading her something out of a guidebook. An Englishman wouldn't do that, at least not in that way."

"In what way?" Steve said.

"In an intense sort of way," May said.

"Maybe he's a Swede," Steve said.

"No," May said, "and I'm almost sure I've seen him before. Please turn around, but don't do it too quickly, because they're looking at us. He's taken off his glasses."

Steve pushed his chair sideways, turning his head slowly, and there, four tables away, was Willis Wayde.

"Well, well," Steve said.

"You know him, do you?" May asked.

He nodded and picked up his glass.

"Yes, I know him," he said. "He's Willis Wayde."

"Oh," May said, "of course he is. Steve, aren't you going to speak to them? Ask them to come and join us."

"Now, listen, May," Steve said, "where would it get us?"

"You always have an inferiority complex about anyone interesting," May said.

Her voice made him squirm in his wicker chair.

"Now, listen, May," he said, "I don't like to push myself on people."

"I wish you wouldn't be small-town," May said. "You sound small-town."

"All right," Steve said, "all right, but he and I don't know each other any more."

"Aren't you even curious?" May asked.

"No," said Steve.

"But you always talk about the time you used to know him," May said. "Don't you care what happened to him?"

"Everybody knows what happened to him."

"Steve," May said, "can't you be natural for once, in a perfectly friendly way? Can't you walk over to that table and say . . ."

"Say what?" Steve asked.

"Just say, 'You're Willis Wayde, aren't you? I'm Steve Decker. We used to know each other back in Clyde.'"

Steve sighed.

"And then I'd say, 'I remember your wife too. Don't you remember me, Sylvia? I used to know you in Cambridge, Massachusetts.'"

"You never told me you knew her," May said.

"You never asked me," Steve answered. "She was Sylvia Hodges. It doesn't matter, May."

"You've never told me anything about her," May said.

"There isn't anything to tell," Steve answered. "They were a family that lived off Brattle Street. Bill Harcourt brought Willis around, and Willis finally married Sylvia."

"Bill Harcourt?" May repeated.

"Yes," Steve said, "Bill Harcourt."

The names had a strange sound in the café.

"Steve, I'm tired of seeing you acting scared," May said.

"Who?" Steve asked. "Me? Of the Waydes?"

"Then go ahead and speak to them," May said.

"All right," Steve said, "all right."

He wished that he could make it clear to May that he did not have an inferiority complex. The physical problem of threading his way past a few tables to reach the spot directly behind him was not only a problem of time and space but one of human relationship, which involved a strain on memory. It was a little like trying to get a home motion picture into focus and on the center of the screen.

Steve had only seen Sylvia once since she had married, and Sylvia was no longer dressed in a tweedy shirtwaist way. Once she had told him she did not like jewelry, but now she wore a diamond-and-sapphire clip that looked inconspicuous but expensive against the scarf around her throat. Steve had never thought of her as being particularly pretty, except occasionally when they had been arguing about something, but now her features looked more distinguished.

He would have known Sylvia anywhere and also he would have known Willis, but Willis, too, looked more distinguished. It was hard to remember that he had ever been awkward and that his hair had been frequently overlong. He still looked young but no longer naïve or hesitant or impelled to make nervous efforts to be agreeable. Everything about him was under control, and after all, why not? The Waydes were becoming clearer and at the same time less approachable. Steve Decker was living in his past as he walked toward them.

"Hello," he said.

The Waydes both gazed up at him. Willis looked up without a trace of blankness. A light of welcome shone from his eyes, registering pleasure and perfect recall.

"Why, hello," Willis said. There was the faintest beat of hesitation, but everything was streamlined. "Why, hello, Bill. Sylvia, I don't believe you have ever met my old friend, Bill Jerrod. How's everything in Akron, Bill?"

Steve Decker was maliciously amused, but at the same time he had an embarrassed wish that he might have been Bill Jerrod from Akron. Willis Wayde was half out of his chair, half holding out his hand, when his gaze faltered, and then before he could speak Sylvia interrupted.

"Willis," she said, "don't you remember Steve Decker?"

Willis knew when the joke was at his expense, and he gave way to disarming mirth.

"Why, of course, it's Steve," Willis said. "Fancy meeting you in Paris." But obviously Willis was still trying to place him. Given a second Willis might very well have come up with the right answer, but instead Sylvia spoke again.

"Steve Decker, Willis," she said again.

But Willis was on the beam at last, and there was no annoyance, or grinding of the gears.

"Steve," he said, "forgive me, will you? Faces out of the past get blurred occasionally. Sweetness, it's all straight now. Say, Steve, it's wonderful to see you. It's like being back in high school, isn't it?"

"Well, not exactly," Steve said.

"Miss Wilson's room," Willis said, "and Cambridge. Sunday evenings at the Hodgeses'. Say, Steve, you were there the first night I came to the Hodgeses'. Bill Harcourt brought me. Remember?"

"That's right," Steve said. "Bill Harcourt."

"How is old Bill?" Willis asked, and he spoke more quickly. "It's just wonderful to see someone from the old town. You can't ever forget any place where you lived as a kid, can you? Let's see, you were at Harcourt for a summer, weren't you? That was a fine old manufacturing establishment, an ideal old plant."

"Yes, it used to be quite a place," Steve said.

"Yes," Willis said, "you always have a soft spot in your heart for the place where you got your first chance. Let's see, when did I see you last, Steve?"

"About ten years ago," Steve said. "You were up for a directors' meeting or something. We just met for a minute."

"That's right," Willis said. "I was staying at the Harcourt place. It's a beautiful old home, isn't it?"

"It still is," Steve said. "It's quite a place."

"Is Bill living there now?" Willis asked.

"No," Steve answered. "Bess has it now, since Mrs. Harcourt died. She stays there every summer, and Ed comes down for week ends."

"Well, well," Willis said. "How's Bess?"

"She's fine as far as I know," Steve said.

"Willis," Sylvia said, "aren't you going to ask Steve to sit down?"

"Of course," Willis said. "I've been so interested I forgot completely. *Garçon!*"

"Darling," Sylvia said, "not in French."

Willis laughed again.

"Sylvia's sensitive about my French," he said. "She spent a year in Paris."

"Did she?" Steve asked. "With a French family?"

"Yes," Sylvia said, "on the rue de l'Université."

"That's the way to develop an accent, isn't it?" Steve said.

"It certainly is," Willis said. "But let's not get off the beam, Steve. What are you doing with yourself?"

"Why, nothing much," Steve said, "since my father died."

"Oh," Willis said, "I'm sorry. I always admired Mr. Decker."

"That's right," Steve said. "Well, he left quite a lot more money than I ever guessed he would. That's why I'm not doing much."

[403]

"Well, well," Willis said, "good for Mr. Decker."

"And then I got married," Steve said, "and May had a little something. I never was much good at working anyway."

"May?" Sylvia said. "Is she your wife?"

A waiter had brought a chair, and when Steve saw it he realized that he could not stay.

"Oh yes," he said, "I guess I've been married so long that I take it for granted that everyone knows May."

"That's right," Willis said. "I remember now. Bess mentioned that you were married, or maybe it was Bill. Let's see—May. I don't seem to remember anyone in town named May."

"She isn't a native," Steve said. "She's a Brookline girl."

"Well," Willis said, "time marches on, doesn't it?"

"I wish you two would sit down," Sylvia said.

"Well, thanks just as much," Steve said, "but I can't stop, really. I just came over to say hello. You see, May's waiting."

"Do you mean she's here?" Sylvia said. "Why didn't you say so?"

"I was just about to suggest," Steve answered, and he felt himself squirming inwardly, "that you come over and join us. We've just come from the races and I came out ten thousand francs ahead, and we're having a little champagne."

"Well, well," Willis said, "that sounds like a real party. I wish we had time but I'm afraid . . ." He looked at Sylvia. "Sweetness, aren't we having dinner with friends somewhere near Neuilly?"

He did not pronounce the name correctly.

"Neuilly," Sylvia said. "But that isn't until nine, dear. We'd love to, Steve. I think it would be awfully nice."

"It's always great to see someone from home," Willis said. "Yes, this is a swell idea of yours, Steve. I'll call our waiter."

"I'll speak to him," Sylvia said.

"All right, sweetness," Willis said. "Sylvia means my French isn't what it ought to be, and she's right, although I'm sentimental about Paris. At the risk of being—bromidical—Paris is a magnificent city, isn't it?"

"It certainly is," Steve said.

"It keeps reminding you of the past, doesn't it?" Willis said. "Although there are some pretty bright industrialists around here—in a foreign way, I mean."

They continued talking while Sylvia conversed with the waiter.

"It's always been a dream of Sylvia's and mine," Willis said, "to take time off, and to absorb some Old World atmosphere. That's why we're here in Paris—just puttering around and recharging our batteries."

"Willis," Sylvia said, "will you give the waiter six hundred francs?"

As it turned out, nothing was awkward about the meeting, because May and Sylvia each could show the other that she was at home in Paris.

"I can't tell you what fun it is to see you," May said to Sylvia. "Steve has told me so much about you."

"It's so nice to hear a Boston accent again, after the Middle West," Sylvia answered.

"Well, almost Boston," May said. "Brookline."

"It's queer we never met at dances or somewhere," Sylvia said. "But then I always used to be afraid of Brookline girls. I suppose you must have gone to Miss Winsor's?"

"Yes," May said. "Winsor's was a sort of conditioned reflex around Brookline."

It was at least moderately funny, and they all laughed in unison.

"Well, now we're here," Steve said, "we'd better have some more champagne. Where's the waiter? *Garçon!*"

"Don't, dear," May said. "I'll order it. You know, Steve is wonderful in many ways but not in French."

"It's just the same with Willis," Sylvia said. "Willis just doesn't try."

"Look, sweetness," Willis said. "I never had the chance to board with a French family when I was young. Let's not get back to that *rue.* What was it—the rue de l'Université?"

"Don't tell me you're in that alumnae association," May said. "Don't tell me you stayed at the Bouchers', too."

"Indeed I did," Sylvia said. "Weren't they darlings? Especially Papa Boucher."

"And Grandmère," May said.

"Oh yes," Sylvia said. "Dear Grandmère. And Tante Elise."

It all went to show how small the world was, and the coincidence was assisted by the champagne.

"I can't get Willis to see the Picassos," Sylvia was saying. "Men never seem to feel at home in Paris."

As a matter of fact they were all feeling at home, by this time.

"I've got an idea, Steve," Willis said. "We ought to turn the girls loose together some day and you and I do the town by ourselves. How about it, girls?" But the girls no longer wanted to hear what the men were saying.

"From my observation," Willis said, "there's always something queer about women when they get to Paris."

"American husbands don't understand women," Steve said. "They aren't good lovers. Did you ever hear that one?"

"I certainly have," Willis said, "but still I like a lot of things about Paris."

"And I like Paris," Steve said. "I understand it in my own way. For instance, I was here in the war and May wasn't."

"Oh," Willis said, "what were you doing in the war, Steve?"

"Hell, Willis," Steve said, "I was in the Chemical Warfare Service. Nobody our age can do anything much."

"Don't say that, boy," Willis said. "You've always had a lot on the ball."

It made Steve Decker laugh.

"I guess you're confusing me again with that Mr. Jerrod in Akron," he said.

Willis shook his head and his expression was almost serious. He looked at Steve Decker steadily for a moment with a bright and slightly glassy alertness. There seemed to be something both watchful and pleading in Willis's look, and Steve had the idea that Willis wanted to be liked.

"I'm not confusing you with anyone," he said. "Frankly, I always used to envy you, and you're the same old Steve Decker still."

He made it sound sincere. Willis had learned how to make people listen to everything he said.

"Well," Steve said, "times have certainly changed since then."

Willis was silent for a minute, as though he were thinking of changing times, comparing then with now.

"If you mean I'm not what I used to be," he said, "you're right, but partially everyone stays what he used to be. There were two people I used to envy—you and Bill Harcourt, frankly."

"Me and Bill?" Steve said. He looked at Willis's right hand, beating on the marble top of the café table, and Steve was sure that Willis's nails were professionally manicured.

"To put it simply," Willis said, "I envied you two boys because you never had to worry. Me, I always had to."

"I don't see you have to worry now," Steve said.

"Not about myself now," Willis said, "but about a lot of other people. One thing always leads to another."

For a moment the thread of conversation was broken, but May and Sylvia were still talking.

"Steve wouldn't go to the château country," May said. "He said if he went he would just sit in the car."

"There's one thing about Willis," Sylvia said. "He makes a most fearful effort, but we're not doing much serious sightseeing. He needed to get away from things."

Willis took a small sip of his champagne.

"That's right," he said. "You've got to get away now and then and recharge your batteries—at least I do. It gets your mind on another tack. How's Bill Harcourt, Steve?"

It occurred to Steve that it was the second time that Willis had asked the question.

"Bill's pretty well," he said. "He's living in Marion, you know. He likes the sailing and the golf."

"How's his game?"

"Not much," Steve told him. "Somewhere in the nineties."

"That means I could beat him," Willis said. "I've got to look up old Bill sometime. I've always had a warm spot—that is, a deep affection for Bill." Steve did not answer, but Willis was going on. "He's the nicest person in the world, with all the right instincts, and generosity and integrity, and a lovely sense of humor, but Bill never had what it takes in a business way."

"Well, he doesn't have to," Steve said.

"That's right," Willis answered. "Other people have done it for him. Why, I'm working for Bill right now."

"Yes," Steve said, "and I own a few shares of Simcoe myself."

"Well, that's fine," Willis said. "I'm glad you're a member of the Simcoe family. I wish you'd come out sometime and see what we're doing."

"Why, thanks," Steve said, "I'd like to sometime." Willis was looking across the table at Sylvia, but Sylvia paid no attention to his signal.

"I'm always loyal to the Harcourt family," Willis said. "I guess you know what I owe them. They don't make families like that any more. How does the old house look now?"

"It looks pretty well," Steve said. "Bess gives a lot of thought to it, keeping up the grounds and everything."

Willis stared at the traffic moving down the avenue.

"That's fine," he said. "I'm glad it's all in order. It's sort of a shrine to me in a way, frankly. Sometimes before I go to sleep I can shut my eyes and walk right up the drive."

The definition was aesthetically disturbing, but the tribute was entirely honest.

"Lovely lawn planting," Willis said. "Those groups of rhododendrons by the gates. It's time that does it, time. Now at my own home I've tried to get that same effect with rhododendrons. Sylvia and I put in a lot of fifty-year-old specimens. They are lovely but they don't give the same effect. It's time."

"It isn't such an old house," Steve said. "It isn't as old as parts of the mill."

"Maybe," Willis said. "But in a home obsolescence has a wholly different meaning. You can have sentiment about a home but not about a factory. I wish some people would see that."

"I suppose you're right," Steve said.

Willis moved his hand and drummed his fingers on the table.

"I'm deeply sorry about the Harcourt Mill decision," he said. "It was like cutting off my arm to close that plant."

Steve Decker did not answer, and Willis looked at him for a moment in a bright impersonal way.

"Naturally there were repercussions," he said. "There always are, but things like that are happening all the time. There was no future in the plant—only past—not the slightest chance of its getting out of the red."

"If you live there," Steve said, "it's harder to take an objective view."

Willis coughed. "We had a dog a while ago," he said—"a retriever. He almost brought up the children. Then he got blind and we had to call the vet to put him out of the way. You have to do things like that."

"Yes," said Steve, "I suppose so."

"I'll always have a warm—er—memory in my heart for that old factory," Willis said. "It's ironical, you might say, that I should have to be the one to take the step, but you have to do things like that."

"Yes," Steve said, "it must have been hard for you."

The trouble was that Steve could always see two sides of a question at the same time. There was no use arguing with someone like Willis Wayde.

"Of course," Willis said, "I can't blame some people for not sharing my point of view. Well, it's great to have had a glimpse of you, Steve, and I'm glad of the opportunity to have expressed a few of my thoughts on the subject. Sylvia, sweet, I'm afraid we ought to be going now."

"Oh dear," Sylvia said. "Must we? I'm so sorry." She pushed back her chair and looked questioningly at Willis, obviously asking mutely whether he wanted her to do anything about the Deckers.

"I hope we can have a chance to return your kindness," Willis said. "We really ought to start right in where we left off. Sylvia, sweet, what are we doing tomorrow?"

Sylvia raised her eyebrows slightly.

"Why, you're having lunch with those textile people, Willis, and there's a dinner for you in the evening."

"That's right," Willis said. "I'd completely forgotten about that, and then we're off for Switzerland, and I haven't had a chance to say a word to Mrs. Decker."

He pushed back his chair and stood up, gently smoothing out the folds in his double-breasted coat, smiling, looking like someone who had been asked by the toastmaster to say a few words. He had that same professional assurance, and May had been right—his suit had undoubtedly been made in London by a tailor accustomed to American whims. For a second Willis dominated the scene, modestly and sincerely. His ease was the best thing about him. You could not tell, Steve was thinking, how much of his cordiality was real. There was no way of gauging the depth of his sincerity. It might very well have been that he did have a soft spot in his heart, and that he had honestly meant what he had said about loyalty, and about being deeply sorry. On the other hand he might have had no heart at all. Authority and success had made him strangely impervious, since success had smoothed down all his rough edges, turning him into a type interchangeable with any photograph on the financial page of the *New York Times*. It was hard to tell about those people, who had all been processed in the same way, but he was essentially an American type.

"Well," Willis said, "good-by, and many thanks. This has been perfectly wonderful."

If that was all there had been to the incident, it never would have been worth repeating. It was what happened next that gave it value and suspense. You never could tell, as May often said, whom you would run into in Paris, and you always ran into the most unlikely people, purely through coincidence. They were all standing up when Steve Decker felt May's hand on his arm.

"My God, Steve," she said, "look who's coming."

There was an aisle between the closely grouped tables leading from the street, since after all there had to be a passage for patrons and waiters, and there, moving straight toward them, were Bess Harcourt and her husband, Edward Ewing. To anyone who knew her she would always be Bess Harcourt, and you thought of her still as young Bess Harcourt, although her yellow hair was much darker and her face more florid, and even in Paris she seemed to bring something of the Harcourts with her. There was something arrogantly provincial in the way she walked. At least she was not trying to be a Continental woman. They must have been shopping, because Edward was carrying an armful of packages. Whenever you saw Ed Ewing, he seemed to be carrying packages for Bess.

There was no way of avoiding the encounter, because the Waydes were only a few feet away from them. They were bound to meet head on. Willis Wayde stepped forward immediately. He had put on his gray felt hat, and now he took it off in a quick, courtly way which was not like him, and all his measured reserve had left him. For once there was no need to guess what he was thinking. He was meeting an old friend. He was obviously perfectly delighted to see Bess Harcourt there.

"Well, if this isn't like Old Home Week," he said. "Why, Bess, fancy seeing you in Paris! And Edward! Hello, Ed."

Willis held out his hand and for a moment you could not tell what might happen. Bess had a pleasant way of looking at people, and the upward tilt of her mouth was always good-natured, and when she spoke her voice was good-natured too.

"You're in my way, Willis," she said. "Get out."

"Now, Bess," Willis said, "please. I haven't the least idea—"

He could not have looked more completely shaken if Bess had slapped him across the face.

"You're in my way," Bess said again, and then she laughed in that bright malicious way of hers. "Get out, Uriah Heep."

Steve Decker said that you could not help but admire Willis Wayde. Willis had gone a long way since he had lived at the Harcourt place. It was plain that that jibe of Bess's about the Dickensian crook had made a very deep impression on Willis, because his face flushed so darkly that he looked as though he had spent the day at the seashore. Nevertheless his manner was composed and his voice was polite, gentle and considerate. Success had certainly worn the rough edges from Willis Wayde.

"Certainly, if that's the way you want it," he said, "but I'm truly very sorry, Bess. Come, sweetness, or we'll be late for dinner." And then the Waydes walked slowly to the street. Willis's shoulders were held back, and his coat did fit him to perfection.

Steve had a final glimpse of them, before they disappeared among the pedestrians on the sidewalk. Willis had put on his hat, and Sylvia was asking him some question. Willis appeared to be listening to her very carefully, and then he shook his head. That was all there was to it, but if you knew something about the component parts and personalities of the individuals involved it made quite a story, and one that could only have happened in America. Steve Decker often wondered what Willis Wayde had thought about it, and how much or how little that brief encounter had affected him. It was the ending of a story that Steve had witnessed, which made no particular sense without knowing the beginning.

XXXI

WILLIS, WHENEVER he had occasion to exchange ideas with acquaintances about life in Paris, always said he had fallen in love with the Ritz at first sight. It was exactly what he had dreamed it would be, and none of the theatrical magnificence of his suite overlooking the Place Vendôme had ever made him ill at ease. When Sylvia, on first seeing it, had said that the whole thing was ostentatious and expensive, he could not help but remind her that her reaction had been just the same when they went honeymooning at Chieftain Manor. The idea was the same, though their sitting room, all gold and old rose, bore not the slightest resemblance aesthetically or ideologically to The Old Chief. It did not take long, however, for Sylvia to get into the mood of the Ritz, and finally she admitted that the Ritz and its surroundings were magnificent, in an old-regime manner. In fact, the atmosphere was so old-regime that Sylvia was surprised both by the rather peculiar people she occasionally saw at the Ritz and by the excellent plumbing. From the very first minute in their suite, Willis had loved looking out on the Place Vendôme, and he knew now that he would never tire of the prospect. There was no security in France any longer, and yet the Place Vendôme epitomized security. The whole thing was in order. There was balance and reason in the expansive façades surrounding that fine square, all paying constant tribute to the victory column of Napoleon in its center. The calmness of age only added to the enclosed security. Once, sipping cocktails in the June dusk and watching that lovely *place*, Willis had said jokingly to Sylvia that he supposed she thought Napoleon's column was ostentatious. She had replied, to his dismay, that, except for Napoleon's tomb, it was the most ostentatious thing in Paris. Perhaps she was right technically, for the idea of copying Trajan's column in Rome may have been egocentric, but the bronze décor made from the cannons of Austerlitz was a concept as magnificent as the Ritz itself. The column belonged right where it was, in the middle of the Place Vendôme, even if the buildings around the *place* were very much older.

The atmosphere of the Place Vendôme was reassuring to Willis when he and Sylvia finally arrived at the Ritz after the painful incident at the Champs Elysées café. The sight of the column reminded Willis that there had been a good many people who had not liked Napoleon, and Napoleon himself had been obliged to make decisions.

"Sweetness," he said to Sylvia, "will you fix it up with the taxi driver? I don't feel much like doing mental arithmetic."

"Why, yes, of course, dear," Sylvia said. "I've got just the right change in my purse."

He was grateful that Sylvia had not once alluded to his meeting with Bess during their taxi ride. He still felt sick and utterly defeated. He was still thinking that it was inconceivable that Bess Harcourt could retain such power to give him pain; but it would pass. He was sure of this now that he saw the Place Vendôme again. In fact he could come close to imagining that nothing untoward had happened, once they were inside the Ritz. The smiling doorman and the prodigious concierge, who knew everything there was to know about anything, were not unlike the personnel of his own office—efficiency-wise. The Ritz literally was a home away from home. The long Paris twilight was still enough illumination for the suite, more peaceful than the formal glitter of the Louis XVI chandeliers.

"Well, sweetness," Willis said, "I'm going to ring for a couple of cocktails, because I feel a little tired, what with one thing and another. It's nice to be back here, isn't it—even if it's ostentatious?"

"Yes, dear," Sylvia said. "I've almost forgotten now that it is ostentatious." She sat down in the gilded armchair that Willis moved near the window for her so that they could both sit side by side and look at the Place Vendôme. "You know I eventually end by loving all the things you love, Willis."

"That's a very lovely thing of you to say, darling," Willis said. "Sweetness, I only wish you and I could be alone here tonight, just looking at the Place Vendôme."

"Why can't we, dear?" Sylvia asked.

He was still surprised when Sylvia did not conquer absent-mindedness.

"Don't you remember, honey?" Willis said. "We have to go out to dinner with those people at that place whose name you don't like me to pronounce."

"I do like you to pronounce it," Sylvia said. "Go ahead and say it. Please say it, Willis."

Willis shook his head. The truth was he was not in the mood for French.

[412]

"Go ahead and say it, please," Sylvia said again. "I really think you are doing very well with your French, dear."

"Sweetness," Willis told her, "you don't have to be as loyal to me as that, but I still wish you and I could sit here and not go to that place to dinner."

Sylvia stood up and kissed the top of his head. It was a gesture that he could not recall her having made before.

"I really don't see why we have to go, dear," she said. "They're only some of those people you met at the convention, and if a couple drops out they can always rearrange the table. If you'll give me your notebook, I'll get the concierge to call them for us. Here come the cocktails, dear. You take yours while I call."

"Well, if you don't mind, sweetness," Willis said, "I think perhaps I will start on mine right away."

He was glad to be alone for the minutes while Sylvia was telephoning, and his gratitude toward her increased, now that she was getting them out of that dinner.

Willis did not want to face a crowd at the moment, let alone a foreign crowd. He wanted to be alone, but at the same time he did not want to think. He wanted to push the ceaseless repetition of the scene at that café from his mind, and stop imagining how he might have acted differently, and what he could have said but did not say. The strange truth, the inescapable fact, was that there was nothing different he could have said. The encounter was one of those things one simply had to take on the chin and absorb the way one absorbed any punishment. Willis could not forget the injustice. That was what hurt the most. After all his years of loyalty to the Harcourts, he could not conceive how Bess could ever have reacted to him in such a way; but then she had, and there was nothing to do but accept it. Given time, only a day or two perhaps, and he could adjust to the fact. The situation was a casualty which was perhaps inevitable, but he had not realized how much he valued the good opinion of the Harcourts. He could not see why the things that Bess said appeared to fall into the category of personal rebuke, which reflected on his own integrity. This was irrational, of course, because he had done absolutely nothing of which he was ashamed. The worst thing Willis had to face was that the whole thing had happened directly in front of Sylvia. Consequently he would have to take the whole thing up with Sylvia. There was no conceivable way of avoiding it.

He finished his cocktail, but it did not appreciably relax the tensions within him. If he were to order another and another—as many people he knew frequently did in times of distress—he had sense enough to know that this would not relieve his troubles. The buildings of the

Place Vendôme, designed by architects for noblemen of whose lives Willis knew nothing save for a few facts from the pages of Nagel's *Paris*, were a greater consolation than alcohol. (He was thinking that he must tell old P.L., facetiously, that he had not known P.L. wrote guidebooks on the side.) Those façades surrounding the Place Vendôme reflected a point of view that got through to Willis. They assured him that the men who had lived behind those cornices had been as aware as Napoleon that there was no such thing as perfect justice. Something always went by the board. There was a real meeting of minds between Willis and the Place Vendôme.

"Sylvia," Willis said, "that was a very lovely idea of yours, getting us out of that dinner, and just across there near Morgan and Cie. in a jeweler's window is something I'm going to get you tomorrow just for thinking of it."

"Oh, Willis," Sylvia said. She was standing beside him, and he could not see her face, and at first he thought she was laughing, but he was not exactly sure. "You don't have to say it with jewelry, darling. You know you only have to say it."

"That's a very sweet thing for you to say," Willis said. "Somehow you've always been kind of allergic to jewelry."

"Oh, darling," Sylvia said, and she sat down in the gold-and-rose armchair near him, "don't you see it's only an act? Don't you know I always love everything you give me?"

Willis turned toward her, but the dusk made it hard for him to see her face.

"You don't have to be as kind to me as all that, sweetness," he said. "Maybe I don't deserve it, basically."

"Well, I know what you do deserve, dear," Sylvia told him. "You deserve another cocktail, and I think maybe I do, too. In fact, when you ordered them I told the waiter to bring two apiece, and here's another now."

"So that's what you were saying to him?" Willis said. "It's funny, I can read a French newspaper, but I don't seem to understand the speech."

"Darling," Sylvia said, and she put her hand on his, "you're awfully sweet. I know better than anyone else how basically sweet you are, and that's one of your favorite words, isn't it—basically?"

There was no use delaying any longer. He had to take the subject up with Sylvia, and the worst of it was he was not sure his reluctance to do so might not have had something to do with shame.

"Sweetness," he said, "I'm dreadfully sorry about that scene this afternoon, and particularly that you should have been present."

She put her hand over his again. He had not realized, until that talk at the Ritz, how dependent he had grown upon Sylvia. After all, perhaps two people always grew together if they had been through enough together, long enough.

"There's nothing to be sorry about," Sylvia said. "If someone acts in a hysterical and unreasonable manner it isn't your fault, Willis."

"I know it, sweetness," Willis said, and he did not look at her when he spoke, but out across the square, "but a thing like that sort of pulls the rug out from under you. I suppose it is irrational for my emotions to be so much involved; yet after what Bess said, I can't help sort of wondering if anything I've done has been worthwhile."

"Why, darling," Sylvia said, "you don't have to wonder anything like that, because you've always been wonderful. No one knows better than I do how wonderful you've been."

Willis cleared his throat. Even though he liked what she said, it was a time to face facts; and perhaps his trouble, now that he thought of it, was that he was sometimes reluctant to face them absolutely squarely.

"That's very sweet of you to say so, honey," he said, "but occasionally it's seemed to me you've had a few reservations. God knows I've tried to do a lot of things the right way, and God knows I'm not perfect."

"Why, darling," Sylvia said, "no one's perfect. It's what I've been telling you, dear. No one knows how wonderful you are as well as I do. I'm an authority."

Willis heard what she said, but he was so involved in his own thoughts that he did not answer her directly.

"I've tried to be sincere, sweetness," he said—"I really have—in all my dealings, but sometimes it's a problem—how to be sincere."

"I know you've always tried, dear," Sylvia said. "Let's ring for the waiter and have some supper. We can think this all through tomorrow, Willis."

But Willis was very sure that the time to think of it was now.

"Of course you were right, sweetness," he said. "I should have gone to Boston and seen them personally at the time. I would have, of course, if I'd had the remotest idea that Bess would react like this."

"Of course you would have, dear," Sylvia said, "but you were awfully busy right then, if you remember."

Willis sighed and crossed his right knee over his left, and rotated his ankle nervously. He was relieved that it was growing darker—so dark that Sylvia could not see him clearly. He could still feel her presence, and he was glad that she was right beside him.

"What hurts me especially," he said, "is that I don't think they've been very loyal to me. They don't seem to look on both sides of the ledger. They forget the years I've worked. They forget, sweetness, that I've worn my fingers to the bone for them. Apparently all they remember is that I closed up that mill."

"I know," Sylvia said. "It isn't fair, but then I don't suppose anybody ever looks on both sides of a ledger—even you or I—and they'd always lived with the mill."

Willis turned his head toward her.

"You don't mean," he said, "that you're taking their side in this? You can't be Sylvia."

He knew the minute that he said it that it was a petulant remark, and he was sorry.

"I was just saying, dear," Sylvia said, "that none of us can see both sides of anything. I'm on your side always, dear, but let's not go on about it now. How would it be if I rang for the waiter? And you have some eggs and some of those *croissants* you love so much, and some chocolate, and then I'm going to give you a Nembutal. You'll see everything much more clearly after a good sleep."

"I'd like that," Willis said, "because, frankly, I do feel tired, and I'm sorry to elaborate on this subject, precious. I have a sort of suspicion that the Harcourts have the idea that I had always intended to close the mill. Maybe I'd better tell you something frankly, darling, because you've been very sweet to me, and I would like to be frank. I'm disturbed about this angle, because frankly, sweetness, I don't know whether they are right or not. I honestly can't remember."

"Why, darling," Sylvia said, "of course you couldn't tell what you were going to do at a future time, and you've always done everything for the Harcourts, darling. Please don't think about it any more." And then she kissed him on the top of the head again, just as she had before. "Let's think about what we're going to do tomorrow."

"That's right," Willis said. "You're dead right. Let's look forward, sweetness, and not back. You know, come to think of it, that's exactly what I wrote to Bess."

"Darling," Sylvia said, "it's all right. It really is all right. Let's not worry about it any more. And when you've had your Nembutal, I'll tell you what we'll do. We'll call up the children's camps and talk to them. It's wonderful that we're both so crazy about the children. Willis, isn't it queer to think it's only early afternoon back there?"